The Fatal Series by Marie Force
Now available in ebook and print
Suggested reading order

One Night with You
(prequel novella, available in print with *Fatal Affair*)

Fatal Affair

Fatal Justice

Fatal Consequences

Fatal Destiny
(available in print with *Fatal Consequences*)

Fatal Flaw

Fatal Deception

Fatal Mistake

Fatal Jeopardy

Fatal Scandal

Fatal Frenzy

Fatal Identity

Praise for the Fatal Series
by *New York Times* bestselling author Marie Force

"Force's skill is also evident in the way that she develops the characters, from the murdered and mutilated senator to the detective and chief of staff who are trying to solve the case. The heroine, Sam, is especially complex and her secrets add depth to this mystery... This novel is *The O.C.* does D.C., and you just can't get enough."

—*RT Book Reviews* on *Fatal Affair* (4.5 stars)

"Sizzle, mystery and suspense...*Fatal Affair* has it all! Nick and Sam are a perfect pair and Marie Force is definitely an author to watch!"

—Christy Reece, *New York Times* bestselling author, on *Fatal Affair*

"This book starts out strong and keeps getting better. Marie Force is one of those authors that will be on my must-read list in the future."

—*The Romance Studio* on *Fatal Affair*

"The author makes the reader part of the action, effortlessly weaving the world of politics and murder in which the characters come alive on the pages. The plot was addictive and scandalous with so many family secrets... Drama, passion, suspense—*Fatal Affair* has it all!"

—*Book Junkie*

"This is a suspense that never stops. Add it to your book list today."

—*NightOwlRomance.com* on *Fatal Affair* (Top Pick)

Recycling programs for this product may not exist in your area.

ISBN-13: 978-0-373-00415-7

Fatal Affair

This edition published by arrangement with Harlequin Books S.A.

www.CarinaPress.com

Printed in U.S.A.

MARIE FORCE

AFFAIR

PREQUEL NOVELLA
ONE NIGHT WITH YOU
INCLUDED

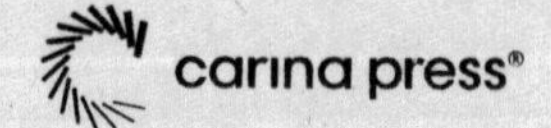

CONTENTS

FATAL AFFAIR

For Sam and Nick, who've taken me on
an unforgettable journey—in more ways than one.

ONE

THE SMELL HIT him first.

"Ugh, what the hell is that?" Nick Cappuano dropped his keys into his coat pocket and stepped into the spacious, well-appointed Watergate apartment that his boss, Senator John O'Connor, had inherited from his father.

"Senator!" Nick tried to identify the foul metallic odor.

Making his way through the living room, he noticed parts and pieces of the suit John wore yesterday strewn over sofas and chairs, laying a path to the bedroom. He had called the night before to check in with Nick after a dinner meeting with Virginia's Democratic Party leadership, and said he was on his way home. Nick had reminded his thirty-six-year-old boss to set his alarm.

"Senator?" John hated when Nick called him that when they were alone, but Nick insisted the people in John's life afford him the respect of his title.

The odd stench permeating the apartment caused a tingle of anxiety to register on the back of Nick's neck. "John?"

He stepped into the bedroom and gasped. Drenched in blood, John sat up in bed, his eyes open but vacant. A knife spiked through his neck held him in place against the headboard. His hands rested in a pool of blood in his lap.

Gagging, the last thing Nick noticed before he bolted

to the bathroom to vomit was that something was hanging out of John's mouth.

Once the violent retching finally stopped, Nick stood up on shaky legs, wiped his mouth with the back of his hand, and rested against the vanity, waiting to see if there would be more. His cell phone rang. When he didn't take the call, his pager vibrated. Nick couldn't find the wherewithal to answer, to say the words that would change everything. *The senator is dead. John's been murdered.* He wanted to go back to when he was still in his car, fuming and under the assumption that his biggest problem that day would be what to do about the man-child he worked for who had once again slept through his alarm.

Thoughts of John, dating back to their first meeting in a history class at Harvard freshman year, flashed through Nick's mind, hundreds of snippets spanning a nearly twenty-year friendship. As if to convince himself that his eyes had not deceived him, he leaned forward to glance into the bedroom, wincing at the sight of his best friend—the brother of his heart—stabbed through the neck and covered with blood.

Nick's eyes burned with tears, but he refused to give in to them. Not now. Later maybe, but not now. His phone rang again. This time he reached for it and saw it was Christina, his deputy chief of staff, but didn't take the call. Instead, he dialed 911.

Taking a deep breath to calm his racing heart and making a supreme effort to keep the hysteria out of his voice, he said, "I need to report a murder." He gave the address and stumbled into the living room to wait for the police, all the while trying to get his head around the image of his dead friend, a visual he already knew would haunt him forever.

Twenty long minutes later, two officers arrived, took a quick look in the bedroom and radioed for backup. Nick was certain neither of them recognized the victim.

He felt as if he was being sucked into a riptide, pulled further and further from the safety of shore, until drawing a breath became a laborious effort. He told the cops exactly what happened—his boss failed to show up for work, he came looking for him and found him dead.

"Your boss's name?"

"United States Senator John O'Connor." Nick watched the two young officers go pale in the instant before they made a second more urgent call for backup.

"Another scandal at the Watergate," Nick heard one of them mutter.

His cell phone rang yet again. This time he reached for it.

"Yeah," he said softly.

"Nick!" Christina cried. "Where the *hell* are you guys? Trevor's having a heart attack!" She referred to their communications director who had back-to-back interviews scheduled for the senator that morning.

"He's dead, Chris."

"Who's dead? What're you talking about?"

"John."

Her soft cry broke his heart. *"No."* That she was desperately in love with John was no secret to Nick. That she was also a consummate professional who would never act on those feelings was one of the many reasons Nick respected her.

"I'm sorry to just blurt it out like that."

"How?" she asked in a small voice.

"Stabbed in his bed."

Her ravaged moan echoed through the phone. "But who…I mean, *why?*"

"The cops are here, but I don't know anything yet. I need you to request a postponement on the vote."

"I can't," she said, adding in a whisper, "I can't think about that right now."

"You have to, Chris. That bill is his legacy. We can't let all his hard work be for nothing. Can you do it? For him?"

"Yes…okay."

"You have to pull yourself together for the staff, but don't tell them yet. Not until his parents are notified."

"Oh, God, his poor parents. You should go, Nick. It'd be better coming from you than cops they don't know."

"I don't know if I can. How do I tell people I love that their son's been murdered?"

"He'd want it to come from you."

"I suppose you're right. I'll see if the cops will let me."

"What're we going to do without him, Nick?" She posed a question he'd been grappling with himself. "I just can't imagine this world, this *life,* without him."

"I can't either," Nick said, knowing it would be a much different life without John O'Connor at the center of it.

"He's really dead?" she asked as if to convince herself it wasn't a cruel joke. "Someone killed him?"

"Yes."

OUTSIDE THE CHIEF'S office suite, Detective Sergeant Sam Holland smoothed her hands over the toffee-colored hair she corralled into a clip for work, pinched some color into cheeks that hadn't seen the light of day in weeks, and adjusted her gray suit jacket over a red scoop-neck top.

Taking a deep breath to calm her nerves and settle her chronically upset stomach, she pushed open the door and stepped inside. Chief Farnsworth's receptionist greeted her with a smile. "Go right in, Sergeant Holland. He's waiting for you."

Great, Sam thought as she left the receptionist with a weak smile. Before she could give into the urge to turn tail and run, she erased the grimace from her face and went in.

"Sergeant." The chief, a man she'd once called Uncle Joe, stood up and came around the big desk to greet her with a firm handshake. His gray eyes skirted over her with concern and sympathy, both of which were new since "the incident." She despised being the reason for either. "You look well."

"I feel well."

"Glad to hear it." He gestured for her to have a seat. "Coffee?"

"No, thanks."

Pouring himself a cup, he glanced over his shoulder. "I've been worried about you, Sam."

"I'm sorry for causing you worry and for disgracing the department." This was the first chance she'd had to speak directly to him since she returned from a month of administrative leave, during which she'd practiced the sentence over and over. She thought she'd delivered it with convincing sincerity.

"Sam," he sighed as he sat across from her, cradling his mug between big hands. "You've done nothing to disgrace yourself or the department. Everyone makes mistakes."

"Not everyone makes mistakes that result in a dead child, Chief."

He studied her for a long, intense moment as if he was making some sort of decision. "Senator John O'Connor was found murdered in his apartment this morning."

"Jesus," she gasped. "How?"

"I don't have all the details, but from what I've been told so far, it appears he was dismembered and stabbed through the neck. Apparently, his chief of staff found him."

"Nick," she said softly.

"Excuse me?"

"Nick Cappuano is O'Connor's chief of staff."

"You know him?"

"*Knew* him. Years ago," she added, surprised and unsettled to discover the memory of him still had power over her, that just the sound of his name rolling off her lips could make her heart race.

"I'm assigning the case to you."

Surprised at being thrust so forcefully back into the real work she had craved since her return to duty, she couldn't help but ask, "Why me?"

"Because you need this, and so do I. We both need a win."

The press had been relentless in its criticism of him, of her, of the department, but to hear him acknowledge it made her ache. Her father had come up through the ranks with Farnsworth, which was probably the number one reason why she still had a job. "Is this a test?

Find out who killed the senator and my previous sins are forgiven?"

He put down his coffee cup and leaned forward, elbows resting on knees. "The only person who needs to forgive you, Sam, is you."

Infuriated by the surge of emotion brought on by his softly spoken words, Sam cleared her throat and stood up. "Where does O'Connor live?"

"The Watergate. Two uniforms are already there. Crime scene is on its way." He handed her a slip of paper with the address. "I don't have to tell you that this needs to be handled with the utmost discretion."

He also didn't have to tell her that this was the only chance she'd get at redemption.

"Won't the Feds want in on this?"

"They might, but they don't have jurisdiction, and they know it. They'll be breathing down my neck, though, so report directly to me. I want to know everything ten minutes after you do. I'll smooth it with Stahl," he added, referring to the lieutenant she usually answered to.

Heading for the door, she said, "I won't let you down."

"You never have before."

With her hand resting on the door handle, she turned back to him. "Are you saying that as the chief of police or as my Uncle Joe?"

His face lifted into a small but sincere smile. "Both."

TWO

SITTING ON JOHN'S SOFA under the watchful eyes of the two policemen, Nick's mind raced with the staggering number of things that needed to be done, details to be seen to, people to call. His cell phone rang relentlessly, but he ignored it after deciding he would talk to no one until he had seen John's parents. Almost twenty years ago they took an instant shine to the hard-luck scholarship student their son brought home from Harvard for a weekend visit and made him part of their family. Nick owed them so much, not the least of which was hearing the news of their son's death from him if possible.

He ran his hand through his hair. "How much longer?"

"Detectives are on their way."

Ten minutes later, Nick heard her before he saw her. A flurry of activity and a burst of energy preceded the detectives' entrance into the apartment. He suppressed a groan. *Wasn't it enough that his friend and boss had been murdered? He had to face* her, *too? Weren't there thousands of District cops? Was she really the only one available?*

Sam came into the apartment, oozing authority and competence. In light of her recent troubles, Nick couldn't believe she had any of either left. "Get some tape across that door," she ordered one of the officers. "Start a log with a timeline of who got here when. No one comes in or goes out without my okay, got it?"

"Yes, ma'am. The Patrol sergeant is on his way along with Deputy Chief Conklin and Detective Captain Malone."

"Let me know when they get here." Without so much as a glance in his direction, Nick watched her stalk through the apartment and disappear into the bedroom. Following her, a handsome young detective with bed head nodded to Nick.

He heard the murmur of voices from the bedroom and saw a camera flash. They emerged fifteen minutes later, both noticeably paler. For some reason, Nick was gratified to know the detectives working the case weren't so jaded as to be unaffected by what they'd just seen.

"Start a canvass of the building," Sam ordered her partner. "Where the hell is Crime Scene?"

"Hung up at another homicide," one of the other officers replied.

She finally turned to Nick, nothing in her pale blue eyes indicating that she recognized or remembered him. But the fact that she didn't introduce herself or ask for his name told him she knew exactly who he was. "We'll need your prints."

"They're on file," he mumbled. "Congressional background check."

She wrote something in the small notebook she tugged from the back pocket of gray, form-fitting pants. There were years on her gorgeous face that hadn't been there the last time he'd had the opportunity to look closely, and he couldn't tell if her hair was as long as it used to be since it was twisted into a clip. The curvy body and endless legs hadn't changed at all.

"No forced entry," she noted. "Who has a key?"

"Who *doesn't* have a key?"

"I'll need a list. You have a key, I assume."

Nick nodded. "That's how I got in."

"Was he seeing anyone?"

"No one serious, but he had no trouble attracting female companionship." Nick didn't add that John's casual approach to women and sex had been a source of tension between the two men, with Nick fearful that John's social life would one day lead to political trouble. He hadn't imagined it might also lead to murder.

"When was the last time you saw him?"

"When he left the office for a dinner meeting with the Virginia Democrats last night. Around six-thirty or so."

"Spoke to him?"

"Around ten when he said he was on his way home."

"Alone?"

"He didn't say, and I didn't ask."

"Take me through what happened this morning."

He told her about Christina trying to reach John, beginning at seven, and of coming to the apartment expecting to find the senator once again sleeping through his alarm.

"So this has happened before?"

"No, he's never been murdered before."

Her expression was anything but amused. "Do you think this is funny, Mr. Cappuano?"

"Hardly. My best friend is dead, Sergeant. A United States senator has been murdered. There's nothing funny about that."

"Which is why you need to answer the questions and save the droll humor for a more appropriate time."

Chastened, Nick said, "He slept through his alarm

and ringing telephones at least once, if not twice, a month."

"Did he drink?"

"Socially, but I rarely saw him drunk."

"Prescription drugs? Sleeping pills?"

Nick shook his head. "He was just a very heavy sleeper."

"And it fell to his chief of staff to wake him up? There wasn't anyone else you could send?"

"The senator valued his privacy. There've been occasions when he wasn't alone, and neither of us felt his love life should be the business of his staff."

"But he didn't care if you knew who he was sleeping with?"

"He knew he could count on my discretion." He looked up, unprepared for the punch to the gut that occurred when his eyes met hers. Her unsettled expression made him wonder if she felt it, too. "His parents need to be notified. I'd like to be the one to tell them."

Sam studied him for a long moment. "I'll arrange it. Where are they?"

"At their farm in Leesburg. It needs to be soon. We're postponing a vote we worked for months to get to. It'll be all over the news that something's up."

"What's the vote for?"

He told her about the landmark immigration bill and John's role as the co-sponsor.

With a curt nod, she walked away.

AN HOUR LATER, Nick was a passenger in an unmarked Metropolitan Police SUV, headed west to Leesburg with Sam at the wheel. She'd left her partner with a staggering list of instructions and insisted on accompanying Nick to tell John's parents.

"Do you need something to eat?"

He shook his head. No way could he even think about eating—not with the horrific task he had ahead of him. Besides, his stomach hadn't recovered from the earlier bout of vomiting.

"You know, we could still call the Loudoun County Police or the Virginia State Police to handle this," she said for the second time.

"No."

After an awkward silence, she said, "I'm sorry this happened to your friend and that you had to see him that way."

"Thank you."

"Are you going to answer that?" she asked of his relentless cell phone.

"No."

"How about you turn it off then? I can't stand listening to a ringing phone."

Reaching for his belt, he grabbed his cell phone, his emotions still raw after watching John be taken from his apartment in a body bag. Before he shut the cell phone off, he called Christina.

"Hey," she said, her voice heavy with relief and emotion. "I've been trying to reach you."

"Sorry." Pulling his tie loose and releasing his top button, he cast a sideways glance at Sam, whose warm, feminine fragrance had overtaken the small space inside the car. "I was dealing with cops."

"Where are you now?"

"On my way to Leesburg."

"God," Christina sighed. "I don't envy you that. Are you okay?"

"Never better."

"I'm sorry. Dumb question."

"It's okay. Who knows what we're supposed to say or do in this situation. Did you postpone the vote?"

"Yes, but Martin and McDougal are having an apoplexy," she said, meaning John's co-sponsor on the bill and the Democratic majority leader. "They're demanding to know what's going on."

"Hold them off. Another hour. Maybe two. Same thing with the staff. I'll give you the green light as soon as I've told his parents."

"I will. Everyone knows something's up because the Capitol Police posted an officer outside John's office and won't let anyone in there."

"It's because the cops are waiting for a search warrant," Nick told her.

"Why do they need a warrant to search the victim's office?"

"Something about chain of custody with evidence and pacifying the Capitol Police."

"Oh, I see. I was thinking we should have Trevor draft a statement so we're ready."

"That's why I called."

"We'll get on it." She sounded relieved to have something to do.

"Are you okay with telling Trevor? Want me to do it?"

"I think I can do it, but thanks for asking."

"How're you holding up?" he asked.

"I'm in total shock...all that promise and potential

just gone…" She began to weep again. "It's going to hurt like hell when the shock wears off."

"Yeah," he said softly. "No doubt."

"I'm here if you need anything."

"Me, too, but I'm going to shut the phone off for a while. It's been ringing nonstop."

"I'll email the statement to you when we have it done."

"Thanks, Christina. I'll call you later." Nick ended the call and took a look at his recent email messages, hardly surprised by the outpouring of dismay and concern over the postponement of the vote. One was from Senator Martin himself—"What the fuck is going on, Cappuano?"

Sighing, he turned off the cell phone and dropped it into his coat pocket.

"Was that your girlfriend?" Sam asked, startling him.

"No, my deputy."

"Oh."

Wondering what she was getting at, he added, "We work closely together. We're good friends."

"Why are you being so defensive?"

"What's your *problem?*" he asked.

"I don't have a problem. You're the one with problems."

"So all that great press you've been getting lately hasn't been a problem for you?"

"Why, Nick, I didn't realize you cared."

"I don't."

"Yes, you made that very clear."

He spun halfway around in the seat to stare at her. "*Are you for real?* You're the one who didn't return any of my calls."

She glanced over at him, her face flat with surprise. "What calls?"

After staring at her in disbelief for a long moment, he settled back in his seat and fixed his eyes on the cars sharing the Interstate with them.

A few minutes passed in uneasy silence.

"What calls, Nick?"

"I called you," he said softly. "For days after that night, I tried to reach you."

"I didn't know," she stammered. "No one told me."

"It doesn't matter now. It was a long time ago." But if his reaction to seeing her again after six years of thinking about her was any indication, it *did* matter. It mattered a lot.

THREE

THE LOUDOUN COUNTY seat of Leesburg, Virginia, in the midst of the Old Dominion's horse capital, is located thirty-five miles west of Washington. Marked by rolling hills and green pastures, Loudoun is defined by its horse culture. Upon his retirement after forty years in the Senate, Graham O'Connor and his wife moved to the family's estate outside Leesburg where they could indulge in their love of all things horses. Their social life revolved around steeplechases, hounds, hunting and the Belmont Country Club.

The closer they got to Leesburg, the tenser Nick became. He kept his head back and his eyes closed as he prepared himself to deliver the gruesome news to John's parents.

"Who were his enemies?" Sam asked after a prolonged period of silence.

Keeping his eyes closed, Nick said, "He didn't have an enemy in the world."

"I'd say today's events prove otherwise. Come on. Everyone in politics has enemies."

He opened his eyes and directed them at her. "John O'Connor didn't."

"A politician without a single enemy? A man who looks like a Greek god with no spurned lovers?"

"A Greek god, huh?" he asked with a small smile. "Is that so?"

"There has to be *someone* who didn't like him. You can't live a life as high profile as his without someone being jealous or envious."

"John didn't inspire those emotions in people." Nick's heart ached as he thought of his friend. "He was inclusive. He found common ground with everyone he met."

"So the privileged son of a multi-millionaire senator could relate to the common man?" she asked, her tone ripe with cynicism.

"Well, yeah," Nick said softly, letting his mind wander back in time. "He related to me. From the moment we met in a history class at Harvard, he treated me like a long lost brother. I came from nothing. I was there on a scholarship and felt like an imposter until John O'Connor took me under his wing and made me feel like I had as much reason as anyone to be there."

"What about in the Senate? Rivals? Anyone envious of his success? Anyone put out by this bill you were about to pass?"

"John hasn't had enough success in the Senate to inspire envy. His only real success was in consensus building. That was his value to the party. He could get people to listen to him. Even when they disagreed with him, they listened." Nick glanced over at her. "Where are you going with this?"

She mulled it over for a moment. "This was a crime of passion. When someone cuts off a man's dick and stuffs it in his mouth, they're sending a pretty strong message."

Nick's heart staggered in his chest. "Is *that* what was in his mouth?"

Sam winced. "I'm sorry. I figured you'd seen it..."

"Jesus." He opened the window to let the cold air in, hoping it would keep him from puking again.

"Nick? Are you all right?"

His deep sigh answered for him.

"Do you have any idea who would have reason to do such a thing to him?"

"I can't think of anyone who disliked him, let alone hated him that much."

"Clearly, someone did."

Nick directed her to the O'Connors's country home. They drove up a long, winding driveway to the brick-front house at the top of a hill. When he reached for the door handle, she stopped him with a hand on his arm.

He glanced down at the hand and then up to find her eyes trained on him.

"I have to ask you one more thing before we go in."

"What?"

"Where were you between the hours of ten p.m. and seven a.m.?"

Staring at her, incredulous, he said, "*I'm* a suspect?"

"Everyone's a suspect until they aren't."

"I was in my office all night getting ready for the vote until five-thirty this morning when I went to the gym for an hour," he said, his teeth gritted with anger, frustration and grief over what he was about to do to people he loved.

"Can anyone confirm this?"

"Several of my staff were with me."

"And you were seen at the gym?"

"There were a few other people there. I signed in and out."

"Good," she said, seeming relieved to know he had an alibi. "That's good."

Nick took a quick glance at the cars gathered in the driveway and swore softly under his breath. Terry's Porsche was parked next to a Volvo wagon belonging to John's sister Lizbeth, who was probably visiting for the day with her two young children.

"What?"

"The whole gang's here." He pinched the bridge of his nose, hoping to find some relief from the headache forming behind his right eye. "They'll know the minute they see me that something's wrong, so don't go flashing the badge at them, okay?"

"I had no plans to," she snapped.

Nonplussed by her tone, he said, "Let's get this over with." He went up the stairs and rang the bell.

An older woman wearing a gray sweat suit with Nikes answered the door and greeted him with a warm hug.

"Nick! What a nice surprise! Come in."

"Hi, Carrie," he said, kissing her cheek. "This is Sergeant Sam Holland. Carrie is like a member of the family and keeps everyone in line."

"Which is no easy task." Carrie shook Sam's outstretched hand and sized up the younger woman before turning back to Nick, her approval apparent. "I've been telling Nick for years that he needs to settle down—"

"Don't go there, Carrie." He made an effort to keep his tone light even though his heart was heavy and burdened by what he had to tell her and the others. How he wished he were here to introduce his "family" to his new girlfriend. "Are they home?"

"Down at the stables with the kids. I'll give them a call."

Nick rested his hand on her arm. "Tell them to leave the kids there, okay?"

Her wise old eyes narrowed, this time seeing the sorrow and grief that were no doubt etched into his face. "Nick?"

"Call them, Carrie."

Watching her walk away, Nick sagged under the weight of what he was about to do to her, to all of them, and was surprised to feel Sam's hand on his back. He turned to her and was once again caught off guard by the punch of emotion that ripped through him when he found her pale blue eyes watching him with concern.

They stared at each other for a long, breathless moment until they heard Carrie coming back. Nick tore his eyes off Sam and turned to Carrie.

"They'll be here in a minute," she said, clearly trying to maintain her composure and brace herself for what she was about to hear. "Can I get you anything?"

"No," Nick said. "Thank you."

"Come into the living room," she said, leading the way.

The house was elegant but comfortable, not a show place but a home—a place where Nick had always been made to feel right at home.

"Something's wrong," Carrie whispered.

Nick reached for her hand and held it between both of his. He sat that way, with Carrie on one side of him and Sam on the other, until they heard the others come in through the kitchen.

Hand-in-hand, John's parents, Graham and Laine O'Connor, entered the room with their son Terry and daughter Lizbeth trailing behind them. Graham and Laine, both nearly eighty, were as fit and trim as people half their age. They had snow-white hair and year-round tans from spending most of their time riding horses. When they saw Nick, they lit up with delight.

He released Carrie's hand and got up to greet them both with hugs. Terry shook his hand and Lizbeth went up on tiptoes to kiss his cheek. He introduced them to Sam.

"What're you doing here?" Graham asked. "Isn't the vote today?"

Nick glanced down at the floor, took a second to summon the fortitude to say what needed to be said, and then looked back at them. "Come sit down."

"What's going on, Nick?" Laine asked in her lilting Southern accent, refusing to be led to a seat. "You don't look right. Is something wrong with John?"

Her mother's intuition had beaten him to the punch. "I'm afraid so."

Laine gasped. Her husband reached for her hand, and right before Nick's eyes, the formidable Graham O'Connor wilted.

"He was late for work today."

"That's nothing new," Lizbeth said with a sisterly snicker. "He'll be late for his own funeral."

Nick winced at her choice of words. "We couldn't reach him, so I went over there to wake him up."

"Damned foolish of him to be sleeping late on a day like this," Graham huffed.

"We thought so, too," Nick conceded, his stomach clutching with nausea and despair. "When I got there..."

"What?" Laine whispered, reaching out to grip Nick's arm. *"What?"*

Nick couldn't speak over the huge lump that lodged in his throat.

Sam stood up. "Senator, Mrs. O'Connor, I'm so very sorry to have to tell you that your son's been murdered."

Nick knew if he lived forever, he would never forget the keening wail that came from John's mother as Sam's words registered. He reached for Laine when it seemed like she might faint. Instead, she folded like a house of cards into his arms.

Carrie kept saying, "No, no, no," over and over again.

With Lizbeth crying softly behind him and Terry's eyes glassy with tears and shock, Graham turned to Sam. "How?"

"He was stabbed in his bed."

Nick, who continued to hold the sobbing Laine, was grateful that Sam didn't tell them the rest. He eased Laine down to the sofa.

"Who would want to kill my John? My beautiful, sweet John?"

"We're going to find out," Sam said.

"Sam is the lead detective on the case," Nick told them.

"Excuse me," Graham mumbled as he turned and rushed from the room.

"Go with him, Terry," Laine said. "Please go with him."

Terry followed his father.

Lizbeth sat down on the arm of the sofa next to her mother. "Oh, God," she whispered. "What will I tell the kids?"

Painfully aware of how close John was to his niece and nephew, Nick looked up at her with sympathy.

"That he had an accident," Laine said, wiping her face. "Not that he was killed. You can't tell them that."

"No," Lizbeth agreed. "I can't."

Laine raised her head off Nick's shoulder. "Where is he now?" she asked Sam.

"With the medical examiner."

"I want to see him." Laine wiped furiously at the tears that continued to spill down her unlined cheeks. "I want to see my child."

"I'll arrange it tomorrow," Sam said.

Laine turned to Nick. "There'll be a funeral befitting a United States senator."

"Of course."

"You'll see to it personally."

"Anything you want or need, Laine. You only have to ask."

She clasped his hand and looked at him with shattered eyes. "Who would do this, Nick? Who would do this to our John?"

"I've been asking myself that question for hours and can't think of anyone."

"Whoever it is, Mrs. O'Connor, we'll find them," Sam assured her.

"See that you do." As if she couldn't bear to sit there another second, Laine got up and made for the door with Lizbeth and Carrie following her. At the doorway, Laine turned back to Nick. "You know you're welcome to stay. You're a part of this family, and you belong here. You always will."

Touched, Nick said, "Thank you, but I'm going to head back to the city. I need to spend some time with the staff."

"Please tell them how much we appreciate their hard work for John."

"I will. I'll see you tomorrow."

"Mrs. O'Connor," Sam said, rising to face Laine.

"I'm so sorry to have to do this now, but in this kind of investigation, the first twenty-four hours are critical…"

"We'll do whatever we can do to find the person who did this to John," Laine said, her tear-stained face sagging with grief.

"I need to know the whereabouts of you and the other members of your family between the hours of ten p.m. last night and nine o'clock this morning."

"You aren't serious," Laine said stiffly.

"If I'm going to rule out any family involvement—"

"Fine," Laine snapped. "The senator and I entertained friends until about eleven." She glanced at Carrie, who nodded in agreement.

"I'll need the name and number of your friends." She handed Laine her card. "You can leave the information on my voicemail. And after eleven?"

"We went to bed."

"You, too, ma'am?" Sam asked Carrie.

"I watched television in my room until about two. I couldn't sleep."

"And you?" Sam asked Lizbeth.

Her expression rife with indignation, Lizbeth said, "I was at home in McLean with my husband and children."

"I'll need a phone number for your husband."

Lizbeth met Sam's even gaze with a steely stare before she stalked from the room and returned a minute later with a business card.

"Thank you," Sam said.

The three women left the room.

"You really had to do that today?" Nick asked Sam when they were alone. "Right now?"

"Yes, I really did," she said, looking pained. "I have

to play by the book on something this high profile. Surely you can understand that."

"Of course I do, but they just found out their son and brother was murdered. You could've given them fifteen minutes to absorb that before you went into attack cop mode."

"I have a job to do, Nick. When I make an arrest, I'm sure they'll be relieved that his killer is off the streets."

"What the hell difference will that make to them? Will it bring John back?"

"I need to get back to the city. Are you coming?"

Taking a long last look around the room, remembering so many happy times there with John, Nick followed her out the front door.

FOUR

FEELING AS IF the world had quite simply come to an end, Graham O'Connor leaned against a white split-rail fence to look out over the acres that made up his estate but saw nothing through a haze of tears and grief. *John is dead. John is dead. John is dead.*

From the moment Carrie called them to say Nick was waiting at the house, Graham had known. With the most important vote of John's career scheduled for that day, there was only one reason Nick would have come. Graham had known, just as he had always known there was something shameful about a father loving one of his children more than the others. But John had been extraordinary. From the very earliest hours of his youngest child's life, Graham had seen in him the special something that inspired so many others to love him, too.

His face wet with tears, Graham wondered how this could have happened.

"Dad?"

The sound of his older son's voice filled Graham with disappointment and despair. God help him for thinking such a thing, but if he'd had to lose one of his sons why couldn't it have been Terry instead of John?

Terry's hand landed on Graham's shoulder, squeezed. "What can I do for you?"

"Nothing." Graham wiped his face.

"Senator?"

Graham turned to find Nick and the pretty detective approaching them.

"We're going back to Washington," she said, "but before we do I need to confirm your whereabouts last night. After ten."

He somehow managed to contain the hot blast of rage that cut through him at the implication that he could have had something to do with the death of the one he loved above all others—except for Laine, of course. "I was right here with my wife. We had friends over, played some bridge and went to bed around eleven or so."

She seemed satisfied with his answer and turned next to Terry. "Mr. O'Connor?"

"I was…ah…with a friend."

Terry's womanizing had gotten completely out of hand since a DUI derailed his political aspirations weeks before he was supposed to declare his candidacy for the Senate. It made Graham sick that Terry was no closer to settling down and having a family at forty-two than he had been at twenty-two.

"I'll need a name and number," the detective said.

Terry's cheeks turned bright red, and Graham knew what was coming next. "I…ah…"

"He doesn't know her name," Graham said, casting a disgusted look at his son.

"I can find out," Terry said quickly.

"That'd be a good idea," the detective said.

"It's not a coincidence, is it, that this happened on the eve of the vote?" Graham said.

"We're not ruling anything out," the detective said.

"Check Minority Leader Stenhouse," Graham said.

"He hates my guts and would begrudge my son any kind of success."

"Why does he hate you?" she asked.

"They were bitter rivals for decades," Nick told her. "Stenhouse has done everything he could to block the immigration bill, but it was going to pass anyway."

"Take a good look at him," Graham said, his chest tight with rage and his voice breaking. "He's capable of anything. Taking my son from me would give him great joy."

"Can you think of anyone else?" she asked. "Anyone who might've tangled with your son, either on a personal or professional level?"

Graham shook his head. "Everyone loved John, but I'll think about it and let you know if anyone comes to mind."

Nick stepped forward to embrace him.

Graham wrapped his arms around the young man he loved like a son. "Find out who did this, Nick. Find out."

"I will. I promise."

As Nick and Sam walked away, Graham noted the hunched shoulders of his son's closest friend and trusted aide. To Terry he said, "Get the name of your bimbo, and get it now. Don't show your face around here again until you do."

"Yes, sir."

ON THE WAY BACK to Washington, Nick checked his cell phone and read through the statement his office had drafted.

With tremendous sorrow we announce that our colleague and friend, Senator John Thomas O'Connor, Democrat of Virginia, was found murdered in his Wash-

ington home this morning. After Senator O'Connor failed to arrive for work, his chief of staff, Nicholas Cappuano, went to the senator's home to check on him. Mr. Cappuano found the senator dead. At the request of the Metropolitan Police, we'll have no further statement on the details of the senator's death other than to say we will do everything within our power to assist in the investigation. Subsequent information on the investigation will come from the police.

We will make it our mission to ensure passage of the landmark immigration legislation Senator O'Connor worked so hard to bring to the Senate floor and to continue his work on behalf of children, families and the aged.

Our hearts and prayers are with the senator's parents, Senator and Mrs. Graham O'Connor, his brother Terry, sister Lizbeth, brother-in-law Royce, niece Emma and nephew Adam. Funeral arrangements are incomplete but will be announced in the next few days. We ask that you respect the privacy of the O'Connor family at this difficult time.

Nick nodded with approval and read it again before he turned to Sam. "Can I run this by you?"

"Sure." She listened intently as he read the statement to her. "Sounds like they covered every base."

"The part about the investigation was okay?"

"Yes, it's fine."

Nick placed a call to Christina. "Hey, green light on the statement. Go ahead and get it out."

Christina replied with a deep, pained sigh. "This'll make it official."

"Tell Trevor to just read it and get out of there. No questions."

"Got it."

"You guys did a great job. Thank you."

"It was the hardest thing I've ever had to do," she said, her voice hoarse.

"I'm sure."

"So, um, how'd it go with his parents?"

"Horrible."

"Same thing with the staff. People are taking it really hard."

"I'm on my way back. I'll be in soon."

"We'll be here."

Nick ended the call.

"Are you all right?" Sam asked.

"I'm fine," he said stiffly, still pissed that she had talked alibis with the O'Connors so soon.

"I was just doing my job."

"Your job sucks."

"Yes, a lot of times it does."

"Do you ever get used to telling people their loved ones have been murdered?"

"No, and I hope I never do."

As bone-deep exhaustion began to set in, he put his head back against the seat. "I appreciated you saying the words for me back there. I just couldn't bring myself to do it."

She glanced over at him. "You were very good with them."

Surprised by the unexpected compliment, Nick forced a weak smile. "I was in uncharted waters, that's for sure."

"You're close to them."

"They're family to me."

"What does your own family think of that?"

They hadn't taken the time to compare life stories

the first time they met. They'd been too busy tearing each other's clothes off. "I don't have much of a family. I was born to parents who were still in high school and was raised by my grandmother. She passed away a few years ago."

"What about your parents?"

"They breezed in and out of my life when I was a kid."

"And now?"

"Let's see, my mother is married for the third time and was living in Cleveland the last time I heard from her, which was a couple of years ago. My father is married to a woman who's younger than me, and they have three-year-old twins. He lives in Baltimore. I see them once in a while, but he's hardly a father to me. He's only fifteen years older than me."

Her silence made him realize she was waiting for him to say more.

"I remember the first weekend I spent with the O'Connors. I thought families like theirs only existed on TV."

"They always seemed almost too good to be true."

"They're not, though. They're real people with real faults and problems, but they have such a strong belief in giving back and in public service that it's impossible to be around them for any length of time and not be sucked in. They changed my whole career plan."

"What were you going to do?"

"I'd considered accounting or finance, but after a few meals at Graham O'Connor's table, I was bitten by the political bug."

"What's he like? Graham?"

"He's complicated and thoughtful and demanding.

He loves his family and his country. He's fiercely patriotic and loyal."

"You love him."

"More than any man I've ever known—except his son."

"Tell me about John."

Nick thought for a moment before he answered. "If his father is complicated, thoughtful and demanding, John was simple, forgetful and lackadaisical. But like his father, he loved his family and his country and was proud to serve the people of Virginia. He took those responsibilities seriously but didn't take himself too seriously."

"Did you like working for him?"

"I liked being around him and helping him to succeed. But from a political staff perspective, he could be a bit of a handful."

"How so?"

Nick paused, considered and decided. "Right now, my chief goal is to protect his legacy and ensure he's afforded the dignity and stature he deserves as a deceased United States senator."

"And *my* goal is to figure out who killed him. If I'm going to do that, I'll need you and the rest of your staff to be forthcoming. I can do it faster and more efficiently with your help than without it. I need to know who he was."

Nick wished he couldn't smell her, wished he wasn't so aware of her. And more than anything, he wished he didn't so vividly remember the night he'd spent lost in her. "I was furious," he said in a soft tone.

"When?" she asked, confused.

"On my way to his place this morning. If he hadn't

been dead when I got there, I might've killed him myself."

"Nick..." Her tone was full of warning, reminding him not to forget who he was talking to.

"If you want to know who John O'Connor was, the fact that his chief of staff was on his way to haul him out of bed—*again*—should tell you everything you need to know."

"It doesn't tell me everything, but it's a start."

FIVE

SAM'S MEMORIES OF Nick Cappuano should have faded over the years, but they hadn't. He remained a larger-than-life character from a single night that shouldn't have meant as much as it had. But she *had* forgotten the reality of him—his height, easily six-three or-four, broad shoulders, chocolate brown hair that curled at the ends, hazel eyes that missed nothing, olive-toned skin, strong, efficient hands that changed forever what she expected from a lover, crackling intelligence, and the cool aura of reserved control she'd found so fascinating the first time she met him.

Cracking that control had been one of the best memories from her night with him. When he didn't call, she'd wondered if their intense connection had scared him off. But now that she knew he *had* called, that he *had* wanted to see her again…that changed everything.

"Can I ask you something that has nothing to do with the case?" she said as they cut across the District on the way to the Watergate where he'd left his car. Along the way, they noticed a few American flags already lowered to half-mast in John's honor. The word was out, and the official mourning had begun.

"Sure."

Her heart raced as she picked at a scab she'd mistakenly thought healed long ago. "When you called me…

after…that night…do you remember who you talked to at my house?"

He shrugged. "Some guy. One of your roommates maybe."

Knowing the answer before she even asked, she said, "You didn't get his name? I lived with three guys."

"Shit, I don't know. Paul maybe."

"Peter?"

"Yes. Peter. That was it. I talked to him a couple of times."

Gripping the steering wheel so tightly her knuckles turned white, Sam wanted to scream.

"Was he your boyfriend?"

"Not then," she said through gritted teeth.

"Later?"

"He's my ex-husband."

"Ah! Well, now it all makes sense," he said but there was a bitter edge to his voice that she understood all too well. She was feeling rather bitter herself at the moment.

"Too bad you didn't give me your cell number instead of your home number."

"I only had a department cell then, and I never used it for personal business." They were quiet until she pulled into the Watergate. "I'd like to interview your staff in the morning," she said as the car idled.

"I'll make sure they're available." He rattled off the Hart Senate Office Building address where she could find them.

"In the meantime, here's my card in case you think of anything that might be relevant. No matter how big or how small, you never know what'll crack a case wide open."

He took the card and reached for the door handle.

"Nick," she said, her hand on his arm to stop him from getting out.

Looking down at her hand and then up to meet her eyes, he raised an eyebrow.

"I would've liked to have gotten those messages," she said, her heart racing. "I would've liked that very much."

He sighed. "I can't process this on top of everything else that's happened today. It's just too much."

"I know." She raised her hand to let him go. "I'm sorry I brought it up."

He surprised her when he reached for her hand and brought it to his lips. "Don't be sorry. I really want to talk about it. Later, though, okay?"

Sam swallowed hard at the intense expression on his handsome face. "Okay."

He released her hand and opened the car door. "I'll see you in the morning."

"Yes," she said softly to herself when he was gone. "See you then."

FREDERICO CRUZ WAS a junk food addict. However, despite his passion for donuts, his ongoing love affair with the golden arches, and his obsession with soda of all kinds except diet, he managed to maintain a wiry, one-hundred-seventy-pound frame that was usually draped by one of the many trench coats he claimed were necessary to staying in character.

In some sort of cosmic joke, Sam had drawn the dietary disaster area known as Freddie for a partner. In the midst of the HQ detective pit chaos, Sam watched fascinated and envious as he chased a cream-filled donut with a cola. She swore that spending most of every day with him for the last year had put ten unneeded pounds on her. "Where are we?" she asked when he put down the soda can and wiped his mouth.

"Still at square one. The neighbors didn't hear anything or see anyone in the elevator or hallways. I sent a couple of uniforms to pick up the security tape—not an easy task, I might add. You'd think we were planning to send G. Gordon Liddy back in there or something. I had to threaten them with warrants."

"What was the hang up?" Sam asked, eyeing his second donut with lust in her heart.

"Resident privacy, the usual bull. I had to remind them—twice—that a United States senator had been murdered in his apartment and did they really want any *more* unfavorable publicity than they're already going to get?"

"Good job, Freddie. That's the way to be aggressive." She was forever after him to get in there and get his hands dirty. In turn, he nagged her about getting a life away from the job.

"I learned from the best."

She made a face at him.

"We also seized everything from the senator's home and work offices—computers, files, etc. The lab is going through the computers now. We can hit the files tomorrow."

"Good."

"What's your take on the O'Connors?"

"The parents were devastated. There was nothing fake about it. Same with his sister."

"What about the brother?"

"He seemed shocked, but he says he was with a woman whose name he doesn't remember."

"He'll have to produce her if he's going to rely on her for an alibi."

"He's painfully aware of that," Sam said, smirking at her recollection of Terry O'Connor's discomfort and Graham's obvious disapproval.

"That's what he gets for sleeping with a stranger. Imagine going up to someone you slept with to ask for her name."

Sam's face heated as memories of her one-night stand with Nick chose that moment to resurface. "Easy, Freddie. Don't get all proper on me."

"It's just another sign of the moral decline of our country."

Groaning at the familiar argument, she said, "Any word from the M.E.?"

"Not yet. Apparently, they had a backlog to get through."

"Who comes before a murdered U.S. senator?"

He shrugged. "Don't kill the messenger."

"My favorite sport."

"Don't I know it? The guy who found him checked out? Cappuano?"

"Yeah." Sam decided right in that moment not to tell Freddie about her history with Nick. Some things were personal, and she didn't want or need Freddie's disapproval. She was still dealing with her own disapproval for bringing up their former personal relationship in the midst of a murder investigation. "He was at work all night with other people from the staff, which I'll confirm tomorrow."

"So what's next?"

"In the morning, we'll interview O'Connor's staff and pay a visit to the senate minority leader," she said, filling him in on Graham O'Connor's long-running feud with Stenhouse.

Freddie rubbed his chiseled cheek. On top of his many other faults, he was *GQ* handsome, too. Life wasn't fair. "Interesting," he said.

"Senator O'Connor questioned the timing—on the eve of the biggest vote of his son's career as a senator."

"Someone didn't want that vote to happen?"

"It's the closest thing to a motive I've seen yet. When we talk to his staff tomorrow, we need to cover both sides—the political and the personal. Who was he dating? Who might've had an axe to grind? You know the drill."

"What's your gut telling you, boss?"

He knew she hated when he called her that. "I'm not loving the political angle."

"The timing works."

"Yeah, but would a political rival cut off his dick and stuff it in his mouth?"

Freddie cringed and covered his own package.

"We're going to keep that detail close to the vest and see where it takes us. But my money's on a woman."

"You know what's bugging me?" Freddie asked.

"What's that?"

"No sign of a struggle. How does someone get a hold of your dick and do the Lorena Bobbitt without you putting up a fight?"

"Maybe he was asleep? Didn't see it coming?"

"Someone grabs my junk, I'm *wide* awake."

"Spare me the visual, will you, please?"

"I'm just saying..."

"That it was someone he knew, someone he wasn't surprised to see."

"Exactly." He picked up the second donut and took a bite. With a dollop of white cream on his lower lip, he added, "He had one of those butcher block knife things in his kitchen. The butcher knife was the one holding him to the headboard."

"So the killer didn't arrive armed."

"It doesn't seem so. No."

Standing up, Sam said, "I want to see those tapes. What the hell is taking them so long?"

DRIVING FROM THE Watergate to the office, Nick should have been thinking about what he was going to say to his staff. They'd be looking to him for leadership, for answers to questions that had no answers. But rather than prepare himself for what would no doubt be an emotional ordeal, he kept hearing Sam's voice: "I would've liked to have gotten those messages."

Pounding his hand on the steering wheel, he let loose with an uncharacteristic string of swears. Like it wasn't enough that John had been murdered. To also have to face off with the one woman from his past who he'd never worked out of his system was…well, calling it unfair wouldn't do it justice.

He knew she wanted to talk about what happened all those years ago and why they never saw each other again. It made him so mad to think about her malicious ex not giving her the messages. But he couldn't process the implications of this discovery in the midst of the mayhem caused by John's murder. Dealing with Sam Holland solely on a professional level would take all the fortitude he could muster, never mind getting personal.

Years ago, when she failed to return his calls, he'd been angry and hurt—so much so that he hadn't pursued it any further, which he now knew had been stupid. He couldn't help but wonder what might have been different for him—for both of them—if she had gotten his messages and returned his calls. Would they still be together? Or would it have burned out the way all his relationships inevitably did?

He realized, with a clarity he couldn't explain or understand, that they would probably still be together. He'd never had that kind of connection with anyone else, which was why he'd been so acutely aware of her all day today.

SIX

AFTER SPENDING AN excruciating hour with his grieving staff, Nick sent them home with orders to be back to work at nine in the morning to meet with the detectives and to plan the senator's funeral. He instructed them not to discuss the case or the senator with anyone and to avoid the press in particular.

He lowered himself into his desk chair, every muscle in his body aching with fatigue as the sleepless night and agonizing day caught up to him.

"Have you eaten?" Christina asked from the doorway.

Nick had to think about that. "Not since the bagel I puked up this morning."

"There's pizza left from before. Want me to get you some?"

Not at all sure he'd be able to get it down, he said, "Sure, thanks."

"Coming right up."

She returned a few minutes later with two slices that she had warmed in the microwave.

"Thank you," he said when she handed him the plate and a can of cola. Her blue eyes were rimmed with red, her face puffy from crying. "How're you doing?"

With a shrug, she collapsed into a chair on the other side of his desk. "I feel like all the air has been sucked out of my lungs, and I can't seem to breathe."

"I know you cared for him a great deal," Nick said haltingly. They'd never discussed Christina's feelings for John.

"For all the good it did me."

"He loved you, Chris. You know he did."

"As a friend and colleague. Big whoop."

"I'm sorry."

"So am I because now I have to live the whole rest of my life wondering what might've happened if I'd had the courage to tell him how I felt."

"I'm kind of glad you didn't."

"I'm sure you are," she said with a laugh.

"Not because of work. I loved him like a brother. You know that. But he wasn't good enough for you. He would've broken your heart."

"Probably," she said. "No, definitely."

"If it makes you feel any better, I was confronted with a blast from my romantic past today. We spent a memorable night together six years ago, and I haven't seen her since—until she walked into John's apartment this morning as the detective in charge of the case."

Christina winced. "Awkward."

"To say the least."

"Do you trust her to handle the case?"

"Sam's a damned good detective."

"I thought you hadn't seen her in six years."

"Doesn't mean I haven't read about her."

"Hmm," she said, studying him.

"What?"

"Oh, nothing." Her eyes widened all of a sudden. "What's her last name?"

"Holland."

"Oh my God! She's the one who ordered the shoot-out at that crack house where the kid was killed!"

"Yes."

"But, Nick, do we really want *her* investigating John's murder? Couldn't we get someone else?"

"I trust her," Nick said. "She has one blemish on an otherwise stellar career. And think of it this way, she's got something to prove right now."

"I guess you're right," she said, still wary. The phone on Nick's desk rang, and Christina reached for it. "Nick Cappuano's office." Once again her eyes widened, and she stammered as she said, "Of course. One moment please."

"Who is it?" Nick asked.

"The president," she whispered.

Nick quickly swallowed a mouthful of pizza and reached for a napkin and the phone at the same time. "Good evening, Mr. President." He had met President Nelson on several occasions—mostly in receiving lines at Democratic Party fundraisers—but a phone call from him was unprecedented.

"Hello, Nick. Gloria and I just wanted to tell you all how sorry we are."

"Thank you, sir. I'll pass that along to the staff. And thank you for the statement you issued to the press."

"I've known John since he was a little boy. I'm heart-broken."

"We all are."

"I can only imagine. I also wanted to make myself available for anything you might need over the next few days."

"I appreciate that. I know Senator and Mrs. O'Connor would be honored if you could speak at the funeral."

"*I'd* be honored."

"I'll work with your staff on the details."

"Let me give you my direct number in the residence. Feel free to use it."

Nick took down the number with a sense of disbelief. "Thank you."

"I spoke earlier with Chief Farnsworth and made the full resources of the federal government available to the Metropolitan Police. I'm sure you'll be close to the investigation. If there's anything you feel they could be doing that they're not, don't hesitate to contact me."

"I won't, sir."

The president released a deep sigh. "I just can't imagine who would do such a thing to John of all people."

"Neither can I."

"Do you think Graham and Laine would be up for a phone call?"

"I'm sure they'd love to hear from you."

"Well, I won't keep you any longer. God bless you and your staff, Nick. Our thoughts and prayers are with you all."

"Thank you so much for calling, Mr. President." Nick put down the phone and looked over at Christina.

"Unreal," she said.

"Surreal," he added, filling her in on what the president had said.

She began to cry again. "I keep waiting for John to come bounding in here asking why we're all sitting around."

"I know. Me, too."

"I actually had a few people ask me today how this affects their jobs," she said with disgust.

"Well, you can't blame them. They have families to support."

"Couldn't they have waited a day or two to bring that up?"

"Apparently not. I'll talk to them about it tomorrow and tell them we'll do our best to get them placed somewhere in government."

"What'll you do?" she asked.

"Shit, I don't know. I can't think about that until after we get through the funeral. The two of us, maybe a couple of others, will be needed for a while until the governor appoints someone to take John's place. Whoever it is will want to bring in their own people, so we'll help with the transition and then figure out what's next, I guess."

Christina looked so sad, so despondent that Nick felt his heart go out to her. "Why don't you go home, Chris? There's nothing more we can do here tonight."

"What about you?"

"I'll be going soon, too."

"All right," she said as she got up. "I'll see you in the morning."

"Try to get some sleep."

"As if."

He walked her to the door and sent her off with a hug before he wandered into John's office. The desk had been swept clean and the computer removed. If it hadn't been for the photo of John with his niece and nephew on the windowsill, there would've been no sign of him or the five years he'd spent working in this room. Nick wasn't sure what he hoped to find when he sat in John's chair. Swiveling to look out the window, he could see the Washington Monument lit up in the distance.

Resting his head back, he stared at the monument and finally gave himself permission to do what he'd needed to do all day. He wept.

SAM ARRIVED HOME exhausted after a sixteen-hour day and smiled when she heard the whir of her father's chair as he came out to greet her.

"Hi, Dad."

"Late tonight."

"I'm on O'Connor."

The side of his face that wasn't paralyzed lifted into a smile. "Are you now? Farnsworth's got you right back on the horse."

She kicked off her boots and bent to kiss his cheek. "So it seems."

Celia, one of the nurses who cared for him, came out from the kitchen to greet Sam. "How about we get ready for bed, Skip?"

Sam hated the indignation that darted across the expressive side of his face. "Go ahead, Dad. I'll be in when you're done. I've got a couple of things I want to run by you."

"I suppose I can make some time for you," he teased, turning the chair with his one working finger and following Celia to his bedroom in what used to be the dining room.

Sam went into the kitchen and served herself a bowl of the beef stew Celia had left on the stove for her. She ate standing up without tasting anything as the events of the day ran through her mind like a movie. Under normal circumstances, she'd be obsessed with the case. She'd be thinking it through from every angle, searching out motives, making a list of suspects. But instead, she thought of Nick and the sadness that had radiated from him all day. More than once she had wanted to throw her arms around him and offer comfort, which was hardly a professional impulse.

Deciding it was pointless to try to eat, she poured the rest of the soup into the garbage disposal and stood at the sink, her shoulders stooped. She was still there twenty minutes later when Celia came into the kitchen.

"He's ready for you."

"Thanks, Celia."

"He's been kind of…"

"What?" Sam asked, immediately on alert.

"Off. He hasn't been himself the last few days."

"The two-year anniversary is coming up next week."

"That could be it."

"Let's keep an eye on him."

Celia nodded in agreement. "What do you know about Senator O'Connor?"

"Not as much as I'd like to."

"What a tragedy," Celia said, shaking her head. "We've been glued to the news all day. Such an awful waste."

"Seemed like a guy who had it all."

"But there was something sort of sad about him, too."

"Why do you say that?"

"No reason in particular. Just a vibe he put out."

"I never noticed," Sam said, intrigued by the observation. She made a mental note to find some video of O'Connor's speeches from the Senate floor and TV interviews.

"Go on in and see your dad. He so looks forward to his time with you."

"The stew was great. Thank you."

"Glad you liked it."

Sam went into her father's bedroom where he was propped up in bed, a respirator hose snaking from his throat to the machine on the floor that breathed for him at night.

"You look beat," he said, his speech an awkward staccato around the respirator.

"Long-ass day." Sam sat in the chair next to the hospital bed and propped her feet on the frame under the pressurized mattress that minimized bedsores. "But it feels good to be doing more than pushing paper again."

"What've you got?" he asked, reverting to his former role as the department's detective captain.

She ran through the whole thing, from the meeting with Chief Farnsworth to reviewing the tapes the Watergate had finally produced. "We only got traffic in the lobby. Nothing jumped out at us, but I'm going to show them to his chief of staff in the morning to see if he can ID anyone."

"That's a good idea. Why do you get a funny look in those blue eyes of yours when you mention the chief of staff? Nick, right?"

"I went out with him once." She spared her father a deeper explanation of what "going out" had meant in this case. "A long time ago."

"But it was hard to see him?"

"Yeah," she said softly. "I found out he *did* call me after that night. Guess who took the messages and never gave them to me?"

"Oh, let's see, could it be our good friend Peter?"

"One and the same, the prick."

Skip's laugh was strained. "You able to be objective on this one with your Nick from the past part of the mix?"

Surprised by the question, she glanced up at him and found him studying her with sharp, blue eyes that were just like hers. "Of course. It was six years ago. No biggie."

"Uh huh."

She should have known he would see right through her. He always did.

"You need to get some sleep," he said.

"Whenever I close my eyes, I'm back in that crack house with Marquis Johnson screaming. And then I break out in a cold sweat."

"You did everything right, followed every instinct." He gasped for air. "I wouldn't have done it any differently."

"Do you ever think about the night you got shot?" She had never thought to ask that until she'd been haunted by her own demons.

"Not so much. It's all a blur."

Her cell phone rang. Sam reached for it on her belt and checked the caller ID. She didn't recognize the 703 number. "I need to take this."

"Go on."

She kissed her father's forehead and left the room. "Holland."

"Sam, it's Nick. Someone's been in my house."

Her heart fluttered at the sound of his deep voice. This was *not* good. "Has it been ransacked?" she asked, making an effort to sound cool and professional.

"No."

"Then how do you know someone's been there?"

"I *know*. Stuff's been moved."

"Where do you live?"

He rattled off an address in Arlington, Virginia.

Even though it was out of her jurisdiction, she grabbed her coat. "I'm on my way."

SEVEN

THIRTY MINUTES LATER, Sam stormed up the stairs to Nick's brick-front townhouse.

He waited just inside the door and held it open for her. "Thanks for coming."

"Sure." She stole a quick glance around a combined living room/dining room where it appeared nothing was out of place. In fact, the space seemed better suited to a furniture showroom rather than someone's home. "How can you—"

He grabbed her hand. "Come."

Startled, she let him lead her into his office, which was as neat as the other rooms but more lived in than what she had seen so far.

"See that?"

Following the direction of his pointed finger, she studied a small stack of books on the desk. "What about it?"

"It's at an angle."

"So?"

"It's not supposed to be."

"*Seriously?* You called me over here at eleven o'clock at night because your stack of books isn't anally aligned?"

With a furious scowl, he grabbed her hand again and all but dragged her upstairs to his bedroom. *Now we're talking! Relax, Sam, he's not dragging you off to bed as much as you wish he were.* Reminding herself that she was investigating a break-in at the home of a player in a homicide investigation, she pushed aside her salacious thoughts and tuned in to what he was showing her.

Pointing to the dresser, he said, "I didn't leave it like that."

A tiny scrap of white fabric poked out through the closed drawers. Deciding to humor him, Sam leaned in to inspect the cloth. "It's not possible your tighty whities got caught in the drawer and you didn't notice?"

"No, it's not possible," he said through gritted teeth.

She stood up and studied him like she had never seen him before, as if she hadn't once seen him naked. "Have you always been so anal?"

"Yes."

"Hmm."

"What does that mean? Hmm? Aren't you going to call someone?"

"To do what?"

"To figure out who's been in my house!"

"Nick, come on."

"Forget it. Go home. I'm sorry I bothered you."

His eyes, she noticed, were rimmed with red. She ached at the thought of him alone and heartbroken over his murdered friend. "Fine. If you really think someone's been in here—"

"I do."

"I left my phone in the car. May I use yours?"

He handed her his cell phone.

"This is Detective Sergeant Sam Holland, MPD. I need a Crime Scene unit," she said, giving the address.

When she hung up, she turned to find him watching her intently.

"Thank you."

She nodded, unsettled by the heat coming from his hazel eyes. Had she caused that or was it the fault of the person who had supposedly invaded his private space?

AN HOUR LATER, Sam sat with Nick on the sofa, out of the way of the Arlington cops who were dusting for prints.

"How do you think they got in?" Desperate to maintain some semblance of distance from him, she spoke in the clipped, professional tone she used to interview witnesses.

"I have no idea."

"Does anyone have a key?"

"John had the only other one."

"Where did he keep it?"

"I'm not sure. I gave it to him in case I ever locked myself out."

"Which probably never happens."

"It hasn't yet."

"You don't use the security system?" she asked.

"It came with the place. I've never had it turned on."

"You might want to think about that."

"Really? Gee, thanks for that advice, Sergeant."

She shot him a warning look.

"I'm sorry," he said, dropping his head to run his fingers through thick dark hair.

Sam licked her lips, wishing she could do that for him.

"I don't mean to snap at you. It's just the idea of someone in my *home*, going through my stuff…It has me kind of skeeved out."

"Any idea what they might be looking for?"

His shoulders sagged with fatigue. "None."

Sam's heart went out to him. He'd had a horrible, painful day, and she wished she could find an appropriate excuse to hug him. She made an effort to soften her tone. "Is it possible someone is trying to find something here they couldn't find at the senator's place?"

"I can't imagine what. Neither of us ever took anything sensitive out of the office. There're all kinds of rules about that."

"What kind of sensitive stuff was he involved with?"

"After the midterm election, he was appointed to the Senate Homeland Security Committee, but most of his work was in the areas of commerce, finance, children, families and the aged. None of that was overly sensitive."

Watching his tired face with much more than professional interest, she was dying to address the elephant in the room—the six years' worth of unfinished business and the tension that zipped through her every time she connected with those hot hazel eyes of his. "Is it possible he was involved in something you didn't know about?"

Nick scoffed. "Highly doubtful."

"But possible?"

"Sure it is, but John didn't operate that way. He relied on us for everything."

"You alluded earlier to him being high maintenance for the staff. Other than having to wake him up in the morning, how did you mean?"

Nick was quiet for a long moment before he glanced at her. "This is all for background, right? I won't read about it in tomorrow's paper?"

"I think we've missed the deadline for the morning edition."

"I'm serious, Sam. I don't want to say or do anything to cause his parents any more grief than they're already dealing with."

"It's for my information now, but I can't guarantee it'll stay that way. If something you tell me helps to make this case, it's apt to come out in court. As much as we might wish otherwise, murder victims are often put on trial right along with their killers."

"That's so wrong."

"Unfortunately, it's just the way it is."

Nick made an A-frame out of his hands and rested his chin on the point. "John was a reluctant senator. He used to joke that he was Prince Harry to Terry's Prince William. Terry was the anointed one, groomed all his life to follow his father into politics. While Terry always lived in the public eye, John had a relatively normal life. For some reason, the press took an unusual interest in Terry's comings and goings. His name was mentioned on the political and gossip pages almost as often as his father's, and this was long before his father announced his retirement."

"It must've been tough to deal with all that attention."

Nick laughed, which chased the tension from his face. "Terry loved it. He ate it up. He was Washington's most eligible bachelor, and he took full advantage, let me tell you."

"That doesn't sound like a smart political strategy."

"Oh, it wasn't. He and the senator—his father, I mean—had huge, knock-down brawls over his lifestyle. I witnessed a few of them. But somehow Terry managed to stay one step ahead of the scandalmongers—that is until he got arrested for drunk driving three weeks before he was supposed to announce his candidacy for his father's seat. No amount of spin can get you out of that."

"Ouch. I remember this. It's all coming back to me now."

"Graham was devastated. Before today, I've never seen him so crushed. That this son he'd placed all these hopes and dreams on had so totally let him down…"

"How did Terry take it?"

"Like a wounded puppy, like it was someone else's fault. He was full of excuses. John was totally disgusted by him. At one point, he said, 'Why doesn't he just be a man and admit he made a mistake?'"

"Did he say this to Terry?"

"I doubt it. They were never really close. Terry loved all the attention, and John did his best to stay well below the radar."

"Until Terry forced him into the spotlight," Sam said, starting to get a clearer picture of the O'Connor family.

"Yes, and forced is the right word. John wanted nothing to do with running for the Senate. In fact, I remember him grousing about how 'lucky' he was that he'd just turned thirty, which is the minimum age to run for the Senate. He was sitting atop a nice little technology firm that made a chip for one of the DoD's weapons systems. He and his partner were very successful."

"What happened to the company when John ran for Senate?"

"His partner bought him out and later sold the company."

"Would he have any reason to want John dead?"

"Hardly. He made hundreds of millions when he sold the company. The last I knew, he was living large in the Caribbean."

"What about Terry? Is he still harboring resentment that his younger brother got the life he was supposed to have?"

"Maybe, but Terry wouldn't have the stones to kill him. At the end of the day, Terry's a wimp."

Regardless of that, Sam made a note to look more closely at Terry O'Connor.

"Sergeant?" The lieutenant in charge of the Crime Scene unit approached them. "We're just about done here. We didn't find any sign of forced entry at either door or any of the ground-floor windows."

"Prints?"

"Just one set." He glanced at Nick. "We assume they're yours, but we'll have to confirm that."

Nick swore softly under his breath.

"Thanks, Lieutenant." Sam handed the other officer her card. "I'll write up what I have if you'll shoot me your report as a courtesy. There may be a connection to Senator O'Connor's murder."

"Of course."

After a perfunctory clean up of the dust left over from the fingerprint powder, the other cops left a short time later.

"Do you want some help cleaning up?" she asked Nick when they were alone.

"That's all right. I can do it."

He stood and extended a hand to help her up.

Sam took his hand, but when she tried to let go, he tightened his grip. Startled, she looked up at him.

"I'm sorry I dragged you over here for nothing."

"It wasn't nothing—" Her words got stuck in her throat when he ran a finger over her cheek. His touch was so light she would have missed it if she hadn't been staring at him.

"You're tired."

She shrugged, her heart slamming around in her chest. "I haven't been sleeping too well lately."

"I read all the coverage of what happened. It wasn't your fault, Sam."

"Tell that to Quentin Johnson. It wasn't his fault, either."

"His father should've put his son's safety ahead of saving his crack stash."

"I was counting on the fact that he would. I should've known better. How someone could put their child in that kind of danger…I'll just never understand it."

"I'm sorry it happened to you. It broke my heart to read about it."

Sam found it hard to look away. "I, um…I should go."

"Before you do, there's just one thing I really need to know."

"What?" she whispered.

He released her hand, cupped her face and tilted it to receive his kiss.

As his lips moved softly over hers, Sam summoned every ounce of fortitude she possessed and broke the kiss. "I can't, Nick. Not during the investigation." *But oh how she wanted to keep kissing him!*

"I was dying to know if it would be like I remembered."

Her eyes closed against the onslaught of emotions. "And was it?"

"Even better," he said, going back for more.

"Wait. Nick. *Wait.*" She kept her hand on his chest to stop him from getting any closer. "We can't do this.

Not now. Not when I'm in the middle of a homicide investigation that involves you."

"I didn't do it." He reached up to release the clip that held her hair and combed his fingers through the length as it tumbled free.

Unnerved by the intimate gesture, she stepped back from him. "I know you didn't, but you're still involved. I've got enough problems right now without adding an inappropriate fling with a witness to the list."

"Is that what it would be?" His eyes were hot, intense and possibly furious as he stared at her. "An inappropriate fling?"

"No," she said softly. "Which is another reason why it's not a good idea to start something now."

He moved closer to her. "It's already started, Sam. It started six years ago, and we never got to finish it. This time, I intend to finish it. Maybe not right now, but eventually. I was a fool to let you slip through my fingers the first time. I won't make that mistake again."

Startled by his intensity, Sam took another step back. "I appreciate the warning, but it might be one of those things that's better left unfinished. We both have a lot going on—"

"I'll see you tomorrow," he said, handing her the hair clip.

Sam felt his eyes on her back as she went to the door and let herself out. All the way home, her lips burned from the heat of his kiss.

EIGHT

EARLY THE NEXT MORNING, as she stood over the lifeless, waxy remains of Senator John Thomas O'Connor, age thirty-six, it struck Sam that death was the great equalizer. We arrive with nothing, we leave with nothing, and in death what we've accomplished—or not accomplished—doesn't much matter. Senator or bricklayer, millionaire or welfare mother, they all looked more or less the same laid out on the medical examiner's table.

"I'd place time of death at around eleven p.m.," Dr. Lindsey McNamara, the District's chief medical examiner, said as she released her long red hair from the high ponytail she'd worn for the autopsy.

"That's shortly after he got home. The killer might've been waiting for him."

"Dinner consisted of filet mignon, potatoes, mixed greens and what looked like two beers."

"Drugs?"

"I'm waiting on the tox report."

"Cause of death?"

"Stab wound to the neck. The jugular was severed. He bled out very quickly."

"Which came first? The cut to the neck or the privates?"

"The privates."

Sam winced. "Tough way to go."

"For a man, probably the toughest."

"He was alert and aware that someone he knew had dismembered him," Sam said, more to herself than to Lindsey.

"You're sure it was someone he knew?"

"Nothing's definite, but I'm leaning in that direction because there was no struggle and no forced entry."

"There was also no skin under his nails or any defensive injuries to his hands."

"He didn't put up a fight."

"It happened fast." Lindsey gestured to O'Connor's penis floating in some sort of liquid.

Sam fought back an unusual surge of nausea. This stuff didn't usually bother her, but she had never seen a severed penis before.

"A clean, fast cut," Lindsey said.

"Which is why the killer was able to get the knife through his neck while he was still sitting up in bed."

"Right. He would've been reacting to the dismemberment. He might've even blacked out from the pain."

"So he never saw the death blow coming."

"Probably not."

"Thanks, Doc. Send me your report when it's ready?"

"You got it," Lindsey said. "Sam?"

Sam, who had reached for her cell to check for messages, looked over at the other woman.

"I wanted you to know how terrible I felt about what happened with that kid," Lindsey said, her green eyes soft with compassion. "What the press did to you…well, anyone who knows you knows the truth."

"Thank you," Sam said in a hushed tone. "I appreciate that."

BY SEVEN O'CLOCK, Sam was in her office wading through four sets of phone records drawn from the senator's home, office and two cell phones. Her eyes blurry from the lack of sleep that she blamed on Nick's kiss and the memories it had resurrected, she searched for patterns and nursed her second diet cola of the day. Most of the calls were to numbers in the District and Virginia, but she noticed several calls per week to Chicago that usually lasted an hour or more. She made a note to check the number.

A few other numbers popped up with enough regularity to warrant a follow up. Sam made a list and turned it over to one of the other detectives who had been assigned to assist her.

Grabbing another soda and a stale bagel left over from yesterday, she stopped to brief Chief Farnsworth before heading out to meet Freddie on Capitol Hill. A crush of reporters waited for her outside the public safety building. When she saw how many there were, she briefly considered going back to ask a couple of uniforms to help her get through the crowd. Then she dismissed the idea as cowardly and stepped into the scrum.

"Sergeant, how close are you to naming a suspect?"

"How was the senator killed?"

"Who found him?"

"What do you think of the headlines in today's paper?"

That last one made her stomach roil as she could only imagine what the papers were saying about the detective the department had chosen to lead the city's highest profile murder investigation in years. She held up a hand to stop the barrage of questions.

"All I'll say at this time is the investigation is proceeding, and as soon as we know anything more, we'll hold a press conference. I'll have no further comment until that time. Now, would you mind letting me through? I have work to do."

They didn't move but also didn't stop her from pushing her way through.

Rattled and annoyed, Sam got into her unmarked department car and locked the doors. "Fucking vultures," she muttered.

Outside the Hart Senate Office Building, she dropped two quarters into the *Washington Post* box and tugged out the morning's issue where a banner headline announced the senator's murder. In a smaller story below the fold, a headline read, Disgraced Detective Tapped to Lead Murder Investigation. Sam released a frustrated growl when the words appeared jumbled on the page as they often did during times of stress or exhaustion. *Goddamned dyslexia.* Taking a deep calming breath, she tried again, taking the words one at a time the way she'd trained herself to do.

The story contained a recap of the raid that had led to the death of Quentin Johnson and stopped just short of questioning her competence—and the chief's.

"Great," she muttered. "That's just *great.*" Tossing the paper into the trash, she took the elevator to the second floor where Freddie enjoyed a glazed donut while he waited for her.

"Did you see the paper?" he asked, wiping the sticky frosting from his mouth with the back of his hand.

She nodded brusquely, and before he could get into a further discussion about the article, she brought him up to speed on the possible break-in at Nick's, the autopsy and the phone records. Gesturing to the door to Senator O'Connor's suite of offices, she said, "Let's get to it."

AFTER A THOROUGH look through the remaining items in John's office where they found nothing useful to the case, Sam and Freddie worked their way up from administrative assistants through legislative affairs people to the staff from the senator's Richmond office to the communications director. They asked each of Senator O'Connor's employees the same questions—where were you on the night of the murder, did you have a key to his apartment, what do you know about his personal life, and can you think of anyone who might've had a beef with him?

The answers were the same with few variations—I was here working (or at home in Richmond with my husband/wife/girlfriend), I didn't have a key, he guarded his privacy, and everyone liked him, even political rivals who had good reason not to.

"Who's next?" Sam asked, feeling like they were spinning their wheels.

"Christina Billings, deputy chief of staff," Freddie said.

"Bring her in."

"Ms. Billings," Sam said, gesturing the pretty, petite blonde to a seat across the conference room table. Sam always felt like an Amazon next to tiny women like her. "Let me begin by saying how sorry we are for your loss."

The sympathy brought tears to Christina's blue eyes. "Thank you," she whispered.

"Can you tell us where you were the night of the senator's murder?"

"I was here. With the vote the next day we had so much to do to get ready for the aftermath—press conferences, appearances on talk shows, interviews…We were doing everything we could to ensure the senator got the attention he deserved." Her shoulders sagged, almost as if life had lost its purpose. "He'd worked so hard."

Intrigued by the gamut of emotions emanating from Christina, Sam said, "You were here in the office the entire night?"

"Except for when I left to get food for everyone."

"What time?" Freddie asked.

"I don't know. Maybe around eleven or eleven-thirty?"

Freddie and Sam exchanged glances.

"Where did you get the food?"

She named a Chinese restaurant on Capitol Hill, and Sam made a note to check it out later. "Did you go anywhere else?"

"No. I picked up the food and came right back. Everyone was hungry."

"Do you have a key to the senator's apartment?" Freddie asked.

Nodding, she said, "He gave it to me some time ago so I could pick up his mail and water the plants when he was in Richmond or Leesburg."

"When was the last time you used it?"

Christina thought about that. "Maybe three months ago. He's been in town for most of the session working on gathering the votes needed for the immigration bill."

"What do you know about his personal life?" Freddie asked. "Was he dating anyone?"

Her expression immediately changed from grief-stricken to hostile. "I have no idea. I didn't discuss his love life with him. He was my boss."

Something in the tone, in the flash of the blue eyes, set off Sam's radar. "Ms. Billings, were you romantically involved with the senator?"

Christina pushed back the chair and stood up. "I'm done."

"The hell you are," Sam snapped. "Sit down."

Trembling with rage, her lips tight, Christina turned and met Sam's steely stare with one of her own. "Or what?"

"Or we'll do this downtown. Your choice."

With great reluctance, Christina returned to her seat, her body rigid, and her hands clasped together.

"Before we continue, I'll advise you of your right to have counsel present during this interview."

Christina gasped. "Am I under arrest?"

"Not at this time, but you may request an attorney at any point. Do you wish to continue without counsel?"

Christina's nod was small and uncertain. Her posture had lost some of its rigidity at the mention of lawyers.

"I'll ask you again," Sam said. "Were you romantically involved with the senator?"

"No," Christina said softly.

"Did you have feelings of a romantic nature for him?"

Christina's eyes flooded. "Yes."

"And these feelings were unrequited?"

"I have no idea. We never discussed it."

"How did you feel about him dating other women?" Freddie asked.

"How do you think I felt?" Christina shot back at him. "I loved him, but he didn't see me that way. To him I was a trusted aide and a friend he could count on to pick up his mail."

"What were your specific duties as his deputy chief of staff?" Sam asked.

"I oversaw his daily schedule, kept his appointment calendar, supervised the administrative assistants, and basically managed his time."

"So you worked closely with him?" Freddie asked.

"Yes."

"More closely than Mr. Cappuano?"

"On many days. Yes."

"And in all this time you spent with him, he had no idea how you felt about him?" Sam asked.

"I went to great lengths to hide it from him and everyone else. He was my boss. I felt like a bad cliché."

"So no one else knew?"

"Nick had figured it out, but I didn't know that until after the senator was...killed," she said, her voice trailing off.

"Why didn't you leave?" Sam asked, working hard to contain her fury at Nick for keeping this from her.

"Because he needed me. He said he'd be lost without me." Christina shrugged. "I know that sounds so pathetic, but it was better than nothing."

"Was it?" Sam asked.

"If you're implying I killed him because he didn't notice me as a woman, you're way off."

"People have killed for less."

"I didn't. I loved him. Receiving that phone call from Nick was the single most devastating moment of my life." After a long moment of silence, Christina started to push back her chair. "May I go?"

"Before you do," Freddie said, "let me ask you this—you say you kept his schedule and managed his life. Did I get that right?"

"Yes."

"So wouldn't you know who he was seeing outside the office?"

Christina's jaw clenched with tension.

"Is that a yes?" Freddie asked.

"There were several," Christina finally said.

"We'll need a list," Sam said. "I'd also like a list of anyone else you know of who had a key to his apartment and his appointment calendar for the last six months—by the end of the day, please."

With a curt nod, Christina got up.

"Stay available," Sam said before the other woman could leave the room.

"What does that mean?"

"Exactly what you think it means."

The moment the door slammed shut behind Christina, Sam turned to Freddie.

"I know what you're going to say." He counted off on his fingers. "A break in the alibi at the same time as the murder, a key to the apartment, unrequited love…"

"It's almost enough to arrest her," Sam said.

"Except?"

Sam sighed. "I believed her when she said his death was the most devastating thing that's ever happened to her."

"Doesn't mean she wasn't responsible for it."

"No, it doesn't."

"I'll do some digging around in Ms. Billings's background."

"Freddie, you read my mind. We also need to look into who would stand to gain financially from the senator's death."

"Would the chief of staff know that?"

"He might. He's next. Do you want to go grab some lunch before we get to him?"

"I thought you'd never ask," Freddie stretched, rubbing his belly with glee. "Something for you?"

"A salad." She slapped a ten-dollar bill into his hand. "Low-fat dressing."

He made a disgusted face. "Coming right up."

The moment he was gone, Sam marched into Nick's office and slammed the door.

"Well, good afternoon to you, too, Sergeant," he said with a small, private smile that let her know he'd been thinking of her since they'd kissed the night before.

"Save the charm for someone who's interested."

He raised a swarthy eyebrow in amusement. "Oh, you're interested. But if you want to play hard to get, don't let me stop you."

"What happened last night can't happen again."

"It can, and it will."

"Not until this case is closed, Nick. I mean that." Deciding it was time to move past their personal debate, she planted her hands on her hips. "Were you planning to mention that your deputy was in love with the senator?"

Nick looked stricken. "She *told* you that?"

"I got it out of her. One of my special talents."

"I'll bet," he said dryly.

"Why didn't you think it was important enough to share with me?"

"It was personal, and I didn't see how it was relevant."

"*Everything* is relevant, Nick! This is a *homicide* investigation!"

"I'm sorry. It never occurred to me that it would matter."

"She left here to get food at the exact time the M.E. has placed the time of death. She had a key to his place. She was in love with him."

Nick's handsome face went pale. "You can't possibly be suggesting—"

"I can, and I am."

"There's no way, Sam. She adored him. She was devoted to him. She could never have harmed him."

"How well do you know her?"

"I've worked with her for five years. She's a great colleague and friend."

"What do you know about her background?"

"She grew up in Oregon, came here for college, and has been working for the legislative branch since she graduated. She's worked her way up from the admin level."

"You trust her?"

"Implicitly."

"What level clearance does she have?"

"Secret."

Sam tugged the notebook from her back pocket and made a note to get a hold of the background check Christina Billings would've been required to undergo for a government security clearance. "What about you?"

"Top secret."

"As of when?"

"As of the senator's appointment to the Committee on Homeland Security and Governmental Affairs. Before that it was secret."

"Who else has top secret?"

"Only the senator."

"Who're his heirs?"

Nick considered that. "Well, I suppose it would be his niece and nephew, Emma and Adam."

"But you don't know for sure?"

He shook his head.

"Who would?"

"Probably his father and their attorney, Lucien Haverfield."

Sam wrote down Haverfield's name.

Freddie came into the room carrying two bags of take out. "Start without me, boss?"

"We're talking heirs," Sam told him. "Mr. Cappuano believes it's most likely the senator's niece and nephew."

"Makes sense," Freddie said. "Are we doing this here or in the conference room?"

Nick gestured to a small table. "Here is fine with me."

"Let me grab the recorder," Freddie said.

"Do you mind if we eat in here?" Sam asked Nick. "Detective Cruz gets cranky if he doesn't get his mid-day influx of grease on time."

Nick smiled but Sam noticed his eyes were tired and sad. "No problem. I eat at that table more often than I do at home."

"Speaking of home, did you notice anything else out of place or missing?"

He shook his head.

"Let me know if you do."

"So you believe me? That someone broke in."

She replied with a small nod and had trouble meeting his intense gaze, startled to realize she was afraid of what she might find in those incredible hazel eyes.

"Am I interrupting something?" Freddie said when he returned with the recorder.

Sam cleared her throat. "No. Let's get this done. We've got a lot of ground to cover today."

NINE

AFTER A QUICK STOP at the Chinese restaurant on Capitol Hill where they confirmed that Christina Billings had in fact picked up take-out around eleven the night before last, Sam drove Freddie back to the office.

"So," he said. "Do you want to tell me what that was all about before?"

"What?"

"You and Cappuano. I felt like a third wheel on a hot date."

Sam shot him a glance. "What the hell are you talking about?"

"Well, gee, let's see." Counting on his fingers, he said, "Pregnant pauses, simmering gazes, and of course the entertaining innuendo. Need I continue?"

Unnerved that Freddie had noticed the sparks flying between her and Nick, she realized she should have known her savvy partner would have tuned in to what she had tried so hard not to encourage during their hour-long interview with Nick. The effort to keep things professional and focused had left her drained. "You're imagining things."

"No, I'm not. What gives, Sam?"

"Nothing. I barely know the man." That much was true—sort of. "Whatever you *think* you saw was the result of your overactive and undersexed imagination."

"Wow," Freddie said on a long exhale. "Who said anything about sex?"

Simmering with retorts she didn't dare pursue, Sam pulled into the parking lot at the public safety complex.

Before she could get out, Freddie stopped her. "What happened on that trip to Loudoun County yesterday?"

"Nothing." Now, *that* was true.

"I'm your partner, Sam." He gripped her jacket to keep her from escaping. "Talk to me."

She tugged her arm free of him. "There's nothing to say! We've got a million things to do, and you've got time to grill me about something you're *imagining?*"

"I'm a trained observer—trained in large part by you. I don't care what you say, there was enough heat in that room to burn down the capitol."

Sam fumed in silence. This was *exactly* why she told Nick that what happened the night before couldn't happen again. She didn't need any more aggravation right now.

In a softer tone Freddie said, "Whatever's going on, I hope you're being careful. You've got a lot at stake right now."

"Thanks, Freddie. I'm glad you reminded me of that. Otherwise I might've forgotten about the child who died on my watch."

"Sam—"

"We have work to do."

"I'm on your side. I hope you know that. If you want to talk—"

"Thank you. Can we get to work now?"

With a deep sigh, he reached for the door handle.

Sam stalked inside, again pushing her way through

the gaggle of reporters gathered in the foyer. Leaving them wanting and frustrated gave her tremendous joy.

She felt bad about being so testy to Freddie who'd been a pillar of support in the wake of the Johnson case, but she didn't want to hear what he'd have to say about her past relationship with a witness—a relationship she hadn't disclosed, knowing that if she did, she'd be taken off the case. That couldn't happen. She desperately needed a big win on a high-profile case like this one to get her career back on track.

That was why she planned to work around the clock, if that's what it took, to break this case as fast as she could—long before anyone found out that she had once spent a night with the man who'd found the senator dead. If she was unsuccessful and her superiors discovered that she'd had yet another lapse in judgment, she could kiss her hard-won career goodbye. And then what would she do? What was she without this job? *Who* was she? No one.

Shaking off that unpleasant thought, Sam told Freddie she'd be back after the press conference and headed for Chief Farnsworth's office. On the way, she stopped in the restroom to splash cold water on her face. Looking up at her reflection, she was startled by the bruised-looking circles under her eyes, the pale, almost translucent skin made more so by weeks of sleepless nights, and eyes that couldn't hide the torment.

She had told them she was ready to come back, had assured the department psychologist she could handle anything the job threw her way. But could she handle seeing Nick Cappuano again? Could she handle how it had felt—even six years later—to be engulfed once again by those strong arms, to be kissed by those soft lips, to be on the receiving end of those heated eyes? *God!* Those eyes of his were flat-out amazing.

"Stop, Sam," she whispered to the face in the mirror, a face she barely recognized. "Please stop. Do your job and stop thinking about him. Think about the senator."

Reaching for a paper towel, she blotted the excess water from her face and took a deep breath. "The senator," she said once more as she prepared to stand next to the chief at the press conference.

THE QUESTIONS WERE BRUTAL.

"How can you trust someone with Sergeant Holland's poor judgment to oversee such an important investigation?"

Chief Farnsworth, bless his heart, made it clear that she was the detective best suited to lead the investigation, and she had his full confidence and trust.

As Sam imagined what he'd have to say about her relationship with a material witness, she swallowed hard. *Enough of that*, she thought. *You've made your decision where he's concerned. It was one night, so stop thinking about it. Yeah, right. Okay.*

Once the reporters were done attacking her, they moved on to more specific questions about the investigation.

"Do you have any suspects?"

The chief nodded at Sam to take the question. "We're considering a number of possible suspects but haven't narrowed it down to one yet."

"What's taking so long?"

"The senator led a complex, complicated life. It's going to take some time to put all the pieces together, but I'm confident that we'll bring the investigation to a satisfactory conclusion."

"Any word on funeral plans?"

"You'll have to ask his office about that."

"Can you tell us how the senator was murdered?"

"No."

"Was his apartment broken into?"

"No comment."

"Was there a struggle?"

"No comment."

The chief stepped in. "That's it for now, folks. As soon as we have more to tell you, we'll let you know." He ushered Sam off the stage and into his office. "You did a good job out there. I know that wasn't easy." Studying her for a long moment, he said, "You're not sleeping well."

She shrugged. "Got a lot on my mind."

"Maybe you should talk to Dr. Trulo about a prescription—"

Sam held up a hand to stop him. "I haven't reached that point yet."

"I need you at the top of your game right now."

"Don't worry. I am."

"I like this Christina Billings for a person of interest."

"I don't know," Sam said, shaking her head. "The people in the office said the food was hot when she returned with it, so it seems like she went straight back. The records at the parking garage show she returned twenty-eight minutes after she left."

"Could she have gone to his place before the restaurant?"

"She'd have had to drive across the District to the

Watergate, kill him and get back with Chinese in half an hour. Not enough time. Plus, the knife severed his jugular. The blow would've sprayed blood all over her. Cappuano, the chief of staff, said she had on the same suit the next morning that she'd worn the day before because they pulled an all-nighter at the office to get ready for the vote the next day. Based on that, I'm on the verge of ruling her out."

The chief rubbed at his chin as he thought it over. "Do some digging into her. She had motive, opportunity and a key. Don't rule her out too quickly."

"Yes, sir."

"Same thing with his brother. Again, we have motive, opportunity and no alibi if he can't produce the woman he says he was with."

"Right. We're going to talk to him more formally. Another thought that's been running around in my head is the sister and brother-in-law, Lizbeth and Royce Hamilton."

"Why?"

"Their kids are most likely the senator's heirs. The O'Connor parents will be here at six to view the body. I'll ask Graham O'Connor about his son's will, and I've got Cruz digging into their finances. Then there's Stenhouse, the O'Connors's bitter political rival. He went home to Missouri for a long-planned fund-raiser today, but we've got an appointment with him in the morning."

"What do you think of that angle?"

"Not much, which is why I didn't stop him from going to Missouri. There's no way he had a key to the place, and I'm convinced that whoever did this was someone John O'Connor was close to."

"Girlfriends?"

"Billings is getting us a list of women he's seen socially in the last six months and anyone who had a key. I'm also going to ask the senior Senator O'Connor if there might be keys still floating around from when he lived there."

"The surveillance videos were no help?"

"We couldn't I.D. anyone and neither could Cappuano. The video captures activity in the lobby and elevator areas but not at individual doors, so that didn't help much. It was a cold night, and everyone was bundled up pretty tight with hats and scarves. We had trouble making out faces."

Startled, the chief looked up at her.

"What?"

"People were bundled up…"

"What about it?"

"Is it possible Christina Billings had a coat she ditched after the killing?"

Intrigued, Sam puzzled that over. "That would explain why the suit wasn't ruined."

"Exactly. Might be time to get a warrant to search her car."

"Jesus," Sam said. "Why didn't I think of this?"

"You would have. I think you've got a timing problem where she's concerned, but it seems to me like you've got every base covered, Sergeant."

"I'm trying."

They were interrupted by a knock on the door.

"Come in," the chief called.

The door opened and Freddie stepped into the room, looking nervous and uncertain.

"Detective Cruz."

"Hello, sir," Freddie stammered. "I'm sorry to interrupt, but the officers going through the documents taken from the senator's apartment have uncovered a life insurance policy that I think you need to see, Sergeant Holland." He handed it to her.

Sam scanned the document, her eyes widening at the two-million-dollar amount. An involuntary gasp escaped when she saw the beneficiary's name: Nicholas Cappuano.

TWENTY MINUTES LATER, Sam stormed past Nick's startled staff straight into his office and slammed the door behind her.

He never looked up from what he was doing when he said, "Back so soon, Sergeant?"

"You son of a bitch!"

He finally glanced at her, but there was steel in his normally amiable eyes. "Care to explain yourself?"

"How about *you* explain *yourself.*" She slapped the insurance policy down in front of him.

Without breaking the intense gaze, he reached for the document. "What's this?"

"You tell me."

He finally looked away from her. "It's an insurance policy."

"To me it looks like a *two-million-dollar* insurance policy," Sam clarified. "Flip to the last page."

He did as she asked. "*I'm* the beneficiary?" he asked with what appeared to be genuine shock.

"As if you didn't know."

"I didn't! I had no idea he'd done this!" An odd expression settled on his face. "So…that's what he meant." His voice faded to a whisper.

She wanted to demand he say more but waited for him to collect his thoughts.

"I once told John, back when I first met him and figured out who his father was, that I couldn't imagine in my wildest dreams ever being a millionaire. He said, 'You never know.'" Nick ran his hand reverently over the pages of the policy. "Then about a month ago, the subject came up again because I made a joke about how rich I'm getting running his office. He said I still had plenty of time to be a millionaire and that what I was doing—what we're all doing—was more important than money." Nick looked over at Sam. "That was the first time it seemed to me that he really embraced the significance of the office he held. Then he said I could be a millionaire sooner than I thought and walked away."

"You didn't ask him what he meant by that?"

He shook his head. "It seemed like a throwaway line at the time, but now it takes on more significance."

"Do you think he knew he was going to die soon?"

"No, but he had a sense that he was going to die young. He'd get into these maudlin discussions when we'd been drinking. We called them his philosophical moods."

"Did he have these moods often?"

Nick considered that. "More often lately, now that you mention it. Christina asked me last week if I thought he might be depressed."

"Did you?"

"Distracted might be a better word than depressed. He definitely had something on his mind."

"And you have no idea what?"

"I tried to talk to him about it a couple of times, but

he brushed it off. Said he was focused on the bill and getting it passed. I chalked it up to stress."

"You really didn't know about the insurance?"

"I swear to God. Give me a polygraph."

Sam studied him for a long moment. "That won't be necessary. Congratulations, looks like you're finally going to be a millionaire."

"Hell of a way to get there," he said softly.

The last of the steam she'd come in with dissipated. "Nick..." She resisted the powerful urge to walk around the desk and embrace him. Clearing the emotion from her throat, she said, "His parents are coming in at six. They want to see him. Do you think maybe you could come, too? It might help them to have a familiar face there."

"Of course."

"I could take you and bring you back later so you don't have to deal with the parking situation over there."

"Sure." He stood up and reached for the suit coat that was draped over the back of his chair.

Sam's mouth went dry as she watched the play of his muscles under the pale blue dress shirt he had worn without a tie. His hands were graceful as he adjusted his collar. She remembered the way those hands had felt moving over her fevered skin so many years ago. The memory shouldn't have been so vivid, but there it was, as bright and as real as if it had happened only yesterday.

He caught her watching him. "What?"

Her face heated. "Nothing."

Without looking away from her, he came around the desk and stopped right in front of her. He reached out and ran a finger over her cheek. "I think about it, too. I never stopped thinking about it."

"Don't." She wondered how it was possible that he had read her mind so easily. "Please."

"Even in the midst of everything else that's going on, even as I plan my best friend's funeral, even as I deal with a traumatized staff and John's parents, I want you. I think about you, and I want you."

"I *can't*, Nick. My job is on the line. My whole career is riding on this investigation. I can't let you do this to me right now."

"What about later? After it's over?"

"Maybe. We'll have to see."

"Then that'll have to do." He gestured for her to lead the way out of his office. "For now."

TEN

"WHAT'S THE PLAN for the funeral?" Sam asked Nick as they sat in heavy traffic on Constitution Avenue.

"He'll lie in state at the capitol in Richmond for forty-eight hours, beginning on Friday. The funeral will be held at the National Cathedral on Monday with burial at Arlington a week or two later. It takes a while to get that arranged."

"I didn't realize he was a veteran."

"Four years in the Navy after college."

"If possible, I'd like to attend the funeral with you in case I need you to identify anyone for me."

"Sure. I'll do what I can."

"Thank you." She wanted to say more but found her tongue to be uncharacteristically tied in knots. After a long, awkward pause, she glanced over at him. "I, um, I appreciate the help you're giving me with background and insight into the senator's relationships."

"Have you spoken to Natalie yet?"

Sam's brain raced through the various lists of friends, family, coworkers, and acquaintances. "I haven't heard of a Natalie. Who is she?"

"Natalie Jordan. She was John's girlfriend for a couple of years."

"When?"

Nick thought about that. "I'd say for about two years

before he ran for the Senate and maybe a year after he was sworn in."

"Did it end badly?"

"It ended. I was never sure why. He wouldn't talk about it."

"Yet you saw fit to toss her name into a homicide investigation."

He shrugged. "You were mad I didn't tell you Chris was in love with him. Natalie was important to him for a long time. In fact, she was the only woman I ever knew of who was truly important to him. I just thought you should know about her."

"Where is she now?"

"Married to the number-two guy at Justice. I think they live in Alexandria."

"Did he ever see her?"

"Sometimes they'd run into each other at Democratic Party events in Virginia."

"Would she still have a key to his apartment?"

"Possibly. They lived together there for the last year or so that they were together."

"Did you like her?"

Nick rested his head against the back of the seat. "She wasn't my type, but he seemed happy with her."

"But did you *like* her?"

"Not really."

"Why not?"

"She always struck me as a social climber. We rubbed each other the wrong way—probably because I couldn't do anything to advance her agenda so she didn't have much use for me."

"Knowing he dated someone like that seems contrary to the picture you and others have painted of him. To me, he wouldn't have had the patience for it."

"He was dazzled by her. She's quite…well, if you talk to her, you'll see what I mean."

"What do you think of his sister and brother-in-law?"

Nick appeared startled by the question. "Salt of the earth. Both of them."

"What's his story? Royce Hamilton?"

"He's a horse trainer. One of the best there is from what I've heard. Lizbeth has been crazy about horses all her life. John always said she and Royce were a match made in heaven."

"Any financial problems?"

"None that I ever heard of—not that I heard much about them. I saw them at holidays, occasional dinners in Leesburg, fund-raisers here and there, but we don't travel in the same circles."

"What circle do they travel in?"

"The Loudoun County horse circle. John adored their kids. He talked about them all the time, had pictures of them everywhere."

"What did Senator O'Connor think of his only daughter marrying a horse trainer?"

"Royce is an intelligent guy. And more important, he's a gentleman. The senator could appreciate those qualities in a potential son-in-law, even if he wasn't a doctor or a lawyer or a politician. Besides, Lizbeth was wild about him. Her father was smart enough to know there'd be no point in getting in the way of that."

"What about her? Could she have had some sort of dispute with John?"

Nick shook his head. "She was completely and utterly devoted to him. She was one of our best campaigners and fund-raisers." He chuckled. "John called her The Force. No one could say no to her when she went out on the stump for her 'baby brother.' There's no way she had anything to do with this." More emphatically, he added, "No way."

"Did she have a key to the Watergate apartment?"

"Most likely. Everyone in the family used the place when they were in town."

"That place has more keys out than a no-tell motel."

"It was just like John to give keys to everyone he knew and think nothing of it."

"Yet he was the only other person in the world who had a key to your place. Can you see the irony in that?"

"He led a bigger life than I do."

"Tell me about your life," she said on an impulse.

He raised that swarthy eyebrow. "Who's asking? The woman or the detective?"

Sam took a moment to appreciate his quick intelligence, remembering how attractive she had found that the first time she met him. "Both," she confessed.

He glanced at her, and even though her eyes were on the road, she felt the heat of his gaze. "I work. A lot."

"And when you're not working?"

"I sleep."

"No one—not even me—is that boring."

He flashed her a funny, crooked grin that she caught out of the corner of her eye. "I try to get to the gym a couple of times a week."

Judging from the ripped physique she had been pressed against the night before, he put those gym visits to good use. "And? No wives, girlfriends, social life?"

"No wife, no girlfriend. I play basketball with some guys on Sundays whenever I can. Sometimes we go out for beers afterward. Last summer, I played in the congressional softball league, but I missed more games than I made. Oh, and every other month or so, I have dinner with my father's family in Baltimore. That's about it."

"Why haven't you ever gotten married?"

"I don't know. Just never happened."

"Surely there had to have been *someone* you might've married."

"There was this one girl..."

"What happened?"

"She never returned my calls."

Shocked and speechless, Sam stared at him.

"You asked."

Tearing her eyes off him, she accelerated through the last intersection before the turn for the public safety parking lot. "Don't say that to me," she snapped. "You don't mean that."

"Yes, I do."

She pulled into a space and slammed the car into park.

He grabbed her arm to stop her from getting out. "Calm down, Sam."

"Don't tell me what to do." She tugged her arm free of his grasp. "And save your cheesy lines for someone who's buying. I don't believe you anyway."

"If you didn't, you wouldn't be so pissed right now."

"Do you want to know what happened to your friend?"

With one blink, his hazel eyes shifted from amused to furious. "Of course I do."

"Then you have to stop doing this to me, Nick. You're winding me up in knots and pulling my eye off the ball.

I need to be focused, one hundred percent *focused* on this case, and *not* on you!"

"What about when you're off duty?" The teasing smile was back, but it didn't steal the sadness from his eyes. "Can I wind you up in knots then?"

"Nick…"

Fixated on the drab-looking public safety building, he sighed. "We're about to go in there and take John's parents to see him laid out on a cold slab, and yet, all I can think about right now is how badly I want to kiss you. What kind of a friend does that make me? To him or to you?"

His tone was so full of sadness and grief that Sam softened a bit. "You were a great friend to him, and in the last twenty-four hours, except for the whole kissing thing, you've been helpful to me, too. Can we keep it that way? Please?"

"I'm trying, Sam. Really I am, but I can't help that I feel this incredible pull to you. I know you feel it, too. You felt it six years ago—as strongly as I did—and you still do, even if you don't want to. If we had met again under different circumstances, can you tell me the same thing wouldn't be happening between us?"

"I have to go in now." Her firm tone hid her seesawing emotions. "His parents are probably waiting for me, and I don't want to drag this out for them. Are you coming?"

"Yeah." He opened the door. "I'm coming."

FREDDIE MET THEM INSIDE. "We've got the O'Connors in there." He pointed to a closed conference room door. "And the Dems from Virginia the senator had dinner with the night he was killed are in there."

Sam glanced back and forth between the two closed doors. "Will you take Mr. Cappuano and the O'Connors to see the senator, please?" she asked Freddie.

"No problem."

She rested a hand on Freddie's arm and looked up at him. "Utmost sensitivity," she whispered.

"Absolutely, boss. Don't worry."

To Nick, she said, "I'll catch up to you."

He nodded and followed Freddie into the room where Graham and Laine O'Connor waited with their daughter and another man who Sam assumed was Royce Hamilton. With a brief glance, Sam noticed that both O'Connors had aged significantly overnight.

"Senator and Mrs. O'Connor, my partner, Detective Cruz, will take you to see your son. I'll join you in a few minutes."

"Thank you," Graham said.

With a deep breath to change gears and force her mind off the intense conversation she'd just had with Nick, Sam entered the room where two portly men sat waiting for her. She judged them both to be in their late sixties or early seventies.

Upon her entrance, they leapt to their feet.

"Gentlemen," she said, reaching out to shake their hands. "Detective Sergeant Sam Holland. I appreciate you coming in."

"We're just *devastated*," drawled Judson Knott, who had introduced himself as the chairman of the Virginia Democratic Party. "Senator O'Connor was a dear friend of ours and the people of the Commonwealth."

"I'm not looking for a sound bite, Mr. Knott, just an idea of how the senator spent his last few hours."

"We met him for dinner at the Old Ebbitt Grill," said Richard Manning, the vice chairman.

"How often did you all have dinner together?"

The two men exchanged glances. "Every other month or so. We offered to reschedule that night because he had the vote the next day, but he said his staff had everything under control, and he had time for dinner."

"How did he seem to you?"

"Tired," Manning said without hesitation.

Knott nodded in agreement. "He said he'd been working twelve-and fourteen-hour days for the last two weeks."

"What did you talk about over dinner?"

"The plans for the campaign," Knott said. "He was up for re-election next year, and although he was a shoo-in, we take nothing for granted. We've been gearing up for the campaign for months, but now..." His blue eyes clouded as his voice trailed off. "It's just such a tragedy."

"What time did you part company after dinner?"

"I'd say around ten or so," Knott said.

"And where was he headed from there?"

"He said he was going straight home to bed," Knott said.

"Who will take his place in the Senate?"

"That's up to the governor," Manning said.

"No front-runners?"

Knott shook his head. "We haven't even talked about it, to be honest. We're all just in a total state of shock right now. Senator O'Connor was a lovely person. We can't imagine how anyone would want to harm him."

"No one in the party was jealous of his success or bucking for his job?"

"Only his brother," Manning said with disdain. "What a disappointment *he* turned out to be."

"Was he jealous enough to kill the senator?"

"Terry?" Knott said with a nervous glance toward the door, as if he was afraid the O'Connors might hear him. "I doubt it. It would require he get his head out of his ass for more than five minutes."

"The O'Connors had their problems, like any family," Manning added. "But they were tight. Terry might've been jealous of John, but he wouldn't have done this to his mother." Shaking his head with dismay, he said, "Poor Laine."

"We saw them outside," Knott said. "Our hearts are broken for them."

"Thank you for coming in." Sam handed each of them her card. "If you think of anything else, even the smallest thing, let me know."

"We will," Manning said. "We'll do anything we can to help find the monster who did this."

"Thank you." Sam saw them out and headed for the morgue.

ELEVEN

FOLLOWING THE O'CONNORS into the cold, antiseptic-smelling room, Nick thought he had properly prepared himself. After what he had seen yesterday, he should have been able to handle anything.

However, nothing could have prepared him for the sight of John lifeless, waxy, and so utterly *gone*. Nor could he have prepared for Laine's reaction.

With one look at her son's face, John's mother fainted into a boneless pile. It happened so fast that no one was able to reach her in time to keep her head from smacking the cement floor.

"Jesus, God!" Graham cried as he dropped to his knees. "Laine! Honey, are you all right?"

"Mom," Lizbeth said as tears rolled down her face. "Mom, open your eyes."

Several tense minutes passed before Laine's eyes fluttered open. "What happened?"

"You fainted," Lizbeth said. "Do you think you could sit up?"

"I need to get out of here. Take me out of here, Lizzie."

Lizbeth and Royce helped her mother up. Without another glance at the body on the table, they escorted her from the room.

"Are you all right, Senator?" Nick asked when they were alone.

His complexion gray, his hands trembling, Graham

O'Connor fixated on the white bandage covering the neck wound that ended his son's life. "It's all so wrong, you know?" the older man said in a hoarse whisper.

"Sir?"

"Standing over the body of your child. It's wrong."

Nick's throat tightened with emotion. "I'm sorry. I wish there was something I could say..." He kept his voice down so Detective Cruz, who was minding the door, wouldn't hear them.

Graham reached out haltingly to caress John's thick blond hair. "Who could've done this? How's it possible someone hated my John this much?"

"I just don't know." Nick looked down at John, wishing he had the answers they so desperately needed.

"Do you think it could be Terry?"

Shocked, Nick whispered, "Senator..."

"He never got over what happened. He resented John—maybe even hated him—for taking his place in a job he felt was his."

"He wouldn't have killed him over it."

"I wish I could be so certain." Graham looked up at Nick with shattered eyes. "If it *was* Terry...If he did this, it'll kill Laine."

Nick could only imagine what it would do to Graham.

"Um, excuse me," Sam said from behind them. "I'm sorry to interrupt."

Nick wondered if she had heard them speculating about Terry.

"Can I get you anything, Senator? Would you like to sit for a minute? I could get you a stool—"

Graham's expression hardened as he turned to Sam.

"You can tell me you've found the person who did this to my son."

"I wish I could," she said. "I *can* tell you we're working very hard on the case. If you want to come with me to the conference room, I can update you and your wife on what we have so far."

The senator turned back to his son and stroked John's hair. Tears pooled in Graham's already-bloodshot eyes. "I love you, Johnny," he whispered, leaning over to press a kiss to John's forehead. Graham's shoulders shook as he clutched the sheet covering John's chest.

Nick had never seen such a raw display of grief. After a moment, he rested a hand on Graham's shoulder. The older man remained hunched over his son until Nick gently guided him up.

"Oh God, Nick," he sobbed, pressing his face to Nick's chest. "What're we going to do without him? *What'll we do?*"

Nick wrapped his arms around Graham. "I don't know, but we're going to figure it out. We're going to get through this." He glanced up to find Sam watching them with an expression of exquisite discomfort. Embarrassed by his own tears, he returned his attention to the senator. "Why don't we let Sergeant Holland fill us in on the investigation?"

Graham nodded and stepped out of Nick's embrace. With a long last heartbroken look at John, Graham headed for the door.

Swiping at his face, Nick followed him.

Sam directed them to the conference room where Lizbeth and Royce sat on either side of a pale and drawn Laine. Someone had gotten her a glass of water and an ice pack for her head.

Graham went to his wife, reached for her hands and drew her up into his arms.

Nick couldn't look. He simply couldn't bear to witness their overwhelming agony. Turning from where he stood in the doorway, he stepped out of the room.

"I'll…ah…give you a moment," he heard Sam say as she followed him.

In the hallway, she joined Nick in resting her head against the cinderblock wall. "Are you all right?"

"I was," he said with a sigh. "I was doing a really good job of convincing myself, despite what I saw yesterday, that he was in Richmond or at the farm. But after that, after seeing him like that…"

"Denial's not an option any more."

"No."

Soft words and sounds of weeping drifted from the conference room.

"I've never before felt like I didn't belong with them. Not once in all the years I've known them, have I ever felt I didn't belong…until in there…just now…" His voice caught, and he was surprised when her hand landed on his arm.

"They love you, Nick. Anyone can see that."

"John was my link to them. That's gone now." His head ached, his eyes burned. Hating the uncharacteristic bout of self-pity but needing her more than he'd needed anyone in a long time, he sighed. "He's gone… my job…everything."

Sam squeezed his arm and then removed her hand abruptly when Freddie came around the corner.

Seeming to sense he was interrupting something, Freddie paused and looked to her for guidance.

"They needed a minute after seeing him," she said.

"Could you do me a favor and find Mr. Cappuano some water?"

"That's not necessary," Nick protested.

A nod from Sam sent Freddie off.

"You didn't have to—"

"It's water, Nick."

"Thank you." He glanced over at her. "How're you holding up?"

"I'm tired."

"And?"

"And what?"

"Something else."

She cast her eyes down at the floor and kicked at the tile with the pointed toe of her fashionable black boot. "I'm pissed. Seeing those people," she nodded toward the conference room. "Others like them. Something like this happens to them and their lives are permanently altered. That bothers me. A lot."

"You care. That's what makes you such a good cop."

"I don't know too many who'd call me a good cop lately."

Taking her hand, he saw that he'd startled her with his public display of affection. "There's no one else I'd rather have on John's case. No one." He surprised her further when he kissed the back of her hand and released it.

Before Sam could chew him out for the risky PDA, Freddie returned with a cold bottle of water for Nick.

"Thank you."

"May I have a word, Sergeant?" Freddie said.

"Of course," Sam said. To Nick, she added, "Tell them we'll be right in."

SAM FOLLOWED FREDDIE into the conference room across the hall and closed the door. "I know what you're going to say, and it's not what you think."

"Guilty conscience, Sergeant?"

Since his question was accompanied by a teasing smile she didn't remind him that she outranked him by a mile and an insubordination complaint wouldn't look good on his record. "Not at all."

"The financials came back on all the principal players."

"And?"

"Royce Hamilton is up to his eyeballs in debt."

Sam's heart reacted to the burst of adrenaline by skipping in her chest. "Is he now?"

"There's a lien on their house, which is mortgaged to the hilt."

"And his kids were O'Connor's likely heirs. Very interesting, indeed."

"We also found a regular monthly payment of three thousand dollars from the senator's personal account to a woman named Patricia Donaldson. I ran the name and came up with hundreds of hits, which I've got some people checking into."

"We can ask his parents who she is."

"Third thing, the tox screen on the senator was clean, except for the small amount of alcohol we already knew about. No drugs, prescription or otherwise."

"Okay, that's good," she said, starting for the door. "One less thing to figure out."

"Wait," he said. "I wasn't done."

She waved an impatient hand to encourage him to proceed.

"They found porn on his home computer. A lot of it."

"Kids?"

"None so far, but what's there is hard core."

She smoothed her hands over her hair. "Christ, can you believe a United States senator would take such chances?"

Freddie frowned at her use of the Lord's name. "What do you suppose it means for the case?"

"I don't know. Let me think about it. Any word on the warrant to search Christina Billings's car and apartment?"

"I just checked when I went back to get the water and nothing yet."

"What the hell is taking so long?" she fumed. "If we don't have it by the time we finish with the parents, I'll get the chief involved."

"What about Hamilton?"

"After we get the wife and in-laws out of there, we'll go at him."

Freddie's eyes lit up with anticipation. "Good cop, bad cop?"

"If necessary."

"Can I be bad cop this time? *Please?*"

She shot him a withering look that said "as if."

"I *never* get to be bad cop," he said with a pout. "It's so not fair."

"Grow up, Freddie," she shot over her shoulder as she crossed the hall to where the O'Connors waited. Before she opened the door, she took a moment to collect herself, to take her emotions out of the equation. She appreciated that Freddie knew her moods well enough by then not to question what she was doing or why. "Ready?"

He nodded.

Sam opened the door. "I'm sorry to keep you waiting." She did her best to avoid looking directly at the four faces ravaged by grief as she took them through what the police knew so far, leaving out anything that would compromise the integrity of the investigation.

"So you're telling me that after two days, you've got absolutely nothing?" Graham said.

"We have several persons of interest we're taking a hard look at," Sam said as the chief slipped into the room. She nodded at him and returned her attention to the O'Connors. "I wish I could tell you more, but we're working as hard and as fast as we can."

Graham turned to the chief. "I've known you a lot of years, Joe. I need the very best you've got."

Chief Farnsworth glanced at Sam. "You're getting it. I have full faith in Sergeant Holland and Detective Cruz as well as the team backing them up."

"So do I," Nick said quietly from where he stood against the back wall.

Senator and Mrs. O'Connor turned to him.

With his eyes trained on Sam, Nick said, "I've known Sergeant Holland for six years. There's no one more dedicated or thorough."

As Sam fought to keep her mouth from dropping open in shock at the unexpected endorsement, Senator O'Connor held Nick's intent gaze for a long moment before he stood and held out his hand to his wife. "In that case, we should let you get back to work. We'll count on you to keep us informed."

"You have my word, Senator," Chief Farnsworth said. "I'll show you out."

"Before you go," Sam said, "can you tell us who Patricia Donaldson was to your son?"

Graham and Laine exchanged glances but their expressions remained neutral.

"She was a friend of John's," he said.

"From high school," Laine added.

"A friend he paid three thousand dollars a month to?"

"John was an adult, Sergeant," Graham said, appearing nonplussed to hear about the payments. "What he did with his money was his business. He didn't have to explain it to us."

"Where does she live?" Sam asked.

"Chicago, I believe," Graham said.

Interesting, Sam thought, that the senator knew, without a moment's hesitation, the exact whereabouts of his son's friend from eighteen years earlier. She debated pushing him harder and might have had the chief not been in the room. In the end, she decided to pursue it from other angles.

"If there's nothing else, I'd like to take my wife home," Graham said with a pointed look at Sam.

"We realize this is an extremely difficult time for you, but we may have other questions," she said.

"Our door's always open," Graham said, helping his wife from her chair.

Lizbeth and Royce got up to go with them.

"Mr. Hamilton," Sam said. "A minute of your time, please?"

Royce's eyes darted to his wife.

"Go ahead, Daddy." Lizbeth kissed her parents. "Take Mom home. We'll be by after a while."

After Graham and Laine left the room with Chief Farnsworth and Nick following them, Sam turned to Lizbeth. "We'd like to speak to your husband alone, Mrs. Hamilton."

Tall, blond, blue-eyed and handsome in a rugged, hard-working way, Royce slipped an arm around Lizbeth's shoulders. "Anything you have to say to me can be said in front of my wife."

Sam glanced at Freddie, who handed her the printout detailing the Hamilton's financial situation. "Very well. In that case, perhaps you can explain how you've come to be almost a million dollars in debt." Only because she was watching so closely did she see Royce tighten the grip he had on his wife's shoulder.

"A series of bad investments," Hamilton said through gritted teeth.

"What kind of investments?"

"Two horses that didn't live up to their potential, and a land deal that's tied up in litigation."

"We're handling it," Lizbeth said.

"By mortgaging your house?"

"Among other things," Lizbeth said, her tone icy.

"What other things?"

"We're considering a number of options," Royce said, adding reluctantly, "including bankruptcy."

"You expect us to believe the daughter of a multimillionaire is on the verge of bankruptcy?"

"This has nothing to do with my father, Sergeant," Lizbeth snarled. "It's our problem, and we're handling it."

"Are your children the heirs to your brother's estate?"

Lizbeth gasped. "You think..." Her face flushed, and her eyes filled. "You're insinuating that we had something to do with what happened to John?"

"What I'm asking," Sam said, "is if your children are his heirs."

"I have no idea," Lizbeth said. "We weren't privy to the terms of his will."

"But he was close to your children?"

"He adored them, and they him. They're heartbroken by his death. And you think we would've done that to them—to *him*—over *money?*"

Sam shrugged. "He had it, you needed it."

Shaking with rage, Lizbeth moved out of her husband's embrace and stepped toward Sam. Speaking in a low, fury-driven tone, she said, "I had only to ask, and he'd have given me anything. *Anything.* There would've been no need for me—or Royce—to kill him for it."

"So why didn't you? Why didn't you ask him for help?"

"Because it was *our* problem, our business. Other than my husband and children, there was no one in this world I loved more than John. If you think my husband or I killed him, I encourage you to prove it. Now, if there isn't anything else, I need to take care of my parents."

"Stay available," she said to their retreating backs.

After they were gone, Sam turned to Freddie. "Impressions?"

"Pride goeth before the fall."

"My thoughts exactly. They'd rather declare bankruptcy than let her family know they're in trouble."

The door opened, and the chief stepped into the room. "What was that about with the son-in-law?"

"Nothing," Sam said, deciding it was just that. "Tying up a loose end."

"You know Nick Cappuano?" the chief asked.

Sam cleared her throat. "Technically, yes. I met him once, six years ago. I hadn't seen him since until yesterday. He's been a tremendous asset to the investigation."

"That was quite a show of support from someone you hardly know."

She shrugged. "It seemed to be what the senator needed to hear."

"Indeed." The chief's shrewd eyes narrowed as he studied her. "Is there anything else you want to tell me, Sergeant?"

He was handing her the opportunity to come clean. But if she told him she'd slept with Nick, had feelings for him—then and now—she'd be off the case and maybe off the force. It was too much to risk. "No, sir," she said without blinking an eye.

"Anything I can do to help?"

"We're waiting on a warrant to search Billings's car and apartment. If you could exert some muscle to speed that up, we'd appreciate it."

"Consider it done." He started to leave, but turned back. "Get me an arrest, Sergeant. Soon."

"I'm doing my best, sir."

TWELVE

SAM SPENT TWO HOURS with Freddie and the other detectives assigned to the case going over everything they had so far. While she was with the O'Connors, the lab came back with the report from John's apartment—nothing was found in the sheets, the drain, or elsewhere in the apartment that didn't belong to the victim.

Beginning to feel frustrated, Sam doled out assignments, told Freddie to meet her at Senator Stenhouse's office at nine the next morning, and sent him home. Fifteen hours after she'd started her day, she returned to her office to find Nick in her chair with his feet on the desk.

"Comfortable?" she asked, leaning against the doorframe.

He dropped his cell phone into his suit coat pocket. "You were my ride."

"Oh shit. Sorry. You waited all this time? You could've grabbed a cab."

"I was hoping to talk you into dinner."

"I can't. I've still got a million things I need to do." She paused, looked closer. "Did you *clean* my desk?"

"I just straightened it up a bit. How can you work in such a messy space?"

"I have a system. Now I won't be able to find anything!"

"You need to eat, and you need to sleep. What good will you be to anyone if you make yourself sick?"

"So in addition to bringing your anal retentiveness to my workplace, you've put yourself in charge of making sure I eat and sleep?"

His face lifted into a cocky, sexy grin. "Happy to oblige on both fronts."

"Food, yes. Sleep? No way in hell."

He shrugged, apparently pleased with the half victory. "Who's this?" he asked, picking up a photo from her desk.

"My dad." In the picture, Sam stood to the side of her father's chair, her arm around his shoulders. "He was injured on the job almost two years ago."

"I'm sorry. What happened?"

Stepping into the cramped office, she bumped his feet off the desk and sat. "He was on his way home in his department vehicle and saw a car weaving through traffic. He followed it for a mile or two before he pulled it over."

"He was a traffic cop?"

She shook her head. "He was deputy chief and three months shy of retirement. Anyway, he approached the vehicle, knocked on the window, and the driver responded with gunfire. He doesn't remember anything after stopping the car. The bullet lodged between the C3 and C4 vertebrae. He's a quadriplegic, but through some miracle, he can breathe on his own when sitting up. We've learned to be grateful for the small things."

"I remember reading about it, but I didn't realize he was your father. Happened on G Street?"

"Yes."

"Did they ever get the guy?"

"Nope. It's an open investigation. I work on it whenever I can, and so does every other detective in this place. It's personal to me, to all of us."

"I can imagine. I'm sorry."

She shrugged. "Life's a bitch."

He stood up, stepped around her, pushed the door closed, reached for her and held her tight against him.

Appalled by the lump that settled in her throat, she wrestled free of him. "What was that for?"

He kept his arms around her. "You seemed to need it."

"I don't." She placed her hands on his chest to put some distance between them and to calm her racing heart. "I can't be alone in here with you. People will talk, and I don't need that."

He reached for the door and opened it. "Sorry."

Sam was relieved to find no prying eyes on the other side of the door and annoyed to realize she *had* needed the comfort Nick offered, that it somehow helped. The discovery left her unsettled.

"What?" he asked, studying her with those intense hazel eyes that made her melt from the inside out. "You're staring."

"I was just thinking..."

He tipped his head inquisitively. "About?"

"You've aged well. Really well."

"Gee, thanks. I think."

"That was a *compliment*," she said, rolling her eyes.

"Thanks for clarifying. Of course, I could say the same to you. You're even sexier than I remembered—and I remembered *everything*." He took a step to close the distance between them.

Her heart tripping into overdrive, she held up a hand to stop him. "Stay out of my personal space."

"You're the one who started handing out the *compliments*," he said with a grin that she much preferred to the grief she'd witnessed earlier.

"Temporary lapse in judgment brought on by fatigue and hunger."

"Then how about that dinner?"

"Pizza and you're buying."

"That could be arranged."

"Speaking of arranged, the M.E. is set to release the senator's body to the funeral home in the morning."

Nick immediately sobered, and Sam was sorry she'd dropped it on him that way. "Okay. Once the funeral home is done, the Virginia State Police will accompany him to the state capitol in Richmond," he said. "I was going to ask you if I could get into his place to get some clothes. The funeral director needs them."

"After dinner. I'd like to go back there anyway. Poke around some more."

"It's a date."

She turned off her computer and the lamp on her desk. "It's not a date."

"Semantics," he said as he followed her from the office.

"It's *not* a date."

OVER THICK-CRUST veggie PIZZA and beer at a place where everyone seemed to know Nick, Sam asked him about Patricia Donaldson.

"Who?"

"According to his parents, she was a high school friend of John's who lives in Chicago."

His eyebrows knit with confusion. "I've never heard of her."

"He sent her three thousand dollars a month, has for years, called her several times a week and talked for as much as an hour."

Nick shook his head. "I don't know anything about her." He seemed puzzled, distressed even. "How's that possible?"

"Did you know he was into porn? Big time into it?"

Pausing mid-bite, he returned the pizza to his plate and wiped his mouth. "No. How do you know?"

"It was on his home computer."

His expression shifted from startled to disgusted. His breathing slowed as he fixated on a spot behind her. He was quiet for a long time. "I wish I could say I'm totally surprised, but I'm not. He took such chances with his reputation and his career."

"What else besides this?"

"Women. Lots of them. It was like he was looking for something he just couldn't seem to find. He'd be all hot over someone and a week later she'd be history."

"Did they have anything in common?"

"They were all blonde and well endowed. Every one of them. One Barbie doll after another. It got so I didn't even bother to make the effort to remember their names."

Sam swallowed the last of her beer in one long sip and had to admit she felt recharged after the meal. "Christina Billings sent over a list of the women he'd dated during the last six months. We're working through it now. I bet we'll find his killer among the Barbies."

"I doubt it."

"Why do you say that?"

"You said it was a crime of passion, right?"

She nodded.

"None of them were around long enough to feel the kind of passion you'd have to feel to do what was done to him—except Natalie, but that was over and done with years ago. If she were going to kill him, she probably would've done it a long time ago."

"We're going to talk to her tomorrow."

"How do you do it?" he asked.

"Do what?"

"Keep up this pace. It's relentless."

"You spent a night in your office this week. You do what it takes to get your job done. That's all I'm doing. Usually it's worse than this. I often have multiple cases going, but thanks to the forced vacation my load has been light lately."

"But dealing with murderers and victims and medical examiners…It's got to be so draining."

"It can be. Other times it's exhilarating. There's nothing quite like putting all the pieces together and coming out with a picture that leads to conviction."

"Did you always want to be a cop?" He hadn't asked that question the first time they met, when she had just made detective.

"That subject is kind of complicated."

"How so?"

She fiddled with the handle on her mug. "I'm the youngest of three girls. I think I was about twelve when it dawned on me that the only reason I'd been born was because my father wanted a son so desperately."

"You can't know that for sure."

"Oh, yes I can. My mother all but told me."

"Sam…"

She hated the sympathy that radiated from him. "So, knowing I'd disappointed him just by being born, I set out to win his approval every way I could think of. Name a high school sport—I played it. I went with him to Redskins games, Orioles games. He even branded me with a boyish nickname."

"You'll be Samantha to me," Nick declared. "From this moment on."

She sneered at him. "I don't let *anyone* call me that."

"You're going to have to make an exception because to me there's nothing boyish about you. You're *all* woman. Every beautiful, sexy inch of you."

Her face heated under the intensity of his gaze. "I'll allow an occasional Samantha, but don't overdo it. And not in front of anyone else."

"I'll save it for only the most important, *private* moments," he said with a grin that melted her bones. "So, you became a cop to please him, too."

"Huh?" she asked, captivated by his hazel eyes.

"Your father."

"Oh. Right. At first that's what it was about. I won't deny that. But I discovered I have a knack for it—or I thought I did until recently."

"You do. You can't let one incident shake your confidence or your faith in yourself."

"You sound like the department shrink," she said with a chuckle. "And while I know you're both right, there's something about a dead kid that shakes you to the core even when you know you did everything right." Sam fixated on a spot on the wall as the horror of it all came back to haunt her once again. She'd never forget the sound of Marquis Johnson's agonized shrieks after his son was hit by gunfire.

"What happened that night?"

The sick weight of it settled over her and turned a

stomach so recently satisfied by food. She'd had a hard time choking down anything for weeks after the incident. "I'm not supposed to talk about it. I have to testify at the probable cause hearing next week."

Under the table, he took her hand, linked his fingers through hers and resisted her efforts to break free. "Stop," he said softly. "Just stop, will you?"

"Someone might see," she hissed.

"No one's looking at us, and the tablecloth hides a world of sin. There's nothing quite like a good tablecloth."

Sam gently extricated her hand and folded her arms while pretending not to notice the wounded look that crossed his face. "I'll bet you've done your share of public sinning."

"I'll never tell," he said, his lips quirking with amusement. "Is it so difficult for you?"

"What?"

"Sharing the burden."

"It's impossible," she confessed. "My inadequacy in that regard has caused me some major problems in my life."

"What kind of problems?"

"The marriage kind for one." She wished for something else to drink since her mouth was suddenly as dry as the desert. Glancing at Nick, she found him watching her with the patience of a man who had nothing but time. She reached for his half-empty glass of beer and took a long drink.

"Why'd you get divorced?"

Sam mulled it over, wondering if she should have this conversation with a man she was wildly attracted to but who was off limits to her. After a long pause, she decided what the hell? Why not? "My ex-husband claimed I didn't need him."

"And did you?"

"No," she snorted. "He turned out to be a total loser."

"Since he failed to deliver a couple of critically important messages, I'd have to agree with you there."

"I made such a big mistake with him," she sighed. "I didn't see him for what he really was until it was too late. I didn't listen to people who tried to warn me."

Nick straightened out of the slouch he'd slipped into. "Was he…I mean…He didn't *hit* you, did he?"

"No, but it almost would've been easier if he had. At least I could've fought back against that. His thing was passive aggression. He wanted total control over me. I let it go on for far longer than I should have because I didn't want to admit I'd been so incredibly wrong. Damned foolish Irish pride."

Despite her resistance, Nick moved closer. "I want to wrap my arms around you right now," he said gruffly against her ear, his warm breath sending goose bumps darting through her. "I hate the idea of someone making you feel inadequate."

"I let him," Sam said, the pillars of her resistance toppling like Dominoes. She wanted Nick's arms around her, wanted to lean her head on that strong, capable shoulder. For the first time in longer than she could remember, she wanted the comfort he offered. No, she *needed* it. What should have been terrifying was actually rather exhilarating. "Can we go?"

"Sure." He put some bills on the table, got up and offered her his hand.

"We've left the safety of the tablecloth," she reminded him as she stepped around his outstretched arm on her way to the door.

Grinning, he followed her out.

Heads bent against the blustery cold, they walked a block to where they'd parked her department vehicle. An odd chill that had nothing to do with the cold ran up her spine as she unlocked the door on the dark street. Glancing around, she expected to find someone watching her, but saw no one. Just her overactive imagination, she thought, as she reached over to unlock the passenger door for Nick.

He slid in next to her. "Before we go to John's place, I need to get my car."

"Okay." Sam started the car to get the heat going, but sat with her hands propped on the wheel.

"What's wrong?"

She gripped the wheel. "I'm sorry I can't give you more right now, Nick." Glancing over, she found him watching her intently. "It's not because I don't want to."

He reached over to caress her face. "I know that."

His touch sent a burst of longing sizzling through her, but she tamped it down. "Can you be patient with me?"

"I spent years wishing for another chance with you, Sam. I'm not about to bail just because it isn't going to be easy."

She released a deep sigh of relief. "Good."

"But after this case is closed…"

"I'll be right there with you."

"What we had six years ago is still there," he said, gazing into her eyes.

"So it seems."

"Whatever it is, I've never had it with anyone else."

"I haven't either. I was so sad when you didn't call. I couldn't believe I'd been so wrong about you."

"*Ugh.* That makes me furious. When I think about what we might've had, all these years…"

"Let me close this case," she said, her voice hoarse and tense. "The minute I close this case…"

Nick seemed to be resisting the urge to haul her into his arms. "Samantha?"

Surprisingly, the dreaded name didn't sound so bad coming from him. "Hmm?"

"We steamed up the windows."

"And we didn't even do anything!"

"Yet," he said, his voice full of promise.

Finding him harder to resist with every passing second, she shifted the car into drive and forced herself to focus on the road.

THIRTEEN

SAM LEFT NICK at the congressional parking lot, and timed her drive across the city to the Watergate. At that hour of the night, traffic was light but an accident on Independence Avenue screwed up her timing. She'd have to try again tomorrow night to determine whether Christina Billings would've had enough time to drive across the city, commit murder, and drive back with a stop to pick up Chinese food in twenty-eight minutes.

Reaching for her cell phone, she called to check on the search of Billings's car.

"I was just going to call you," Detective Tommy "Gonzo" Gonzales said. "We got a hit for blood on the front seat."

"I knew it!" Sam cried. "I'll bet she wrapped up her coat and left it on the seat. The blood soaked through!"

"Wait," Gonzo said. "Before you get too excited, she said she cut her hand scraping ice off her car two weeks ago and had to get three stitches. She has a raw-looking pink scar on her right hand and produced the form from the E.R. with wound care instructions. We're checking the blood anyway, but I'll bet a month's pay it's going to be hers. She willingly gave us a sample."

"*Son of a bitch.* We can't catch a single break in this one."

"We've narrowed down Billings's list of the senator's

recent girlfriends from six to two. The other four could prove they weren't in the city that night."

Sam added visits to the two remaining Barbies to her ever-growing to-do list for the morning. "Do me a favor and set up some plain-clothes coverage for the senator's wake. Make sure you coordinate with Virginia State Police and Richmond."

"Sure thing. Do you want observation and video or just observation?"

"Let's tape it. Make sure the officers you send have the photos of the senator's family and girlfriends, so they'll know who to watch for."

"I'm on it."

"Thanks for the good work, Gonzo."

"You got it. Try to get some sleep tonight, Sam."

"Yeah, sure."

As she sat in the tangle of cars held up by the wreck, Sam banged her fist on the wheel in frustration that came from multiple sources. She couldn't stop thinking about Nick and how understanding he'd been when she put their fledgling relationship on hold. How often did she allow herself to lean on someone? Never. However, she couldn't lean on someone who was a material witness in the homicide case she was investigating. As much as she wanted to, she just couldn't.

She edged the car forward and finally cleared the accident. When she arrived at the Watergate, Nick was waiting for her in his black BMW.

"What took so long?" he asked as he stepped out of the car.

"Accident on Independence."

"You should've taken Constitution."

"Well, I know that *now*. Nice ride," she said, admiring the gleaming Beamer. "The taxpayers take good care of you."

"I have few vices," he said with a grin as he slid an arm around her. "Cars are one of them."

She scooted out from under his arm before they entered the lobby. "No PDA," she growled. Flashing her shield to the officer at the security desk, she gestured to the bank of elevators. "We're taking another look at the senator's apartment."

The officer nodded and waved them through.

They rode to the sixth floor where the door to John's apartment was blocked by yellow crime scene tape. Sam plugged in the code to the police lock and pushed open the door. Lifting the yellow tape, she encouraged Nick to go in ahead of her.

She heard his deep inhale and watched his broad shoulders stoop as the memories came flooding back to him. Placing her hand on his arm, she stopped him. "You don't have to be here. I can get the clothes for you."

"No," he said softly. "I can do it."

"Take a minute. I'm going to wander."

Sam walked through the luxurious apartment where a light sheen of fingerprint dust remained. Picking up knickknacks, opening drawers and checking behind the television, she looked for anything that might have been missed the first time through. She had no doubt the place had been put together by a decorator—probably when the senior Senator O'Connor lived there. It was odd, really, how little of John O'Connor could be found in the apartment.

In the senator's bedroom, the bed linens had been stripped and sent off for DNA analysis. A single hair could have blown the case wide open, but all the fingerprints, fibers and DNA were John's. Since the apartment had not yet been cleaned, blood stained the wall behind the bed as well as the beige carpeting, and coagulated on the bedside table. The blow to the jugular would've been messy. Blood would have burst like a geyser from the wound, soaking the killer.

Sam stood at the foot of the bed and let her mind wander. Had he fallen asleep sitting up? Or had he sat up in surprise when the killer appeared? Obviously, he'd been naked in bed. Had he thought he was going to have sex with the woman who appeared in his bedroom? Is that how she gained easy access to his privates? Sam was absolutely convinced it was someone he knew well, which is why he hadn't had much of a reaction to finding her in his apartment.

"What's going on in that head of yours, Sergeant?" Nick asked from behind her.

"He was asleep," Sam said, her eyes fixed on the headboard where the gaping hole in the beige silk upholstery was a glaring reminder of what had happened there almost forty-eight hours ago. "Dozing. The TV was probably on."

"It wasn't on when I got here."

"She could've shut it off. Whoever it was, she was someone he wasn't surprised to see."

"She?"

"They were lovers." Sam spoke in a monotone as the scene played itself out in her imagination.

"Did he let her in?"

Sam shook her head. "She was waiting for him and took him by surprise. She had the knife behind her back. Maybe she was naked, too, which is why there's no one on the security tapes leaving with blood on their clothes. He thought he was going to get lucky, and that's how she managed to get a hold of his penis. By the time he became aware of the knife, she had already severed it. The pain would've been monstrous. He probably lost consciousness. If he came to before she killed him, he would have asked why. Maybe she told him, maybe she let him wonder."

"Would she have been strong enough to get a knife through his neck with one shot?"

"Good question. And you're right—it would've taken a tremendous blow to go all the way through his neck and lodge in the headboard. She would've been enraged by something he did or failed to do. Rage and adrenaline breeds strength. It could've been a promise he made and didn't deliver on or maybe she caught him with another woman. People have killed over less. When she was done, she took a shower to get rid of the blood that would've been all over her. Then she cleaned the bathroom and scrubbed it so well there wasn't so much as a hair on the floor. The water in the tub had dried by the time he was found, so we can only speculate that she showered. But none of the towels had been used. If she used one, she took it with her. Before she left, she might've taken a long last look at him. She was filled with regret that he couldn't be what she needed him to be, but at the same time she was angry with him for making her do this."

"You're good, Sam," Nick said, his tone reverent.

As if she had been in a trance, Sam looked up at him. "What?"

"The way you describe it...If I were a juror, I'd convict."

"All I have to do now is prove it and figure out who did it."

"You will." He moved to the closet, opened the doors and contemplated the row of dark suits, dress shirts in white, various shades of blue and some with pinstripes. There were easily a hundred ties to choose from.

Peeking into dresser drawers, Sam asked, "Did he ever wear anything besides suits? Where're the jeans? The sweats?"

"He didn't keep a lot of that stuff here."

"Where else would it be?"

"At his place in Leesburg."

"He has a second home?"

Nick nodded. "A cabin near his parents' property. We both use it as a retreat from the insanity of Washington."

"Why didn't you say anything about it the other day?"

"To be honest, it never occurred to me. I'm sorry. I wasn't thinking clearly then. I'm still not. Between what happened to John and seeing you again…"

"Take me there."

"Now?"

She nodded.

"It's almost midnight. You've been at it for eighteen hours. I can take you tomorrow."

Shaking her head, she said, "I won't have time tomorrow. If you drive, I'll nap in the car—if you can stay awake that is."

"I'm fine. I do my best work from midnight to three a.m."

His comment was rife with double meaning that Sam refused to acknowledge. Her face, however, heated with embarrassment as she helped him decide on a dark navy suit, pale blue silk dress shirt and a tie decorated with small American flags. They unearthed a garment bag, and Sam zipped it over the suit.

"Underwear?" she asked.

"He didn't wear it in life."

"How in the hell do you know that?"

Nick laughed. "We were at a luncheon with the Daughters of the American Revolution a year or so ago, and everyone was starting to leave when one of the blue hairs came to tell me the senator needed me at the head table. I went into the room, and he was sitting all by himself."

"How come?"

"Apparently, he'd managed to split his pants and was in need of an exit strategy."

Sam laughed at the picture he painted. "Let me guess—he was in commando mode?"

"You got it. So I found him an overcoat—not an easy feat in July, I might add—and got him out of there with his pride intact."

"Where did that fall in your job description?"

"Under 'other duties as assigned,'" he said with a sad smile that tugged at her heart.

"All right then. No underwear. Shoes?"

"Would you want to spend eternity with your feet encased in wingtips? The tie will be bad enough. I'm sure I'll hear plenty about that when we meet up again in the afterlife." He reached for her hand and linked their fingers. "Thank you for helping me with this."

Flustered, she extracted her hand and jammed it in her pocket. "It's no problem."

"Is choosing clothes for the deceased part of *your* job description?"

"This is definitely a first."

On their way out of John's bedroom, Nick looked at her in a way that reminded Sam of what he wanted from her. A burst of yearning took her by surprise. Sam wasn't a woman who yearned, especially for a man. She was focused, efficient, dedicated to her work and her family, hard nosed when she needed to be, and independent—fiercely and completely independent. So it should have been unsettling to want a man as much as she wanted Nick.

Truth be told, she had fantasized about him for years after the night they spent together. She had followed Senator O'Connor's career and watched hours of congressional coverage in the hopes of catching a glimpse of the senator's trusted aide. But only rarely had she seen Nick. He apparently kept a much lower profile than his illustrious boss.

In the parking lot, he held the passenger door of his car for her.

She slid into the buttery soft leather seat and sighed with contentment. When he turned the car on, she quickly discovered the seats were heated and felt like she'd gone straight to heaven. "This car suits you."

"You think so?"

"Uh huh. It's classy but not showy."

"Is that a compliment, Samantha?"

She shrugged.

He reached for her hand as they headed out of the city. When she tried to resist, he held on tighter. "No one but us, babe."

"There's no tablecloth to hide under."

He flashed that irresistible grin and laced his fingers through hers. "Give me just this much, will you?"

Since he'd asked so nicely and it really wasn't much, she didn't argue with him even if the simple feel of his hand wrapped around hers set her heart to galloping and put her hormones on full alert. Guilt was mixed in there, too. She had no business spending this much time with him or wanting him so fiercely. But since it was dark and she was tired and no one was looking, rather than push him away, she tightened her grip on his hand.

FOURTEEN

SAM HADN'T EXPECTED to sleep. But the combined lull of the moving car, the heated seats, Nick's hand wrapped companionably around hers…

"Wake up, Sleeping Beauty. We're here."

Coming to, Sam looked out at the vast darkness and was able to make out the shape of a cabin in front of the car. "Let's get to it."

The rush of frigid air slapped at Sam's face. She followed Nick up the gravel path to the door and stood back while he used his key in the lock.

Inside, he flipped on lights.

Sam blinked a comfortable living area into focus. Big, welcoming sofas, a flat-screen TV mounted on the wall, overflowing bookshelves on either side of the stone fireplace, framed family photos and a couple of trophies. Here, at last, was Senator John Thomas O'Connor.

She shrugged off her coat, pushed up the sleeves of her sweater, tugged the clip from her hair and got to work. Two hours later, she had discovered that John loved Hemingway, Shakespeare, Patterson and Grisham. His musical taste ran the gamut from Mellencamp to Springsteen, Vivaldi to Bach. She had sifted through photo albums, yearbooks and a file cabinet that seemed to have no rhyme or reason to anyone other than its owner.

She perused a series of essays John wrote for his senior project at Harvard, detailing the roles of government and the governed. The essays were bound into a small navy blue volume with smart gold embossing.

"He was proud of that," Nick said from the doorway to the office.

Startled, she glanced up at him. She had *almost* forgotten he was there.

"His father had the book made and gave it to everyone who was anyone." Nick stepped into the room and handed her a steaming mug.

"*Oh*, is that hot chocolate?" she asked, soaking in the mouthwatering aroma.

"I figured it was too late for coffee." He had removed his suit coat and released the top buttons on his dress shirt. Her eyes fixated on a dark tuft of chest hair.

"You figured right. Fat free, calorie free, I hope." Swirling her tongue over the dollop of whipped cream on top, she took a moment to appreciate the taste. Looking up at him again, she found his hazel eyes locked on her. "What?" she asked, her voice shakier than she intended it to be.

"It's just…you…and whipped cream. It's giving me ideas."

She swallowed, hard.

"I like your hair down like that," he added.

Choosing to ignore the comments and the flush of heat that went rippling through her body, she returned her attention to the book John had dedicated to his father. A photo slid out from between the pages and fell to the floor. Sam put her mug on the desk and leaned over to retrieve the picture of a strapping blond boy of about sixteen in a football uniform.

"What've you got there?" Nick asked.

"Looks like a photo of John when he was in high school." She turned it over to find the initials "TJO" and a date from four years earlier. "Oh. It's not him. Who's TJO?"

Nick took the photo from her, studied the likeness, and then turned it over. "I have no idea, but he could *be* John when I first met him."

"Did he have a son, Nick?" She thought of Patricia Donaldson and the three-thousand-dollar-a-month payments.

"Of course not."

"You're sure of that?"

"I'm positive," he said hotly. "I've known him since he was eighteen. If he had a son, I'd know it."

"Well, if that's not his son, whoever he is, he bears a striking resemblance to John." Sam tucked the photo into her bag with plans to ask the senator's parents about it in the morning. "He had quite a thing for Spider-Man, huh?" She gestured to the shelves in the corner that housed John's extensive stash of Spiderman collectibles.

Nick smiled. "He was obsessed."

She picked up a carved placard from the desk that bore Spider-Man's signature saying, With Great Power Comes Great Responsibility. Studying it for a long moment, she glanced at Nick. "Did he believe this?"

"Very much so. Despite his sometimes lackadaisical approach to his job, he took his responsibilities as seriously as he was able to."

"But not as seriously as you would have."

"Let's just say if our roles had been reversed, I would've done a lot of things differently."

"Have you ever wanted to be the one in the corner office?"

"God no," he said with a guffaw. "I work much better as the guy behind the guy." He seemed to sober when he remembered he had lost his guy when John died.

"With his parents' okay, I'd like to have a team go through here more methodically tomorrow." She stretched and got up. "I'm running out of gas after twenty hours."

"I'm guessing you'll want to talk to his parents about that photo," Nick said, "so why don't we crash here and go see them in the morning?"

Her eyes darted up to meet his. "I'm not sleeping with you."

"I'm not asking you to," he said with a sexy smile. "There's a guestroom I use when I'm here. I'll take John's room."

Sam ran it around in her mind as she finished her hot chocolate. Technically, the cabin wasn't a crime scene, so she didn't have an issue there. She was exhausted, he didn't look much better, and she *could* knock a few things off her to-do list in the morning if she stayed in Leesburg, including another discussion with Terry O'Connor if he was available.

"All right," she said, even though she would've preferred separate hotel rooms, but hotels were in short supply in that corner of the county. She got up to follow Nick down the hallway to the bedrooms.

"Bathroom's in there," he pointed. In the guestroom, he rooted through an antique chest of drawers and pulled out a large T-shirt. "One of mine if you want something to sleep in. There're extra toothbrushes and anything else you might need in the bathroom closet."

"Thanks," she said, embarrassed and shy all of a sudden—two emotions she rarely experienced.

He slid a hand around her neck to draw her in close to him. For a long, breathless moment he just looked at her before he kissed her forehead. "I'll see you in the morning. Holler if you need anything."

Devastated by the simple kiss, she watched him cross the hall, her heart pounding and her hands damp. She hated being off balance and out of kilter, which of course was why he had done it. Feeling defiant, she used the bathroom and then left the shirt he had given her on the bed as she stripped out of her clothes and slid naked between the cool sheets.

Less than a minute later, she was out cold.

"SAM. HONEY, WAKE UP. You're dreaming."

Sam could hear him but couldn't seem to force her eyes open.

"Babe."

Her eyes fluttered open to find Nick sitting on the bed.

When he brushed the hair back from her face, she realized she was sweating and her heart was racing.

"Are you okay?" he asked.

"Mmm, sorry." It occurred to her that she must've been loud if she had woken him. She glanced at him, noticing he wore only a pair of sweats, and let her eyes take a slow journey over his muscular chest.

"It was a doozy, huh? The dream?"

"I don't know. I never remember the details, just the fear." She rubbed a weary hand over her cheek and wished for a glass of water. "Did I…um…say anything?"

He replaced the hand she had on her face with his own. "You kept saying, 'Cease fire, hold your fire.'"

"Shit," she said with a deep sigh.

He stretched out next to her on top of the comforter and settled her head on his shoulder. "It was a traumatic thing, Sam, but it wasn't your fault."

Steeped in the masculine scent of citrus and spice, she closed her eyes against the rush of emotion and absorbed the comfort he offered. Just for a minute. His chest hair brushed against her face, making her want him so fiercely. "If only I could forgive myself as easily as you've forgiven me."

He brought her closer to him.

"Um, Nick?"

"Hmm?"

"I'm kind of naked under here."

"Yeah, I noticed."

As all the reasons this was a bad idea came crashing down on her, she attempted to struggle out of his embrace. "I can't," she whispered. "I can't have this. I can't have you."

"Yes, you can."

Her face still pressed to his chest, Sam gave herself another second to wallow in the scent that she'd never forgotten. "Not here. Not now."

He released a deep, ragged breath. "I missed you, Sam. I thought about you, about that night, so often."

"I did, too," she said, her eyes closed tight against the onslaught of emotions she'd only felt this acutely once before.

"I've never wanted anyone the way I want you. If you're in the room, I want you."

"I seem to have the same problem."

"We've got a few hours until daybreak. Would it be okay if I just held you until then?"

"I'd love nothing more, but it's too tempting. *You're* too tempting."

Sighing again, he released her and sat up. He leaned down to press a soft kiss to her lips. "See you in the morning."

Sam watched him go, knowing she'd never get back to sleep with every cell in her body on fire for him.

FIFTEEN

SAM CORRALLED HER hair into a ponytail, strapped on her shoulder holster, clipped the badge to her belt, and adjusted her suit jacket over the same scoop-necked top she'd worn yesterday. When she was ready, she took a long look around to make sure she wasn't leaving behind any sign that she had spent the night for the team she planned to send in there later that day. Satisfied by the quick sweep of the room, she emerged to find Nick waiting for her in the living room. Somehow he managed to appear pressed and polished in yesterday's clothes. His face was smooth and his hair still damp from the shower.

"Ready?" he asked.

She nodded.

Wrapping her coat and his arms around her, he hugged her from behind and pressed kisses to her neck and cheek before he finally let go.

The spontaneous demonstration of affection caught her off guard. Unless it was leading to sex, Peter had never bothered with the random acts of affection that Nick doled out so effortlessly. Nick seemed to *need* to touch her if she was near him. That she liked it so much was just another reason to keep her distance.

The O'Connors's home was located two miles up the main road from John's cabin. Once again, Carrie met them at the door and was surprised to see them out so early.

"Are they up?" Nick asked.

"They're having breakfast. Come on in." She led them into the cozy country kitchen where Graham and Laine sat at the table lost in their own thoughts. Neither of them seemed to be eating much of anything.

Both had dark circles under their eyes. Weariness and grief clung to them.

"Nick?" Graham said. "You're out early. Sergeant."

Carrie handed mugs of coffee to Sam and Nick.

"Thank you," Nick said.

"I'm sorry to barge in on you so early." Sam stirred cream into her coffee and wished it was a diet cola. "But I have something I need to ask you."

"Of course," Laine said. "Whatever we can do to help."

Sam retrieved the photo from her bag. "Who is this?" She placed the photo on the table between them.

They looked at the photo and then at each other.

"Where'd you get this?" Graham asked.

"At the cabin," Nick said. "The photo was tucked into the essay book you had made for him."

"It's John's cousin, Thomas," Laine said, glancing up at Sam with cool patrician eyes. "His father is Graham's brother Robert."

"I don't remember John mentioning a cousin that young," Nick said.

Laine shrugged. "There were almost twenty years between them. They were hardly close."

"He looks an awful lot like your son," Sam said, testing for reactions.

"Yes, he does," Graham said, his expression neutral. "Is there anything else?"

"Do you know where I can find Terry?" Sam said.

The question seemed to startle both O'Connors.

"I believe he's working in the city this morning," Graham said.

"The address?"

He rattled off the name and K Street address of a prominent lobbying firm, which Sam wrote down in the small notebook she pulled from her back pocket. "If you have no objection, I'd like to send a team into the cabin today to make sure we're not missing something that could help with the case."

"Strange people in John's home?" Laine asked, visibly disturbed by the notion.

"Police," Sam clarified. "They'll be as respectful as possible."

"That's fine," Graham said with a pointed look at his wife. "If it'll help the investigation, do it."

"Can you tell me, Senator, who might still have keys to the apartment at the Watergate from when you lived there?"

Graham pondered that for a moment. "Only my family."

"No staffers or aides?"

"My chief of staff had one, but I distinctly recall him giving it back to me when we left office."

"Any chance he might've had others made, given them to other people?"

"No. He was a guard dog about my privacy. He didn't even like having the key himself."

"Are you aware, either of you, that John spoke with

Patricia Donaldson in Chicago several times a week for an hour or more each time?"

Again the O'Connors exchanged glances.

"No, but I'm not surprised," Graham said. "They were close friends as children."

"Just friends?"

"Yes," Laine said pointedly, so pointedly in fact that it raised Sam's hackles and her radar. There was more to this story. Of that she had no doubt. She'd be speaking to Patricia Donaldson as soon as she could arrange a trip to Chicago.

"John is still due to be moved today to Richmond?" Laine asked Nick.

He nodded. "The motorcade is leaving Washington at noon."

"We'll be going down to Richmond this afternoon," Graham said. "The state police are escorting us and clearing the way for us to get in and out before they open it to the public."

"The staff will have a private viewing in the morning," Nick said.

"You got the clothes they needed?" Laine asked.

"Yes. I'm heading to the funeral home from here. Um, about the funeral…Have you decided who you want to have speak on behalf of the family?"

"You do it," Laine said with a weary sigh.

"Are you sure? You wouldn't rather have a family member?"

"You *are* family to us, Nick," Graham said. "You'll do him proud. We know that."

"I'll do my best," he said softly. "We should let you get back to your breakfast."

"We'll see you Monday, if not before," Laine said.

Nick leaned over to kiss her cheek. "I'll be in touch."

She squeezed the hand he rested on her shoulder. "Thank you for all you're doing. I know it can't be easy for you."

"It's an honor and a privilege."

Patting his hand once more, she released him.

Nick hugged Graham and kissed Carrie on his way out of the kitchen. With his hand on the small of her back, he steered Sam to the front door. Once they were outside, he took a deep, rattling breath of cold air.

Since there was little else she could do to comfort him, she held his hand between both of hers all the way back to Washington.

AFTER FIGHTING THEIR WAY through rush-hour traffic, Nick pulled up to the Watergate with fifteen minutes to spare before Sam's appointment with Senator Stenhouse.

"So much for going home to change first," she grumbled. "Freddie will have a field day with this."

"Tell him you worked all night. Won't be a total lie."

"It'll be a good excuse to remind him that I outrank him and can order him to shut up. He likes that."

Nick smiled and reached for the inside pocket of his suit jacket. He withdrew a small leather case and handed her his business card. "Call me? My cell number is on there."

She took the card, stuffed it in her pocket and reached for the door.

He stopped her before she could get out. "Talk to me before Monday so we can arrange to go to the funeral together if you still want me to help you ID people."

"I do. I'll be in touch."

"Remember to eat and sleep, will you?"

"Yeah, right," she said on her way out the door.

Nick waited, probably to make sure her car started because he was polite that way, and then pulled into traffic just ahead of her.

On the way to Capitol Hill, Sam called Gonzo and asked him to oversee the sift through John O'Connor's cabin.

"It's not a crime scene, so I'm not interested in fingerprints or DNA. I'm just looking for anything we don't already know about him."

"Gotcha. So we got confirmation that the blood in Christina Billings's car was her own."

"Well, I guess that closes that loop," Sam said. "There's no way she made it across town, killed him, showered, cleaned up the bathroom and got back with Chinese food in twenty-eight minutes. Not in this town with this traffic, even at midnight."

"No way is right," Gonzo agreed. "I'll get a team together and get out to Leesburg this morning."

"You'd better notify Loudoun County, too, so we don't have jurisdictional trouble." She paused before she added, "Full disclosure—I crashed in the guestroom there last night. I needed to see his parents in the morning, and it saved me some time. Cappuano slept in the senator's room."

"Okay."

"If you could keep that tidbit to yourself, I'd owe you one."

He laughed. "I like having you indebted to me. Just let me know if there's anything else I can do."

"There is one thing," she said, playing the hunch. "Do a run on Graham O'Connor's brother, Robert. I need the deal on his family, offspring in particular. If you can get photos, even better."

"Will do," Gonzo said. "I'll call you with what I find out. So, um, you saw the papers this morning I assume..."

Sam's stomach took a queasy dip that reminded her she hadn't eaten or had either of the two diet colas she usually relied upon to jumpstart her day. "No, why?"

"Destiny Johnson is calling you a baby killer."

"Is that so?" Sam growled, the dip in her stomach descending into the ache that dogged her in times of stress. Two doctors had been unable to determine the cause. One had suggested she give up soda, which simply wasn't an option, so she lived with her stomach's annoying ability to predict her stress level.

"Don't take it to heart, Sam. Everyone knows that if she'd been any kind of mother, her kid wouldn't have been hanging out in a crack house in the first place."

"But she has the nerve to call *me* the baby killer." Of all the things she could've said, that hurt more than anything.

"I know. She made some pretty serious threats about what she'd do if you testify against her deadbeat husband next week. I'm sure you'll be hearing from the brass about it."

"That's great." She rubbed her belly in an effort to find some relief. "Just what I need right now."

"Sorry. You know we're all standing behind you. It was a clean shoot."

"Thanks, Gonzo." Her throat tightened with emotion she couldn't afford to let in just then. Clearing it away, she said, "Call me if you find anything useful at the cabin. I did a surface run last night, but I was operating on fumes. I could've missed something."

"Leave it to me. I'll let you know when we finish."

She gave him the O'Connors's phone number so he could get a key to the cabin from them and signed off. Weaving her way through traffic, she made it to Capitol Hill with minutes to spare and took off running for the Hart Senate Office Building.

Freddie was pacing in the hallway outside Senator Stenhouse's office suite. "There you are! I was just about to call you." His astute eyes took in her day-old suit and landed on her face.

"I worked all night, I haven't been home to change yet, and yes, I've heard about Destiny Johnson," she snapped. "So whatever you're going to say, don't bother."

"As usual, a night without sleep has done wonders for your disposition."

"Buzz off, Freddie. I'm truly not in the mood to go ten rounds with you."

"What were you doing working all night? And why didn't you call me? I would've come back in."

"I went through O'Connor's place again and then his home in Leesburg."

Freddie raised an eyebrow. "By yourself?"

"Nick Cappuano was with me. He told me about the place in Leesburg and took me there. Otherwise I never would've found it. Do you have a problem with that?"

"Me?" Freddie raised his hands defensively. "I've got no problems, boss."

"Good. Can we get to work then?"

"I'm following you."

"Nice digs," she muttered under her breath as Stenhouse's assistant showed them into a massive corner office that was triple the size of that assigned to the junior senator from Virginia.

Stenhouse, tall and lean with silver hair and sharp, frosty blue eyes, stood up when they came in. He dismissed the assistant with orders to close the door behind her. "I'm on a tight schedule, Detectives. What can I do for you?"

Wants to play it that way? Sam thought. *Well, so can I.* "Detective Cruz, please record this interview with Senate Minority Leader William Stenhouse." She rattled off the time, date, place and players present.

"You need my permission to record this," Stenhouse snapped.

"Here or downtown. Your choice."

He glowered at her for a long moment before he gestured for her to proceed.

"Where were you on Tuesday evening between ten p.m. and seven a.m.?"

"You can't be serious."

Turning to Freddie, she said, "Am I serious, Detective Cruz?"

"Yes, ma'am. I believe you're dead serious."

"Answer the question, Senator."

Teeth gritted, Stenhouse glared at her. "I was here until ten, ten thirty, and then I went home."

"Which is where?"

"Old Town Alexandria."

"Did you see or speak to anyone after you left here?"

"My wife is at home in Missouri preparing for the holidays."

"So that's a 'no'?"

"That's a 'no,'" he growled.

"How did you feel about the immigration bill Senator O'Connor sponsored?"

"Useless piece of drivel," Stenhouse muttered. "The bill has no bones to it, and everyone knows that."

"Funny, that's not what we've been told, is it Detective Cruz?"

"No, ma'am." Freddie flipped open his notebook and rattled off the statement the president had issued days earlier, calling the immigration reform bill the most important piece of legislation proposed during his first term.

Stenhouse's glare could've bored a hole through a lesser cop, but Sam barely felt the heat. "Were you irritated to see Graham O'Connor's son succeeding in the Senate?"

"Hardly," he said. "He was nothing to me."

"And his father? Was he nothing to you as well?"

"He was a prick who overstayed his welcome."

"How did you feel when you heard his son had been murdered?"

"It's a tragedy," he said in a pathetic attempt at sincerity. "He was a United States senator."

"And the son of your longtime rival."

Awareness dawned all at once. "Did he tell you I did this? That bastard!" He stalked to the window and stared out for a moment before he turned to them. "I hate his fucking guts. But do I hate him enough to kill his son? No, I don't. I haven't given Graham O'Connor a thought in the five years since we saw the last of his sorry ass around here."

"I'm sure you've had cause to give his son more than a passing thought in the same five years."

"His son was in the Senate for one reason and one reason only—his pedigree. The O'Connors have the people of Virginia snowed. John O'Connor was even more useless than his father, and that's not just my opinion. Ask around."

"I'll do that," Sam said. "In the meantime, stay available."

"What does that mean? Congress will be in holiday recess after tomorrow. I'm heading home to Missouri the day after."

"No, you're not. You're staying right here until we close this case."

"But it's Christmas! You can't keep me here against my will."

"Detective Cruz, can I keep the senator here against his will?"

"I believe you can, ma'am."

"And do we have a jail cell with his name on it if we hear he leaves the capital region?"

"Yes, ma'am. We absolutely do."

Stenhouse breathed fire as the detectives had their exchange.

Sam took three steps to close the distance between them. Looking up at the senator, she kept her expression passive and calm. "Neither your rank nor your standing mean a thing to me. This is a homicide investigation, and I won't hesitate to toss you in a cage if you fail to cooperate. Stay available."

With that, she turned, nodded at Freddie to follow her, and left the room.

She was gratified to hear Stenhouse yell to his assistant, "Get Joe Farnsworth on the line. Right now!"

TERRY O'CONNOR SPENT the days he was sober in a closet-sized office on Independence Avenue. Judging from the lack of anything much on his desk, Sam deduced the job was bogus and most likely a favor to his illustrious father.

Terry's already pasty complexion paled when the detectives appeared at his door.

"Good morning, Mr. O'Connor," Sam said. "We're sorry to interrupt your work, but we have a few follow-up questions for you."

"Um, sure," he said, gesturing to a chair.

Sam took the chair while Freddie hovered in the doorway.

"I have to leave soon," Terry said. "We're going to Richmond."

"Yes, I know. We won't keep you long. Have you made any headway in producing the woman you were with on the night of the murder?"

Terry seemed to shrink further into his chair. "No."

"Did you kill your brother, Terry?"

Misery turned to shock in an instant. "No!"

"You had good reason to want him dead. I mean, after all, he was living the life that should've been yours and was about to know real success as a senator when the immigration bill passed. Maybe that was just too much for you."

"I loved my brother, Sergeant. Was I jealous of him? You bet I was. I wanted that job. I *wanted* it. Down here, you know?" He gestured to his gut. "I'd prepared for it my whole life, so yeah, it bothered me that he had it when he didn't even want it. But killing him wouldn't change anything for me. You don't see the Virginia Democrats lined up outside my office wanting me to take his place, do you?"

"No."

"So what was my motive in killing him?"

"Pleasure? Revenge?"

"Do I look like I've got the energy to care that much about anything?" he asked, his tone heavy with utter defeat.

Sam stood up. "I'd still like the name of the woman you say you were with that night."

Terry sighed. "So would I, Sergeant. Believe me. So would I."

OUTSIDE, SAM TURNED to Freddie. "What do you think?"

"I don't want it to be him. I mean, think of those poor parents if it *was* him…"

Freddie's endless compassion could be alternatively comforting and aggravating. "He's a lot more than jealous of his brother. Check out that hole-in-the-wall office. You think it didn't bug the shit out of him that baby brother was snuggled into that suite in the Hart Building?"

"Enough to kill him?"

"I don't know. I still see a woman for this, but I'm not ruling out the brother angle. Not yet. I'm giving him until the funeral is over to produce his alibi and then he and I are going to have a more formal chat." She paused before she added, "I need to go home and get changed. Do you mind if we make a quick stop?"

"Nope. You know I like seeing the deputy chief."

"He likes you, too, for some unknown reason."

"My wit and charm are hard to resist."

"Funny, I seem to have no problem resisting."

"You are a rare and unique woman, Sergeant."

"And you'd do well to remember that."

Freddie laughed and followed her to the car.

SIXTEEN

SAM WASN'T SURPRISED to receive a call from Chief Farnsworth as she drove home.

"Good morning, Chief. I assume you've heard from Senator Stenhouse."

"You assume correctly. Is it really necessary to retain him, Sergeant?"

"I believe it is, sir. He had a number of political reasons to want to see John O'Connor dead, not the least of which was his hatred for the senator's father."

"Hate is a strong word."

"It's his word." Glancing at Freddie she said, "Correct me if I'm wrong, Detective Cruz, but I believe the senator's exact words in reference to Graham O'Connor were, 'I hate his fucking guts.'"

Freddie nodded his approval.

"Detective Cruz has confirmed my account, sir."

"Tread carefully on this front, Sergeant. Stenhouse can make my life difficult, and if my life is difficult, so is yours."

"Yes, sir."

"The media is burning a hole in the back of my neck clamoring for information. How close are we to closing this one?"

"Not as close as I'd like to be. I don't have a clear-cut suspect at the moment—a few who had motive and opportunity—but no one's popping for me just yet."

"I'd like to see you when you get back to HQ."

"About what was in the paper this morning?"

"Yes."

"I can handle that, sir. There's no need—"

"My office, four o'clock," the chief said and ended the call.

"Shit," she muttered as she returned the cell phone to her coat pocket.

"They have to take those kinds of threats against an officer seriously, Sam," Freddie said. "They have no choice."

"She's a grieving mother who's looking for someone to blame. I'm convenient."

"Too bad she can't see that her crack head husband is the one to blame, not you."

Sam parked on Ninth Street, rested her hands on the wheel, and looked over at Freddie. "Listen, in the event that she's not blowing smoke, there could be some trouble in the form of stray bullets flying at me. I'd understand if you wanted to partner up with someone else until this blows over."

"Nice try, Sergeant, but you're stuck with me."

"I could have you reassigned."

"You could," he conceded. "But let me ask you this—if someone was taking pot shots at me, would you bail?"

"No."

"Then why do you think I would?"

Under his junk food-loving, cover-boy exterior, Freddie Cruz was made of stuff Sam respected. "All right then," Sam said, attempting to return things to normal. "When you get your pretty head blown off, don't come crying to me."

He stuck out his jaw. "You really think my head is pretty? You've never told me that before."

"Shut *up*," she groaned, reaching for the door handle. "Jesus."

"I've asked you to refrain from using the Lord's name in vain."

"And I've asked *you* to refrain from preaching your Holy Roller crap to me." There. Back to normal.

The ramp that led to Skip Holland's front door was a stark reminder of the changes wrought by an assailant's bullet. Inside, Sam called for him and smiled when she heard the whir of his chair.

"There's my daughter who blows her curfew and stays out all night."

"I left a message that I know you got." She bent down to kiss his forehead. "So don't give me any grief."

"Morning, Detective Cruz. Have you eaten?"

"Earlier." Freddie squeezed Skip's right hand in greeting. "But you know me, there's always room for more."

"Celia made eggs. I think there's some left."

"Don't mind if I do." Freddie flashed Sam a grin as he headed for the kitchen.

She rolled her eyes. "Why do you have to encourage him?" she asked her father.

"He's a growing boy. Needs his protein."

"I hope I'm around when his metabolism slows to a crawl the way mine has." She reached for the mail stacked on a table. "You look tired."

"I could say the same for you, Sergeant. What kept you out all night?"

"Working the case. You know." She glanced at him, caught a hint of something in his wise eyes. "What?"

"I can still read."

"Oh." She released her hair from the ponytail and combed her fingers through it in an attempt to bring some order to it. "You saw the thing in the paper. She's looking for someone to blame."

"What's being done?"

She knew he meant by the department and wanting to quell his fears she told him of the meeting Farnsworth had called.

"He'll take you off the streets. Off O'Connor until you've testified."

"He'll take me off kicking and screaming. I can't let a useless excuse for a mother like Destiny Johnson get in the way of the job."

"She has a lot of friends—angry friends with guns. Farnsworth won't have any choice but to put you under protection after the threats she's made."

"If I go under, the case goes with me. I'll be surprised if they haven't already picked her up for threatening the life of a police officer."

"No doubt, but just because she's locked up doesn't mean the threat's been neutralized."

Sam leaned over to press another kiss to his forehead. "Don't worry."

A look of fury crossed the expressive side of his face. "You can say that to me? When I'm sitting in this chair incapable of doing a goddamned *thing* when the life of my daughter, *my child*, has been threatened by someone who has not only the will but the means to follow through? Worry is all I've got. Don't take that away from me, Sam, and don't patronize me. I expect better from you."

"I'm sorry. You're right." She expelled a long deep

breath as her stomachache returned with a vengeance. Navigating his new reality was a slippery slope, even almost two years later. "Of course you're right."

"You're to take this seriously and do whatever you're told by your superior officers. I'm trusting Joe to do his part, so I need your word that you'll do yours."

She reached for his hand and squeezed the one finger that could still feel it. "You have it."

"Go get changed and then come down to have some breakfast."

Because he was her dad and needed to feel like he still had control over something, she did what she was told without reminding him that she was thirty-four and didn't have to.

Over eggs and toast, she and Freddie hashed out the case with Skip while Celia helped him with a cup of coffee.

"I agree with you about the female angle, the act of passion," Skip said.

"We haven't encountered a woman yet with the emotional baggage toward O'Connor that this would've required," Freddie said.

"We're talking to some ex-girlfriends when we leave here, so we're hoping to get lucky," Sam said.

"You're looking for a cool customer," Skip said, slipping into the zone. "Someone who keeps tremendous anger bottled up under a refined exterior. You'll find she's been abused or had complicated relationships with the significant men in her life—father, ex-husband, ex-lover. Men have disappointed her in some way and whatever the senator did was the final straw. The breaking point."

"Damn," Freddie said reverently. "You two are something else. She sees these things as clearly as you do."

Celia smiled at him. "It's in their genes. I wonder sometimes if I should be afraid, spending as much time as I do with people who can slide inside a criminal's mind as easily as these two can."

"Enough about our genes." Sam stood as she downed a last swallow of soda. "Thanks, Celia, for the chow, and you for the consult." She kissed her father's cheek. "See you tonight."

"I won't hold my breath," he said with a dry chuckle. To Freddie he added, "She uses me for a place to keep her considerable wardrobe."

"Seems to me she uses you for a lot more than that. Always a pleasure, Chief."

"All mine, Detective. The Skins are playing at home Sunday night if you want to stop by to watch the game. Celia tells me there'll be snacks. Maybe even a beer or two if I'm good."

"Snacks, beer *and* football?" Freddie reached out to squeeze Skip's hand. "Hard to resist an offer like that. I'll do my best to come by. Thanks for breakfast, Celia. It was fabulous as usual."

"Anytime, Detective," Celia said, blushing a little as even the strongest of women tended to do when on the receiving end of Freddie's formidable charm.

Outside, Sam paused before she got into the car. "I, ah, I just wanted to say thanks for that in there."

Freddie's eyebrows knitted with confusion as he studied her over the top of the car. "For what? Eating your food like I just got rescued from a deserted island?"

"No." She struggled to find the words. "For treating him like he's still a normal guy, a normal person."

"He is." Freddie maintained the puzzled air of innocent befuddlement. "Why would I treat him any other way?"

"You'd be surprised the way people treat him sometimes." They got into the car. "I'm only going to say this once, and if I hear you repeated it I'll deny it with everything I've got. Understand?"

"Gee, I can't wait to hear this. You leave me breathless with anticipation."

"Your sarcasm and significant dietary failings aside, you're a special guy, Freddie Cruz. A one-in-a-million good guy." She glanced over to find him staring at her with his mouth hanging open. "Now that we've got that bullshit out of the way, what do you say we get back to figuring out who killed the senator?" When Freddie failed to reply, she said, "For Christ's sake, will you quit looking at me like I just hit you with the Taser?"

"Might as well have," he muttered. "Might as well have."

That he didn't mention her disrespectful use of the Lord's name told her she'd truly shocked him with the compliment, which made for a satisfying start to what promised to be a shitty day.

THEY FOUND NATALIE JORDAN at home alone in Belle Haven, an upscale development of stately colonial homes in Alexandria. Red brick, white columns and black wrought iron fronted hers. The home reeked of old money and Virginia aristocracy.

"Nice crib," Freddie said, gazing around at the well-kept grounds.

"Looks like Natalie landed herself a sugar daddy after all," Sam said as she rang the doorbell. Chimes pealed inside.

Natalie answered the door dressed in a salmon-colored silk blouse, winter white wool pants and two-inch heels. A gold chain bearing a diamond the size of Sam's thumb encircled her slender neck, and her blond hair was cut into a sleek bob that perfectly offset her thin, angular face. Sharp blue eyes were rimmed with red and dark circles marred her otherwise flawless complexion. Sam could see what Nick had meant when he'd described Natalie as "quite something."

No slouch in the fashion department herself, Sam was immediately intimidated. Her stomach twisted. Willing the pain away with a quick deep breath, Sam flashed her badge. "Detective Sergeant Holland and Detective Cruz, Metro Police."

"Come in," Natalie said in a honeyed Southern accent. "I've been expecting you."

"Is that so?" Sam said as they followed her to a living room ripped from the pages of the *Town & Country* holiday issue.

"Senator O'Connor and I were involved for a number of years. I assumed you'd want to speak to me at some point. May I offer you something? Coffee or a cold drink?"

Before Freddie could accept, Sam said, "No, thank you. Do you mind if we record this conversation?"

Natalie shook her head, and Sam gestured for Freddie to turn on the recorder.

Sam began by noting the people present and the location of their interview. "Can you tell me where you were on Tuesday between the hours of ten p.m. and seven a.m.?"

While Natalie might have been expecting them, she clearly hadn't been expecting that. "I'm a *suspect?*"

"Until we determine otherwise, everyone is. Your whereabouts?"

"I was here," she stammered. "With my husband."

"His name?"

"Noel Jordan."

"And where might we find him to confirm this?"

"He's the special assistant attorney general at Justice." She rattled off an address in the city. "He's at work right now."

With the wave of her hand to encompass the room, Sam said, "Swanky digs for a guy on a government salary."

"His family has…they're wealthy."

"Can you tell me the nature of your relationship with Senator O'Connor?"

Hands twisting in her lap, Natalie said, "We were involved, romantically, for just over three years."

"And it ended when?"

"About four years ago," she sighed. "A year or so after he was elected."

"Were you in love with him?"

"Very much so," she said with a wistful expression that had Sam speculating that Natalie's feelings for the senator remained intact.

"Why did the relationship end?"

"I wanted to get married. He didn't." She shrugged. "We argued about it. Several times. After one particularly nasty disagreement, he said our relationship had run its course and we should think about seeing other people."

"And how did you feel about that?"

"Devastated and shocked. I loved him. I wanted to spend my life with him. I had no idea he was that unhappy."

"Did he love you?"

"He said he did, but there was always something… off, I guess you could say. I was never entirely convinced he loved me the same way I loved him."

"Must've pissed you off to get dumped by the guy you'd planned to marry."

Raw blue eyes flashed with emotion. "I was too crushed to be pissed, Sergeant. And if you're wondering if I killed him, I can assure you I didn't. In fact, I was quite certain I was over him until I heard he was dead." Tears suddenly spilled down her porcelain cheeks. She wiped at them with a practiced gesture that indicated she'd done a lot of crying in the last few days. "Since then, I can't seem to turn off the waterworks." Pausing for a moment, she added, "I have a nice life now with a man I adore, a man who's good to me. I'd have nothing to gain by harming John."

"Do you still have a key to the senator's apartment at the Watergate?"

"I, um, I don't know." She appeared genuinely perplexed. "I might."

"So you had one when you were dating?"

"I lived with him there for the last year or so of our relationship." Red blotches formed on her cheeks. "I don't recall giving the key back to him when I moved out."

"I need to ask you something of a personal nature, and I apologize in advance if it offends you."

"Everything about this offends me, Sergeant. A good man, a man I loved, has been murdered. It offends me on a very deep level."

"I understand. However, my job is to find out who killed him, and to do that I have to ask you about his sexual preferences."

Taken aback, Natalie said, "What do you mean?"

"Was he into anything kinky?"

Her cheeks went from blotchy to flaming. "We enjoyed a satisfying sex life if that's what you're asking."

"Did he tie you up?" Sam asked, playing a hunch based on the type of porn they'd found on his computer. "Did he get rough? Want more than the usual deal?"

"I don't have to answer that," Natalie stuttered. "It's my personal business, *his* personal business."

"Yes, it is, but aspects of his murder were intensely personal, so if you'd answer the questions, I'd appreciate it."

Natalie took a long deep breath and exhaled it as she spun a huge diamond engagement ring around on her finger. "He was a creative lover."

Sam used her trademark steely stare to let Natalie know she'd have to do better than that.

"*Yes*," she cried. "He tied me up, he could be rough, he asked for more than the usual deal." Descending into sobs, she added, "Are you satisfied?"

"Were *you?* Did you go along with it because you wanted to or because you felt you had to?"

"I loved him," she said in a defeated whisper that set Sam's already frazzled nerves further on edge. "I loved him."

"Did he ever bring other people into the relationship? Male or female?"

"Of course not," Natalie sputtered. "No!"

"Mrs. Jordan, I'm going to need you to stay available until we close this case."

"My husband and I are due to leave for Arizona in a few days to visit his parents for Christmas."

"You're going to have to change those plans."

Wiping her face, she said, "Do I need an attorney, Sergeant?"

"Not at this time. We'll be in touch."

SEVENTEEN

"Go ahead and say it," she muttered to Freddie when they were back in the car.

"Say what?"

"I was too hard on her. I'm a mean, insensitive bitch. Whatever's on your mind."

"I feel sorry for her."

She hadn't expected that. "Other than the obvious, why?"

"Did you notice the one thing she *didn't* say?"

"How about we skip the Q&A, and you tell me what you observed, Detective."

"She said she 'adored' her husband. She never said she loved him. How many times did she say she loved O'Connor? Four? Five?"

Startled, Sam could only stare at him.

"What?" he asked, squirming.

"We might just be making a detective out of you yet."

Freddie flashed that *GQ* smile, and damn it if her heart didn't skip a beat. He was so goddamned cute.

She started the car. "You know, you can feel free to jump in when we're interviewing people."

"And interrupt your groove? I wouldn't dream of it. Quite a pleasure to watch you work, Sergeant Holland. Shame on me if I spend a day with you and don't learn something."

"Are you sucking up?" She shot him a suspicious

glance as she drove through Belle Haven. "What do you want?"

"Other than lunch, I couldn't ask for anything more than I already have. Where are we heading now?"

"We've got two more ex-girlfriends to knock off the list, and then I'd like to have a word with Noel Jordan."

"Are we going to ask the exes about their sex lives?"

"Damn straight."

He sighed. "I was afraid of that."

TARA DAVENPORT, AGE twenty-four, worked the lunch shift at a high-end restaurant that catered to the Capitol Hill crowd. Sam presented her badge to the maître d'. "We need a few minutes with Tara Davenport."

"She's working. Can you come back at end of shift? Around five?"

"This isn't a social call. I can speak with her in a private space you'll provide or I can haul her out of here in cuffs and take you with us for interfering with a police investigation. What's it going to be?"

Looking down his snooty nose at her, the stiff said, "Wait here and keep your voice down, will you?"

"Mean and scary," Freddie murmured, drawing a laugh from Sam.

"Thank you."

"You would see that as a compliment."

"How else should I see it?"

They watched the stiff tap a slender but well-endowed young blonde on the shoulder and point to Sam and Freddie. He signaled to them, and they followed Tara to the back of the busy restaurant. On the way, more than a few patrons took notice of them. For some reason, that pleased Sam, so much so she hitched her hands into her pockets and put her weapon and badge on full display.

"Class act, Sergeant," the maître d' seethed.

"The next time myself or any of my colleagues appear at your door, perhaps you'll consider cooperating."

"You have fifteen minutes. After that you'll need a warrant to set foot in here again."

"Will I need a warrant if I wish to return for a follow-up visit, Detective Cruz?"

"No, ma'am, in most cases an informal interview of a potential suspect in a homicide investigation doesn't require a warrant."

The stiff paled. "Homicide?"

"Step aside and let me do my job," Sam said in a low growl. "So much as knock on that door and I'll haul your skinny ass downtown and put you in a cage with some guys who'd love nothing more than to make you their bitch."

He swallowed hard and moved to let them by.

"Mean *and* scary," Freddie said again.

Choking back a laugh, Sam opened the door to the break room where Tara Davenport waited, pale and trembling. As she introduced herself and Freddie to Tara, Sam questioned whether the woman had the physical strength to put a butcher knife through John O'Connor's neck.

"Is this about John?" she asked softly after agreeing to allow them to record the conversation.

"It is. Can you provide your whereabouts on the night of the murder? Tuesday, from ten p.m. to seven a.m.?"

Rattled but firm, Tara said, "I was out with some friends, early in the evening, but home by ten."

"I'll need you to give Detective Cruz a list of the people you were with. Do you live alone?"

She nodded.

"So no one can verify your whereabouts after ten?"

"No."

"No one saw you arriving home? Neighbors?"

"Not that I can recall."

"How and when did you meet Senator O'Connor?"

"I met him about six months ago. He was a regular here. He and his chief of staff, Nick, came in for lunch a couple of times a week when the Senate was in session."

Sam's belly twisted at the mention of Nick, whom she'd studiously tried to block from her mind all day. Remembering his muscular chest and the tender way he'd cared for her after the dream infused her with heat. She shrugged off her coat and slung it over a chair.

"John always asked to be seated in my section. He liked to tease and flirt. After a few months of that, he asked me out to dinner."

"Did that surprise you?"

"It did. I mean, he's a United States senator. What does he want with a waitress?"

"What *did* he want?"

"At first, I thought he was lonely," she said, her green eyes filling. "The first few times we went out, we talked for hours. He took me to nice places."

"You must've felt like Cinderella," Freddie said.

"In some ways, I did. He was a perfect gentleman, and so very handsome."

"Did you fall for him?" Sam asked.

"Yes," she whispered. "If you knew John at all, you'd know it would be hard not to."

"So what happened?"

Playing with her fingers, Tara said, "We had dated for a few weeks when he asked me to spend the night with him."

"And did you?"

Looking down at her lap, she nodded. "It was lovely. *He* was lovely." She swiped at tears. "We couldn't get enough of each other."

"Did you have a key to his place?"

"He gave me his once when I was meeting him there, but I gave it back to him that same night."

"Why did it end?" Freddie asked.

"He, ah…he was looking for more than I was willing to give."

"In the relationship?" Sam knew the answer before she asked.

Tara shook her head, her cheeks blazing with color. "In bed."

"What happened to lovely?"

"I wish I knew. After a few times, it changed. He became rough, almost aggressive. And he wanted… things…that I'm not into."

"What kind of things?"

"Is this really necessary?"

"I'm sorry, but it is."

"He…"

"I know this is terribly difficult for you, Ms. Davenport, but we're looking for a killer. Anything you can tell us that will aid in our investigation is relevant."

Tara took another moment to collect herself. "He wanted bondage and…anal."

"Did you have anal sex with the senator, Ms. Davenport?"

"No! I said no! I don't do that. I'm not into that."

"And how did he take it when you refused him?"

"He was mad, but he didn't try to force me."

"Honorable," Freddie muttered. "Did you see him again after you refused?"

She shook her head. "I never heard from him again."

"How did you feel about that?" Sam asked.

"I was sad, devastated. I thought we had something special, and then it was

just…over. Like you said. For a few weeks, I felt like Cinderella. It was right out of a fairy tale."

"But he wasn't your Prince Charming," Freddie said.

"No."

"Did he ever ask you about bringing other people into your sexual relationship?" Sam asked.

Tara's face lit up, her cheeks flaming. Bingo.

"Ms. Davenport?"

"Once," she said softly. "He said it would be amazing for me to have two guys at the same time." A shudder rippled through Tara's petite frame.

"Did it seem to you that he'd done that before?"

"Yes."

"And you said what to this request?"

"I told him that I was perfectly satisfied with just him. He seemed annoyed that I said no."

"That must've been disappointing," Sam said.

"It was."

"Were you disappointed enough to kill him, Ms. Davenport?"

She blanched. "*Kill him?* You think I *killed* him?"

Her shock was so genuine that it all but knocked her off the list of suspects. "If you could just answer the question."

"No, I wasn't disappointed enough to kill him. I didn't kill him."

"Have you told anyone else about why your relationship with the senator ended?"

"No. It's not something I'd ever talk about with even my closest friends. It's mortifying, to be honest."

"How did you feel when you heard he was dead?"

"Sad. I was overwhelmed with sadness. But to be honest, I wasn't entirely surprised that someone killed him. If you treat people the way he treated me, it's going to catch up to you eventually."

"I need you to stay available and in town for the time being."

"I'm working through the holidays," she said, her voice flat, devoid of hope or animation. "I'll be here."

"I HAVE TROUBLE understanding his type," Freddie said when they left the restaurant.

"You would. Do you think he was gay?"

"And in the closet? Working it out on women?"

"He certainly went for a type. The porcelain blonde. No way Tara is strong enough to get a knife through him on one stroke."

"I was thinking that very same thing." He paused and seemed to be pondering something. "So you know how we always joke that we spend more time together than we do with our own families?"

"*You're* the joker. I'm the serious law enforcement professional."

"Yeah, whatever."

"Your point?"

"I've known you a long time. Partnered with you over a year."

"Do you have a point? 'Cause if you could get to it in this decade, I'd like to get back to work."

"I have a point," he huffed. "It's just when she mentioned Cappuano in there, your face got all red and you had to take your coat off."

"I was hot! So what?"

"You were *flustered*. And you're *never* flustered."

Her stomach picked that moment to make its presence known. *Never flustered? Ha!* She spent half her life flustered but apparently did a good job of hiding it.

Freddie stopped on the sidewalk and turned to her. "Tell me the truth, Sam. Are you into him?"

She chose her words carefully. "The job, it takes almost everything I have. I work, I take care of my father, I help my sisters with their kids whenever I can. That's my life."

"Do you think I'd begrudge you wanting more?" His warm brown eyes flashed with emotion. "You think that?"

"He's off limits. There's no point talking about something I can't have."

"Why can't you have him?"

"He's a witness! He found O'Connor. He'll be wrapped up in this until sentencing."

"He didn't kill anyone. He's on our side."

She shook her head. "It's a murky ethical pit, and you know it."

"You're right. It's not clean. Few things in life ever are. But he wants this closed as much as we do, if not more. He *flusters* you, Sam. That's an amazing thing, if you ask me."

"I'd say unsettling is a better word." Glancing up at

him, she added, "You won't say anything about this at HQ, will you?"

"Give me some credit, and while you're at it, ask your friend Cappuano if there's any chance the senator was gay."

"He'll say no."

"Humor me, and before you drag me into another interview that includes questions about peculiar sexual appetites, you're going to have to do something about mine."

She turned up her nose. "Your sexual appetite?"

"Nope." He chuckled and rubbed his belly. "The other one."

SAM PULLED RANK, insisted they have lunch at a vegetarian sandwich shop and was treated to Freddie's vociferous complaints about the lack of grease.

"Can't even get a stinking French fry in this place," he muttered as Sam downed her small veggie sub and wondered if it really had fewer than six grams of fat. No doubt every gram would find its way to her ass.

"If you're done sulking, we need to hit Total Fitness on Sixteenth."

He raised an eyebrow. "Are you taking up working out to go with this diet you're on?"

"Just because I choose to eat healthily doesn't mean I'm on a diet. Another of the senator's ladies works at the gym as a personal trainer." She consulted her notebook. "Elin Svendsen."

Freddie perked right up. "Swedish?"

"Sounds like it."

"Blonde, buff *and* Swedish? This day is suddenly on the upswing."

"Why, Freddie, I thought you were above such base human emotions as lust."

"Just because I'm choosy doesn't mean I don't enjoy a little eye candy as much as the next guy."

"This insight into the male psyche is fascinating. Truly."

"I'm here to serve."

Elin Svendsen was not only buff, she looked like she'd be capable of kicking some serious ass when provoked. Easily five-ten or-eleven, with white blonde hair, icy blue eyes and a figure that could stop a train dead on its tracks, Sam decided she wouldn't want to meet up with Elin in a dark alley.

They caught her between clients and followed her into the club's juice bar, which wasn't due to open for another hour. They declined her offer of fruit smoothies.

"Do you mind if I make one for myself? My energy is starting to flag. Been a long morning."

"Not at all," Sam said. "Do *you* mind if we record this?"

"Nope."

Noticing Freddie had his eyes glued to Elin's every movement, Sam nudged him to get his head back in the game.

He replied with a chagrinned smile.

Elin joined them at the table with a strawberry smoothie. "If you're here to ask if I killed John O'Connor, I didn't."

"Where were you the night of the murder, between ten p.m. and seven a.m.?"

"I had a date and was home by two or so."

"Alone?"

She nodded.

"Your date's name?"

"Jimmy Chen. He's a member here. We go out once in a while. No biggie."

"You never left your house after you got home?"

"Not until I left for work the next morning."

"Where did you meet the senator?"

"Here. He hired me to train him, we hit it off, one thing led to another..."

"And how long ago was this?"

"Three or four months ago." Sam did some quick math and realized he was seeing Elin and Tara at the same time.

"Do you have a key to his apartment?"

"I set him up with some home workout equipment, and he gave me a key so I could get in when he was at work to put it together."

"Did you give the key back to him?"

She thought about that for a moment. "You know, I don't think I ever did. Hmmm."

With a glance, Sam handed the ball to Freddie.

"Oh, um, what was the nature of your relationship with the senator, Ms. Svendsen?" he asked.

Sam had never seen him so tongue-tied around a woman and planned to poke at him about it the moment they left.

"Mostly we had sex."

Freddie's face flushed with embarrassment.

Sam sat back to enjoy the show. Folding her arms, she sent the message that she had no plans to bail him out.

"Could you, or I mean, would you mind if I asked

you to be more specific about the, ah, sex you had with the senator?" Using Sam's words, he added, "Was it, um, the usual deal or more?"

Seeming to cue in to Freddie's exquisite discomfort, Elin smiled as she leaned toward him. "It was more, Detective. Much more. We were very well matched sexually."

Freddie cleared his throat.

"Were you still tearing up the sheets with the senator when he was killed?" Sam asked, realizing they were going to be there all day if she waited for Freddie to get on with it.

"No, we called it off a month or so ago."

"Who's doing?"

"Mine." She shrugged. "I was getting bored. It was time to move on."

"How did he take it when you ended it?"

"He was fine with it. This wasn't a love match, Sergeant. It was purely physical."

"Did he ever try to bring other people into the relationship."

"He did more than try." Elin seemed to be enjoying the effect she was having on Freddie. "We had a couple of memorable threesomes."

Sam glanced at Freddie to find his mouth hanging halfway open. She wanted to smack it shut.

"Male or female?" Sam asked.

"One of each on two separate occasions."

"Who sought out the extra parties?" Sam asked.

"I did. I know a lot of people from working here, and it was easier for me in light of who he was."

"What was his interaction with the other guy?"

"Hardly any. He was for me, not John."

"So John didn't have any kind of sex with him?"

Elin thought about that for a minute. "I think the guy sucked John's dick, but John didn't do anything to him."

"Did these 'extras' know who he was?"

"Nope. We just introduced him as 'John.' We didn't get into our life stories."

Sam left her with the standard line about staying available.

"Detectives?" Elin said as they headed for the door.

They turned back to her.

"He wasn't 'the one' for me, but he was a good guy. He didn't deserve to be murdered."

Sam nodded and pushed open the door, thinking the definition of "good guy" was all a matter of perspective.

"Did you enjoy that?" Freddie snapped the moment they were back in the cold air.

"Enjoy what?"

"Making me ask her those questions."

Sam stopped and turned to face him. "If you can't ask the questions, *any* question, *any* time, you shouldn't be carrying a gold shield, Detective."

"You're right." He sagged a bit as the anger seemed to leave him all at once. "I know you are, but it's just so freaking embarrassing asking a woman I've never met about what kind of sex she had with a dead senator."

"You think I like it any more than you do? It's part of the job. The best way to figure out who killed him is to figure out who and what he was."

"You're right, and I apologize for going queasy on you. It won't happen again."

"Yes, it will," she said with a sigh. "The day it doesn't bother you to ask those kind of questions is the day you're no longer Freddie Cruz. It's supposed to bother you. Just don't let it stop you from doing what needs to be done."

"I won't," he vowed. "See what I mean about learning from you? That's what I meant. Right there."

"Kiss my ass, Cruz."

"While that's a lovely offer and one I take very seriously, I don't think it would be appropriate in light of our professional relationship. You know, with you being my superior officer and all."

She used her best withering look to shut him up. "If you're quite through, can we go see what Noel Jordan has to say about his wife's ex?"

"One thing we can say for Svendsen is that she certainly would've had the strength to get that knife through him in one shot."

"No doubt. And she had a key."

"The part about her breaking up with him threw me, though. I can see her being pissed if he dumped her, like he did with Davenport, but if she's the one who pulled the plug, what's her motive in offing him?"

"That's only her side of the story. Who knows how it really went down? She can tell us she dumped him because he's not here to refute it."

"Here again, I find myself learning from you."

"Keep that up and you're going to piss me off. I like her for the murder. So far, more than anyone else, I like her."

"I liked her, too," he joked.

"I could tell by the tongue hanging out of your face, but she's too scary and experienced for an innocent boy like you. She'd chew you up and spit you out."

"And that would be bad how exactly?"

"Pardon me while I get busy poking out my mind's eye."

EIGHTEEN

GONZO CALLED AS they made their way toward the Justice Department on Pennsylvania Avenue.

"What've you got?" Sam asked.

"Nothing so far at the cabin, but I did that run you asked for on Robert O'Connor. Sixty-five years old, lives in Mechanicsville with his wife Sally, age sixty-three. They have three grown children—Sarah, forty, Thomas, thirty-six and Michael, thirty-four. Five grandchildren."

"Son of a bitch," Sam muttered. "They lied to me."

"Do you want me to do some more digging?"

"No, that's okay. Were you able to get pictures of the kids?"

"Yeah, I shot them to your email."

"Thanks, Gonzo. Let me know if you turn up anything at the cabin."

"It's slow going. I'll call you when we're done."

"Who lied to you?" Freddie asked when she had ended the call.

"O'Connor's parents." She explained about the photo she had found at the cabin. "I think John had a son they swept under the rug. I'm going to Chicago tomorrow to find out."

"Want me to tag along?"

"No, I can take this one alone. I need you to confirm the info we got from Davenport and Svendsen about the people they were with the night of the murder. I'd also like you to check security at both their buildings. See if you can catch them coming home that night—or more importantly, going back out."

"Got it," he said, making notes. "I would've done that run you had Gonzo do."

"Don't pout, Freddie. An investigation of this magnitude requires we make use of all available resources."

After navigating building security and handing over their weapons—something that always left Sam feeling twitchy—she and Freddie were escorted to Jordan's office. As special assistant attorney general, he sat right next door to the attorney general himself. Jordan was tall with an athletic build, short blond hair that looked like it would be wildly curly if left to grow and sharp blue eyes. He wore a dark pinstriped suit that had clearly been cut just for him. *Nothing off-the-rack for this guy*, Sam thought, as she noted his almost startling resemblance to John O'Connor. Apparently, the late senator wasn't the only one who went for a "type."

"Detectives," he said, standing to shake their hands. He gestured for them to make use of the chairs in front of his desk. "What can I do for you?"

"You're aware that your wife had a long-term relationship with Senator O'Connor?"

"I am."

"Did she ever talk to you about him?"

"Occasionally, but nothing more than an off-hand comment or two. She respects me too much to throw him in my face. My wife and I are happily married, and none of our former relationships factor into our marriage."

"Did you ever meet the senator?"

"A few times. I'm active in the Virginia Democratic Party, and obviously he was as well."

"Did you like him?"

"I didn't dislike him, but neither would I say we were anything more than casual acquaintances. So he dated my wife? Big deal. She's a beautiful woman who had several relationships before me. I don't expect that her life—or mine—began the day we met. Although," he said, softening, "in many ways, mine did begin with her."

"Can you confirm your whereabouts on the night of the murder? Tuesday between ten p.m. and seven a.m.?"

He consulted a brown leather book. "On Tuesday evening we attended the annual Christmas fund-raiser/ silent auction for the Capital Region Big Brothers and Big Sisters here in the city. We were home by ten, in bed by ten-thirty. We made love and went to sleep. Is that enough information?"

"Has your wife ever mentioned anything about her relationship with the senator that made her uncomfortable?"

For the first time, Jordan's cool composure wavered. "Uncomfortable in what way?"

"Any way."

"No, but like I said, we've never felt the need to share the intimate details of our past relationships."

When Sam stood up, Freddie followed her lead. "I know you had plans to be out of town for the holidays," she said, "but you'll need to remain in the area."

"I'm due to leave for Europe on the third of January. Work-related travel."

"Hopefully by then we'll have cleared this up. Until we do, you and your wife are required to stay local."

"THOUGHTS?" SHE ASKED FREDDIE after they had reclaimed their weapons. Relieved to have her gun back, Sam slid hers into her hip harness.

"First, he knew we were coming. Had that appointment book nice and handy."

"No doubt the wife tipped him. But guess what? He lied about one thing."

"What's that?"

"The Big Brothers/Big Sisters thing?"

Freddie nodded.

"That was *last* Tuesday. I know because I was there."

Freddie released a low whistle.

"It doesn't mean one of them killed the senator, though. It only means there's something he doesn't want us to know or his date book is messed up. We still can't place either of them at the Watergate."

"So we file this tidbit away and continue to work the case?"

"Exactly. The thing between the senator and Natalie was over years ago. Where's the motive?"

"True," Freddie said.

"My take is that he's crazy in love with her, still wonders how he ever managed to snag her and he's glad O'Connor's dead. He didn't kill him, but he sees it as a favor that someone else did."

"So you think he was threatened by the senator?"

"Big time," Freddie said. "He knows he wasn't the love of Natalie's life."

"Good. That's good. Crazy how much he looks like O'Connor, huh?"

"I'd say creepy would be a better word."

"Agreed. I want you to look into those 'other relationships' of hers that he referred to. Find out if any of the other men in her life met with an untimely demise, and while you're at it, do a search for unsolved cases involving dismemberment. The senator might not have been the first."

"Local or national?"

"Start local and see what pops. I'll be authorizing overtime for both of us, so while you're at it, get me everything you can find on the three women we met today. No detail is too big or too small. If they have a tattoo, I want to know what it is and where."

"Tramp stamps," he wrote as she snickered at the term. "Got it. You're really sure it was a woman, aren't you?"

"Every fiber of my being tells me this was a love affair gone very wrong."

"Or someone wants us to *think* that."

"We can't rule that out," she conceded.

"In light of what we've learned today, we also can't rule out that it might've been a love affair with a *man* that went very wrong."

"Right again," she said. "Nothing is ever as cut and dried as we'd like it to be, is it?"

"Nope."

"You've had a few girlfriends."

"So?" he said warily.

"Don't you compare notes on past relationships?"

His face flooded with color. "Depends on how serious it is with the new one and whether or not she asks."

"Is it weird that Natalie Jordan never told her husband that things got kinky with the senator?"

"I don't know, Sam. That falls into a serious gray area. What guy would want to know that his woman did it *all* with the ex?"

"Hmm. It just seems strange to me that she's never even alluded to it. I mean, they're *married.* And you saw his face. He had no idea what I was talking about."

"Did you share that kind of stuff with Peter?"

"Bad example. We weren't your typical married couple."

"Sorry to dredge up the past, but I think you'd be in a better position to answer your own questions than I would be, having never been married myself."

"Yeah, I guess, but I hardly had the kind of marriage where major sharing factored in."

"So what's next?" he asked, seeming anxious to change the subject.

"I need to go back to HQ, write up what we have so far, and deal with the brass on this thing with the Johnson case."

"What'll you do if they put you under?"

"*If* they do, it'll only be for a couple of days at most—one of those days I'll be in Chicago, another one we're taking off because we'll need to recharge, and then Monday is the senator's funeral. With all the local police and Secret Service who'll be there, I can't imagine they'll stop me from going. I can pull the strings from the sidelines, but I'm not letting it go."

"Even if they order you to?"

"Especially then."

"Righteous."

BACK AT HER DESK, Sam downed a soda, opened the email Gonzo had sent, and discovered the real Thomas O'Connor was a thirty-six-year-old man with dark hair and eyes. She made a note to ask Nick whether John had ever mentioned having a cousin of the same age.

Regardless, the man on her screen was not the boy in the picture, and she now had positive confirmation that Graham and Laine O'Connor had lied to her about the boy. But why? Why would they deny their own grandchild? Sam had no idea, but she intended to find out.

Her stomach clenched with pain as she read—and then re-read—an email from the chief's admin, confirming her four o'clock appointment. Checking her watch, she realized she had just a few minutes to get there on time. She stood up, but the pain had other ideas. Collapsing back into her chair, she put her head down and tried to breathe her way through it. A bead of sweat slid down her back.

This was a bad one, but it had been getting progressively worse over the last few months despite her best efforts to ignore it. Sooner or later, she was going to have to do something about this "nervous stomach" situation, possibly even give up diet cola as she'd been told to do. But not now. No time for that now. When the worst of the pain had passed, she tested her shaky legs, took another long deep breath and set out for the chief's office.

She was waved right in but stopped short just inside the door. When Farnsworth called in the brass, he called in the brass. Seated in a wide half-circle in front of Farnsworth's desk were Deputy Chief Conklin, Detective Captain Malone, Lieutenant Stahl and Assistant U.S. Attorney Miller. Sam glanced at Miller's shoes, saw the stiletto heel, and confirmed it was Charity, one of the identical triplets who worked for the U.S. Attorney. Neither Faith nor Hope would be caught dead in stilettos.

"Well," Sam said, as the pain resurfaced with an

ugly vengeance. Determined to stay cool, she took shallow breaths and slipped into the remaining chair. "You didn't tell me we were having a party, Chief. I would've brought snacks."

"Sergeant," Farnsworth said, his handsome face tight with stress that only added to Sam's. "Before we get into the Johnson matter, go ahead and brief us on the status of the O'Connor investigation."

Folding her hands tightly in her lap, she brought them up to speed, holding back the details about the senator's peculiar sexual appetites. She had decided to do her best to keep that out of the official record in deference to his parents and family.

"So almost seventy-two hours out, we don't have so much as a suspect?" Stahl said.

Sam made an effort not to show him what a jackass she thought him to be. "We have several individuals of interest we're actively pursuing. In addition, I believe the senator had a son who was kept hidden from the public. I request permission to travel tomorrow to Chicago to further investigate this thread."

"How's it relevant?" Stahl snapped.

Repulsed by the roll of fat around his belly and the huge double chin that wiggled when he talked, Sam said, "If it's true, the senator's relationship with the mother could be very relevant."

"I'll authorize the travel," Malone said, pulling rank on Stahl who fumed in silence.

"Thank you, Captain," Sam said.

"The Feds are sniffing around," Farnsworth said. "I've managed to hold them off thus far, but with every passing day, it's getting harder."

"Understood. We're moving as fast as we can."

"All available resources are at your disposal, Sergeant," Farnsworth added. "Use whatever you need."

"Yes, sir. Thank you."

"Now, on the other matter, we've got Mrs. Johnson on a seventy-two-hour hold."

"You aren't planning to charge her, are you, sir?" Sam asked.

"AUSA Miller is considering charges."

"If I may, sir," Sam said. "While no one would mistake Destiny Johnson for mother of the year, I have no doubt her heartbreak is genuine."

"That doesn't give her the right to threaten the life of a police officer," Farnsworth said.

"She has good reason to be pissed with Sergeant Holland and the department," Stahl said.

"Lieutenant, I find your attitude counterproductive," Farnsworth said. "You can get back to work."

"But—"

Captain Malone flipped his thumb toward the door.

With an infuriated glance at Sam, Stahl hauled himself out of the chair and waddled to the door. After it closed behind him, Farnsworth returned his attention to Sam. "We have to take her threats seriously, Sergeant. You're extremely vulnerable in the field, so until you've testified on Tuesday, we're putting you under. Limited duty, permission to work from home, no field work."

"Since I'm going to Chicago tomorrow, taking Sunday off, and attending the senator's funeral on Monday, that shouldn't be a problem."

"About the funeral..." Deputy Chief Conklin said.

"I believe the local and federal security required to bring in the president will be sufficient to protect a lowly District sergeant," Sam said with what she hoped was a confident smile.

"The Secret Service will have to be made aware of the threat and your planned presence at the service," Conklin said. "I'll take care of that."

"Appreciate it," Farnsworth said. He leaned forward to address Sam. "I want you to take this very seriously. Johnson has a lot of friends, and all of them—fairly or unfairly—blame you for what happened in that house. They don't care that you didn't fire the shot. They care that you gave the order."

"Yes, sir." Since she blamed herself, too, she could understand where they were coming from.

"AUSA Miller, has Sergeant Holland been adequately prepared for Tuesday's court appearance?"

"She has, Chief. We've been through it several times, and she's never wavered from her initial statement."

"I'll let you get back to work then," Farnsworth said. "Thanks for being here."

"No problem." With an encouraging smile for Sam, Charity got up and left the room.

"If there's nothing else, I've got a few more threads to tie up before my tour ends," Sam said.

"There's just one more thing," Farnsworth said, reaching for a file on his desk.

Sam refused to acknowledge the twinge of pain that hovered in her gut. "Sir?"

"I had lunch with your father earlier this week."

"Yes, sir, he mentioned that. I know he appreciates your visits." To the others, she added, "All of you."

"And I know you go out of your way to downplay your family's history with this department."

"I don't want nor do I expect special treatment because of the rank my father attained prior to being injured in the line."

Farnsworth replied with a hint of a smile. "Regardless, he was curious as to whether I'd gotten the results of the lieutenant's exam."

Just those words were enough to override any success she'd had in keeping the pain at bay. It roared through her, leaving her breathless in its wake. When she was able to speak again, she said, "I'm aware it's a source of embarrassment to my father and to you as my superior officers that I've been unable to pass the exam on two previous attempts."

"What I'd like to know is why the fact that you're dyslexic isn't mentioned anywhere in your personnel file."

Stunned, Sam opened her mouth and then closed it when the words simply wouldn't come.

"I've done some basic research on dyslexia and discovered that standardized tests are one of the dyslexic's greatest foes."

"Yes, but—"

"Allow me to finish, Sergeant. I have to admit this information was a relief to me." He gestured to the deputy chief and captain. "To all of us. We've been hard pressed to understand how the best detective on this force has been unable to attain a rank that should've been hers some time ago."

"I...um..."

"You passed this time," Farnsworth said. "Just barely—but you did pass."

Sam stared at him, wondering if she had heard him correctly.

He rifled through some other papers until he found

what he was looking for. "With the distinct exception of Lt. Stahl, you've received outstanding superior officer recommendations, high marks on your interviews and evaluations. We also factored in the graduate degree in criminal justice you earned from George Washington. All in all, you make for an ideal candidate for promotion." He looked up at her. "Under my discretion as chief of police, I'm pleased to inform you that your name will be included in the next group of lieutenants."

"But, sir," Sam stammered, "people will talk. They'll scream favoritism."

"You met the criteria. The test score is only one element, and no one but the people in this room will know it was low."

"I'll know," she said softly.

"Sergeant, do you believe you've earned the rank of lieutenant?"

"If I didn't, I wouldn't have sat for the exam in the first place, but—"

"Then you should have no further objection to a promotion you have earned and deserve. You'll be taking command of the detective squad at HQ."

Staggered, Sam stared at him. "But that's Lieutenant Stahl's command."

"He's being transferred to internal affairs."

The rat squad, Sam thought, her stomach grinding under the fist she had balled tight against it. "You're setting me up to have a powerful enemy."

"Lieutenant Stahl is skating on very thin ice these days," Captain Malone said. "I don't believe he'll give you any trouble, and if he does, he'll deal with us. Let me add my congratulations, Sergeant, on a well-earned and highly deserved promotion. I look forward to working with you in your new role."

"Thank you, sir," Sam said, still shocked as she shook his outstretched hand and then Conklin's.

"Ditto," Conklin said, following Malone from the room. "You've earned it."

"Thank you, sir."

When they were alone, Sam turned to the chief.

"You'll piss me off if you ask if this is because I'm your chief or your Uncle Joe," he said, his tone full of friendly warning.

"I was just going to say thank you," Sam said with a smile that quickly faded. "Will the, ah, dyslexia be added to my jacket?"

"It'll remain your personal business, provided it continues to have no bearing on your ability to do the job."

"It won't."

Farnsworth sat back in his big chair and studied her. "I have to ask how you managed to get two degrees while battling dyslexia."

"I got lucky with professors who worked with me, but everything took me twice as long as it took everyone else. And I've always choked on standardized tests. I just can't get them done in the time allotted."

"I can only imagine how much harder you've had to work to compensate. Knowing that only adds to my respect for you and your work." He stood up, came around the big desk, and offered his hand. "Congratulations."

Sam's throat closed as her hand was enfolded between both of his. "Thank you, sir. I'll do my very best to be worthy."

"I have no doubt. Let me know what you uncover in Chicago."

"I will, sir. Thank you again. For everything." She closed the door behind her, managed a nod to the chief's admin, and made for the nearest ladies' room. The relief, the sheer overwhelming relief, left her staggered. She gave herself ten minutes to fall apart before she pulled it together, wiped her face and blew her nose.

Studying her reflection in the mirror, she whispered, "Lieutenant," as if to try it on for size. For once her stomach had no comment. Taking that as a positive sign, she splashed cold water on her face and decided to leave on time for a change. The report could be written and transmitted from home. Besides, she needed to go tell the only other person in the world who would care as much as she did that she would soon become Lieutenant Holland.

NINETEEN

Before Sam could call for him, she heard the chair.

"What's this? Home on time?"

She went to him, rested her hands on his shoulders and was startled to encounter sharp bones where thick muscle used to be. Jarred by the discovery, she bent to kiss his forehead. Eye to eye, she said, "I should be furious with you."

"For?"

"Don't play coy with me."

"It should've been in your jacket. From day one. I've always said that."

"It wasn't for a reason. I don't want people feeling sorry for me or treating me differently. You know how I feel about it."

"That fierce pride of yours is only going to get you so far."

"And my daddy is going to get me the rest of the way?"

"I simply gave him a piece of information he didn't have. What he did or didn't do with it was up to him."

"No, Dad, it was up to *me*. I don't want you interfering in my career. How many times do I have to say it before you get the message?"

"I've been duly chastised. Now, are you going to tell me what he did with it?"

"Not until you've suffered a little first. What's for dinner?"

He followed her to the kitchen. "That's mean, Sam."

"Are you being mean to your father again?" Celia asked.

"Believe me, he deserves it. Oh, jeez, is that *roast beef?*"

"Sure is. Are you hungry?"

"Starving. I didn't even realize it until right this very minute." She peeked into a pot and groaned. "Mashed potatoes? God, my ass is growing just smelling it."

"Now you stop that," Celia said as she served the meal. "You have a lovely figure that I'd kill for. How was your day?"

"The usual chaos."

"Nothing special?" Skip asked. "Nothing different?"

Sam pretended to give that some significant thought. "Not really. Freddie and I are working the case, pulling the threads. Got a couple of good angles to pursue."

"What are they doing about Johnson?" Skip asked.

Hanging on their every word, Celia fed him and herself with a practiced hand.

"I was ordered to 'lay low' until I testify on Tuesday."

"To which you said…?"

She shrugged. "I'm fine with it. I have to go to Chicago tomorrow, I'm taking most of Sunday off, and have the funeral on Monday. I should be fine."

"Should be isn't good enough." He swallowed, cleared his throat and turned his steely blue eyes on his daughter. "Anything else happen at your meeting with Farnsworth?"

Deciding she had tortured him long enough, she said, "Oh, you mean about the promotion?"

He growled.

"I got it." She took another bite of mashed potatoes and tried not to think about the calories. "You can soon call me Lieutenant, Chief."

"Yes," he whispered. "Yes, indeed."

"Oh that's wonderful, Sam!" Celia jumped up to hug and kiss her. "That's just wonderful, isn't it, Skip?"

He never took his eyes off his daughter. "It sure is. Come give your old man a hug."

Pained that he'd had to ask and embarrassed by Celia's effusiveness, Sam got up and did her best to work around the chair. With her lips close to his ear, she whispered, "Thank you."

"For?"

Sam pulled back to smile at him. "Love you."

"When you're not being mean to me, I love you, too."

TWO HOURS LATER, Sam was laboring her way through the report of the day's activities on her laptop when Celia knocked on the door.

"Sorry to interrupt your work, but I thought you might enjoy some warm apple pie. It's so darned cold out."

Sam moaned. "Tell me it's fat free, calorie free and can't find an ass with a roadmap."

Chuckling, Celia handed her the plate. "All of the above. I swear."

"If the nursing gig doesn't pan out, you might consider a life of crime. You're a convincing liar."

"You've made your father very proud tonight, Sam. He's always proud of you, but he wanted this promotion for you. More, I think, than you wanted it for yourself."

"I don't doubt it." Sam used a finger to swirl a dollop

of whipped cream off the pie and pop it into her mouth. "Sometimes I feel so selfish where he's concerned."

Celia lowered herself to the edge of Sam's bed. "How do mean? You're here for him every day, despite a demanding, time-consuming job."

"It would've been better…for him anyway…if the shot had been fatal. I can't imagine how he stands living the way he does, confined to four small rooms and wherever he can go in the van the union bought him. But I wasn't ready to lose him, Celia. Not then and not now. I thank God every day that bullet didn't kill him. As much as I hate the way he has to live now, I'm so grateful he's still here."

"In his own way, he's accepted it and come to terms."

"I wish you could've known him." Sam sighed. "Before."

"I did," Celia said with a smile, her pretty face blazing with color and her green eyes dancing with mirth.

"You've never told me that! Neither of you ever did!"

"I met him at the Giant, about two years before he was wounded. I helped him pick some tomatoes in the produce aisle, he asked me out for coffee and that was the start of a lovely friendship."

Sam slipped into detective mode as she narrowed her eyes. "Just friends?"

Laughing, Celia said, "I'll never tell."

"You dirty dogs! How did you slide this by me? By everyone?"

"You weren't looking," Celia said, her expression smug. "Why do you think I asked to be assigned to his case?"

"You love him," Sam said, incredulous.

"Very much. In fact, we've been talking about maybe…getting married."

Sam's mouth fell open. "Seriously? You said he's been down lately, worried about something. Is this it?"

"It's one of several things. He's been terribly upset about what happened to you in the Johnson case and fretting over your safety as well as the promotion he thinks you've been due for some time now."

"I wish he wouldn't spend so much time worrying about me."

"Sam," she said with a smile. "You're his life. His heart. He loves your sisters and their children very much, but you…"

"I know. I've always known that."

"And you've always struggled to live up to it."

Startled, Sam stared at her. "Been doing a lot more than nursing around here, haven't you?"

"I hope I haven't overstepped."

"Of course you haven't. You're already family, Celia. I don't know what we would've done without you the last two years."

"So you wouldn't mind too much if I married him?"

Sam put down the plate and reached for the older woman's hand. "If you make him happy and can bring some joy to whatever time he has left, the only thing I can do is thank you for that."

"Thank *you*," Celia said, her eyes bright with emotion. "It matters to him, to both of us, that you'd approve."

"I guess I need to get busy looking for another place to keep my clothes."

"Why?"

"You crazy kids won't want me underfoot."

"He wants you to stay. We both do. There's no reason for you to move out. I'll take one of the other bedrooms up here. We'll work it out. I'm here most of the time anyway. I don't expect much will change."

"This'll change everything for him, Celia. It'll give him a reason to keep fighting."

"Perhaps. I'll consider myself blessed for whatever time we get."

"Did he bully you into telling me?"

"He was afraid it would upset you, so I offered."

"You can tell him that not only am I fine with it, I'm thrilled for him. For both of you."

"That means a lot, Sam. I'm tired of hiding it. He's the most remarkable man I've ever known and the best friend I've ever had."

"Ditto," Sam said with a smile as Celia got up to leave. "Thanks for the pie."

"My pleasure. Don't work too hard."

When she was alone, Sam had to resist the urge to call her sisters to share the huge scoop that had just fallen into her lap. "Not my news to tell," she muttered, deciding that maturity wasn't much fun at all.

While Celia's news had surprised her, Sam realized it shouldn't have. With hindsight, she could see there was something special between her father and his devoted nurse. Their banter, the carefree caresses Celia showered him with even though he couldn't feel them, the genuine affection.

Comforted by Celia's disclosures, Sam finished the pie and turned back to her report. She ran through it twice more before she sent it off to Freddie, who always checked them for her before she passed them up the food chain. If he wondered about the random mistakes, odd phrasings or twisted wording, he never said.

Rather, he corrected the errors and returned the reports to her without comment.

Might be time to bring him into the loop, she thought. Dyslexia had cast its long net over every corner of her life, and until its diagnosis in sixth grade, she had believed herself to be as stupid as she was made to feel by teachers who had no idea what to do with her and parents who had been frustrated by her less-than-stellar performance in school.

Giving it a name had helped somewhat, but the daily struggles that went along with it were exhausting at times.

With the report finished, she finally allowed her thoughts to drift to Nick. As if floodgates had opened, she was overwhelmed by emotions and yearnings she had managed to resist all day. She had a list of questions she wanted to run by him, so she had every reason to take out the card he had given her. The call was about the case, right? There was nothing wrong with reaching out to him in a strictly official capacity. If she was also dying to tell him about her promotion and her father's pending marriage, what did that matter?

She flipped the card back and forth between her fingers for several minutes until her stomach twisted with the start of the dreaded pain. Thinking of the case and *only* the case, she dialed his cell number.

He sounded groggy when he answered.

"Oh God, did I wake you?"

"No, no." A huge yawn made a liar out of him. "I was hoping you'd call."

Deciding to keep it strictly business, she said, "I have some questions. About the case."

"Oh."

She winced at the disappointment reverberating from that single syllable. "You sound…I don't know…kind of lousy."

"It's been a lousy day, except for the very beginning when I was with you."

Without saying much of anything he had managed to say it all. And she knew she couldn't tell him what she needed to tell him over the phone. "You're at home?"

"Uh huh."

"Do you mind if I come by? Just for a minute?"

"Are *you* at home?"

"At the moment."

"You're just going to 'drop by' all the way over here in Arlington? And only for a minute?"

"I need to talk to you, Nick. I need…Oh hell, I don't even know what I need."

"Come. I'll be waiting. And babe? You don't ever, *ever* have to ask first. Got me?"

She melted into a sloppy, messy puddle of need and want and desire. "Yeah," she managed to say. "I'll be there. Soon." Her heart doing back flips, Sam reached for her weapon, badge and cuffs. She released her hair to brush out the kinks and primped for a few more minutes before she headed downstairs to tell her dad she was going into work for a while. Celia told her he was already asleep.

"He was especially tired tonight." She held Sam's coat for her. "You'll be careful, won't you?"

"Always." Impulsively, she turned to kiss Celia's cheek on her way to the front door. "See you."

HE'D TURNED ON the outside light for her. A simple thing, but it evoked such a powerful sense of homecoming that

Sam sat there for several minutes reminding herself of why she was there—and why she wasn't. "It can't be about you," she whispered. "Not now. This is about finding justice for John O'Connor. Nothing more."

But when Nick came to the door looking so…well… *lost* was the best word she could think of, nothing else mattered but him.

"Nick." Closing the door behind her, she let her coat drop to the floor and reached for him.

They stood there, arms wrapped around each other, comfort seeping through to warm the chill she had brought in with her.

Raising her hands to his face, she looked up at him. "What is it?"

Shrugging, he said, "Everything." He leaned his forehead against hers. "I've gone from having every minute of every day programmed to not knowing what the hell to do with myself, which gives me way too much time to think."

Even after what she had learned that day about John O'Connor, she was still able to feel Nick's pain over the loss of his friend and boss. Used to his unflappable, polished demeanor, seeing him disheveled in a ratty Harvard T-shirt and old sweats was jarring. Sometime in the course of that long day, the shock apparently wore off and gritty grief set in.

"I'm glad you're here." He shifted to press her against the closed door. "I've been worried about you. That stuff in the paper…"

"We're handling it."

"I don't like the idea of you being unsafe." The light caress of his hand on her cheek caused her heart to lurch. He leaned in, bringing with him the scent of spice and soap.

"Nick, wait—"

His lips came down hard and insistent on hers, sucking the breath from her lungs and the starch from her spine. If he hadn't been holding her up with the weight of his body, she might have slid to the floor. Somehow he maneuvered them so her legs were hooked over his hips, his hands were full of her breasts and his tongue was tangled up with hers—all in the scope of thirty seconds.

Having forgotten everything she'd vowed in the car the moment she saw his grief-stricken face, Sam wove her fingers through his damp, silky hair and pressed hard against his straining erection. Then they were moving, falling. She yelped against his lips and clung to him as he lowered them to the sofa.

Tearing at clothes, desperate for skin, for contact, for relief, they wrestled through layers until there was nothing left between them but raging desire.

"You're just like I remembered." His tongue darted in circles around her nipple, and his hands seemed to be everywhere at once. "Tall and curvy and strong… soft in all the right places." Nick gazed with reverence at breasts that had always seemed too big to her, but he appeared to like what he saw.

Need zipped through her, leaving her desperate and panting. "Nick…" She tugged at him to align them for what she wanted more than the next breath. "Now."

"Condom," he said through gritted teeth. "Wait a sec."

She stopped him from getting up. "I'm on the pill. We get tested—"

"So do we." He slid one arm under her shoulders while his other hand cupped her bottom and tilted her into position to receive him.

Overwhelmed by desire, Sam let her legs fall open to take him in.

He held her gaze as he entered her with one swift stroke.

She cried out as an orgasm ripped through her with more force and fury than anything she'd ever experienced.

He froze. "Oh, God, did I hurt you?"

"No, *no!* Don't stop. *Please.*"

Watching him, feeling him, there were no recriminations. There wasn't room for thoughts of anything but him as he began to move, slowly at first and then faster as his closely held control seemed to desert him. She remembered that from the last time, how he'd let go with her, in a way she suspected he didn't often allow himself.

With his arms wrapped tight around her, he pounded into her, the smack of flesh meeting flesh the only thing she could hear over the roar of her own heartbeat.

Sam met each thrust with equal ardor, and when he sucked hard on her nipple, she cried out with another climax that took him tumbling over with her.

"Jesus," he whispered when he'd recovered the ability. "Jesus Christ. I didn't even offer you something to drink."

She laughed and tightened the hold she had on him, letting one hand slide languidly through soft hair still damp from an earlier shower. "What kind of host does that make you?"

"A crappy one, I guess," he said, turning them over in a smooth move.

Stretched out on top of him, still joined with him, Sam breathed in his warm, masculine scent and reveled in the comfort of strong arms wrapped tight around her. It was almost disturbing to accept that she had never experienced anything even remotely close to this, except during the one night she spent with him so many years ago. How foolish she had been then to assume that what she'd shared with him would show up again with someone else. She was wise enough now, old enough, jaded enough, to know better.

But even as the woman continued to vibrate with aftershocks and tingle with the desire for more, the cop resurfaced with disgust and dismay. "This was a very bad idea," she muttered into his chest.

He curled a lock of her hair around his finger. "Depends on your perspective. From my point of view, it was the best idea I've had in six years."

Sam studied him. "It must be the politician in you."

Eyebrows knitting with confusion, he said, "What must?"

"The way you always seem to have the right words."

He framed her face with his big hands. "I'm not feeding you lines, Sam."

His sweet sincerity made her heart ache with something she refused to acknowledge. "I know." The emotions were so overwhelming and new to her, she did the first thing that came to mind. She tried to escape.

His arms clamped around her like a vise. "Not yet." He brushed his lips over hers in a gesture so tender it all but stopped her heart. Her eyes flooded with tears that she desperately tried to blink back.

"What?"

She shook her head.

"Sam."

Letting her eyes drift up to meet his, she said, "I like this. I know I shouldn't because of everything… but I like it."

"Sex on the sofa?"

"This." She had to look away. It was just too much. "You. Me. Us."

"So do I." He kissed her softly. "So does this mean we're together now?"

A stab of fear went through her. She just wasn't ready for the magnitude of what this had the potential to be. "Why does it need a label? Why can't it just be what it is?"

Once again, the flash of pain she saw on his face bothered her more than it should have. "And what is it exactly, Sam? I want far more from you than just a sex buddy."

"That might be all I can give you right now."

He sighed. "I suppose I'll take whatever I can get." When his lips coasted up her neck, he made her shiver. "We could move this somewhere more comfortable. There's a big soft bed in the other room."

Her stomach ached as reality stepped in to remind her of why she'd needed to see him. "There're things we need to talk about. Stuff about the case."

"We'll get to it. Can I just have a few more minutes of this first?"

Because he seemed to need it so much, she said, "Okay."

TWENTY

THE BED, AS ADVERTISED, was big and soft. How he managed to coax her into it was something she planned to think about later when she reclaimed her sanity. It would be so easy, so very easy indeed, to curl into him and sleep the sleep of the dead. But the grinding sensation in her gut was an ever-present reminder of the conversation she needed to have with him.

"What's wrong?" he asked as his talented hand worked to ease the tension in her neck.

"Nothing, why?"

"I had you on the way to relaxed, and now you're all tight again."

"We need to talk."

"So you've said. I'm listening."

"I can't do cop work naked."

Laughing, he said, "Is that in the manual?"

"If it isn't, it should be."

Sitting up, he reached for the pile of their clothes he had deposited on the foot of the bed, found the T-shirt he'd been wearing when she arrived, and helped her into it. "Better?"

Engulfed in the shirt that carried his sexy, male scent, she was riveted by his muscular chest. "Um, except you're still naked."

"I'm not the cop." He reached for her hand, brought it to his lips. "Talk to me, Sam."

The dull ache sharpened in a matter of seconds.

"Something's wrong," he said, alarmed. "You just went totally pale."

"It's nothing." She tried and failed to take a deep breath. "Just this deal with my stomach."

"What deal?"

"It gives me some grief from time to time. It's nothing."

"Have you had it checked?"

"A couple of times," she squeaked out.

"Babe, God, you're in serious pain! What can I do?"

"Gotta breathe," she said as the pain clawed its way through her, making her feel sick and clammy. "Sorry."

"Don't be." He fitted himself around her, held her close and whispered soft words of comfort that eased her mind.

She closed her eyes, focused on the sound of his voice and drifted. The pain retreated, but the episode—worse than most—left her drained and embarrassed. "Sorry about that."

"I told you not to apologize. You have to do something about that. You might have an ulcer or something. I can get you in with my friend. He's awesome."

"It seems to crop up whenever I'm nervous about something, which I'm finding is fairly often."

"You're nervous about what you have to say to me?"

She tilted her head and found his pretty hazel eyes studying her intently. "I guess I am."

He sat up, propped the pillows behind him and snuggled her into his chest. "Then let's get it over with."

"Cops don't snuggle."

"Make an exception."

"I think I've already made quite a few," she said dryly.

"Make another one."

Before the pain could come back to remind her she was powerless against it, she took the plunge. "I have to ask you something. It's probably going to upset you, and I hate that, but I have to ask."

"Okay."

"Is there any chance John was gay? Or maybe bi?" She felt the tension creep into his body, and then just as quickly it was gone.

He laughed. He actually *laughed*. "No. Not only no, but *no fucking way*."

"How can you know that for sure? Some men hide it from their friends, their families..."

"I would've known, Sam. Believe me. I would've known."

"You didn't know he had a son."

And just that quickly he was tense again. "You don't know that, either."

"I'm all but certain of it. The picture?"

"What about it?"

"His parents lied. His cousin Thomas, the son of Robert O'Connor? He's thirty-six, dark hair, dark eyes." She sat up straighter and shifted so she could see his face. "Surely you must have heard him talk about a cousin who was the same age as him?"

Nick mulled that over. "I can't say I ever did. Maybe they weren't close. I don't think Graham and his brother are."

"Either way, the kid in the picture isn't his cousin. His mother lied to me today, and his father didn't refute it. The monthly payments—stretching twenty years—

the weekly phone calls, catching his parents in a big, fat lie, the startling resemblance to the senator…It doesn't take a detective to add it all up, Nick."

"But why…wait." He went perfectly still. "One weekend a month."

Baffled, she said, "Excuse me?"

"He required one weekend a month with no commitments. Usually the third weekend. Never would say what he did with the time. In fact, he was always kind of weird about it, now that I think about it."

"And you just thought to mention this now? What the hell, Nick?"

"I'm sorry. It was just so much a part of our routine that I didn't think anything of it until right now."

"I bet if I do some digging, I'll find him booked on a regular flight to Chicago."

All the air seemed to leave Nick in one long exhale. "Why didn't he tell me? Why would he keep something like this hidden from me? From everyone?"

"I don't know, but I'm going out there tomorrow to find out."

"You are?"

"I'm on an eleven o'clock flight."

"Does she know you're coming?"

Sam shook her head. "Element of surprise. I don't want to give her time to put away the pictures or send the kid out of town."

"And you think this has something to do with his murder?"

"I can't say for sure until I've spoken to the mother, but for some reason they've kept him hidden away for twenty years. I want to know why."

"Politics, no doubt."

"How do you mean?"

"A teenaged son with a baby would've been a political liability to the senator. I should know. As the offspring of teenaged parents, I can attest to the embarrassment factor in a family with zero public presence."

Sam ached from the pain she heard in his voice.

"Graham O'Connor would've wanted this put away in a closet," he concluded.

"His own grandchild?"

"I don't think it would've mattered. The O'Connor name wasn't always the powerhouse it is now. He had a few contentious campaigns around the mid-point of his career. If the timing coincided, this could've ruined him. He would've acted accordingly."

"At the expense of his own family?"

"Power does strange things to people, Sam. It can be addicting. Once you get a taste of it, it's hard to give it up. I've always found Graham to be a kind and loving—albeit exacting—father, but he's as human as the next guy. He would've been susceptible to the seduction of power." Nick paused, as if he was pondering something else.

"What are you thinking?"

"I'm wondering how, considering you're certain he had a son, you also think he might've been gay."

"Just a vibe we've picked up on the investigation. Nothing concrete. I've told you my gut says it was a woman he'd wronged, but then Freddie goes and ruins that by pointing out that it could've just as easily been a love affair gone wrong with a guy."

Nick shook his head. "I can't imagine it. There was

never anything, *anything* in almost twenty years of close friendship that would make me doubt his orientation. Nothing, Sam. He was a skirt-chasing hound."

"So I've discovered. But he wouldn't be the first guy to use that as a front to hide his real life."

"I suppose."

"You're upset. I'm sorry."

He shrugged. "It's just…you think you know someone, really know them, only to find out they had all these secrets. He had a son. A *child.* And in twenty years, he never mentions that to his closest friend? It's disappointing at the very least."

It was also a betrayal, she imagined. That the family he'd considered his own—his only—had kept something of this magnitude from him.

As if he could read her thoughts, he said, "Did they think I'd tell anyone?"

"You shouldn't take this personally, Nick. It won't do you any good."

"How else should I take it?"

Looping an arm around him, she bent to press her lips to his chest and felt the strong, steady beat of his heart. "I'm sorry this is hurting you. I hate that."

He enfolded her in his arms. "It goes down easier coming from you." Tilting her chin, he fused his mouth to hers.

"I should go," she said when they resurfaced.

"Stay with me. Sleep with me. I need you, Samantha." He dropped soft, wet kisses on her face and neck. "I need you."

"You're playing dirty."

"I'm not playing."

Something other than pain settled in her gut, something warm and sweet. This was a whole new kind of powerlessness, and it felt good. Really good. She let her hand slide over the defined chest, the ripped abdomen and below. Finding him hard and ready, her lips followed the path her hand had taken. His gasps of pleasure, his total surrender, told her she had succeeded in taking his mind off the pain and grief, which made everything that was wrong about this feel right.

THEY BEGAN THE next day the same way they finished the one before.

As her body hummed with rippling aftershocks, she pressed her lips to his shoulder. "This is getting out of hand."

"We've got six years of lost time to make up for."

His lips moving against her neck made her tremble. "I need to go soon," she said. "I have to shower and change and get to the airport."

"I'm taking the staff to Richmond today to see John," he said with a deep sigh. "I'd rather be going with you."

"I wish you could." She reached up to caress his face and found the stubble on his jaw to be crazy sexy. Replacing her hand with her lips, she said, "I forgot to tell you my news."

"What news?"

"I made lieutenant."

His face lit up with pleasure. "That's awesome, Sam! Congratulations."

"It won't be official for a week or so." For a moment, she thought about telling him how it happened but decided against it. "And my dad is marrying one of his nurses."

"Wow. Do you like her?"

"Yeah. A lot."

"Where's your mother?"

"She lives in Florida with some guy she hooked up with when I was in high school. They ran off together the day after I graduated. Nearly killed my dad. He had no idea."

"Ouch. That sucks. I'm sorry."

"Yeah, I guess I should be grateful that she stuck around long enough to get me through school, but it wasn't like she was *there* for me or anything."

"I saw my mother three times when I was in high school."

Sam cursed herself for being insensitive. "I'm sorry. I didn't mean to complain."

He shrugged. "It was what it was."

"At least you had your grandmother."

"And she was a real treat," he said with a bitter chuckle.

Intrigued, she shifted so she could see him. "She wasn't good to you?"

"She did what she could, but she always made it clear that I was a burden to her, that I was keeping her from traveling and enjoying her retirement." He paused, focused on her fingers. "When I was about ten, I heard her talking to my dad—her son. She said she'd done enough, and it was time for him to step up and take over, that he was an adult now and there was no reason he couldn't take care of his own child. He said he would, and I got all excited, thinking I was going to get to go with him."

Her stomach twisted with anxiety for the ten-year-old boy. "What happened?"

"I didn't see him again for a year."

"Nick…I'm sorry."

"He sent money—enough for me to play hockey, which I loved. I poured all my energy into that and school. Ended up with an academic scholarship to Harvard and played hockey there, too. That was my escape."

Listening to him, she wanted to give him everything he'd been denied as a child and wished she had it to give.

"Anyway," he said, running a hand through his hair, "someday hopefully I'll have my own family and it won't matter anymore."

And that, she thought, *is my cue to go.* She sat up and reached for her clothes at the foot of the bed.

"It's only seven. You've got time yet." His hand slid from her shoulder to land on her hip. "I could make you some breakfast."

"Thanks, but I've got to go home, take a shower, get changed, check in at HQ," she said as she jammed her arms into her shirt and dragged it over her head. *Air and space*, she thought, *and we're not talking about the museum. That's what I need. Some air, some space, some perspective. Distance.*

Twirling her bra on his index finger, his full, sexy mouth twisted into a grin. "Forget something?"

She snatched it away from him and jammed it into her pants pocket.

Laughing, he reclined on the big pile of pillows.

She felt the heat of his eyes on her as she ducked into the bathroom. Re-emerging a few minutes later, she found him out of bed and wearing just the sweats he'd had on the night before. The pants rode low on narrow hips, and that chest of his…It should've been gracing the covers of erotic romance novels rather than spending its days hidden behind starched dress shirts and silk ties. Tragic. Truly a waste of good—no, *great*—man chest.

"You're staring."

"And you're hot. Seriously. Hot."

"Well, um, thanks. I guess."

His befuddlement amused and delighted her until she remembered that she'd been plotting her escape. Suddenly, morning-after awkwardness set in, leaving her tongue-tied and uncertain as she tugged on her sweater. "Good luck with your staff. Today. In Richmond."

"Thank you." He reached for her hand, brought it to his lips. "Will you tell me what happens in Chicago?"

"If I can, I will. That's the best I can do."

"That's all I can ask." Releasing her hand, he caressed her cheek. "When will I see you?"

Before she knew it the words were tumbling from her face as if her mouth was on autopilot. "There's this thing tomorrow. Family dinner at my dad's. If you want to come." All but stuttering now, she added, "I'd understand if you didn't want to because there're so many of us—"

He stopped her with a finger to her lips. "What time?"

"Dinner's at three." Her cheeks grew warm with embarrassment. "But if you want to come earlier, we could take a walk. Check out the market. If you want."

"I want." He slid his arms around her waist and brought her in snug against him. "I really want."

She should've been prepared by then for the way her legs turned to jelly when he kissed her in that particular proprietary way, but the sweep of his tongue, the pressure of his hands on her ass holding her tight against his instant arousal…no way in hell she could prepare for that.

"So," he asked, peppering her face and lips with kisses, "does *this* mean we're together? I mean, *you're* asking *me* to do stuff." His teasing grin did nothing to offset the serious look in his eyes.

With her hands on his chest, she managed to extricate herself. At the bedroom door, she paused and turned back to him. "I've crossed every line there is to cross here, Nick."

"I know that," he said, his expression pained.

"If the job requires it, I won't hesitate to cross back."

"I wouldn't expect anything less."

Satisfied that he understood, she left him with a nod and a small smile.

He followed her downstairs. "Sam?"

She swung open the inside door. "Hmm?"

Framing her face with his hands, he said, "Fly safely."

She winced.

"What?"

"I hate to fly. Hate it with a passion. I've been trying not to think about it."

Grinning, he leaned his forehead against hers. "Just close your eyes and try not to think about it."

"Yeah, right," she said, rolling her eyes. "Okay, I'm going now."

"Okay, I'm letting you." Except he didn't. He hung on for a moment longer. "Be safe. This thing with that Johnson woman…Be careful." He kissed her. "Please."

"I always am."

"Guess what?"

"What?"

His lips landed on hers for another mind-altering kiss. "You're pretty damned hot yourself."

Sam gave herself one last minute to sink into the kiss.

With what appeared to be great reluctance, he finally released her.

TWENTY-ONE

NICK STAYED AT the door to watch her walk to her car. *Damn*, if the woman didn't make his mouth water with that curvy body and long-legged gait. The whole package was a huge turn-on. He acknowledged they were walking a fine line that was causing her great ethical conflict, but Nick could only be grateful for the second chance they'd been given. And despite her reluctance to acknowledge that this was an actual relationship, he had no intention of messing it up this time.

Long after she should have driven away, she sat at the curb. He wondered if she was on the phone. Tipping his head so he could better see her face, he noticed it was tight with frustration. He cracked the door, heard the unmistakable click of a dead car battery and waved at her to come back in.

Furious, she got out, slammed the car door and started back up the stone pathway to his door. She was halfway there when the car exploded.

The blast was so strong it shattered the storm door and propelled him backward onto the floor. His head smacked hard on the tile, but he fought through the fog to remain conscious so he could get to her.

Barefooted, shirtless and panic-stricken, he crawled through the glass calling for her. The quiet neighborhood had descended into bedlam. He heard people screaming and could smell the acrid smoke coming from the burning car. "Sam! *Sam!*"

Blood flowed from a cut on his forehead. He swiped at it and started down the stairs, ignoring the pain of jagged glass under his feet. *"Samantha!"* Frantically, he scanned the small front yard, the street, the neighbors' yards.

A moan from the bushes behind him caught his attention. "Sam!" He rushed to the huddled form in his garden and had the presence of mind to realize that the miniature evergreens he had planted the summer before had most likely saved her life. "Sam! Sam, look at me." With the scream of sirens in the distance, he gently turned her head. Other than a knot on her forehead and a shocked glow to her eyes, he didn't see any obvious injuries.

"Bleeding," she whispered. "You're bleeding."

"I'm fine." He picked branches from her hair, brushed dirt from her cheek. "Do you hurt? Anywhere?" Releasing a long deep breath, he swayed with lightheadedness. "Babe. Jesus." Sitting with her in the garden, he did battle with the blood pouring from his forehead. He held her tight against him and whispered soothing words as she trembled in his arms.

"Need to call. HQ. Report it."

"I'm sure someone called 911. Just stay still until we get you checked out."

"My ears are ringing."

"Mine, too. You didn't hurt anything else?"

"Chest hurts." She trembled. "God, Nick. Oh my God." Clutching her stomach, she rocked in his arms.

He tightened his hold on her. "Shh, babe." The blood

coming from the cut on his forehead seemed to finally be slowing. "Breathe. Deep breaths."

An Arlington police officer approached them. "Are you folks all right?"

"I'm on the job." She showed him the badge she pulled from her tattered coat pocket. "Detective Sergeant Holland. Metro."

"Are you hurt, Sergeant?"

"I don't think so, but it was my car that went up. I need to get word to my brass."

"I'll call it in for you." Until the cop handed Nick a blanket, he'd forgotten he was wearing only the now-torn sweats. "And I'll send the paramedics right over."

"Thank you, Officer…"

"Severson."

"Thank you," Sam said again. When they were alone, she glanced at Nick. "I'm sorry."

"What the hell for?"

"For bringing this to your home." She sniffed and wiped her nose. "I never thought they'd really try to kill me. I never imagined they had the balls."

"Don't you dare apologize to me, Samantha. You're a victim here."

"Your windows are broken. Your neighbors', too."

"Screw that. It's glass. It can be replaced. But you…" His voice hitched with emotion. Brushing his lips over the lump on her forehead, he took a deep shuddering breath. "There's no replacing you. I ought to know. I tried for six years."

"Nick," she said, haltingly, "I'm supposed to hold it together and do my job, but this…" She fixed her eyes on the firefighters hosing down what was left of her car.

"Nothing's going to happen to you. I won't let it."

Smiling now but still shaky, she turned to him and wiped the drying blood from his brow. "And how do you intend to do that?"

"By not letting you out of my sight."

"Nick—"

"Sergeant Holland?" Officer Severson said. "The paramedics are ready for you."

"We're not finished," she told Nick as she gestured the paramedics over. "We'll talk about this later."

"You bet your fine ass we will."

REMARKABLY, NICK'S INJURIES were more serious than Sam's. He required five stitches to close the cut over his left eyebrow and stitches in his right foot after doctors removed several slivers of glass. In addition, he had a slight concussion and a minor case of hypothermia from the hour he spent half-dressed in the cold.

Sam, on the other hand, had only a bump on the head and an ugly bruise on her breastbone where she'd connected with the bushes. When she allowed her mind to wander to what could've happened, she was beset by the shakes. She decided it was better if she didn't think about it until she had to. Standing at Nick's bedside, watching the plastic surgeon stitch his forehead, Sam's knees went weak as the needle passed through his flesh. Nothing freaked her out more than needles—not even airplanes.

The TV was tuned to John's public wake in Richmond, with special coverage of the O'Connor family's poignant visit the day before. Nick was riveted to the coverage, but Sam was riveted to the needle.

"You'll have a scar," she whispered.

"No way," the doctor protested. "He'll be good as new."

"Damn," Nick said with a grin. "I was hoping for a gnarly scar."

"It's not funny," Sam snapped.

"Hey." He squeezed her hand. "Why don't you wait outside? You're pale as a ghost."

"I'd rather stay in here where there're needles than face what's waiting for me out there."

"And that would be?"

"I heard the lieutenant and the captain are here, no doubt media, too. It'll be all over the news that I spent the night with you."

"We'll deal with it, babe."

"*I* will deal with it. *You* will say nothing, you got me?"

"I'm not going to let you get reamed for something we both had a hand in."

"You're a *civilian*. You won't help me if you try to fight my battles for me, Nick. You have to promise me you'll resist the urge to speak."

"Or?"

"I'll have Freddie toss you in the can until the dust settles."

"You wouldn't dare."

"Oh no?" She leaned in close to his battered face, but not too close to the needle. "Try me."

The doctor smiled. "I think I'd listen to the lady if I were you—unless you want to be back for more stitches."

"The *lady*," Nick said, never taking his eyes off Sam, "is sadly deluded if she thinks she can order me around like one of her collars."

"Ohhh," Sam said. "Listen to him spewing cop talk." Reaching behind her, she grabbed her cuffs and snapped them on him and the bed rail so fast he never saw it coming.

"What the fuck?" He tugged on the cuffs, clanked them against the metal rail. *"Goddamn it, Sam!"*

"Ah, you need to stay still unless you want a needle straight through to your brain," the doctor said.

"I'll be back to get him after I've dealt with my bosses," Sam said to the doctor. "Keep him quiet until then."

"Yes, ma'am," the doctor said, seeming awestruck by her brassiness.

"You're going to pay for this, Samantha," Nick growled.

She brushed a kiss over the uninjured side of his forehead. "Be back soon." Over her shoulder, she added, "Behave." As she walked away, the furious clatter of cuffs made her smile. "That'll teach him to screw with me." Her smile faded when she encountered Lieutenant Stahl's angry scowl in the waiting room. Realizing she was still braless, she pulled her tattered coat closed and crossed her arms.

Stahl gestured her to a deserted corner. Captain Malone followed them.

"Sergeant," Stahl said. "I'd like an explanation for what you were doing at the home of a material witness—overnight."

"Yes, sir, Lieutenant, I'm fine. Thanks for asking."

"How about we add a rap for insubordination to your growing list of problems?" Stahl retorted.

"Lieutenant," Captain Malone said, the warning clear in his tone. To Sam, he said, "Your injuries were minor?"

"Yes, sir. Bump on the head, bruised sternum."

"And your companion?"

Sam gave him a rundown of Nick's injuries. "Was anyone else hurt?"

"No. The street was deserted. Luckily, it was a weekend."

Yes, luckily, Sam thought, feeling a tremble ripple through her as she realized how truly lucky she—and Nick—had been. "Has Explosives gotten anything on the car?"

"They're there now. Our people are bumping heads with Arlington. The chief was on the phone with their chief asking for some latitude when I left."

"I'm sorry to have caused all this trouble, sir."

"You start down that path, you're gonna piss me off."

"What were you doing with Cappuano?" Stahl asked.

This time, Malone didn't bail her out. Rather, he watched her with wise gray eyes that she knew from experience didn't miss a thing.

"We're friends," she said haltingly. "We met at a party six years ago. I hadn't seen him again until the, ah, until the senator was murdered. Cappuano has been cleared of any involvement and has been a tremendous asset to the investigation in a civilian capacity. Sir."

"I'm taking you off the O'Connor case, effective immediately," Stahl said, puffed up with his own importance.

"But—"

"Not so fast, Lieutenant," Captain Malone said.

"This is my call, Captain," Stahl huffed. "She's *my* detective."

"And I'm *your* captain." Malone dismissed Stahl by turning his back to him.

The foul look Stahl directed at Sam would have reduced a lesser woman to tears. Fortunately, Sam wasn't a lesser woman. She directed all her attention and focus on the much more rational captain.

"Sergeant, I'm disappointed in the judgment you've exhibited by getting involved with a witness," Malone said.

"Exactly—" Stahl sputtered.

"Lieutenant!" the captain roared. "Get back to your squad." When Stahl didn't budge, Malone added a fierce, *"Now."*

With one last hateful glance at Sam, Stahl stalked out of the emergency room.

"As I was saying," Malone continued, "you've shown poor judgment with this involvement, but in the more than twelve years you've been under my command, I've never once had reason to question your judgment. I know you, Holland. I know how you think, how you operate and have had many an occasion over the years to appreciate your high ethical standards. So, the way I see it, the only way you hook up with a witness in the midst of the most important case of your career is if it's serious."

Sam might've swallowed her tongue—if she could've opened her mouth. "Sir?" she squeaked.

"Are you in love with this guy? Cappuano?"

"I…ah…I…"

"It's a simple yes or no question, Sergeant."

"Don't be ridiculous. Of course I'm not in love with him," Sam sputtered, but the words rang hollow, even to her. Apparently, they did to him, too.

Looking satisfied, he studied her again, long and hard. "I'm going to give you the benefit of the doubt.

I'm going to assume you've done nothing to compromise this investigation, that when you say Cappuano has been invaluable to you, you're being completely aboveboard with me."

"I am, sir."

"In that case, for now you're to have no comment to the press about your relationship with him. We'll let the media folks spin it. I'll take care of that." He sat and gestured for her to take the chair next to him. "As for the bombing—"

"If you take me off O'Connor, you're going to have to take my badge, too."

"Sergeant, there's no need for ultimatums. You've been through a traumatic thing."

"Yes, I have, and by tomorrow morning, everyone in the city will know who I'm sleeping with. They'll know Destiny Johnson meant it when she said she'd get even with me for what happened to her kid. They'll know I'm no closer to a suspect in the O'Connor case today than I was the day it happened. They'll know all that, and then they'll hear that my own command didn't have enough confidence in me to let me close this case. Where will that leave me?"

"You're a decorated officer. Soon to be a lieutenant. This is a setback. That's all it is."

"On top of another setback. You want me to take command of the detective squad. I won't have an ounce of authority left if you take this case away from me."

"Your safety has to be a consideration. They've come at you once. They'll come at you again."

"Next time, I'll be ready. I screwed up this time because I didn't take her seriously. I know better now."

"I've got to talk to the chief about this. He's having a

fucking cow. Gonzo and Arnold have Destiny Johnson in interview right now. Because we've had her in lock-up since yesterday, she's playing dumb on the bombing."

Freddie came rushing into the Emergency Room, looking pale and panicked. "Oh, thank God," he said when he saw Sam talking with Malone. "Thank you, Jesus."

"If you hug me, I'll have you busted down to Patrol," Sam snarled at him.

Freddie stopped just short of the embrace, bent at the waist and propped his hands on his knees. "I heard it on the radio," he panted. "Scared the freaking shit out of me."

"He's swearing," Sam commented to Malone. "He only does that in extreme circumstances. I'm honored."

Freddie tipped his face, met Sam's eyes. "You almost got blown up. I'm sorry if I don't find that funny."

"I'm fine, Cruz," she said, touched by his concern. "You can relax."

"What are we doing?" he asked Malone, his eyes hot with anger and passion. "What can I do?"

"Gonzo's got Destiny in interview," Sam told him.

"I was thinking on the way over here," he said, still breathing heavily. "What if it's not Johnson?"

"How do you mean?" Malone asked.

Freddie stood up straight. "Destiny spews in the paper yesterday, right?"

Sam and the captain nodded.

"So say someone wants to hose up the O'Connor investigation? What's the fastest way?" Before they could answer, he said, "Take out Sergeant Holland and have the full wrath of the department focused on Johnson.

Presto. O'Connor is back burner. Senator or not, no one takes precedence over a dead cop."

"That's an interesting theory, Detective," Malone said, clearly impressed.

Sam was filled with pride. Young Freddie was coming along very well. Very well, indeed.

"You think it's possible?" Freddie asked, full of youthful exuberance.

"It's solid, Cruz," Sam said. "Good thinking." She paused, thought for a moment and decided. "I want you to go to Chicago and talk to Patricia Donaldson. I want to know if her kid is John O'Connor's son. I want the whole story. Tell her she can either spill it to you, or we'll get a warrant for DNA. Don't come back until you know every detail of her relationship with O'Connor. He went out there the third weekend of every month. I want to know if he was banging her. I want to know how. You got me?"

"Without you?" His normally robust complexion paled again.

"A bomb just blew off your training wheels, Detective." Sam winced at the pain in her chest as she rose. "Get your ass to Chicago." She grabbed the lapels of his ever-present trench coat and pulled him down so his face was an inch from hers. "You get yourself hurt in *any* way, and I'll kill you. You got me?"

"Ma'am." He swallowed hard. "Yes, ma'am."

She retrieved the paper with her ticket information from her purse. "Be on that eleven o'clock flight and get back here as fast as you can. Report in tonight."

"Watch your back, Cruz," Malone added. "If they've got eyes on Sergeant Holland, they're on you, too."

"Yes, sir." Freddie stood there for a second longer, beaming at the two of them.

"What the hell are you standing there grinning like a goon for?" Sam asked.

"I'm going. I won't let you down. I'll call you as soon as I've got anything."

"Go!" After he scrambled through the ER doors, she glanced at Malone. "Sheesh, was I ever that green?"

"Nope," he said without hesitation. "You came in with the sensibilities of a captain. Why do you think I've been watching my back all these years?"

Staggered by the compliment, Sam stared at him. "I'm sorry if I've let you down."

"I'll bet your friend is wondering where you are. Why don't you go on back and check on him? I'll give you both a lift when he's sprung."

She rested a hand on his arm. "Don't let them take me off O'Connor, Captain. Don't let them."

"I'll do what I can."

TWENTY-TWO

SAM MADE HER WAY back down the long hallway, pausing just before Nick's room to lean against the wall and collect herself. She couldn't stop thinking about what Malone had said. Was she in love with Nick? Is that why she'd allowed things with him to progress even though she knew it was wrong and could get her into a shit load of trouble? Had she maybe always loved him? Way back to the first time they met?

With a soft groan, she tipped back her aching head. She hadn't loved Peter but discovered that far too late. When Nick failed to call her after their night together—or so she thought—she'd been seriously depressed. Peter came to the rescue, offering a shoulder to cry on and a friend to lean on. It had been easy, too easy she later realized, to get swept up by him.

Now, on top of everything else she'd learned about him, she knew he intercepted Nick's calls while pretending to offer comfort, proving he was an even bigger asshole than she had given him credit for being. He had robbed her of a lot more than four years of her life. He had taken her self-esteem, caused her to question her judgment, stolen her self-respect and left her confidence in tatters.

A smart woman would be leery of making another mistake after the whopper she'd made with Peter. A smart woman would go slow with Nick, would take her time, would make sure she was doing the right thing. As the clank of metal against metal reminded her she had a very angry man to deal with, she decided she clearly wasn't as smart as she'd always thought.

Pasting a big smile on her face, she stepped into the room, her stomach aching from the tension. "Great! You're all done."

All but smoking with rage, Nick said, "Get these things off me, Sam. Right now."

"I'd be happy to." She dug the key out of her pocket and dangled it in front of him. "But before I do, let's get one thing straight. I need you to stay out of my work stuff. Agree to that, and I'll let you go."

"How do you know I don't plan to let *you* go once you unlock me?"

The question sent a surprising jolt of fear through her. "Well, I guess that'll be up to you, won't it?" she said with more bravado than she felt.

"Unlock me. Now."

"Not until you agree."

"I'm not agreeing to anything while I'm locked to a bed. If you want to unlock me and talk this through like rational adults, then that's fine."

She studied his furious, handsome face for a long moment. "You're awfully sexy when you're pissed." Leaning down, she kissed the bandage over his left eye.

The kiss seemed to defuse him, but only somewhat.

"I'm sorry I locked you up." When his face twisted with skepticism, she said, "I *am* sorry. But you have no idea how difficult it is to be a woman in this profession or the daughter of a fallen hero. The last thing I need is some guy on a white horse riding to my rescue as if I can't handle things myself. As it is, I spend most of every day waiting for it all to blow up in my face."

"Like it did today?"

"A joke?" she asked, incredulous. "You're joking about a bomb?"

"Sorry," he said with chagrin, "it was too good to pass up. Doesn't mean I think it's funny. Quite the contrary." With his free hand, he captured one of hers and brought it to his lips. "Unlock me. I promise not to kill you."

Knowing that was the best she was going to get and encouraged by the tender gesture, she released the cuffs.

He made a big dramatic show of rubbing his sore wrist for a minute before he got up to reach for his jeans and sweater.

Still uncertain about just how angry he really was, Sam stayed on the far side of the bed while he got dressed. She winced at the flash of pain that crossed his face as he slid his injured foot into an old running shoe the cops had brought from his house.

"Um, Captain Malone is going to take us…well…I guess to my house if you don't mind."

"I don't mind," he said in a testy tone.

Swallowing the lump in her throat, she added, "I'd appreciate it if you don't discuss what happened earlier with him."

"What? That my girlfriend or sex buddy or whatever you are was nearly blown to bits in my front yard? I shouldn't mention that?"

She rubbed at eyes gone gritty with exhaustion. After an almost-sleepless night with him, she'd planned to catch a couple of hours on the plane if her nerves allowed it. "I'm asking you to do this for me. He was a lot cooler about me getting caught with you than I expected him to be. It would just be better if you stayed out of it."

He came around the bed and backed her up to the wall. "You want me to stay out of it?"

"Um, yeah, that would help." Only her hands on his chest kept him from completely invading her space.

"Let's get one thing straight, Samantha. I've been the guy behind the guy my whole career, and that's fine with me. But if you think, for one second, I'm going to ride shotgun in my personal life, you've got the wrong lapdog on your leash."

While she should have been pissed at a comment like that, she was ridiculously turned on. She looped a hand around his neck and brought him down for a kiss intended to make him forget all about being mad with her.

With his hands on her hips, he jerked her tight against him.

"I don't want a lapdog," she said when she finally came up for air. "That's not what I'm asking you to be."

"What *are* you asking me to be?"

"Do we have to decide that right now? It's bad enough the whole town's going to know we're sleeping together."

"Damage done," he said with a bitter laugh that jangled her already frazzled nerves.

"That's easy for you to say. Your job isn't on the line."

"No, it's not. I lost my job when my boss got himself murdered. Remember?"

"I don't want to do this. I don't want to be sniping with you when we've got so many bigger things to deal with."

"See what you just said there? *We* have so many bigger things to deal with? You just made my point."

She studied the floor for a moment before she found the courage to bring her eyes back up to meet his. "I'm not used to *we*."

He laughed, but at least the anger seemed to be gone. "And you think I am? This is all new ground for me, too, babe."

"I'm sorry we're being forced to go public before we're ready."

"Something tells me that nothing about you and me is going to be simple or easy. We may as well get used to it. At least you're calling us 'we' now. That's progress."

Ignoring that, she said, "So you'll be cool with the captain?"

"I'll be cool."

With her eyes fixed on his, she kissed him softly. "You really are super sexy when you're all steamed up."

"Is that so?"

She loved how embarrassed he got when she said stuff like that. "Uh huh." After patting his face, she headed for the door.

"Samantha?"

She turned back.

"You owe me twenty-six minutes in handcuffs, and I fully intend to collect."

DAMN HIM! WHEN ALL her attention and focus was needed to deal with the captain and whatever was waiting for her at home, all Sam could think about was being cuffed and at Nick's mercy for twenty-six minutes. Her whole body tingled with anticipation.

Turning to glare at him, she was rewarded with a shit-eating grin that told her he knew he had rattled her.

"You really are super sexy when you're all steamed

up," he whispered, earning another furious glare. When he tried to hold hands with her, she tugged hers free and jammed it into her coat pocket where she encountered the cuffs and her bra. Her head pounded, and she began to believe it was possible for a head to actually blow off a neck. As they approached the waiting area, her stomach took a nasty dip that caused her to gasp with pain.

"What?" Nick asked, taking her arm to stop her.

"Stomach."

"Why don't we get someone to look at that while we're here?"

She tugged her arm free. "It's been checked."

"It needs to be checked again," he said, rubbing his hands up and down her arms.

"It's better." She stepped out of his embrace. "No PDA in front of the captain or anyone else."

"You're not giving me orders, remember?"

"Nick—"

"Sam."

With a growl of frustration, she marched into the waiting room several strides ahead of him.

Captain Malone put down the *Time* magazine he'd been flipping through and stood up. "Ready?"

"Yes, sir. Ah, this is Nick. Nick Cappuano." Gesturing to Nick without looking at him, she added, "Captain Malone."

While Sam's stomach grinded, the two men sized each other up as they shook hands and mumbled, "Nice to meet you."

"On behalf of the department," Malone said, "I apologize for your injuries and the damage to your home."

"Not your fault," Nick said. "However, I'd like to

know what's being done to find the person who tried to kill Sam."

Sam stared at him, her mouth hanging open. Was *that* how he planned to stay out of it?

"Let's get you two out of here, and we'll talk about it on the way." He waved his hand and two uniformed officers appeared. "We've got press up the wazoo outside the E.R., so Officers Butler and O'Brien are going to get you out through the main door upstairs. I'll get my car and meet you there."

"Thank you, sir," Sam said. The moment the captain was out of earshot she pounced on Nick. "*That's* you staying out of it and being cool?"

"What? He knows we're sleeping together. Wouldn't I look like a jerk if I didn't even ask? Do you want him to think I'm a jerk? Wouldn't it be better for you if he likes me? If he can see why you'd risk so much to be with me right now?"

"Ugh!" She stalked after the uniforms, pretending not to hear him laughing behind her.

By the time they had parked in front of her father's Capitol Hill home, Nick was the captain's new best friend. They'd bonded over their shared concern for Sam's safety as well as their passion for the Redskins, politics and imported beer. If Sam hadn't already been on the verge of puking, she would be now for sure.

She suspected they were using the small talk to mask the underlying tension that surrounded them all as they contemplated what could have happened that morning and the staggering array of implications they were left to contend with. For that reason, and that reason only, she decided not to kill Nick for defying her.

Her stomach clutched when she saw the chief's car parked on Ninth Street. No doubt he and her father were in there concocting a plan to lock her up somewhere until she testified.

As they approached the house, Sam glanced at Captain Malone. "Um, sir, could you give us just a second?"

"Sure. I'll see you in there."

After he had gone inside, Nick turned to her. "I know what you're going to say, but I was just trying to make conversation—"

She went up on tiptoes to plant a kiss on him.

Startled, he said, "What was that for?"

"Just wanted to."

"Are you intentionally trying to keep me off balance?"

"It's not intentional, but if it's working…"

"I figured I was in for another tongue-lashing—and not the good kind."

She smiled. "I just wanted to tell you that my dad has some feeling in his right hand, so when I introduce you…" She shrugged. "If you wanted to squeeze his hand, it'd mean something to him. And to me."

Nick put his arms around her, drew her in close and kissed the top of her head. "Thank you for telling me."

"He's going to be all wound up about the bomb and stuff, so he might not even notice you. Don't be offended by that."

"I won't."

"I hope you didn't use up all your charm on the captain," she said, rubbing her belly, "because my dad's the one who counts. You know that, right?"

"Of course I do. It's going to be fine, babe. Don't worry or your stomach will start up."

She eyed him with amusement. "Starting to see the pattern?"

"Yep. Let's get this over with before you work yourself into a full-blown episode."

"Might be too late," she muttered. Taking one last deep breath, she led him up the ramp to the front door and stepped into a room full of cops.

Celia pounced on her. *"Oh my God, Sam!"* Her tears dampened Sam's cheek. Stepping back to run her hands over Sam as if to take inventory, Celia said, "Are you all right?"

"I'm fine." She did a little spin. "See? Everything still attached and working."

Celia raised an eyebrow. "You lied to me last night when you said you were going to work."

Sam squirmed under her future stepmother's stern glare. "Um, yeah, I do that every now and then. Lie, that is. Is that going to be a problem for you?"

Celia cast an appreciative glance at Nick over Sam's shoulder and smiled. "If he's the reason, I guess I can forgive you. This one time."

Sam introduced her to Nick, and when she couldn't avoid it for a second longer, she met her father's steely stare from across the room. She went over to him and bent to kiss his cheek. "I'm sorry you were worried."

"I went past worried about three hours ago, but we'll get to that. Who've you got with you?"

Knowing her father was already fully aware of who Nick was, Sam nodded to Nick anyway. "Dad, this is Nick Cappuano."

As instructed, Nick squeezed Skip's right hand. "Pleased to meet you, Deputy Chief Holland."

"Excellent sucking up. I'd say someone prepared you well to meet her old man."

"I wouldn't know what you mean, sir."

Skip's eyes danced with mirth. "That from this morning?" he asked, referring to the bandage over Nick's eye.

"Yeah, but I'll live."

Sam re-introduced Nick to Chief Farnsworth.

"Detective Higgins, ma'am," the other cop said to Sam. "Explosives."

"I've seen you around," Sam said, although she couldn't believe he was a detective. With his sandy hair cut into a flat top over a baby face, he barely looked old enough to be out of the academy. "What'd you find?"

"Two EDs on your car." For the benefit of Nick and Celia, he added, "Explosive devices—one on the ignition and a backup. Only one detonated. Both of them go, we're not having this conversation."

Sam swallowed hard and didn't object when Nick's hand landed on the small of her back.

"That's not all," Higgins said. "When we did a sweep of the other cars in the area, we found two more attached to a black BMW."

Nick and Sam gasped.

"Registered to you, Mr. Cappuano."

As if all her bones had turned to mush, Sam sank to the sofa. "Why?" she whispered. "Why would they target him?"

"We were just discussing that when you came in," Chief Farnsworth said. "If it's Johnson or their pals, the best theory I've heard yet is 'you take mine, I'll take yours.' Revenge, pure and simple. Johnson wanted you either dead or decimated. How would they've known his car?"

"I've been in it," Sam confessed. "Recently. And I've had the feeling someone was watching me a few times."

"Detective Cruz suggested a link to O'Connor rather than Johnson," Malone said. "Worth looking into, especially since they targeted Nick, too."

Farnsworth turned to Nick. "Do you know of anything Senator O'Connor was involved in that had ties to terrorists or terrorism?"

"He was on the Homeland Security Committee, working mostly on the immigration issue, but he was briefed on counterterrorism initiatives. We both were."

"I want to take apart that bill he was sponsoring, line by line," Sam said. "Maybe I've totally missed the boat on this. I've been thinking jilted lover, but they don't tend to plant bombs."

"No," Malone agreed. "They tend to dismember."

"Which is why I've focused most of my attention on his love life." Sam got up to pace. "We've uncovered a slew of recent ex-lovers, a few with complaints about some of his, um, fetishes." She sent a sympathetic glance to Nick since he was hearing this for the first time. "But maybe Cruz is right. Maybe the Lorena Bobbitt was intended to throw us off."

"He was *dismembered?*" Higgins squeaked, his baby face gone pale.

"A detail we've managed to keep out of the press," Farnsworth said with a pointed look at his detective.

"Yes, sir." Higgins got up to leave. "I need to get back to the lab where it's safe."

Sam rolled her eyes. "Run back to your cave, Higgins, and leave the dirty work to those of us in the field."

"You can have it. I'll send you details on the EDs

when I have more, but I can tell you they were crude and you got lucky, Sergeant. Damned lucky."

"Yeah," Sam said. "I know." She saw him out and turned to find every man in the room focused on her.

No doubt sensing a battle royal in the making, Celia stepped into the kitchen.

"Before you all get going," Sam said, "I have something I want to say, and I want you to listen to me without interrupting."

When they agreed with their silence, she pushed her fist into her aching gut and took a second to look each of them in the eye—Dad, her hero and her rock; Chief Farnsworth, beloved friend and respected leader; Captain Malone, boss and mentor; and Nick, quickly becoming more important than anyone. All of them cared about her. She had no doubt about that, just as she had no doubt they'd go to any lengths to keep her safe.

"I'm sure you two have cooked up a plan to toss me into a safe house for the weekend," she said to her father and the chief, "but that's not going to happen." Before they could protest, she held up a hand to stop them. "I'm going to continue to work this case until I close it, and I'm not going to let punks or terrorists or whoever strapped an ED to my car and Nick's take me off the streets. The minute they think they have that kind of power over me, I'm done on this job and you know it."

Pausing, she made eye contact with each of them again. "I know you're worried, and I know you care. But if you care about me at all, don't ask me to be a coward. I won't deny that bomb scared the shit out of me." She let her gaze fall on Nick. "When I saw your face covered with blood, my heart almost stopped. So

I'm going to get them. If for no other reason than they hurt you, and that's simply unacceptable to me."

Nick's hard expression softened into a smile that engaged his eyes and filled her heart with emotions she had never experienced quite so strongly before.

To Farnsworth, she said, "Let me do my job. I'll take every precaution I can. I'll run things from here, stay as close to home as I can, but I won't hide out. I dare any of you to tell me you wouldn't rather go down in the line than run scared from scum who think they can take us out like yesterday's garbage."

A full minute of silence ensued, during which she noticed Farnsworth and Malone watching her dad and understood they were going to take their cues from him.

"I'd like to see that immigration bill," Skip finally said. He glanced at Nick. "I'm a political junky in my spare time. I might catch something in there we can use."

"I'll get it for you." Nick checked his watch as he stood up. "My staff should be back from Richmond by now, so let me make a call. What format do you prefer?"

"A fax would work. We can pop it right into my reading device. I can see two pages at once that way. Skip rattled off the number and followed Nick into the kitchen.

"I'm going to go lean on the lab to speed things up with the boomer," Malone said as he pulled on his coat.

Sam was left alone with the chief. "I know what you're going to say."

"Do you?"

She squirmed under the heat of his stare. In a rush of words, she said, "I'm sorry I lied to you about Nick. But I was so afraid you'd take me off the case, and after

Johnson I *needed* it. You know I did. I tried to fight what was happening between us, but he was just *there* for me, every step of the way and I, um…Why are you smiling?"

"In some ways, you're exactly the same as you were at twelve, you know that?" He took a step closer to her, the smile fading. "But if you ever, *ever* lie to me again, Sergeant, I'll have your badge. Are we clear?"

"Crystal," she said, swallowing hard. "Sir."

"Get O'Connor cleaned up—and fast. I don't want any more bad publicity for you or the department."

"Yes, sir."

He called out his good-byes to Skip and Celia before donning his coat.

"Chief? Thank you for understanding why I have to do this."

"I would've done the same thing myself. In fact, your dad predicted your little speech almost down to the last vowel. We were ready for you."

"Well, sheesh," she huffed. "Here I was thinking I'd handled you, and *I'm* the one being handled?"

"You gotta get up a lot earlier in the morning to get one past a couple of crusty old vets like us. Truth is, we would've been disappointed if you'd done it any other way. You're a chip off the old block, Holland."

"Thank you, sir. You couldn't pay me a higher compliment."

"I know." He glanced toward the kitchen. "You think about what it would do to him if something happens to you. It'd be the end of him. You think about that."

"Yes, sir," she whispered as she watched him go down the ramp.

TWENTY-THREE

WITH NICK OUTSIDE on the phone, Sam went into the kitchen where her dad was reading the bill.

She bent to kiss his cheek. "Thanks for the help. I hate feeling like I've totally missed the point on this one."

"Don't know for sure yet that you have. Just because it's taken a few twists and turns doesn't mean you aren't on the right path."

"That's true."

"Seems like a nice kid."

"Who? Higgins?"

"No," he said grinning. "Nick."

"Oh, right." She wasn't ready to go down *that* path with him just yet. "So, hey, I hear you've been keeping secrets."

"You're one to talk, and which secrets are you referring to?"

Sam raised an eyebrow as she slipped into a kitchen chair.

"Oh. Celia."

"Uh huh," Sam said, delighted by the faint blush that appeared on his ruddy cheeks.

"Well, I was going to tell you."

"Except you were too chicken so you got her to tell me."

"Something like that."

Sam laughed. "I'm happy for you."

"Really? You are?" His relief was almost as comical as his embarrassment.

"Of course I am. She's terrific. What would we have done without her the last couple of years?"

"No kidding. Thing I can't understand is why she'd want to shackle herself to this?" With his eyes, he took in his useless body, the chair, the whole situation.

"She loves you. I think it's that simple."

"She's not in it for the house or the pension, in case you wondered."

"I didn't."

"Sure you did, because I've trained you to be as cynical as I am."

"Well, maybe it crossed my mind for an instant, but listening to her talk about you…she's genuine."

"I think she is," he said, seeming incredulous. "In fact, she wants to sign something that says she gets nothing, you know, after…"

"Which says to me she should get it."

"See? That's what I think, too. It wouldn't bother you or your sisters if she got a cut?"

Sam stood up to rest her hands on his shoulders and brought her face down to his. "All I want is you, here with us, for as long as we can have you, for as long as you want to be here."

"You haven't forgotten, have you? About our deal?"

Sam thought of the prescription bottle she had stashed in a safety deposit box. "No."

"And you're still willing? If the time comes…"

Fighting back the sting of pain in her belly and her heart, she kept her voice steady when she said, "If the time comes."

He released a long deep breath. "Good. Okay. Let me get back to this. I'll report in if anything jumps out, Sergeant—or should I say Lieutenant?"

"Not quite yet." She kissed his forehead. "Thanks for the help."

"My pleasure."

And she could see that it was. He seemed more vital, more alive in that moment than he had in a long time. She should've been bringing him into her cases on a more formal basis all along and vowed to do so going forward. His mind was as sharp as ever, and if using it gave him a reason to stay in the fight, then she'd use it and no doubt benefit from it.

NICK ENDED THE CALL with Christina and stashed the cell phone he'd borrowed from Sam in his pocket. He rested against the porch rail and let his eyes wander up and down the quiet street. Some of the townhouses were painted in a variety of bright colors while others were fronted by brick or stone. The red brick sidewalks sloped and curved over tree roots. Black wrought iron gates added a touch of class to the Capitol Hill neighborhood.

Was someone out there right now watching him? Hoping to get another shot at Sam? Or at him? The thought sent a chill chasing through him as he contemplated the sudden changes in his life. Last Saturday, he spent the morning in the office and then played in a pickup basketball game at the gym. He went out for a few beers with the guys he'd played with and went home alone.

Now, a week later, John was dead, he was in love with Samantha Holland and someone had tried to kill them both. Any doubt that he was in love with her had evaporated during the interminable trip through shattered glass to get to her after the bombing. He'd had just enough time to imagine a return to the empty existence his life had been without her to be certain he loved her.

Three doors down on Ninth Street, a metal "For Sale" sign caught his attention as it banged against a brick-front townhouse. The creepy sound reminded Nick of ghost towns and spaghetti Westerns. Another trickle of fear crept along his spine as he took a long look up and down the deserted street.

"What're you doing out here in the cold?" Sam asked as she joined him on the porch.

"Nothing much." He extended a hand to her. "Where's your coat?"

"I'll share yours." She slipped her arms around his waist and burrowed into his coat. "Mmm. Warm."

As Nick held her close, he wondered how he had survived, how he had lived without her for all the years since he first met her. He closed his eyes and rested his cheek on the top of her head.

"What are you thinking about?"

He couldn't tell her he loved her. Not now. Not in the midst of murder and chaos and not when she wasn't ready to hear it. Later, he decided. There'd be time. He would make sure of it. "That you showed a lot of spine before, letting them know you planned to stay on the case."

"Yeah, well, apparently they predicted that's what I'd say and had planned for it." She looked up at him. "I just cashed in every good judgment and sterling moral code chip I've earned in twelve years on the force to bring you into my life." With a coy smile, she added, "I hope you're going to be worth it."

Realizing the huge step she was taking, he framed her face with his hands and kissed her. "I will be. I promise."

"I was kidding."

"I wasn't."

She brought him down to her and sucked the breath out of his lungs with a passionate kiss.

"Sam," he gasped, burying his face in the elegant curve of her neck. "God."

"What? What is it?"

"When I think about what might've happened." He raised his head, met her sparkling blue eyes and was grateful. So very grateful. "I know this is all so new, but the thought of losing you…again…I don't want to lose you."

"You won't. Nothing's going to happen to me."

"They could take a shot at you right now. We're totally exposed standing out here."

She reached up to caress his face. "You can't do this. If you're going to be with me—"

"If?"

She smiled. "I get hurt every now and then. I have close calls—not like I did today—but stuff *happens.* You can't let fear rule you. That's no life for you—or me." She hesitated, as if there was something else she wanted to say.

"What?" He sensed her tension before he felt it. "Babe. What?"

"When I was married," she said haltingly, "Peter obsessed about my safety, my whereabouts, my cases. It wasn't healthy, and while it wasn't the only problem we had, it made a bad situation much worse. It was totally suffocating."

"I hear what you're saying, and I understand. I really do. I'll do my best to give you room to breathe, but you've got to give me some time to adjust, okay? I'm not used to the woman I care about being nearly blown up in my front yard. It's going to take me a while to get used to the dangers that go with your job."

"Fair enough."

He brushed his thumbs over the deep, dark circles under her eyes and pressed a gentle kiss to the lump on her forehead. "You're whipped. Do you think you could sleep for a bit?"

"I guess I could try, but my mind is racing. I want to get everyone here later when Freddie gets back to start all over again. We're missing something. I know we are."

"You won't be any good to anyone if you run yourself into the ground. How about a nap to recharge?"

She flashed that coy smile he'd come to love. "Only if you join me."

"*Here?* With your dad in the house?"

"He can't shoot you."

"That's not funny. He can have me killed. Easily."

"I was married, Nick. He knows I've had sex."

"Not with me."

"I'll bet he doesn't think we were baking cookies last night."

"That's what we were doing. If he asks, that's *exactly* what we were doing. Baking cookies—all night long."

Laughing, she took his hand to lead him inside. "We're going to crash for a bit," she said to Celia. "Freddie is due back later tonight. If we conk out big time, will you wake us up when he gets here?"

"I sure will, honey. Can I get you two something to eat?"

"I don't think I could eat yet," Sam said, running her hand over her belly.

"Me either," Nick said. "But thanks anyway." He glanced at the kitchen where Skip was still engrossed in the immigration bill. "If you could fail to mention to Chief Holland that I'm upstairs, too, that'd be cool. In fact, I'd pay you."

Celia chuckled and waved them up. "I'll see what I can do."

Feeling like a teenager sneaking into his girlfriend's room—a goal he'd never managed to achieve back then—Nick followed Sam up the stairs.

She closed the bedroom door and pulled off her sweater.

He winced at the ugly purple bruise on her chest. If he hadn't stopped breathing, he might've enjoyed watching her strip. "I agreed to a nap. I didn't agree to nudity."

"You want me to sleep, right?"

"Uh huh."

She wiggled out of her jeans and panties and came at him with intent in her eyes. "I sleep best in the nude."

He took a step back and encountered wall. "He's going to know. If a babe like you is my daughter, I've got her room bugged to make sure guys like me don't get in." Without allowing his eyes to leave her face, he said, "So he's going to know I'm up here with his daughter—his beautiful, sexy, *naked* daughter—and he'll call some of his cop buddies. They'll drag me into a dark alley to rip the limbs from my body one by one, and then toss what's left of me in the Potomac."

Laughing, Sam slipped her hands under his sweater and eased it up and over his head, catching him off guard when she nuzzled his nipple. That's all it took to make him rock hard.

"With an imagination like that, you should consider a career in fiction."

He kept his hands limp at his sides. Maybe if he didn't leave prints on her he'd walk away with his life.

"You really think you can resist me?" she asked, trailing kisses from his jaw to his collarbone as her breasts rubbed against his chest.

"My life depends on it."

Her lips glided over his chest to his belly. "All that tough talk from before..." She unbuttoned his jeans, pushed them down and sank to her knees in front of him. "I think I'm about to make you my lapdog."

Sensing where this was going, he tried to escape.

In a move that both startled and stirred him, she pinned him to the wall.

He groaned, his fingers rolling into fists as her hot mouth closed around him. "Sam...*please*. I thought you liked me."

"I do," she said, dragging her tongue in circles that made his head spin. "I really do."

A bead of sweat rolled between his shoulder blades, straight down his spine. "He'll *know*, and he'll kill me."

She managed to laugh as she sucked. Hard.

"Jesus." His breathing became labored, the heat of her mouth unbearable. "Sam, honey, come here."

"So you're willing to play now?"

"Yeah." He helped her up, lifted her and sank into her in one easy movement. "Hell, you only live once, right?"

She gasped from the impact.

"Okay?" he asked.

Her arms encircled him, and he bit back a moan when she made contact with the bump on the back of his head. "Yes," she sighed. "*So* okay."

If he had to suffocate, he decided, he wanted to do it between Samantha Holland's spectacular breasts, engulfed in her jasmine and vanilla scent. Dropping a gentle kiss on the bruise, he walked them—carefully, since his jeans were still twisted around his ankles—to the bed and lowered her.

"Nick."

"What, babe?"

"Fast." She clung to him. "I want it fast."

His heart staggered, and he had to bite his lip to keep from losing it right then and there. Knowing she could be noisy, he captured her mouth as he gave her what she wanted. Had *anything* ever been this good? No. Nothing. Ever. She was tough and courageous on the job, yet here with him she was all girl—warm, soft, fragrant girl. Her moan echoed through her and into him the instant before she lifted off.

He muffled her cries, or at least he hoped to God he did, before he pushed hard into her one last time and let himself go.

TWENTY-FOUR

FREDDIE SAT IN FRONT of Patricia Donaldson's two-story home for a long time. He couldn't imagine asking her the questions he needed to ask but knew it was long past time he got over the queasiness that struck him whenever he had to ask people personal questions—especially about their sex lives.

Perhaps if he got a sex life of his own, then he wouldn't be so put off by asking about what other people did in their bedrooms. He'd been raised a Christian, had taken his religion seriously and had saved himself for marriage. That's how he ended up a twenty-nine-year-old virgin, a fact he had shared with no one, lest he be ridiculed by his colleagues.

He'd had plenty of girlfriends and had done his share of fooling around, but he'd yet to have the full experience. Lately, he'd been thinking too much about what he was missing. And with no marital prospects on the horizon, he wondered how much longer he could hold out.

Since they'd interviewed that personal trainer the other day, Elin Svendsen, he had fantasized about her obsessively. The way she hinted at the nasty stuff she had done with Senator O'Connor...What Freddie wouldn't give for one night with her. Maybe once they cleared the case, he'd be in the market for some personal training of a different sort.

In the meantime, he needed to go into that house and

ask Patricia Donaldson if her son was John O'Connor's son, if she'd continued a sexual relationship with the senator and if so, what kind of sex she'd had with him. The thought of asking those questions of a woman he'd never met made him sick.

Even if he sat there all night, he'd never be fully prepared. And since Sam was waiting for him to get this information and get it back to her, Freddie emerged from the rental car and headed up the flagstone walkway. With one last deep breath to settle his nerves, he rang the bell. Chimes echoed through the house. He waited a full minute before a fragile-looking blonde opened the door. Her blue eyes were rimmed with red, her pretty face ravaged with exhaustion. If this woman hadn't recently lost someone she loved, Freddie would turn in his badge.

"Patricia Donaldson?"

"Yes?"

"I'm sorry to disturb you, ma'am. I'm Detective Freddie Cruz, Metro Police, Washington, D.C." He showed her his badge.

She took the badge from him, examined it and handed it back to him. "This is about John."

"Yes, ma'am. I wondered if I might have a few minutes of your time?"

With a weary gesture, she stepped aside to let him in.

Freddie followed her to a comfortable family room, noting the photos of the handsome blond boy scattered throughout the house. The place appeared to have been professionally decorated, but had retained a warm, cozy atmosphere.

When he was seated across from her, Freddie said, "You were acquainted with Senator John O'Connor?"

"We've been friends for many years," she said softly. "I'm sorry for your loss."

Her raw eyes filled with tears. "Thank you." She brushed at the dampness on her cheeks.

"You were just friends?"

"Yes," she said without hesitation.

Freddie reached for a framed photo on an end table. "Your son?"

"Yes."

"Handsome boy."

"Thank you."

"I can't help but notice his striking resemblance to the senator."

She shrugged. "Maybe a little."

Freddie returned the photo to the table. "Is your son at home?"

"He went to do an errand at school. He's a junior at Loyola."

Relieved to know the boy wasn't in the house, Freddie pressed on. "In the course of our investigation, we've uncovered a series of regular monthly payments Senator O'Connor made to you for the last twenty years." Even though he knew the facts by heart, Freddie consulted his notebook. "Three thousand dollars, paid by check, on the first of every month."

Her hand trembled ever so slightly as she reached for the gold locket she wore on a chain around her neck. "So?"

"Can you tell me why he gave you the money?"

"It was a gift."

"That's a mighty big gift—thirty-six thousand dollars a year, totaling more than seven hundred thousand over twenty years."

"He was a generous man."

"Ms. Donaldson, I realize this is a very difficult time for you, but if you were his friend—"

"I was his best friend," she cried, her hand curling into a fist over her heart. "He was mine."

"If that's the case, I'm sure you want us to find the person who killed him."

"Of course I do. I just don't see what you need from me."

"I need you to confirm that your son Thomas is John O'Connor's son."

"Do you, Detective?" she asked softly. "Do you really need me to confirm it?"

Her easy capitulation flustered Freddie. He'd expected to have to work for it. "I'd appreciate if you could tell me about your relationship with the senator, from the day you met him through to his death."

She paused for a long moment, as if she were making a decision, and then began to talk so softly that Freddie had to strain to hear. "My family moved to Leesburg the summer before eighth grade. I met him on the first day of school. He was nice to me when no one else gave me the time of day, but that was John. It was just like him to make the new girl feel welcome." Lost in her memories, she seemed to have forgotten Freddie was there.

He took notes, knowing Sam would expect every detail.

"We became friends—unlikely friends."

"Why unlikely?"

"His father was a United States senator, a multimillionaire businessman. Mine worked at the post office. We weren't exactly from the same universe, but John was the least status-conscious person I ever knew.

He couldn't have cared less about his father's position, which of course drove his father crazy.

"Over time, our friendship grew and blossomed into love. His parents never liked me, never welcomed me into their home or their family. That made John sad, but it didn't keep us apart. He was the love of my life, Detective, and I was the love of his. We knew it at fifteen. Can you imagine?"

"No, ma'am." He couldn't imagine it at twenty-nine. "I can't."

"We were overwhelmed by what we felt for each other and determined to be together forever, no matter what it took." She glanced down at her lap, her fingers twisting nervously. "I was sixteen when I got pregnant. My parents were devastated, but his were outraged. His father was in the midst of an ugly re-election campaign, and all they cared about was the potential scandal. They offered me a hundred thousand dollars to have an abortion."

Freddie kept his expression neutral.

"I refused to even consider it. I was under the illusion that John and I would find a way to be together, to raise our child together. I had no idea then how far people with power could and would go to get what they wanted. Within a week, my father was transferred to a post office in Illinois."

"What did John say about this?"

"What could he say? He was going into his senior year of high school. His parents still had him under their thumb."

"Did he see the baby?"

She nodded. "He and his parents came out for a day when Thomas was born. The senator pitched a holy fit when I named him Thomas John O'Connor, but they had taken John away from me—away from us—they weren't going to deny my son his father's name. I had my limits, too."

"What was your relationship with John like after the baby was born?"

"We talked on the phone as often as we could. We made plans to be together." Her hands trembled in her lap. "After he graduated from high school, his father got him an internship in Congress for the summer and then they shipped him off to Harvard. It was more than a year before we saw each other again."

"He was an adult by then. Why didn't he stand up to his parents?"

"They controlled the money, Detective, the money he was using to support his son while he was in college. He did what he was told."

"And after college?"

"His father threatened to disown him if he married me, because if he did, people would find out about 'the kid' as Graham called him, and there'd be a scandal." Her voice had gone flat and lifeless. "As much as John loved me and Thomas, he wouldn't have been able to live with being disowned by his father." She leaned forward. "Don't get me wrong, Detective. I hate Graham O'Connor for what he denied me, what he denied Thomas and mostly what he denied John. But John loved his father, and more, he respected him despite everything he had done to us. John was a good man, the best man I've ever known, but he didn't have it in him to turn his back on his father. He just didn't. I accepted that a long time ago and learned to be satisfied with what I had."

"Which was what exactly?"

"We had one weekend a month to be a family, and we made the most of it. John was a wonderful father to Thomas. Between visits, he was completely available to him, and they talked most days. My son is devastated by his father's death."

"And no one ever questioned his resemblance to the senator in light of the fact that he had his name?"

"No," she said. "Amazingly, we got away with it. The O'Connors managed to thoroughly bury us here in the Midwest. During John's campaign and the first few months he was in office, we played it cool and didn't see much of each other. Once the attention faded, we were able to pick things up again. The media never caught so much as a whiff of us."

"I'm curious as to why he sent you monthly payments, rather than giving you a lump sum. His parents had money, and he became a wealthy man himself when he sold his company."

"He took good care of us, but he liked sending the monthly payments. He said it made him feel connected to Thomas and to me."

"I apologize in advance for what I'm about to ask you…But I need to know where the senator slept when he was here."

Her eyes flashed with anger and embarrassment. "Where do you think he slept?"

"Was he involved with other women?" Freddie hated the pain his question obviously caused her.

"Yes," she said through gritted teeth. "But my son doesn't know that, and I'd prefer to keep it that way."

"It didn't bother you? That he was with other women?"

"Of course it bothered me, but I didn't expect him to be celibate the other twenty-seven days a month."

"Did you discuss the other women in his life?"

"We did not."

"Not even when he was with Natalie for three years?"

"He had his life, and I had mine," she snapped. "One weekend a month, we belonged to each other."

"Have you ever been married?"

She laughed. "Where do you think I would've stashed my husband on the third weekend of every month when my longtime lover came to visit?"

"So that's a no?"

"I've never been married."

"When he was here," Freddie said, trying not to stumble over the words, "you had sexual relations with him?"

"I don't see how that's relevant to the case."

"It's relevant, and I need you to answer the question."

"Yes, I had sex with him! As much and as often as I could! Are you satisfied?"

"Was there anything, um, unusual about the kind of sex you had with him?"

She stood up. "We're finished here. I won't allow you to come into my home and debase the most important relationship in my life."

Freddie stayed seated to give her the perceived advantage as he dropped the final bomb. "Did he ever try to get you to have rough sex or anal sex with him?"

She stared at him, astounded. "I want you to leave. Right now."

"I'm sorry, ma'am, but you can answer the question here or I can take you back to Washington so you can answer it there. It's your call."

Her hands on her hips, her eyes shot daggers at him. "John O'Connor was never anything but a perfect gentleman with me. Every woman should have a lover as gentle and sweet. Now if there's nothing further, I want you to leave my home."

"Will you be attending the funeral in Washington?"

"Since there's no longer an O'Connor in office, I can't see any reason for my son and me to hide out anymore. We're planning to go. John's attorney called me today to tell me we need to be at the reading of the will the day after the funeral. I'm sure Graham and Laine are thrilled about that."

"Have they ever had any contact with Thomas?"

"Not since the day after he was born."

"The media will be all over you."

He admired the courageous lift of her chin. "John suffered over the fact that he couldn't acknowledge his son. The least I can do for him is rectify that now that he's gone."

"I'm sorry again for your loss, Ms. Donaldson, and I'm sorry to have upset you with my questions."

She shrugged off his apology. "If it helps the investigation, then I guess it will have been worth it."

"You've been a big help."

At the door, she said, "Detective? Get the person who did this to my John." Her eyes filled with new tears. "Please."

"We're doing everything we can."

TWENTY-FIVE

THE WATERGATE LOBBY was mobbed, but when Nick walked in the mob went silent, parting to allow him passage to the elevator. He recognized some of the faces—his grandmother, his father, Mr. Pacheco from seventh grade science, Lucy Jenkins who'd lived next door and Graham O'Connor. Why was he here? With the vote this afternoon, John wouldn't have time for one of their regular lunches.

Nick tried to tell him John was busy, but Graham wouldn't listen. He just smiled, like he knew something Nick didn't know. Behind him, was that…Sam? Sam Holland? She hadn't returned his calls, but that was a long time ago. He'd always wanted to see her again. Reaching out, he tried to get to her.

She smiled and slipped away.

"No! Not again. Come back. Sam!"

John's sister Lizbeth cried and clawed at him, her face red and swollen. "John's hurt! Help him, Nick. Help him!"

Nick ran for the elevator, pushed the up button frantically, but the doors wouldn't open. Banging on the metal doors until his hands were bruised, he finally bolted for the stairs and ran up six flights. Gasping for air, he emerged into the hallway. A woman dashed from John's apartment carrying a bloody knife, her face covered by a knitted scarf.

"John!" Nick sprinted into the apartment.

"Hey, Cappy," John said, emerging from the bedroom, blood coursing from the open wound in his neck. "What's up?"

"John…" Nick pressed his hands against John's neck, trying to make it stop. How could he lose this much blood and stay conscious? "Help! Somebody help us!"

"It's okay, Cappy." John's hand landed on Nick's shoulder. "I'll be all right."

Nick looked up to find John's face morphing into a smiling skeleton. He screamed.

"Nick," Sam said. "Wake up. Babe, wake up."

His head ached, his mouth was dry, his eyes gritty. "What?"

Sam brushed the hair off his forehead and kissed his cheek. "You were dreaming."

Nick rested a hand over his racing heart. "John was there. He was still alive. There was so much blood. I tried to make it stop." His throat tightening, he closed his eyes. "I couldn't stop it."

She held him close, running her fingers through his hair. "You couldn't have stopped it," she whispered.

"The stuff I've found out about him…since it happened…None of it matters. He was my friend."

"Yes." She pressed her lips to his forehead. "That'll never change."

"He was the closest thing to a brother I've ever had. We had this…language. It was all ours. The staff used to shake their heads when we'd get going. They had no idea what we were talking about. But we did. We always did."

Sam tightened her hold on him.

"I miss him," he whispered. "I really miss him. I just can't believe I'm never going to see him again."

"I'm sorry. I wish there was something I could say."

"You're helping." He raised his head, met her eyes.

She leaned in to kiss him. "I want to get the person who did this for his parents and his family. But mostly I want it for you."

"I'm apt to be a bit of a mess for a while."

"That's all right."

He rested his hand over the hideous bruise on her chest. "This is a hell of a time for us to be starting something. You know that, don't you?"

"Worst possible time."

"So it stands to reason we'll be able to deal with just about anything if we can get through this."

"I guess we'll find out." She smiled and caressed his face. "I need to get back to work."

"I know. Did you sleep?"

"Big time. I didn't think I would."

"You needed it. We both did." He leaned in to kiss her once more. "Are you or your dad going to mind that I plan to stay here with you until this is over?"

"No. I like having you here, and he doesn't really care, despite the grief he might give you."

"I need to go home at some point to get some clothes and make sure the condo association took care of getting the windows fixed."

"We can arrange that." She sat up and stretched. "I'm going to grab a shower. Care to join me?"

"I'd love to, but I'm not going to push my luck. I'll go after you."

"Wimp."

"Yep."

She laughed as she slipped into a robe, and the sound warmed him. He was surprised to realize she had made him feel better, even as the sickening images from the dream lingered. After Sam went into the bathroom, he sat up, gripping his pounding head. The concussion they'd called minor was making a major statement, and whatever they'd used to numb the cut over his eye had worn off, leaving a dull, throbbing ache.

He felt kind of foolish about unloading on Sam, but she hadn't seemed to mind. Having someone to share the ups and downs with was something he could get used to—as long as that someone was her.

He stood up and groaned when his injured foot protested. Reaching for his jeans, he pulled them on and took a good look around the messy room. Sam had a way of exploding into a space, which was in direct conflict with his need for order. Beginning with the clothes piled on the floor, he went to work on the clutter. By the time she emerged from the bathroom fifteen minutes later, the place was almost livable.

Her eyes all but popped out of her skull. "It's like you can't help yourself!"

"Just straightening up. No biggie."

"I won't be able to find anything!"

"You couldn't find anything before."

"I knew *exactly* where everything was."

"No way," he scoffed. "You're a slob, Samantha." He bunched the towel she had wrapped around her into his fist and tugged her close enough to kiss. "A sexy, gorgeous slob, but a slob nonetheless."

Pouting, she tried to break free of him. "Just because I'm not an anal retentive freakazoid, doesn't mean I'm a slob."

"Freakazoid? I'm hurt." With another hard kiss he released her so she could get dressed. "This is going to be a problem when we live together."

"*Live* together?" she sputtered, choking on the words. "Where the hell did *that* come from?"

"You don't have to act like the idea is totally repulsive."

She shoved her long legs into jeans. "We haven't even been together a week, Nick. I mean…come on."

Not wanting her to see that she'd hurt him by being so dismissive, he turned away from her to look out the window. He churned with things he'd like to say to her, arguments and persuasions she was clearly not ready to hear. As he stared out into the darkness, a shadow across the street caught his eye. Zeroing in for a closer look, he realized someone was watching the house. He ignored the screaming pain in his foot and the pounding in his head when he bolted for the door and flew down the stairs.

Sam called out to him.

Blasting through the front door and down the ramp, he was almost hit by a car as he ran into the street. The blare of the car's horn startled him, taking his attention off the shadow for just an instant, but that was all it took.

"Watch out, asshole!" the driver yelled out the car window.

By the time Nick recovered his bearings the shadow was long gone.

"*Shit!* Son of a bitch!"

"What're you doing?" Sam screamed from the porch.

"Someone was there," he said, his breath coming

out in white puffs in the cold air. "I saw him. Watching the house."

"So you just run out half-cocked, not to mention half-dressed?"

"What else was I supposed to do?"

She had her hands on her hips in a gesture he recognized by now as her seriously pissed stance. "Um, I don't know. Maybe tell the *cop* who was in the room with you?"

He limped back to the ramp and started up to where she waited for him. "I didn't think of it. All I thought about was getting him."

"And what were you going to do with him once you got him?"

Squirming under the heat of her blue-eyed glare, he shrugged. "I would've figured something out."

"That's *exactly* how civilians get themselves killed by the hundreds every year, thinking they can take the law into their own hands."

"I don't need you to lecture me or to keep using the word *civilian* like it's some kind of vermin."

"Vermin's got to be smarter than you just were."

"I almost had him."

"You almost got flattened by a car!"

Fuming, they stood there spitting nails at each other.

"Um, 'scuse me, but ah, I'm back," Freddie said from the sidewalk. "You said I should come here and, um…"

"Come up," Sam said, never taking her eyes off Nick. "Go in. I'll be right there."

"Gotcha, boss," Freddie said with a sympathetic smile for Nick as he went by them. "Good to see you again, Mr. Cappuano."

"Likewise," Nick said, still focused on Sam. "And you can call me Nick."

"You should've told me what you saw," Sam said after the door closed behind Freddie. "If you had, I could've called it in, and maybe we would've nabbed him. Instead, you go off on a Rambo mission that yielded squat."

Nick contemplated that. "You might have a point."

"I *might?* Really? Wow, thanks."

"I'm sorry, all right?" He ran a hand through his hair in frustration. "I just reacted. So shoot me for wanting to get whoever is stalking you."

"How do you know they're not stalking *you?*"

"Because I'm a whole lot more boring than you are."

"You're not boring. Stupid occasionally, but never boring."

"Thank you. I think."

"Did you get a good look at him?"

He shook his head. "Nothing but a shadow, but that shadow was definitely watching this house."

"If you see him again, *tell me.*" She pinched his chest hair and tugged just hard enough to raise him to his tiptoes and bring tears to his eyes. "Don't you *dare* risk yourself like that again. You got me?"

"I got it," he said through gritted teeth. After she released him, he rubbed a hand over his chest. "I only let you get away with that shit because I was taught it's bad manners to flatten a woman, even if she deserves it."

"Whatever," she retorted on her way back into the house where Skip, Celia and Freddie waited for them.

Skip's sharp eyes skirted over Nick's bare chest and feet.

"Um, I'm going to go find a shirt," Nick said, starting up the stairs.

"Might not be a bad idea," Skip said.

"Leave him alone, Dad," Sam said. "He's already convinced you're going to have him killed."

"Also not a bad idea. Why didn't I think of it?"

"*Dad…*"

"Relax and let me have some fun with the boy, will you? I so rarely get to have any fun these days."

Freddie smirked.

"What're you smiling at, Cruz?"

The smile faded. "Not a thing, ma'am. Not one thing."

"I assume you're not just here to bum another meal. What've you got for me?"

"Some of the others are heading over from HQ to help out," he said. "Want me to wait and brief everyone at the same time?"

"Give me the highlights."

By the time he had run through it, she had paced a path in the living room rug.

"I was thinking on the plane ride home," Freddie said, "that the other women he dated were like substitutes for the one he couldn't have. All of them resemble her in basic features, and I'm no shrink, but maybe he turned on the kink with them because he was frustrated he couldn't be with the one he wanted."

"That's probably why he freaked when Natalie pressured him about getting married. In his own twisted way, he felt like he was already married, even if he was unfaithful to her. I mean, how does he marry someone else when she's off raising his kid in Siberia?"

Nick came down the stairs, his hair wet from the shower.

"You heard all that?" Sam asked, alarmed by his pale face and flat eyes.

"Enough to get the gist."

"I'm sorry," she said, surprised when he shook off her sympathy.

"Don't protect me. Do your job. Find out who did it."

"Okay," she said, understanding that he was absorbing the blow the best way he knew how. Turning back to Freddie, she was interrupted when the front door swung open. In flooded most of the HQ detectives, carrying platters of food, six packs of beer and soda, and armloads of chips. Each of them paused to squeeze Skip's hand on their way into the kitchen to deposit the food.

"What the hell is this?" she asked Gonzo.

"They take a stab at you, they take one at all of us," he said, his chocolate brown eyes fierce. "Everyone's on their own time. Give us something to do."

Touched and on the verge of choking up, she said, "Thank you."

"They posted the LT list today. Congratulations."

"You'll be there soon enough," she said with a twinge of guilt over how she'd gotten there. Gonzo made detective a couple of years after her, so at least she hadn't snagged a spot from him. "For sure."

He shrugged. "We'll see."

"There was someone out there." She gestured to the door. "Nick saw him watching the house. He went vigilante on me and scared the guy off."

"I'll call it in and get someone posted outside."

"If it was just me, I wouldn't want it. But my dad's here and Celia…"

"Say no more. We're on it." He glanced over at Nick. "So. You and the witness, huh?"

She winced. "Don't."

Gonzo's handsome face lit up with amusement. "I won't, but others will. You have to know that."

"Hopefully, the gossip mill will run its course and the story will die a natural death when someone else fucks up."

"Not before you take some serious abuse."

"I can handle it."

"Sam?" Nick said. "Why don't you come have something to eat?"

"He likes to feed me," she whispered to Gonzo.

"Nothing wrong with that."

Thirty minutes later, after everyone had eaten, Sam called them into the living room. "Let's get back to work."

"Before we do that," Freddie raised his Coke bottle in salute to Sam, "a toast to my partner, soon-to-be *Lieutenant* Holland."

As Sam glared at him and plotted his slow, painful death, the room erupted into applause and whistles. She glanced at her father and found him watching her, his eyes bright with emotion.

He nodded with approval and pleasure—more pleasure than she'd seen on his face in two years.

"All right," she said, putting a stop to the merriment before they forgot they were there to work on a homicide. "Thanks for the food, the toast and the help. I appreciate it. Before we go any further, I need to ask if you all mind that Nick is here. He's been very helpful to us on the investigation—"

"He's been critical," Freddie said.

Sam sent him a grateful smile. "Still, if anyone's uncomfortable..."

"No problem for me," Gonzo said.

The others mumbled their agreement.

Sam released a breath she hadn't realized she'd been holding and turned to Freddie. "In that case, Cruz, let's hear what you found out in Chicago."

"You got it, boss."

TWENTY-SIX

"I ALSO DUG INTO the girlfriends like you asked me to," Freddie said, consulting his notebook. "Tara Davenport has no tattoos or unusual piercings. The people she says she was with on the night of the murder confirm her story, and security tapes show her arriving home at 10:18 and leaving again at 9:33 the next morning. Elin Svendsen's date, Jimmy Chen, a major muscle head, confirmed they had dinner and went to a dance club for a couple of hours. He dropped her off at her apartment just after two in the morning. The building has minimal security and no video, so I couldn't confirm that she stayed in for the rest of the night. She has a tattoo on her left breast—a heart with a Cupid's arrow—and both nipples are pierced."

"I don't even want to *know* how you found that out," Sam said, drawing chuckles from the other detectives.

"Not the way I would've preferred, that's for sure."

"Go, Cruz!" Detective Arnold said with a bark of laughter.

"Aw, our little boy's growing up," Gonzo said, dabbing at a pretend tear.

"Up yours, Gonzo."

In deference to her partner, Sam stifled the urge to laugh. "Is that it?"

"You didn't tell me to," Freddie continued, "but I dug a little deeper on Natalie Jordan. St. Clair was her maiden name, and I got a hit on that. Apparently our girl Natalie lost her college boyfriend in a suspicious fire in Maui about fifteen years ago."

"You don't say." Blood zipped through Sam's veins as pieces began to fall into place. Whether they were the right pieces, she'd soon find out.

"She and the senator had been broken up for years when he was killed," Skip said. "Hardly the same thing."

"True," Sam said. "Give us the details on the fire, Cruz."

"Brad Foster, age twenty-one, killed in a suspicious house fire while on a two-week vacation in Maui with Natalie St. Clair."

"Two weeks in Maui for a couple of college kids?" Gonzo asked with a low whistle.

"Apparently, Foster's family was loaded. His parents owned the beach house. Anyway, from the reports I found in the newspaper, Natalie went out for a morning walk and while she was gone the house went up. Police suspected arson but couldn't prove it. Her alibi for the time of the fire was flimsy. They looked really closely at her but never charged her with anything."

"Good work, Cruz," Sam said. "We'll have another chat with Mrs. Jordan tomorrow."

"I should also add that I found no unsolved dismemberment cases in the District, Virginia or Maryland," Freddie said. "I can widen the search if you think it's worth it."

"Hold off on that for now. Gonzo, what do you have from the search of O'Connor's cabin?"

"Nothing other than some additional references to the kid, Thomas—cards, letters, artwork from when he was younger—but you've already got that."

"What about the immigration bill, Dad?"

Skip took them through the finer points of the proposed law. "There's a lot of passion on both sides of this issue. There are those who feel that keeping our borders open to people in need is what this country is all about—'give me your tired, your poor, your huddled masses...'" When he was greeted with blank stares, he added, "Emma Lazarus? The poem engraved on the Statue of Liberty? Did you people go to school?" Rolling his eyes, he continued. "The other side argues that immigrants are a drain on the system, that charity should begin at home and we can't take care of the people who are already here."

"Would killing the senator kill the bill, too?" Sam asked Nick.

"That's exactly what it did. We had it sewn up by one vote. The Senate's in recess until January. Depending on who they get to take John's seat and whether he or she supports the bill, we might get lucky and get it back to the floor for a vote sometime next year. But either way, the supporters will have to start all over to make sure they have the votes. Even a month is a long time in politics—plenty of time for people to change their minds."

"So if someone was out to stop it altogether, killing him would accomplish that," Sam said.

"It'll certainly delay it indefinitely. Getting a bill through committee and on to the floor for a vote is no simple process. It took more than a year of writing, rewriting, compromising, meetings with various lobbies and interest groups, more compromise. Not simple."

Listening to him, Sam had a whole new appreciation for how John's death had affected Nick's professional life. The failure to pass the immigration bill had to be a bitter defeat on top of the personal tragedy. "In that case, his murder seems too well timed to be coincidental."

"Someone couldn't bear to see him get this win, you mean," Freddie said.

"Which takes us right back to his brother Terry," Sam said.

Nick shook his head.

"Speak," Sam said.

"I've said this before—Terry doesn't have the balls to kill his brother. He's an overgrown boy trying to live in a man's world. This would take planning and foresight. Terry's idea of making a plan is deciding which bar to hit on a given night."

"Still," Sam said, "he had motive, opportunity, a key and can't produce his alibi. I want to bring him in tomorrow morning for a formal interview."

"Can't that wait until after the funeral?" Nick asked, beseeching her with those hazel eyes of his.

"No. I'm sorry. I wish I could spare the O'Connors any more grief, but the minute they lied to me about Thomas, they lost the right to that courtesy. In fact, I could charge them with obstruction of justice."

"But you won't," Nick said stiffly.

"I haven't decided yet."

"I noticed Terry never completed the court-ordered safe driving school after his DUI," Freddie said.

Sam smiled as she turned to Gonzo and Arnold. "Will you pick up Terry O'Connor in the morning? While he's our guest, we'll have another chat with him about his alibi. Coordinate with Loudoun County."

"Can do," Arnold said.

"You're barking up the wrong tree," Nick said, frustration all but rippling from him.

"So noted." To the others, she said, "What've we got on the bombing?"

Higgins gave them an in-depth analysis of the four crude, homemade bombs they'd found attached to Sam's car and Nick's. "We got a partial print off one of the EDs on Mr. Cappuano's car, and we're running it through AFIS now," he said, referring to the Automated Fingerprint Identification System.

"We've worked our way through the Johnson family and the majority of their known associates," Detective Jeannie McBride said. "For the most part, they were hardly sympathetic to hear you'd nearly gotten blown up but were adamant that they had nothing to do with it." With a chagrinned expression, she added, "A few said they wished they'd thought of it."

"Nice," Nick muttered.

"We didn't pick up any vibe that an actual order had come from either of the Johnsons," McBride said.

"And it would have," Sam said. "After six months undercover with them, I can tell you nothing happens without one of them ordering it."

"Agreed," McBride said.

Sam ran her fingers through her hair, which she had left down the way Nick liked it. "I've got a bunch of shit running around in my head, so I want to go through it from the top if no one minds."

When the others nodded in agreement, she began with Nick finding the senator's body in his apartment. "He's murdered on the eve of a vote that would elevate his standing in the Senate by passing legislation on a hot-button issue. The murder itself, at least on the surface, is personal, with all the trimmings of a love affair gone wrong. However, as Detective Cruz correctly pointed out, the dismemberment could've been intended to throw us off, to send us down the personal road. Keep in mind there was no forced entry and no sign of a struggle, leading us to believe the killer was someone he knew, someone he was comfortable with and not surprised to see."

"And someone who had one of the many keys he'd given out," Freddie interjected.

"Yes. We've interviewed three of his past lovers, discovered he had a few fetishes, and uncovered a son his family kept hidden from the public for twenty years. The mother of that child appears, for all intents and purposes, to have been the love of his life and, for some reason, the only one who didn't experience his wilder side. It would stand to reason that his often-cavalier treatment of other women and his fixation with Internet porn stem directly from the stymieing of the most important sexual relationship in his life. That it wasn't allowed to flourish or take its natural course, set him up for all kinds of psychological issues that he worked hard to keep hidden from even the people closest to him." She glanced at Nick and found him staring at the wall, his face impassive.

"The senator's relationship with his parents, his father in particular, was complicated by the teenage pregnancy and the resulting child. When John reached adulthood, his father threatened to disown him if he married Patricia Donaldson or acknowledged his son. If Ms. Donaldson is to be believed, protecting his political career and reputation was more important to Graham O'Connor than his own grandchild." She looked to Freddie for confirmation. With his nod, she continued. "On the same night he discovered the senator's body, Mr. Cappuano reported an intruder in his house, which the Arlington police investigated. Toss in Destiny Johnson's threats in yesterday's paper and the bombing today. Is that everything?" She looked to Freddie. "Am I forgetting anything?"

"Stenhouse."

"Right—the O'Connors's bitter political rival. His motive would be derailing the bill and deflecting the accompanying glory that would have fallen on John, the son of a man he told us he hated."

"But he would've had no way into O'Connor's apartment," Freddie said. "Or at least he wouldn't have had a key."

"Which keeps him at the bottom of the list, but still a person of interest," Sam said. "A man in his position could probably get a key if he wanted one badly enough. So how's it all related? How's our dead senator related to a break-in at his chief of staff's house? If we've ruled out Johnson, how's it related to a bombing at the same location?"

"Maybe it isn't," Skip said.

All eyes turned to him.

Sam's brows knitted with confusion. "What do you mean, Dad?"

"Goes back to timing. What else has happened this week?" Before Sam could reply, he said, "In the course of the investigation, you've rekindled an old flame." He glanced at Nick. "Who might be put out by that?"

"We're both single, so other than my superiors, I can't think of anyone," she said, wondering where he was going with this.

"Are you sure?"

And then, all at once, she knew exactly what he was

talking about—or rather *whom*. "Peter," she gasped. "Oh my God." Curling her fist into her stomach, she had to sit when her legs would have buckled under her.

The room fell silent. Her rancorous divorce, complete with restraining orders and accusations of mental cruelty and emotional abuse, was hardly a secret to any of them.

Nick sat next to her, and Sam didn't object when his arm slid around her shoulders.

"He was outside the house," she whispered. "That was him before. He was watching us that night after we had pizza. I felt *something*, but I blew it off, chalked it up to nerves. I'll bet he was in your house, too."

"What would he want there?"

"First rule of combat," she said softly. "Know your enemy."

Nick turned to Skip. "What do we do?"

Skip shifted his furious eyes to Gonzo. "Call Malone. Report in, and then pick up Gibson."

"Yes, sir." Gonzo signaled to Arnold, his partner, and they left.

"I'm going with you," Freddie said, following them.

Sam got up and grabbed her coat off a hook by the door. "I just need some, ah, air." She rushed through the front door.

Nick was right behind her.

She struggled against his efforts to embrace her. "Just leave me alone, will you?"

"The hell I will." He pulled her in close and tightened his arms around her. "Don't push me away, Samantha."

"*He was watching us!* He was in your house! Because of *me!*"

"It's not your fault. Don't take it on."

"*How can I not?* He's obsessed." Another thought occurred to her all of a sudden.

"What?"

"The EDs," she whispered, the ramifications so huge, so monstrous it was almost too much to process.

"You don't think..."

She looked up at him. "That he'd rather kill me than see me with you? Yeah, I do, and if he couldn't take me out, getting rid of you would be the next best thing."

"Jesus."

"I told him everything about you after that night we spent together. When you didn't call, I told him about the connection we'd had, how I'd never had that before with anyone else. I thought he was my friend." She took a deep, rattling breath to stave off the pain circling in her gut. "He'd remember that. He'd know you were important, a real threat. The first real threat since he and I broke up."

"He'd be jealous enough to want to kill us both?"

"Destiny Johnson handed him the perfect opportunity with her tirade in the paper yesterday," Sam said as the whole thing clicked into focus with such startling clarity she wondered how she could've missed it. "If it had worked, the cops would naturally blame her or her friends. No one would've thought to look at him. It was so easy. He wouldn't have been able to resist." The pain gnawed at her insides, making her sick and weak.

"Would he know *how* to build a bomb?"

"You can get how-to instructions for just about anything on the Internet these days." She winced at the claws stabbing her gut. "Higgins said the EDs were crude. I guess we were lucky Peter screwed it up."

"You're in pain."

"Just need to breathe," she panted.

He loosened his hold on her. "What can I do? You're scaring me, Sam."

Clutching her midsection, she looked up at him. "I've dragged you into a nightmare."

"I'm exactly where I want to be—where I've wanted to be since the night I met you. And if I get my hands on that ex-husband of yours before you do, I'll be sure to let him know that he might've sent us on a long detour but we found our way back to each other." He kissed her, gently at first and then with more passion when she responded in kind. "Despite him, we found our way back, and nothing's going to get in our way this time. Nothing and no one."

"Especially not a couple of bombs," she said with a weak smile.

"That's right." He returned her smile. "How's the belly?"

"Better," she said, surprised to realize it was true.

"We're going to do something about that. As soon as this case is closed, you're going to see my doctor friend Harry."

"You and what army will be taking me?"

"You'll find out if you don't go on your own."

Her heart hammered in her chest as she studied him. "There're things...about me...that I need to tell you, stuff you should know before you decide anything."

Cradling her face in his hands, he looked down at her with his heart in his eyes. "There's nothing you could tell me that would make me not want to be with you. Nothing."

"You don't know that—"

His mouth came down hard on hers, stealing the

words, the thoughts, the air and every ounce of reason. When he had kissed her into submission, he said, "I do know that."

"But—"

"I love you, Samantha. I've loved you from the first instant I ever saw you across a crowded deck at that party and for all the years since. Having you back in my life is the single best thing that's ever happened to me. So there's nothing, nothing at all, you could tell me that would change my mind about you or what I want from you."

Sam rarely found herself speechless, but as she looked up at his beautiful, earnest face—the face she had dreamed about during her miserable marriage—she simply couldn't find the words.

Without breaking the intense eye contact between them, he brushed his lips over hers in a kiss so sweet and undemanding that her knees went weak.

"Later," he said. "We'll have all the time in the world. I promise."

TWENTY-SEVEN

THEY BORROWED CELIA'S CAR to go to Arlington. After an upsetting day, the neighborhood had returned to tranquility, and the media had thankfully moved on to the next story. At Nick's house, the windows had been repaired, but broken glass crunched under their feet in the foyer and upstairs in his bedroom. "I'll still be cleaning up glass a year from now," he joked, attempting to make light of it since he could feel the distress radiating from her.

"I'm sorry."

"Don't go there, Samantha." He threw jeans, sweaters, underwear, T-shirts and socks into a large duffel bag. With the funeral scheduled for Monday, he packed a dark suit, dress shirt and tie into a garment bag and tossed a pair of wingtips into the duffel. In the bathroom, he grabbed what he needed as fast he could, not wanting her to be there any longer than necessary after what happened earlier.

He'd told her he loved her. Just blurted it out because he thought she needed to hear it right then. He told himself it didn't matter that she hadn't said it back. She would. Eventually. But what if she didn't? What if she'd been swept up by the craziness of the investigation, and he'd read her all wrong? No. That wasn't possible. Couldn't be possible.

"Nick?"

"What, babe?"

"You just went all still. What're you thinking about?"

He cleared the emotion and fear from his throat. "I'm wondering if they found Peter."

"They'll call me. They know he's mine once they bring him in."

"You're going to confront him?"

"I'm going to nail him."

"Why don't you let someone else do it? Why does it have to be you?"

"Because it does."

"That's it?"

She shrugged. "Yeah."

"What if I ask you not to?"

"Don't."

"Would it matter? If I did ask?"

"It would matter. And I'd take that in with me, and it'd throw me off. I want to be at one hundred percent when I confront that miserable excuse for a human being. So don't send me in there dragging baggage. Don't do that to me."

"Is that what I am? Baggage?"

"What the hell happened between my house and here?"

He zipped the duffel. "Nothing. Not a goddamned thing."

She grabbed his arm and spun him around to face her. "Are you mad that I didn't say it back?"

"What're you talking about?" he asked, his heart aching.

"You know." Her tone softened as she raised her hands to his face. "Everything is so insane—the investigation, my psychopathic ex-husband, your loss and your job situation, my stomach…even the freaking holidays are bearing down on me. After what I went through with Peter, I'm different than I used to be. I'm more cautious. I haven't been cautious with you, though, and that scares me." She laughed. "It terrifies me, actually."

"You have nothing to fear from me."

"I know that, but I've screwed up so badly in the past. I need time, when I don't have fifty other things on my mind, to think and to process everything that's happened this week. I can't do that right now. But if it helps at all, I can tell you I'm moving in the same direction you are."

"It does help to know that." He reached for her hands and brought them to his lips. "Will you promise me one thing?"

"If I can."

"Will you spend Christmas Eve with me here? No matter what happens in the next few days, will you save that one night for me?"

"We usually go to my sister's…"

"We can do whatever you want on Christmas Day."

"All right."

"Promise?"

"I promise." She went up on tiptoes to kiss him. "I can't believe Christmas is Wednesday, and I haven't bought a thing for anyone. What about you?"

"Not too many people on my list. I usually get something for Christina, the O'Connors, my dad's twins, John…"

"I'm sorry. I wasn't thinking. About your family situation."

"Don't sweat it." He shut off the light in the bedroom and led her downstairs.

She stood in the living room with her hands jammed into her coat pockets. "What you said earlier, about us living together?"

"Too much, too soon. I get it."

"What I was going to say is if, you know, we get to that, I couldn't live here. It's too far from the city and my dad."

"Okay."

"That simple?"

"It's just a house."

She studied him. "When are you going to turn into a jerk?"

"Any minute now. I've been meaning to get to that."

Her cell phone rang, and she pulled it from her pocket. "It's Freddie." She put it on speaker so Nick could hear. "What've you got?"

"No sign of him at his place, but we found wires, plastic and fertilizer sitting right out on the table. Gonzo requested a warrant for a full search, and we're just waiting on that now."

She sat down. "I was hoping it wasn't him. I was really hoping…"

"I'm sorry. We've issued an APB. Every cop in the city is looking for him. We'll get him, Sam."

"Thanks. Go on home. Get some sleep. Meet me at HQ at eight. We'll put in a half day."

"I'll be there. Are you okay?"

"Overall, I've had better days, but I'm okay. See you in the morning."

Nick dropped the duffel and suit bag by the front door and joined her on the sofa.

"I was so hoping he was just stalking me and we

wouldn't be able to pin the EDs on him. I didn't want it to be him."

Nick put his arm around her and brought her in to rest against him. "I know, babe."

"The papers tomorrow will be all about me—the bomb, my relationship with you, my psycho ex-husband. They'll rehash Johnson, run through my dad's unsolved case." She scrubbed at her face. "I hate when the story is about me. It's been about me too often lately."

"You're so tired," he said, kissing her brow. "Do you want to sleep here tonight?"

"I'd rather stay close to home until we get Peter. He knows my dad is an Achilles heel of mine."

Standing, Nick held out a hand to help her up.

She surprised him when she wrapped her arms around him. "Can we just do this for a minute?"

He kissed the bruised bump on her forehead. "For as long as you want."

They were interrupted several minutes later by a knock on the door.

"Wonder who's here at this hour." Nick swung the door open and was startled to find Natalie Jordan on his doorstep. "Natalie? What're you doing here?" He wouldn't have thought she even knew where he lived.

Her eyes rimmed with red, she said, "May I come in for a minute?"

Nick glanced back at Sam, who nodded. He showed Natalie into the living room.

"I was hoping you'd be here," Natalie said to Sam. Her face was splotchy, as if she'd been crying for hours.

"What can I do for you?" Sam asked.

To Nick, Natalie said, "Would it be possible to get a glass of water?"

Nick made eye contact with Sam. "Sure." When he returned with the water, Natalie had taken a seat on the sofa and was focused on her hands in her lap.

Sam looked at him and shrugged.

"Here you go," Nick said, handing Natalie the glass of water.

"Thank you."

"It's really late, Natalie," Nick said. "Why don't you tell us why you're here?"

"It's so unreal," she said softly. "I still can't believe it..."

"Mrs. Jordan, we can't help you if we don't know what you're talking about," Sam said.

Looking up at them with shattered eyes, Natalie said, "Noel. I think he..."

"What did Noel do?" Nick asked, his heart beating harder all of a sudden. He wanted to take Natalie by the shoulders and shake it out of her. "What did he do?"

"He might've killed John."

"Why do you say that?" Sam asked.

Nick noticed that she'd slipped into her cop mode, all signs of her earlier dismay over Peter gone.

"He's been acting funny, leaving at odd hours, long silences. He seems very angry, but he won't tell me why."

"When I talked to you earlier in the investigation, you didn't mention any of this."

"I hadn't put two and two together yet."

"Tell me what you think you've put together."

"That night," Natalie said haltingly, "the night John was killed, we went to bed together, but I woke up in the middle of the night and he was gone."

"You never mentioned that before."

"He's my husband, Detective." Natalie's eyes flooded with new tears. "I couldn't believe it was even possible. I didn't want to believe it's possible."

"So what changed?" Nick asked. "Why did you come here?"

"You were John's friend," Natalie said to Nick. "I thought you'd want to help find the person who did this to him."

"Of course I do! But I want the truth!"

"So do I! I loved him! You know I did. Noel was jealous of him. I couldn't even mention John's name without setting him off."

"What do you think set him off enough to want to kill him?" Sam asked.

"We saw John a couple of weeks before he died. It was at a cocktail party the Virginia Democrats had at Richard Manning's house." Natalie wiped new tears from her cheeks. "John came over to me, gave me a friendly hug and kiss. We talked for a long time, just catching up on each other's lives. It was nothing. But I looked over at one point and saw Noel watching us. He looked like he could kill us both on the spot."

"Why didn't you mention any of this to us the other day?" Sam asked.

"I didn't want to believe it."

"You still haven't said what changed your mind."

"I asked him." She ran a trembling hand through her disheveled hair. "Straight out. 'Did you kill John?' He denied it of course, but I don't believe him." To Nick, she said, "I didn't know what to do, so I came over here, hoping you'd put me in touch with Detective Holland."

"Do you have somewhere you can go where you'll be safe?" Sam asked.

Natalie nodded. "My parents' home in Springfield."

"Give me some time to look into this," Sam said.

"He's powerful," Natalie said. "You'll never be able to pin this on him."

"If he did it, I'll pin it on him," Sam assured her.

Natalie stood up to leave. "I'm sorry to barge in on you. I heard about what happened earlier. I'm glad you weren't seriously hurt."

They walked her to the door. "Tomorrow, I'll want to get all of this on the record." Sam pulled her ever-present notebook from her back pocket. "Write down your parents' address and a phone number where I can reach you."

Natalie did as she asked. "Thank you for listening." To Nick, she added, "I know I was never your favorite person—"

"That's neither here nor there."

"Anyway, thank you."

They watched her walk to her car.

"She's full of shit," Nick said, his eyes intensely focused on Natalie's car as it drove away. "I don't believe her for one minute."

"What don't you believe? That her jealous husband could've killed the man his wife never stopped loving? That's as good a motive as I've heard yet."

"I know Noel Jordan. He's not made of that kind of stuff. If you ask me, she is, though. I could very easily see her losing her shit with John and killing him for not loving her enough. After what we heard earlier about her ex-boyfriend dying in a suspicious fire, you believe it's possible, too."

"Why would she come here, seeking out the lead detective on the case, if she was the one who did it? Think about that, Nick."

"Why didn't you ask her about what happened to her boyfriend in Hawaii?"

"I didn't want to tip my hand on that just yet. As long as she thinks we don't know about it, she might be more forthcoming."

"I don't like her. I've never liked her, and I don't care what you say, she's lying. She'll do anything it takes to advance her agenda, even if it means tossing her husband under the bus."

Sam checked her watch. "I wonder what time Noel goes to bed."

"You're actually going to do something with that pile of bullshit she just fed you?"

"Of course I am. This could be the break we've been waiting for."

He ushered her out of the house and locked the door behind them. "You're wasting your time."

"It's my time to waste."

"It's almost midnight."

"I know what time it is. If you'd rather stay here, I can go by myself."

"You're not going anywhere by yourself as long as your ex-husband is out there waiting for another chance to kill you."

"I don't need you to protect me, Nick. I'm more than capable of taking care of myself."

Silently, he ushered her into the car and a few minutes later took the exit for the George Washington Parkway, heading toward Alexandria. "You really think I could go home and go to bed and actually *sleep*, knowing you're out here by yourself confronting a potential killer while your ex waits for his next opportunity?"

"I've been in tighter spots."

"That was before."

"Before what?"

"Before me."

"I'm not one of those women who finds this whole alpha-male act sexy. In fact, it's a major turn off."

"Whatever."

They rode to Belle Haven in stony silence. Sam didn't speak until she had to direct him to the dark house. She retrieved her gun and badge from her purse and tucked them into her coat pockets. "Wait here."

As if she hadn't spoken, Nick emerged from the car and followed her up the walk.

"I told you to wait!"

"You're not going in there alone, Sam. It's either me, or I call 911." He held up his cell phone defiantly. "What's it going to be?"

They engaged in a silent battle of wills until Sam finally said, "Don't say a word. Do you hear me? Not one freaking word." She spun around and marched up the front stairs to ring the bell. It echoed in the big house. They waited a couple of minutes before a light went on upstairs. Through the beveled windows next to the door, Sam watched Noel come down the stairs.

He peeked through the window before he opened the door. "Sergeant Holland?" Blinking, he glanced at Nick.

"Yes," Sam said. "I'm sorry to call on you so late." Begrudgingly, she added, "I believe you know Nick Cappuano."

"Of course. Come in." Noel's blond hair stood on end. He wore a T-shirt from a road race with flannel pajama pants and hardly resembled the second-ranking attorney at the U.S. Department of Justice she had met the other day.

Nick and Noel shook hands as he ushered them into the house.

"What can I do for you?"

"Is Natalie here?" Sam asked, feeling him out.

Noel's genial expression faded. "She flew out of here in a rage after we had a fight earlier. She must be at her parents' house."

"Is that something that happens often?" Sam asked. "The rages?"

"It's not the first time, but I think it's going to be the last. I can't believe what she accused me of! She thinks I could actually *kill* John O'Connor. Can you even imagine?"

"People have killed over jealousy before."

"I see that she's voiced her suspicions to you." Noel ran his hands through his hair. "What do you want, Detective?"

"Why did you tell me that you attended the Big Brother/Big Sister event the night John was killed?"

"Because I had it in my date book."

"Your date book was off by a week."

Noel seemed startled to hear that. "My secretary keeps it up for me." He thought for a moment. "You know, you're right. It was two weeks ago. I'm really sorry about that. Things have been insane at work lately, and at home…"

"What's been going on at home?" Nick asked.

Sam glowered at him. "I'll ask the questions." Turning back to Noel, she said, "Things have been tense between you and Natalie?"

"More so than usual since we saw John at a fundraiser a couple of weeks ago. She knows how I feel about her talking and flirting with him in public, so what does she do? Flaunts her 'friendship' with him right in front of my face—and everyone in the room is talking about the two of them. How do you think that makes me feel?"

"Disrespected?" Nick said.

"I said to be quiet!" Sam hissed.

Noel directed an ironic chuckle at Nick that infuriated Sam.

"I guess you can relate, huh?" Noel said to Nick.

They followed Noel into the living room where he poured himself a drink from a crystal decanter.

Sam shook her head when he offered them one.

"Don't mind if I do," Nick said, earning another glare from Sam.

"Were you jealous of John?" Sam asked, anxious to wrestle the interview back from the old boy's club.

Noel handed Nick a drink and took a seat on the sofa. "I was sick of him. I was sick of hearing about him, sick of running into him. Mostly, I was sick of being her consolation prize."

"Why didn't you tell me any of this the other day?" Sam asked.

Swirling the amber liquor around his glass, Noel glanced at her. "Because I love her." He smiled, but it didn't reach his eyes. "Pathetic, huh? She has almost no regard for me or my feelings, yet I love her anyway."

"Were you sick enough of John O'Connor to kill him, Mr. Jordan?"

"No! Of course not. I didn't kill him."

"I'd like to give you a polygraph in the morning," Sam said.

"Fine. I have nothing to hide."

"Natalie said she woke up in the middle of the night John was killed and you were gone?"

"I was out running. I do that when I can't sleep."

"Do you think Natalie continued to see John after you were married?"

"We ran into him quite frequently. I've told you that."

"I don't mean in public."

Sam watched as her meaning dawned on him.

"You're not suggesting…"

"I'm not suggesting anything. I'm just asking."

"If she'd been seeing him, it's certainly without my knowledge." He took a long sip of whiskey, and Sam noticed a slight tremble in his hand.

"Do you think there's any way she killed him?"

"I'd like to say no way, but I honestly don't know anymore what she's capable of. I used to think I knew her. All I can say is she's been genuinely distraught since we heard he was dead. No doubt she's more upset than she would've been if it had been me who'd been murdered. And I'm the one who actually married her."

"Do you know about her ex-boyfriend who died in Hawaii?"

He nodded. "Brad. She's had more than her share of heartbreak, that's for sure."

Sam stood up. "I'm sorry to have disturbed you, but I appreciate your candor. I'll have someone contact you in the morning about the polygraph."

At the door, Noel said, "I didn't kill him, Sergeant. But it doesn't break my heart that someone else did."

"I KNOW YOU'RE dying to tell me what you think," Sam said as they crossed the 14th Street Bridge on the way back to Capitol Hill.

"I was told to be quiet."

"I don't want to fight with you, Nick. That's the last thing I need right now."

"I don't want that, either. But you're asking a lot expecting me not to worry about you. He tried to *blow you up*."

"We're both kind of raw today," she said, reaching for his hand. "I really do want your impression of Noel."

"So you value my opinion?"

"Yes!"

Laughing, he curled his fingers around hers.

Right away, Sam felt better.

"He didn't do it," Nick said, "but he's not a hundred percent certain that she didn't."

"My thoughts exactly."

"I still say she's the one. She wanted John, he rejected her and she's never gotten over that."

"So why now? What sent her over the edge?"

"Maybe she didn't want to see him get the big win with the immigration bill."

"Why would she care about that? I keep coming back to that, to the timing of it all on the eve of that vote. *Why then?*"

"I can't see how the bill would have any impact whatsoever on Natalie," Nick said.

"Maybe the bill has nothing at all to do with his murder."

"I find that hard to believe."

"Yeah," Sam said, staring out the window. "Me, too."

TWENTY-EIGHT

SAM TOSSED AND TURNED. She dreamed about Peter, Quentin Johnson and Natalie Jordan, and for once she actually remembered the dreams when she awoke with a start, her heart racing. Glancing at the bedside clock, she saw it was just after three and realized Nick wasn't in bed with her. Her eyes darted around the dark room and found him standing at the window, the glow of a street light illuminating his tall frame.

Taking a moment to appreciate his muscular back, she remembered him telling her he loved her and was filled with a warm feeling of contentment and safety that was all new to her. Then she remembered arguing with him over Noel and Natalie, and her stomach took a sickening dip. The soaring highs and crushing lows were just one reason why she'd stayed away from men since she broke up with Peter, who never would've been as civil as Nick had been during a fight. Even though they'd disagreed, Sam didn't doubt for a minute that he loved her. That made him as different from Peter as a man could get.

She got up and went to Nick. Slipping her arms around him from behind, she pressed her lips to his back. "What're you doing up?"

He rested his hands over hers. "Couldn't sleep."

"He's not stupid enough to come back here. By now he knows we're looking for him."

"I think I could kill him if I got my hands on him. I really think I could. Not just because of the bombs, but all those years ago, too. All the years we could've had."

"He's not worth losing sleep over, Nick." She turned him so he faced her and shivered with desire when he ran his hands over her while looking down at her with hot, needy eyes. Looping her arms around his neck, she gasped when he lifted her and carried her back to bed. "I thought you were mad with me."

"I am," he said in an unconvincing tone as he snuggled her against him and pulled the comforter up around them. "Try to get some sleep."

She dragged a lazy finger from his chest to his belly and smiled when he trembled under her touch.

"*Sleep*, Samantha."

"What if I don't *want to,* Nick?" she asked, curling her hand around his erection.

"I'm sleeping," he said with an exaggerated yawn. "And I'm mad with you."

Laughing, she clamped her teeth down on his nipple.

"*Ow!* That hurt!"

"But you're not asleep anymore," she said with a victorious smile as she raised herself up to plant wet kisses on his belly while continuing to stroke him.

His fingers combed through her hair. "You're going to be tired again tomorrow."

"Then I'd better make it count." She straddled him and teased him by sliding her wet heat over his hard length, her nails lightly scoring his chest.

He arched his back, seeking her.

"Maybe you're right," she said, stopping. "We should get some sleep."

Growling, he surged up and entered her with a hard thrust that took her breath away.

"Mmm," she sighed, closing her eyes and letting her head fall back in bliss. "All right, if you insist."

"I insist. Sleep is highly overrated." He brought her down to him and fused his lips to hers, his tongue flirting and enticing.

When she needed to breathe, Sam broke the kiss and moved with painstaking slowness, rising up until they were barely connected, and then taking him deep again. If his sharp intake of air was any indication, he liked it. A lot. So she stopped. "Are you still mad at me?"

"Yes." With his hands on her hips, he tried to control the pace, but she wouldn't be controlled. "Sam..." He moaned, his eyes closed, his jaw tight with tension. "Babe..." Overpowering her, he held her in place and pumped into her. "Come for me. Now."

She rolled her hips, but the orgasm hovered just out of reach. "I *can't*," she whimpered.

Without losing their connection, he turned them over and gave it to her hard and fast, the way she'd told him she liked it, as he sucked her nipple into his mouth and flicked his tongue back and forth.

She cried out when she reached the climax that had eluded her.

Calling out her name, he went with her.

Her fingers danced through the dampness on his back. "You didn't have to do that."

He raised his head and found her eyes in the milky darkness. "Do what?"

"Wait for me." Her cheeks burned with embarrassment, and she was grateful for the dark.

He kissed her. "I'll always wait for you."

"It doesn't always happen."

"It has with me unless you've been faking."

She smacked his shoulder. "I haven't!"

"I know," he said, laughing as he rolled to his side and brought her with him.

"It's been an issue…in the past."

"It's not an issue now."

Reaching up to caress his face, she pressed her lips to his neck and breathed in the warm spicy scent she was quickly coming to crave. "I guess the right partner makes all the difference, even when he's mad with you."

"Especially then." His fingers danced over her hip, sending a new shiver of desire racing through her. "Want to try for a two-fer?"

"That *never* happens."

He eased her onto her back and kissed his way down the front of her. "Baby, I *love* a challenge."

SAM SKIPPED THROUGH her morning routine with far more energy than she should have had. Multiple orgasms had multiple benefits. Who knew? With one last glance at Nick sleeping on his belly, she went downstairs in desperate need of a soda. As the first blessed mouthful cruised through her system, she realized she had no way to get to HQ.

Laughing softly, she called Freddie and asked him to pick her up. Since her dad wasn't up yet, she decided to wait for Freddie on the front porch. She surveyed the quiet street, wondering if Peter was out there somewhere watching her and waiting for his next opportunity. They would've called her if they'd found him, so she knew it was possible he was watching her.

"Come and get me, you bastard. You won't catch me off guard a second time."

As she took another long drink of soda, Freddie's battered Mustang came around the corner with a loud backfire.

"Gonna wake up the whole freaking neighborhood," she grumbled.

He pulled up to the house and leaned over to unlock the passenger door.

"Do I need a tetanus shot before I ride in this thing?"

"What's that they say about beggars and choosers?"

She battled with the seatbelt. "I've got to requisition a new ride."

"I'll take care of that for you, boss." He offered her one of the powdered donuts from the package on his lap.

With a scowl, she took one and turned so she could see him. "You've done some good work on this case, Cruz. Damn good."

His face lit up with pleasure. "Thanks. So after I got home last night, I was kinda wired and couldn't sleep, ya know?"

"Uh huh." Her face flushed when she thought of how she'd worked off her own tension.

"I got to thinking that maybe there's some sort of connection besides the sexual kind between O'Connor and one of our people of interest."

"What kind of connection?"

"A domestic—cook, caterer, cleaning lady, gardener."

"Possible. Where you going with it?"

"I know this is way out there, but what if one of the domestics found out about the kid, Thomas, and told someone who'd be infuriated by it?"

"Worth looking into."

"You think?"

"When are you going to start having some faith in yourself and your instincts?"

"I don't know. Soon. I hope."

"So do I, because you're starting to piss me off."

"You know what pisses me off?" He took his eyes off the road long enough to glance at her. "Your scumbag ex-husband. He pisses me off."

"Yeah," she sighed. "Me, too."

"It's all over the papers."

"I knew it would be."

"I have it there. In the backseat if you wanted to..."

Her stomach twisted in protest. "That's all right. Thanks."

"He had pictures of you all over his place. It was totally creepy. There were shots of you from a distance working crime scenes, and he even had a police scanner."

Sam's stomach took a dive at that news. "I should've known he wouldn't just give up and go away. I should've known that."

"This isn't your fault," he said fiercely.

"So Natalie Jordan paid us a visit last night," Sam said, anxious to change the subject. She relayed what Natalie told them and went over their visit with Noel. "I don't think he did it, but I want to get him on a polygraph today. Will you set that up?"

"Sure thing. I don't see Noel for it, either. Nothing about him screamed 'murderer' to me. Natalie, on the other hand, she's a cool customer."

"Nick said she's lying about Noel, but he's never liked her."

"He's got good instincts, though," Freddie said.

"Do me a favor when we get in, ask Gonzo and Arnold to check out this address." She gave him the slip of paper with Natalie's parents' address. "And have them go by Noel Jordan's house in Belle Haven. Get me a couple of hours of surveillance on him before you bring him in."

"Got it. Will do." As they pulled up to the last intersection before the public safety building, he said, "Shit." He pointed at the street leading to HQ, lined with TV trucks bearing satellite dishes.

"Goddamn it."

He scowled at her choice of words. "Let's go in through the morgue."

"Good plan."

They parked on the far side of the building, entered through the basement door and took a circuitous route to the detectives' pit where Gonzo and Arnold waited for them.

"We've got Terry O'Connor in lockup. He's lawyering up."

"Figured."

"They filmed us bringing him in," Arnold said. "It'll be the lead story this morning."

Captain Malone burst through the door. "The chief just got off the phone with a very angry Senator O'Connor. He's threatening to call the president."

"He can call anyone he wants," Sam said. "His son had motive, a key and can't produce his supposed alibi. If he was anyone else, we would've had him in here days ago, and you know it. I need to rule him out."

They stared each other down for a long moment before Malone blinked. "Get him into interview and either charge him or let him go. And do it quickly."

"Yes, sir." To Gonzo, she added, "Bring him up."

TWENTY-NINE

WHEN SAM AND FREDDIE entered the small interrogation room, Terry O'Connor leaped to his feet. "I didn't kill my brother! How many times do I have to tell you that?"

She pretended to gaze intently into the file she had carried into the room with her. "The reason you're here is you failed to attend the safe driving course the judge ordered after your DUI."

"You aren't serious."

Sam glanced at Freddie.

"She's serious," Freddie said.

"I meant to," Terry stammered.

"Why don't we talk about why we're really here?" the attorney said.

"Give me a lie detector."

Grabbing Terry's shirt, the attorney yanked him into a chair. "Shut up, Terry."

"Mr. O'Connor, have you been advised of your rights?" Sam asked.

"The cops you sent to haul me out of my parents' house before dawn went through all that," he spat back at her.

"Do we have your permission to record this interview?"

"At the advice of counsel," the attorney drawled in

a honeyed Southern accent, "Mr. O'Connor will cooperate with this farce—within reason."

"Isn't that good of him?" Sam asked Freddie.

"Real good," Freddie agreed as he turned on the recorder and noted for the record who was in the room and why.

"It's now been ninety-six hours since your brother's body was discovered in his apartment," Sam said. "You say you spent the night of the murder with a woman you met in a Loudoun County bar. Can you give me her name?"

"No," Terry said, dejected.

"Have you found anyone who can confirm you left the establishment with this imaginary woman?"

"She wasn't imaginary!" he cried, slapping his hand on the table.

"Witnesses?"

He slumped back into his chair. "No."

"That kind of puts you in a bit of a pickle, doesn't it?" she asked as Nick's words echoed through her mind—*you're barking up the wrong tree with Terry.* She had to admit that the buzz she got from knowing she had a suspect's nuts on the block and all she had to do was lower the boom was missing here.

"Is there a relevant question coming any time soon?" the attorney drawled.

Sam hammered Terry hard for ninety minutes, reduced him to a whimpering, sniveling baby, but he never deviated from his original statement. Finally, needing to regroup, she asked for a word with Freddie in the hallway.

Malone waited for them outside the observation room door. "Spring him."

Frustration pooled in her aching belly. She nodded to Freddie. "Tell him to stay local and to get that safe driving class done within thirty days."

"Got it."

When they were alone, she looked up at Malone. "I had to rule him out."

"And you all but have." He lowered his voice. "They brought Peter in thirty minutes ago."

"He's mine."

"No one's saying otherwise. But you know we can take care of him if you aren't up to it—"

"I'm up to it—after he chills in the cooler for a little while longer."

"As a courtesy, I let Skip know we had him."

"Thanks."

"The partial print off the ED on Cappuano's car had similarities to Peter's, but they couldn't make a definitive ID."

"I'll get him to confirm the print is his," she said, more to herself than to Malone.

"With what we found in his apartment, we've more or less already got him." He handed her a rundown of what the warrant had yielded and a folder full of photos that made her sick.

"But he doesn't know that," she said.

"Nope."

She looked up at the captain. "I think I'm going to enjoy this. Does that make me a bad cop?"

"No, it makes you human. Arlington will want him when we're done with him."

With a nod, she left him to go buy another soda and took it back to her office. Closing the door, she dropped into her chair suddenly exhausted and drained. She hadn't seen Peter, except for in court, in almost two years. Their last explosive argument over the time she was spending with her newly paralyzed father had put the finishing touches on what had been a horrible four years for her. The next day, she'd moved her essentials into her father's house and put the rest of her belongings in storage where they remained.

In the ensuing months, Peter had popped up with such annoying regularity that she'd been forced to get a restraining order to keep him from coming around while they hurled accusations back and forth. Since then she'd often had the sensation of being watched or followed, little pinpricks of awareness on the back of her neck that had never materialized into an actual confrontation. In fact, it hadn't occurred to her that he'd still be so invested in her. She should've known better. What made her truly sick was that she had endangered Nick just by spending time with him.

Imagining Peter locked up in a cell in the basement, she smiled. "Let him sit there for a while longer wondering how much we know." The idea infused her with joy as she drank her soda and returned her attention to the O'Connor case.

NICK WOKE UP ALONE in Sam's bed and shifted onto her pillow to breathe in the scent she'd left behind. He contemplated whether he should stay there until she got home or get up to face her father. Staying in bed all day was definitely the more appealing of the two options. But since he didn't want her to think he was a total coward, he got up to take a shower.

He took his time getting dressed in jeans and a long-sleeved polo shirt. How ridiculous was it that he was afraid to go downstairs to face a man in a wheelchair?

"You're being an ass," he said to his bomb-battered reflection in the mirror. Still, he took another ten minutes to make the bed and straighten up the room while marveling that one woman could own so many shoes. When there was nothing left to do, he finally started down the stairs and almost groaned when he found Skip by himself in the kitchen. Couldn't even Celia have been there to provide a buffer?

"Morning," Nick said.

"Morning," Skip muttered. "There's coffee."

"Thanks." As Nick filled a mug that had been left by the pot, he felt the heat of the other man's eyes on his back. "Sam got an early start."

"I heard her leave about seven-thirty. Celia's downstairs doing laundry, but she made bacon and eggs. Plates are up there in the cabinet."

"That sounds good." Wondering if he'd be able to eat under the watchful eyes of Sam's dad, Nick brought the plate and coffee to the table. They sat in awkward silence for several minutes before Nick put down his fork and worked up the courage to look over at the older man. "I love her."

"If I thought otherwise you wouldn't have slept in her bed last night. I don't care how old she is."

Taken aback, Nick stared at him. "I wanted to go with her today."

"She wouldn't have let you."

"Still, until this thing with Peter is cleared up…"

"They snagged him this morning at Union Station, buying a one-way ticket to New York."

"Is that so?"

"Yep."

"Well, that's a relief."

"She's gonna have a go at him. I don't know about you, but I'd kind of like to see that."

"How about I drive you?"

SAM TOOK A series of deep breaths to calm her churning stomach before she picked up the folder of material gathered from Peter's apartment, opened her office door, signaled to Freddie, and headed for the interrogation room where she'd asked the uniforms to put Peter. The quiet in the normally buzzing detectives' cubicles told her she'd have a good-size audience watching in observation.

"He's apt to come at me," Sam said to Freddie before they went in. "Don't stop him."

"Are you out of your freaking mind?"

"Let me handle this my way, Cruz."

"Fine, but if it appears he's about to kill you, you'll have to excuse me if I get in the way of that."

"Deal." With a small smile for Freddie, she stepped into the room. Peter had aged since she last saw him. His sandy hair was now shot through with silver, and the face she'd once found handsome was hard and lined with bitterness.

Nodding to release the officer guarding him, Sam stepped up to the table.

"I want someone else," he said without looking at her.

"Tough."

"This is a conflict of interest."

"We're not married anymore, so no it isn't. Detective Cruz, please record this interview with Peter Gibson."

Freddie clicked on the recorder and returned to his post by the door, sending the signal that this one belonged to Sam.

"You've been advised of your rights, including your right to an attorney?"

"Don't need one. You've got nothing on me." Peter raised his cuffed hands. "Is this really necessary?"

"Detective Cruz, please un-cuff Mr. Gibson." When Freddie didn't immediately comply, she said, "Detective."

Freddie stalked past her and released the cuffs. Scowling at her, he returned to the door.

Peter rubbed his wrists. "Kind of a lot of drama over nothing, Sam," he said in the patronizing tone he'd often used on her when they were together.

"Nothing?" She laid out each of the photos of her that had been found in his apartment, hearing the loud nuts-on-the-block buzz that had been missing with Terry O'Connor. "What do you call this?"

"Amateur photography. Is that a crime these days?"

"No, but stalking is."

He shrugged. "A misdemeanor. So charge me."

"Thanks, I will. Hanging around outside my house? Kind of pathetic, even for you."

His genial blue eyes hardened. "I wasn't outside your house."

"Yes, you were. It's sad that you'd rather stalk the woman who divorced you than find someone new to control. Pathetic, isn't it, Cruz?"

"At the very least," Freddie said. "I'd say it's kind of sick *and* pathetic to be fixated on your ex, especially when she's made it crystal clear to the world that she wants nothing to do with you."

If looks could kill, Freddie would've been a goner.

Sam moved around the table so she was behind Peter. "Pissed you off that I didn't want you anymore, didn't it?"

"I didn't want you, either. You were a shitty wife and lousy in bed." He looked up at the dark glass that masked the observation room. "You hear that?" he yelled. "She sucks in the sack!"

"Nick doesn't think so."

Peter tried to surge to his feet, but she shoved him back down.

"I guess you've figured out that we compared notes and discovered you didn't give me his messages six years ago when you were pretending to be my friend."

"That's not a crime."

"No, but it *is* pathetic. Must've pissed you off this week to see me with him."

"Like I care."

"Oh, I think you do." She leaned in to speak close to his ear. "I think you care a whole lot."

In a jerky motion, he shrugged her off. "Giving yourself a lot of credit, aren't you?"

Returning to the other side of the table, she laid a photo of the bomb-making materials in front of him.

"What's that?" he asked.

"Why don't you tell me?"

A bead of sweat appeared on his upper lip. "I have no idea."

"I think you do." Sam rested her hands on the table and leaned toward him. "You disappoint me, Peter. Four years of living with a cop and you didn't learn a goddamned thing. If you're going to try to kill your ex-wife and her boyfriend, you should know better than to leave fingerprints on the bombs."

"I didn't leave any prints!"

She smiled. Bingo.

His face went purple with rage. "You fucking cunt. Spreading your legs for that asshole ten minutes after you see him again."

Sam leaned closer to him, her stomach burning. "That's right. And guess what?" She lowered her voice so only Peter—and maybe Freddie—could hear her. "When I fuck him, I come every time—sometimes more than once. So it turns out that despite what you always tried to make me believe, *you* were the one who sucked in the sack."

He lunged at her, grabbed her throat and squeezed so hard she saw stars in a matter of seconds.

She heard Freddie moving toward them as she rammed the heel of her hand into Peter's nose, sending him flying backward, blood bursting from his face.

"You *fucking bitch*! You motherfucking frigid whore! You broke my fucking nose!"

"Book him, Cruz." Sam's hand shook as she brought it up to her throat. "Two counts attempted murder, assaulting a police officer, stalking a police officer, possessing bomb-making materials, breaking and entering, violating a restraining order, and anything else you can think of."

Freddie hauled Peter up off the floor and snapped cuffs on his wrists. "With pleasure."

"Does he know you're only half a woman?" Peter screamed. "Did you tell him you're barren?"

Sam's heart kicked into overdrive as pain shot through her gut. "Get him out of here."

Long after Freddie dragged the shrieking Peter from the room, Sam stood there trying to get her shaking hands under control. Finally, she turned to leave the room and found a crowd of coworkers waiting for her.

Captain Malone stepped forward. "Well done, Sergeant."

"Thank you," Sam said, her voice shaky. She heard the whir of the wheelchair before she saw it. *Oh God*, she groaned inwardly at what her father must've heard. The crowd parted to let him through, and her heart almost stopped when she saw Nick with him. "So you heard all that, huh?" Sam said to her dad after the others left them alone.

"Uh huh."

"I'm sorry," she said, her cheeks burning. "It must've been embarrassing for you—"

"That was the most entertaining fifteen minutes of my life—right up until he grabbed you. You should put some ice on your neck. Those bruises are gonna hurt."

"I will." She bent down to kiss his cheek.

"Proud of you, baby girl," he whispered.

She rested her head on his shoulder. How she wished he could wrap his strong arms around her the way he used to. "I think it's finally over."

"I think you're right. Since I'm here, I'm going to go do some visiting. I'll be back in a bit, Nick."

"I'll be right here," Nick said.

"That's what I figured." Skip turned his chair and started down the long corridor, no doubt heading for Chief Farnsworth's office.

Nick held out a hand to her. That he did just that and nothing more finally did it for her. Curling her hand around his, she fell the rest of the way into love with him.

THIRTY

"I'M SORRY," SAM SAID when they were in her office.

"What the hell for?" Nick asked.

"For using you and our relationship to stick it to him. I didn't know you were there. I hate that you heard it."

"You think that bothers me?" His hazel eyes were bright with emotion. "You nailed him. That's all that matters. So what did you say that made him go ballistic?"

"It doesn't matter."

"It matters to me."

Reluctantly, Sam told him what she'd said. "I don't want you to think…"

As if he could no longer resist, he put his arms around her. "What?"

Again her cheeks burned with embarrassment and discomfort, but this had to be said. "That I think of what we do…together…as fucking."

"Baby, come on. I know that."

"Because it's so much more than that," she said, looking up at him.

"Yes." He brushed his lips over hers. "It is."

"I love you, too."

He went perfectly still. "Yeah?"

Pleased to have caught him off guard, she nodded. "Since that night at the party for me, too. I shouldn't have married Peter for many reasons, but mostly because I always loved you. Always."

"Samantha," he whispered, leaning in for a deep, passionate kiss.

"No PDA on duty, or any other time," she mumbled when she came to her senses and remembered where they were.

"Very special occasion." His hands slid down to cup her ass and pull her tight against his erection. "Does that door have a lock?"

With her hands on his chest, she tried to push him back. "Don't even think about it."

"I'm way past thinking."

She went up on tiptoes to roll his bottom lip between her teeth. "I'll make it up to you. I promise."

Groaning, he released her. "I'll hold you to that."

"Um, what he said about me…at the end…We should probably talk about that."

Nick rested a finger on her lips. "Later."

Grateful for the reprieve, she took a deep breath. "So what's with you and my dad?" she asked, grabbing a half-empty bottle of soda from her desk.

"We've reached an understanding of sorts."

Raising a suspicious eyebrow, she studied him. "What sort?"

"That's between me and him."

"I don't like the sound of that."

He tweaked her nose. "You don't have to."

A knock on the door startled them.

"Enter," she called.

Gonzo opened the door. "Um, sorry to interrupt—"

"You're not interrupting anything," she said with a meaningful glance at Nick. "What's up?"

"There's a woman here to see you. Wouldn't give her name, insists on seeing you and only you. Looks shook up."

"All right. Bring her in." To Nick, she said, "Do you mind taking my dad home? I'll be along soon."

"Sure." He leaned in for one last kiss.

"Don't talk about me with him."

"Dream on," he said, laughing as he left the room. "Put some ice on that neck."

Sam took in the view of his fine denim-clad ass and sighed with delight. That he was hers, all hers, was something she still couldn't believe. She wished she had time to indulge in the happy dance that was just bursting to get out.

Gonzo accompanied a distraught woman to the door and showed her in. "This is Sergeant Holland."

"Have a seat." Sam gestured to the chair and dismissed Gonzo with a grateful nod. "What's your name?"

The woman's manicured fingers fiddled with her designer purse as she looked at Sam with dark, ravaged eyes. "Andrea Daly."

"What can I do for you, Ms. Daly?"

"It's *Mrs.* Daly." She looked down at the floor, sobs shaking her petite frame. "I've done an awful thing."

Sam came around her desk and leaned back against it. "If you tell me about this awful thing, maybe I can help you."

Andrea wiped the tears from her face. "The night the senator was killed…"

The back of Sam's neck tingled. "Did you know him? Senator O'Connor?"

Andrea shook her head. "I've never done anything

like this. My family means everything to me. I have children."

"Mrs. Daly, I can't help you if you don't tell me what it is you think you've done."

"I was with Terry O'Connor," she whispered. "I spent that whole night with him at the Day's Inn in Leesburg." She wiped her runny nose. "When I saw him on the news being brought in this morning…I couldn't let that happen. He didn't do it."

"I know."

Incredulous, Andrea stared up at Sam. "I risked my marriage and my family and you *already knew?*"

Sam reached out to her. "You did a brave thing coming here. It was the right thing."

"A lot of good that'll do me when my husband reads about it in the paper."

"It won't be in the paper. If your husband finds out, it'll be because you tell him."

"Do you mean that?"

"Terry O'Connor doesn't remember you. He was so drunk he couldn't even offer a description of the woman he said he'd been with. I'm sorry if that hurts you, but it's the truth. So the only two people who know he was with you are in this room. I know what I'm going to do with the info. What you do with it is up to you."

Overcome, Andrea bent her head. "I've never been unfaithful to my husband before. In nineteen years, I've never so much as looked at another man. But he travels a lot, and we've drifted apart in the last couple of years. I was lonely."

"I understand that feeling—better than you can imagine." Sam raised her fingers to cover bruises on her throat that were starting to hurt. "But if you love your husband and want to make your marriage work, stay out of the bars, go home and fix it. You're lucky this was the worst thing that happened."

"Believe me, I know." She stood and offered her hand. "Thank you."

Sam held Andrea's hand between both of hers. "Thank *you* for coming in. You did the right thing. I had him ninety-nine percent eliminated. You just gave me the one percent I still needed."

"In that case, I guess it was worth it."

"Good luck to you, Mrs. Daly."

"And to you, Sergeant. Senator O'Connor was a good man. I hope you find the person who did this to him."

"Oh, I will. You can count on that." Sam stood at her doorway and watched Andrea leave.

"What was that all about?" Freddie asked.

"Terry O'Connor's alibi."

Freddie's eyes lit up. "No shit?"

"Nope."

"Did you get an official statement?"

"Nope."

"Why not?"

"Because I had nothing to gain, and she had everything to lose. She gave me what I needed. That was enough."

"I continue to be awed not just by your instincts but by your humanity."

"Fuck off, Cruz," she said, rolling her eyes. "Did you get Peter put on ice?"

"Yep. Sent the EMTs down to take a look at his busted schnoz. He's screaming police brutality."

"Self-defense." The fact she had taunted Peter into attacking her wouldn't matter to the U.S. Attorney in light of the evidence they had implicating him in the bombings.

"Damn straight it was."

"What're you hearing from Gonzo and Arnold?"

"Natalie's mother told them she's in seclusion and couldn't come to the door. They didn't push it because all you wanted was confirmation that she was there, and they saw her looking out an upstairs window. Noel spent the day working in his yard and washing his car. No sign of her at the house. Gonzo just took him in for the polygraph."

"Let's set one up for her for tomorrow, after the funeral."

"Got it."

"So where does that leave us?" Sam unclipped her hair and ran her fingers through it. "Our two prime suspects, both with motive and opportunity pointing the finger at each other, but nothing about them is jumping out at us."

"Except her dead boyfriend. That's a red flag."

"If she had anything to do with that, would her husband know about it? Would she have told him all about the boyfriend who'd tragically died in a fire?"

"Hard to say. Murderers can be an arrogant lot. They often want people to know what they've done so they get the credit."

"I didn't get that vibe from Noel. It was more of a 'she was heartbroken' vibe." Sam checked her watch and saw it was after one. "I wanted another go with her, but I think I'll wait until after we polygraph her to see if I need to show my cards on the dead boyfriend. Have Gonzo get her suspicions about her husband on the record at some point today. I'm not liking him for a suspect, but I want it in the file."

"Sounds like a good plan. Do you think it's possible that neither of them had anything to do with it, and she's just trying to get rid of a husband she never should've married?"

"At this point, I'd say anything is possible, but I'm still left without a primary suspect three days into the investigation. That'll really please the chief."

"How about I write up the reports from this morning?"

"I'd appreciate that." She thought for a moment and realized this was as good a moment as there was likely to be. "Can you come in for a minute?"

"Sure." He shut the office door behind him. "What's up?"

"You know I appreciate your help with the reports, right?"

"It's no problem."

"Well, for me it kind of is." She rubbed a hand over her belly. In a rush of words, she said, "I'm dyslexic. I've struggled with it all my life, and it's mostly under control, but I know you must wonder about the weird mistakes and stuff."

"Why didn't you tell me before? I could've been doing all the reports."

"I don't want that. It's enough that you help me as much as you do."

"You still should've told me. We're partners."

"Do I know everything there is to know about you?"

He squirmed under the heat of her glare. "Most everything."

"We've all got our secrets, Cruz, and the last thing

I want is special treatment. I don't expect anything to change now that you know."

"Asking for help doesn't make you weak, Sam. It makes you human."

"That's the second time today someone told me what it means to be human. Don't tell anyone about the dyslexia, all right?"

"Who would I tell?" he huffed. "If you don't know by now that you can trust me—"

"If I didn't trust you, I wouldn't have told you." She paused before she said, "I'm sorry you had to hear that stuff I said to Peter. I know it was embarrassing for you."

"You got him to implicate himself, which is the goal of any interrogation."

"Still..."

"I'm a big boy, Sergeant. I can handle it."

She looked at him with new appreciation. "Copy me on those reports, and you can run your domestic angle in the morning while I'm at the funeral."

"Got it."

"Go home after you finish the paperwork."

He held up a set of keys. "Your new ride, madam."

"Ohhh, what'd you get me? One of the new Tauruses?"

"Yep. Navy blue." He rattled off the parking space number.

"Nice. Thanks."

"I might come by to watch the game later. I mean, if that's all right with you."

"My dad invited you, didn't he?"

"Well, yeah, but..."

"But what?"

He smiled. "Nothing."

She pulled on her coat. "I'll see you later, then. Oh, and thanks for having my back with the scumbag."

"No problem." He followed her out of the office and closed the door behind him. "Sergeant Holland?"

She turned to him, perplexed by his formality.

"It's a great pleasure to work with you."

"Back atcha, Detective. Right back atcha."

ON HER WAY OUT of the detectives' pit, she stopped to peek into the office that would soon be hers. Since the day she made detective, she'd had her eye on the lieutenant's spacious corner office. However, because of her struggles with dyslexia, she hadn't really allowed herself to hope.

She turned to leave and ran smack into Lieutenant Stahl.

"Would you jump in my grave that fast, Sergeant?"

Taken aback by his sudden appearance, Sam stepped aside to let him in and noticed he carried a box.

"You must be feeling quite satisfied." He flipped on the lights and dropped the box on the desk. "Shagged a witness, made lieutenant, stole my command and got away with it—all in the same week."

Sam leaned against the doorframe and let him spew, fascinated by the way his fat chin jiggled in time with his venomous words.

"I mean do you *honestly* think you'd have gotten away with screwing a witness if your daddy wasn't the chief's buddy?" He tossed pictures and mementos into the box. "You can bet internal affairs will be interested in taking a closer look at that. In fact, you might just be my very first order of business."

Sam pretended to hang on his every word while she planned where to put her own things in the space.

"This isn't over, Sergeant. I refuse to turn a blind eye to blatant disregard for basic rules by someone who's gotten where she is because of *who* she is."

Her hand rolled into a fist that she'd love to plant smack in the middle of his fat face, but she wouldn't give him the satisfaction. Instead, she pulled her notebook from her back pocket and reached for a pen.

His eyes narrowed. "What are you writing?"

"Just a note to maintenance. They need to do something about the smell in here." As little red blotches popped up on his fat face, she returned the pad to her pocket. "Good luck in the rat squad, Lieutenant. I'm sure you'll fit right in." Turning, she took her leave.

"Watch your back, Sergeant," he called. "Daddy won't always be there to clean up your messes."

She turned around. "If you so much as look at my father with crossed eyes, I'll personally break your fat-assed neck. Got me?"

He raised an eyebrow. "A threat, Sergeant?"

"No, Lieutenant. A promise."

THIRTY-ONE

FOLLOWING THE CONFRONTATION with Stahl, Sam's stomach burned as she headed for the morgue exit, anxious to avoid the press and get home to Nick. The prospect of a boisterous Sunday dinner with her sisters and their families was looking better all the time. She was on her way to a clean escape when Chief Farnsworth stopped her in the lobby.

"I'm glad I caught you, Sergeant. You need to give the media ten minutes."

She groaned.

"In the aftermath of the bombing, you have to show the public you're alive and actively engaged in the O'Connor case—and you've got to let them know you've cleared Terry O'Connor before the president himself starts calling for my ass in a sling."

"Yes, sir."

"They'll ask about Nick."

Rubbing her hand over her gut, she looked out at the media circus that had taken over the plaza. "I can handle it."

"I'll be right there with you."

"Thank you," she said, knowing his presence would send the signal that the department was firmly behind her.

"You're pale. Do you need a minute?"

"No." She breathed through the pain and buttoned

up her coat. "Let's get it over with." The chief followed her into the maelstrom.

The reporters went wild, screaming questions at her.

Chief Farnsworth held up a hand to quiet them. "Sergeant Holland will answer your questions if you give her the chance."

As Sam stepped up to the microphone, the crowd fell silent. "Today, we ruled out Terry O'Connor as a suspect in his brother's murder. We have a number of other persons of interest we're looking at closely." She really wished that was true, but she couldn't exactly tell the media that the investigation had hit a dead end.

"Can you tell us who they are?"

"Not without compromising the investigation. As soon as we're able to give you more, we will."

"Is there anything else you can tell us about the O'Connor investigation?"

"Not at this time."

"How close are you to making an arrest?"

"Not as close as I'd like to be, but it's far more important that we build a case that'll hold up in court rather than rush to judgment."

"Why did Detective Cruz go to Chicago?"

"No comment." No way was she handing them Thomas O'Connor. They would have to figure that one out for themselves.

"Did the Johnson family play a role in yesterday's bombing?"

"No. We've made an arrest that's unrelated to the Johnsons." She looked down and summoned the strength to get through this. "My ex-husband, Peter Gibson, has been charged with two counts of attempted murder—among numerous other charges—in the bombing."

"Why'd he do it?" one of the reporters shouted.

"We believe he was enraged by my relationship with Mr. Cappuano."

"Did you know Mr. Cappuano before this week?"

Gritting her teeth, she forced herself to stay calm and to not make their day by getting emotional. "We met years ago and had a brief relationship."

"Did you tell your superior officers that you'd had a past relationship with a material witness?" asked Darren Tabor from the *Washington Star*. He'd been particularly harsh toward her in his reporting after the Johnson disaster.

Sam's fingers tightened around the edges of the podium. "I did not."

"Why?"

"I was determined to close the O'Connor case and believed Mr. Cappuano's assistance would be invaluable, which it has been. Thanks to his help, I'm much further along than I would've been without it."

"Still, aren't you walking a fine ethical line especially in light of the publicity you received after the Johnson case?" Tabor asked with a smirk.

"If you examine my more than twelve-year record, you'll find my behavior to be above reproach."

"Until recently."

"Your judgment," Sam said, working to keep her cool while making a mental note to check on his unpaid parking tickets. Issuing a warrant for his arrest would give her tremendous joy.

"Is it true Mr. Cappuano is the beneficiary of a sizable life insurance policy taken out by the senator?" Tabor asked.

Sam clenched her teeth. How the hell had *that* leaked? "Yes."

"Doesn't that give you a motive?"

"Maybe if he had known about it."

"You believe he didn't?"

"He was as surprised by it as we were. Mr. Cappuano has been cleared of any involvement in the senator's murder."

"Is it serious between you and Cappuano?" Sam wanted to groan when she recognized the bottle-blonde reporter from one of the gossip rags.

"It's been a week," Sam said, laughing off the question.

"But is it *serious?*"

What is this? Sam wanted to shoot back at her. *High school?* "Would I have gotten involved if it wasn't? Next question." She looked away from the reporter's satisfied grin, sending the signal that she was finished with the discourse into her personal life.

"Are you concerned by Destiny Johnson's threats?" another reporter asked.

Relieved to be moving on, Sam made eye contact with the new reporter, a woman she recognized from one of the network affiliates. "Mrs. Johnson is a grieving mother. My heart goes out to her."

"How about Marquis Johnson?"

"As I'm due to testify in his probable cause hearing on Tuesday, I have no comment."

"Sergeant, the second anniversary of your father's shooting is coming up next week. Are there any new leads in his case?"

"Unfortunately, no, but it remains an open investigation. Anyone with information is urged to come forward."

"And how's he doing?"

"Very well. Thank you for asking."

Chief Farnsworth stepped forward to rescue her.

Sam held up her hand to stop him. "I just want to say..." She cleared the emotion from her throat. "That it's an honor to serve the people of this city, and while you've taken your digs at me lately, there's nothing I wouldn't do, no risk I wouldn't take, to protect our citizens. If that's not enough for you, well then you can continue to make me the story rather than focusing on real news. That's it."

As they hollered more questions at her, she pushed through them to the staff parking lot where her gleaming new car waited for her. Only when she was safely inside could she begin to breathe her way through the pain.

SAM CALLED NICK from the car.

"Hey, babe," he said.

She took a moment to enjoy the easy familiarity they had slid into, as if they'd been together for years rather than days.

"Sam?"

"I'm here."

"Everything all right?"

"It is now that I'm talking to you. What're you doing?"

"I'm sitting on your bed trying to write what I have to say at the funeral tomorrow. It's just dawned on me that I have to speak in front of the president and most of Congress."

Sam released a low whistle. "I don't think I could do it."

"Sure you could. You just took on the Washington press corps."

"You saw that, huh?"

"Yep. I heard it's serious between us. Did you know that?"

Laughing, she said, "I've heard that rumor."

"Say it again, Sam," he said, his voice gruff and sexy.

Her heart contracted. "Say what?" she asked, even though she knew exactly what he was after.

"Don't play coy with me. Say it."

"When I see you."

"And when will that be?"

"I'm almost home. Want to meet me outside and go for a walk? I promised I'd take you to the market."

"So you did. Was that *only* yesterday?"

"Sure was. Meet me on the corner in five? If I come in, I'll get trapped, and I need some air."

"I'll be right there."

HE WAS WAITING for her when she parked in front of the house and set out toward the corner.

Her heart skipped a beat at the sight of him in jeans and a black leather jacket, and she couldn't help but break into a jog to get to him faster. She hurled herself into his outstretched arms and squealed when he lifted her right off her feet.

His mouth descended on hers for a hot, breathtaking kiss.

"Mmm," she said against his lips. "I missed you."

"You just saw me a couple of hours ago."

"Long time." She burrowed into his neck to nibble on warm skin.

He trembled and tightened his hold on her. "What happened to your ban on PDA?"

"Momentary lapse."

"I like it." He returned her to terra firma and tipped her chin up. "There was something you were going to tell me?"

She thought about playing coy again, but as she looked up at his handsome face, she found she couldn't do it. "I love you. Big."

His hazel eyes danced with delight. "Big, huh?"

"Scary big."

"Not scary." He hugged her. "Because I love you bigger."

"Not possible."

"Bet?" Laughing at the face she made at him, he slipped his arm around her shoulders for the walk to the market.

A melting pot of crafts, colors, nationalities, smells and textures, Eastern Market was mobbed with last-minute Christmas shoppers braving the damp chill to bargain with bundled-up vendors.

"You aren't going to believe this, but I've never been here," he confessed as they passed a row of fragrant Christmas trees.

She stared up at him. "Are you serious? You've worked a few blocks from here for how long?"

"Well, I worked for a congressman before John, so I guess almost fourteen years."

"That's sad, Nick. Truly pathetic. The flea market is open every weekend, year round."

"So I've heard," he said with a sheepish grin. "I figured, you know, flea market—junk. I never expected all this hand-crafted stuff."

"You can get anything here, and it's usually better than what you can buy in a store."

"I can see that."

"Hey, Sam," one of the vendors called.

"How's business, Rico?"

"Booming, thank God. Heard about you on the news last night. You okay?"

"Just fine. No worries."

"Glad to hear it. Bring your dad down one of these weekends."

"I will."

After several similar exchanges, Nick said, "Do you know *all* these people or does it just seem that way?"

She shrugged as she sorted through a table of fluffy knitted scarves. "This is my hood. I'm a regular." Twisting a hot pink scarf around her neck, she pirouetted in front of him. "What do you think?"

He turned up his nose. "Not your color, babe."

"My niece Brooke firmly believes that no one over the age of four should wear pink."

"That's funny. How old is she?"

"Fifteen going on thirty. You'll meet her later." Returning the scarf to the table, she glanced over at the next kiosk and spotted a beautifully framed painting of the Capitol that she had to have for him. Dying to get a closer look at it, she rubbed her hands together and blew into them. "Do you feel like some hot chocolate?"

"Sure."

"They're selling it right over there."

Eyeing her suspiciously, he looked over to where she pointed. "All right."

Flashing a brilliant smile, she went up on tiptoes to kiss him. "Thank you, honey."

"What're you up to?"

"Nothing." She gave him a little push. "Go."

The moment he crossed the street, she spun around and pounced on the unsuspecting artist in the neighboring booth. "That one. Right there. How much?"

"Three-fifty."

"Sold. Will you take a check?"

"With a license."

"Be quick."

They completed the transaction in record time, and Sam accepted the package wrapped in brown paper moments before Nick returned with two steaming cups of hot chocolate.

"What did you buy?"

"Something for my dad."

"You're a terrible liar, Samantha. Does this mean I have to buy something for you, too?"

"Only if you plan to get lucky in the New Year," she said with a saucy smile.

"In that case, what looks good to you? Sky's the limit."

Laughing and teasing, they were navigating the crowd on their way to the indoor food market when a flash of metal caught Sam's eye. Everything shifted into slow motion as she realized it was a gun. In the span of a second, she shoved Nick out of the way, dropped the painting and her hot chocolate, drew her own weapon and lunged at the shooter.

"Baby killer!" the woman shrieked as she fired an erratic shot.

People screamed and dove for cover as Sam wrestled the heavy-set woman to the ground and struggled to disarm her. Out of the corner of her eye, she saw Nick's black shoe.

"Get back!" she cried as the woman's elbow connected with her cheekbone.

Nick stomped on the woman's hand, and the gun clanked to the cobblestone street.

"Don't touch it!" Sam said to him as she cuffed the crying woman.

"You killed Quentin! *You killed our baby!*"

Something about the voice was familiar. "Marquis killed Quentin," Sam growled into the woman's ear as she tightened the cuffs. Flipping her over, she wasn't surprised to find Destiny Johnson's sister Dawn under her. "Was anyone hit?" Sam asked Nick.

"I don't think so." He looked down at her with a pale face and big, shocked eyes. "I heard someone call 911."

"Thanks for the assist."

"No problem."

As the market slowly returned to normal around them, Sam sat on a curb with Dawn until a couple of uniforms arrived to take statements and cart her off. Sam promised to write up her portion of the report and get it to them later.

"Nice job, Sam," one of the vendors called to her.

"Thanks," she said as Nick helped her up.

The moment she was upright, the pain she had managed to stave off during the confrontation with Dawn roared through her, leaving her breathless and weak in its wake.

"Jesus Christ, Sam," Nick muttered.

"S'okay," she said, bent in half as she took deep breaths. "Just give me a second." It took several minutes, but she was finally able to straighten only to find his hazel eyes hot with dismay and anger. "I'm fine."

"You're not fine." He took hold of her arm to steer her toward home. "And don't you ever push me out of the way again so you can dive at a gun, do you hear me? Don't ever do that again."

Startled by his tone, she stopped and turned to face him. "It's instinct and training. You can't fault me for that."

"How do you think it makes me feel, as a *man*, when the woman I love pushes me out of harm's way so she can throw herself in front of it? Huh?"

"I have no idea," she said sincerely.

"Well, let me tell you, it makes me feel like a useless, dickless moron."

"I'm not the kind of woman who needs a big strong man to protect her, Nick. If that's what you want or need, you've got the wrong girl."

"And you think I'm the kind of man who needs his *woman* to protect him? Is that what *you* want?"

"Why are we fighting?" she asked, perplexed. "I saw a shooter. I took her down. What the hell did I do wrong?"

"You pushed me out of the way!"

"Excuse me for not wanting your dumb ass to get killed. Next time I'll let her blow your head off. Would that be better?"

"Now you're just being a jerk."

Stunned and dismayed, she stared at him and said a silent thanks a lot to Dawn for turning their romantic afternoon to shit. "*I'm* the jerk? Whatever." Without a care as to whether he followed her or not, she stomped off toward home. When she got there, she heard voices in the kitchen and figured her sister Tracy's family had arrived. But rather than go see them, Sam went straight upstairs, needing a few minutes to get herself together first.

What's his problem anyway? She fumed as she shrugged off her coat, tossed it over her desk chair and flopped down on the bed. *What did I do besides try to protect his sorry ass?* The ache in her stomach was no match for the pain in her heart. This was exactly why she had stayed away from relationships since she split with Peter. If she never felt this shitty again, it would be just fine with her.

Nick came in a few minutes later, carrying the package she had abandoned in the chaos. "I believe this is yours," he said as he put it on her desk and took off his coat.

She couldn't believe she had forgotten all about the painting. "Thanks."

He sat down on the edge of the bed and brushed his fingers over her sore cheek.

Sam winced when he grazed the spot where Dawn's elbow had connected.

"You should put some ice on that." He laced his fingers through hers. "Between the bump on your head, the bruises on your chest and neck, and now this, you're quite a colorful mess."

"It's not usually like this. I swear to God, it's never this crazy."

"That's good to know, because I don't think I could handle this much drama on a daily basis." He brought their joined hands to his lips and kissed each of her fingers. "I'm sorry I overreacted."

Sam's mouth fell open. "Did you just *apologize?*"

"Yeah," he huffed. "So?"

"I didn't think guys did that. This is a first for me. You'll have to excuse me while I take a moment to enjoy it."

His eyes narrowed. "I'm about to take it back."

She laughed. "Please don't." Reaching up to touch the soft hair that curled over his ear, she studied the face she had come to love so much in such a short time. "I'm trying to understand why you got so upset."

"You did what you were trained to do, and just because I didn't like it doesn't mean you were wrong."

"Wow. This is truly quite a moment for me."

"Samantha…"

"I'll always push you out of the way, Nick. If you can't deal with that, we're going to have problems."

"We're going to have problems anyway. So how about we handle it this way? When I'm wrong, I'll say so. And when you're wrong, you'll say so."

"I will?"

"Uh huh. That's how it works. That's the *only* way it works."

"Is this you being anal again and cleaning things up?"

"If that's how you want to see it."

"Fine," she conceded. "On the sure-to-be rare instances when I'm actually wrong about something, I'll do my best to admit it. Are you happy?"

"For some strange reason," he said, bending to kiss her, "I really am."

She slid her fingers into his hair to keep him there. "So am I."

THIRTY-TWO

AFTER DINNER, SAM JOINED her sisters on the porch to share a cigarette. She leaned in to block the air as Tracy lit up while Angela flanked her other side. Each of them took a long drag before passing it on.

"Oh, I needed that," Tracy, who at forty was the oldest, said as she exhaled a steady stream of smoke. She shared Sam's height but had held on to ten extra pounds after each of her three children.

Angela, at thirty-six, had bounced right back to her svelte shape after giving birth to her son Jack five years earlier.

The door swung open, and Angela stashed the cigarette behind her back.

"Mom, Jack is walking back and forth in front of the TV and won't stop," whined fifteen-year-old Brooke, brimming with indignation. Her long dark hair, bright blue eyes and porcelain skin gave her a delicate beauty that was a source of great consternation to her parents as the boys began to take an avid interest in her.

"Sorry," Angela said. "I'll get him."

Tracy stopped her sister and said to her daughter, "Turn off the TV and spend some time with your cousin. All he wants is your attention."

In a huff, Brooke stomped back inside.

"Sorry about that," Angela said. "He loves being with the kids."

"Don't worry about it," Tracy said. "They watch enough TV at home. They don't need to do it here, too."

The door opened again, and this time Sam stashed the cigarette behind her back when she saw it was Nick.

"I was wondering where you all had disappeared to, and your father suggested I check the front porch where I'd find the three of you sharing a cigarette that you think no one knows about. I said, 'What do you mean, Skip? Samantha doesn't smoke.'"

Behind her back, Sam transferred the cigarette to Angela in a move they had perfected over the years. She smiled at Nick. "Of course I don't smoke. Did you need me?"

"I was going to ask if you'd mind if we go to my place tonight."

"I don't mind. I'll be in shortly, and we can take off."

"Okay."

The moment the door closed behind him, Angela took a drag off the dwindling cigarette. "Mmm. Hubba hubba."

Her sisters stared at her.

"Did you seriously just say 'hubba hubba'?" Tracy asked.

"Well, come on. He's yummy. And did he call you *Samantha?*"

Sam shrugged as her cheeks heated with embarrassment. "He likes to call me that."

"You must really dig him to put up with that," Ang said. "How's the sex?"

"Angela!" Tracy said.

"What? Don't tell me you don't want to know, too."

They waited expectantly for Sam.

"It's…you know…amazing."

"I remember amazing sex," Tracy said with a sigh. "At least I think I do."

"Stop," Angela said, bumping Tracy with her hip. "Mike's still hot for you."

"Yeah, I guess. So, Sam, I didn't want to ask in front of the kids, but this insanity with Peter…Are you okay?"

"It's kind of overwhelming to know he hates me enough to want to kill me."

"I think it's more that in his own sick, twisted way he *loves* you that much," Tracy said.

Angela nodded in agreement.

Sam told them about meeting Nick years ago and what Peter had done to keep them apart.

"Motherfucker," Angela muttered.

Sam laughed as she extinguished the cigarette. The sick feeling in her stomach and the lingering foul taste reminded her of why she'd quit smoking years ago. "Tell me how you really feel, Ang."

"I hate that bastard."

"So do I," Tracy said. "Divorcing him was the best thing you ever did. I couldn't stand the way he always had to know where you were and what you were doing. He never would've gone back inside the way Nick did just now. He would've wanted to know what we were talking about."

"I know," Sam said. "When I think about him not giving me those messages…I really wanted to hear from Nick after that night."

"You might've missed the whole Peter saga altogether," Tracy said.

"Maybe everything that happened with Peter, with the babies and stuff, would've happened with Nick and it would've screwed us up just as bad."

Her sisters each slid an arm around her.

"There's no point in going there, Sam," Tracy said.

"I haven't had a chance to tell Nick the whole story."

"It won't matter to him," Ang assured her. "He's mad about you. He never takes his eyes off you, but not in the creepy way Peter used to. More of an adoring way."

"He didn't have a family growing up, and I know he wants one."

"There're other ways, hon," Tracy said. "You know that. Don't worry about it right now. Enjoy this time with him. You deserve to be happy after everything you've been through."

"Thank you," Sam said, hugging them. "I'm so glad you guys like him."

"Hubba hubba," Ang said again, and they all laughed.

"Now how about Dad and Celia?" Sam said.

JUST AS SAM and Nick were getting ready to leave Skip's house, Freddie called. "We've got another body, Sergeant."

A burst of adrenaline zipped through Sam. "Who?"

"Tara Davenport."

"Oh, shit," Sam sighed, remembering the timid Capitol Hill waitress they'd interviewed. "Where?"

"Her apartment." Freddie rattled off the address. "It's bad, Sam. Whoever did this made sure she suffered."

"I'm on my way."

Nick insisted on driving her to the scene. On the way, Sam pumped him for information about Tara.

"She was so sweet," he said. "We always requested her section when we went in for lunch. I can't believe anyone would want to harm her."

"No way this is a coincidence. This has got to be tied to O'Connor. Did he tell you he was dating her?"

"He never came right out and discussed it with me, but I knew. He was so much older than her. I'm sure he thought I wouldn't approve."

"Did you?"

"Not really, but they were both consenting adults, so I kept my opinions to myself."

Since emergency vehicles had surrounded Tara's apartment building, Sam told him to double-park.

Freddie met them at the door to Tara's apartment, his expression grim. "Beaten, bound, raped and strangled."

Steeling herself, Sam followed him into the bedroom. "God almighty," she whispered at the sight of a bloodbath.

Behind her, Nick gasped.

Sam spun around. "You need to step back." Realizing he was on the verge of passing out, she rushed him into a chair and pushed his head between his knees. "Breathe."

"I'm okay," he muttered, looking up at her. His eyes glazed with shock, he shook his head. "Who could do that? Who?"

"I don't know, but I'm going to find out."

"Go ahead. Sorry to wimp out."

Sam left him in the living room and returned to the bedroom as Freddie took photos of the scene. Tara had been bound, gagged and, judging by the bloody pool between her legs, repeatedly raped.

"Who found her?" Sam asked Freddie.

"One of her coworkers got the super to let her in when she didn't show up for work for the second day in a row."

Dr. Lindsey McNamara, the medical examiner, stepped into the room. "Damn. Just when you think you've seen it all..."

"No kidding," Sam said.

One of the Crime Scene officers lifted a baseball bat from the floor. Blood stained the thick end of the barrel. "Looks like this was used for the beating, among other things..."

The women in the room winced.

Sam studied the young waitress who'd been so distraught over her breakup with John O'Connor. "How long has she been dead?"

Lindsey pulled on latex gloves and reached out to close Tara's eyes. "Looks like twenty to thirty hours, but I won't know for sure until I get her into the lab."

"I need a time of death ASAP so I can get a timeline going."

Lindsey nodded. "Who did this to you, sweetie?" the kind-hearted doctor whispered. "Don't you worry. We'll get them." Lindsey shifted her green eyes to Sam. "Won't we?"

"You bet your ass we will."

"Go pick up Elin Svendsen," Sam said to Freddie, working a hunch.

"Really?" The spark of excitement in his voice wasn't lost on Sam. "Will I get hardship duty pay for that?"

"Take her to a hotel and arrange for round-the-clock coverage."

"Got it—take goddess to hotel and watch over her. I think I can handle that."

Sam was relieved to hear him joking again after the

hideous two hours they'd just put in at Tara's. "I'm going to send Gonzo out to Belle Haven to pick up the Jordans, too. I want her under protection."

"Noel passed the polygraph."

"Yeah, I got that word an hour ago."

"What're you thinking, boss?"

"Did Patricia Donaldson tell you where she'd be staying in the city when she came for O'Connor's funeral?"

His brows furrowing with skepticism, he said, "No, but I can try to find out."

"Do that. I could be wrong, but I'm going to pull her credit card records to see if she recently bought a plane ticket to Washington."

"Come on, Sam, you're not thinking it's her...That woman was madly in love with him."

"And he was fucking his way through the city while she raised his son in Siberia." Here was the buzz that came when all the pieces started to fall into place. "I'll pull the records, you find Elin."

Sobering, Freddie said, "You can count on me to take very good care of her."

Sam rolled her eyes. "Go easy. You might sprain something."

EMERGING FROM TARA'S apartment building, Sam found Nick leaning against her car. "Aren't you freezing?"

"The cold feels good." His face was pale, his eyes watering from the cold or maybe the emotion.

"You shouldn't have followed me in there. I told you to stay here."

"I don't know how you do it," he said softly. "How

you can stand seeing stuff like that day after day? I'll never forget what I saw in there."

"I wish I could say it's the first time I've seen something like that."

He reached for her, but Sam shook him off. "No PDA when the place is swarming with cops," she growled.

Jamming his hands into his pockets, he seemed to be making an effort to bite his tongue.

Sam unclipped her hair and ran her fingers through it. "I need some computer time. Do you mind dropping me at HQ?"

"Does it have to be there? You could get online at my house."

She consulted her watch. Ten-forty. "I suppose that would work."

Nick offered to drive her car to Arlington, and Sam was tired enough after the long, draining day to let him.

"This is the time to be on the road." She gestured to the deserted stretch of I-395 as they passed the Jefferson Memorial on their way to the 14th Street Bridge.

"If only it was like this in the morning."

She turned her head so she could see his profile in the orange glow of the streetlights. Anxious to get both their minds off the horror they'd witnessed at Tara's, Sam said, "So tell me, did my family overwhelm you?"

"What? No, of course not. Everyone was really nice."

"They liked you."

"What's the story with your brother-in-law Spencer?"

Sam smiled. "He's a bit much, huh?"

"Ah, yeah. Got a big opinion of himself."

"We only put up with him because he worships the

ground Angela walks on. There's nothing he wouldn't do for her."

"Mike's a lot more normal."

"I adore him."

Nick shot her a meaningful glance.

"Not like that," Sam said, laughing. "I just give him so much credit. He's raising Brooke like she's his own—"

"She's *not?*"

Sam shook her head. "Her father was a guy Tracy dated briefly. When they found out she was pregnant he hit the road, and she never heard from him again. She met Mike a couple of years later. After they got married, he adopted Brooke."

"You'd never know she wasn't his."

"That's why I love him so much. We all do. He doesn't treat her any differently than he does Abby or Ethan."

"No, he certainly doesn't," Nick agreed. "I like him even more knowing that about him."

"He's the big brother I never had."

"Which is why he thoroughly grilled me about where I came from, where I'm going and what my intentions are toward you."

"He did *not*," Sam said, astounded.

"Yes, he did. And he made sure your father was able to hear the interrogation. In fact, I'll bet Skip put him up to it."

"I wouldn't doubt it." Turning in her seat, she leaned over to plant a wet kiss on his neck. "Thank you for putting up with that." Because he deserved it after dealing with her family, she tossed in some tongue action, too.

The car swerved. "Hello? I'm going seventy over here!"

She ran her hand up his thigh. "Want to go for eighty?"

He caught her hand the instant before it reached the promised land. "Behave."

"So what did you tell Mike?" she asked, resting her head on his shoulder.

Bringing their joined hands to his lips, he pressed a kiss to the back of hers. "That I've always loved you, and I always will."

Sam sighed with contentment. "I like hearing that."

"Do you know why I wanted to go home tonight?"

"Nope."

"I found out today that you love me, too. I wanted to be alone with you tonight."

A tremble of anticipation rippled through her. "You knew before today."

"I suspected and I hoped, but I didn't know for sure. I worried that maybe we were both caught up in the craziness of the last week."

She raised her head from his shoulder. "Did you really think that was possible?"

He shrugged. "I was afraid I wanted you too much and that somehow I'd screw it up. I almost did a few times."

"I hate knowing you felt that way." Returning her head to his shoulder, she was struck by how alone he was and how badly she wanted to surround him with the love he'd missed out on while growing up without a family. A lump formed in her throat when she thought of one thing he wanted that she couldn't give him.

They rode the rest of the way in silence, both wrapped up in their own thoughts.

Entering his house through the front door, he took her coat and hung it in the hall closet.

"What happened to all the glass?" she asked.

"I paid my cleaning lady double to come in today and deal with it, but we probably shouldn't walk around barefoot for a while."

"How's your foot?"

"Sore."

She winced. "And I had you out walking on it earlier. I never even thought about it. I'm sorry."

He leaned in to kiss her. "No worries, babe. Computer's in the office. I'll take our stuff upstairs."

"Thanks. I'll be quick."

"Take your time. I've got to finish my eulogy."

She went up on tiptoes to kiss him while wishing there was something she could say to ease his pain. But knowing only time could do that, she let him go and headed for his office. Kicking off her shoes, she sat down to boot up his computer. Before she got to the research she planned to do, she wrote the report on the incident at Eastern Market and saved it to Nick's desktop.

While she waited on the police department system to log her in, she took note of the fastidious order on the dark cherry wood desktop. Feeling mischievous, she nudged the pile of books out of alignment, shifted the container of paperclips so it was off center, turned all the black pens in the pen cup upside down and drew a heart with an arrow through the Sam loves Nick she had written on the blotter.

Pleased with her handiwork, she turned her attention to Patricia Davidson's credit card records. Scanning through the pages, her eyes began to blur with fatigue until she stopped short on an airline charge from two days before John's death. "Well, look at you, Miss Patricia," Sam whispered, the kick of adrenaline making her heart beat faster. "Gotcha!"

She took a moment to look the woman up online to get a visual on her before she called Freddie. "Have you got Elin?"

"We're on our way." He named one of the city's best hotels.

"Jeez, spare no expense, why dontcha," she muttered, imagining the grief she'd get when that expense report landed on Malone's desk.

"Just following orders, Sergeant."

"Patricia Donaldson bought a seat on a flight from Chicago to Washington the day before O'Connor's murder."

Freddie released a long deep breath. "Wow. I totally missed this one. I'm sorry."

"We all missed it."

"But I interviewed her. I should've caught the vibe—"

"Knock it off, Cruz."

"I don't see her having the strength to get that knife through O'Connor's neck. She was almost fragile."

"Rage can make people a lot stronger than normal."

"Yeah, I guess. Would she have a key to his apartment?"

"Maybe she came for conjugals once in a while. It wouldn't surprise me that she had a key—I mean who *didn't* have a key to that place?"

"Right. And don't forget, he could've let the killer in after he got home."

"I still say he was taken by surprise since he was

murdered in bed. Anyway, don't let Elin out of your sight, do you hear me?"

"It's a tough job, but someone's got to do it."

THIRTY-THREE

SAM ENDED THE call and sat back in the big leather chair. Closing her eyes, she let her mind wander through the parts and pieces, hoping something would start to add up. The frustration was starting to get to her as day after day went by without the big break she needed to wrap this up. *I'm missing something. Something big. But what?*

"Everything all right babe?" Nick asked from the doorway.

Holding out her arms, she invited Nick to join her. "We might be starting to get somewhere. Patricia Donaldson bought a ticket on a flight to D.C. the day before John's murder. We've got people trying to figure out where she's staying in the city. Nothing on the credit report shows her hotel."

"You'll figure it out." He kneeled down in front of her and leaned into her embrace. "What brought on this spontaneous show of affection?"

"I just needed it," she said, resting her cheek on his shoulder. "I'm frustrated, aggravated, pissed that it's taken me so long to hone in on her, that someone else had to die..."

"Well, I'm happy to provide comfort any time you need it." He suddenly stiffened.

"What's wrong?" she asked, pulling back to look at him.

"What did you do to my desk?"

"Nothing," she said, all innocence.

"You did, too. You moved things, and you probably did it on purpose to screw with me."

Sam dissolved into laughter. "You're *such* a freak show." When he would've gotten up to fix it, she stopped him. "Leave it. See if you can do it." She gripped his hands. "Come on. Be strong."

"Why does it bother you so much that I require order?"

"What you require is so far beyond order the sphincter police haven't invented the word for it yet."

"Fine. If you want to make a mess and walk away, that's your problem. It doesn't bother me."

"Yes, it does," she said, laughing to herself at his definition of a mess. He hadn't the slightest idea of what she was capable of in that regard. "I bet you'll sneak down here when I'm sleeping tonight and fix it."

"No, I won't," he said, his eyes flashing with the start of anger.

"It's okay if you do," she cooed. "I'll still love you and all your anal retentive freakazoidisms."

At her words of love, he softened, but only a little.

She ran her fingers through his hair and leaned in to kiss him. "Will you do me a favor?"

"What?" he asked in a terse tone.

"Will you read my report about the shooting at Eastern Market for me? See if I made any mistakes?"

He looked at her oddly as he got up to take her place at the desk.

Sam stood behind him, hanging over his shoulder as he went through the events of earlier, making tweaks here and there. She was relieved that he found no blatant errors.

When he was done, he turned to her. "Want to tell me what that was all about?"

She pursed her lips, wanting to tell him, but feeling shy all of a sudden. "Well, you were there. I was just making sure I didn't miss anything."

He reached for her hand and brought her down to sit on his lap. "You don't need me for that. What is it, babe?"

"I'm dyslexic," she said for the second time that day. "Freddie usually checks me, but since he wasn't involved in this, I didn't feel right asking him. Plus he's baby-sitting one of John's girlfriends at the moment."

"I'm glad you asked me. I'll do it for you any time."

She attached the file to an email to the arresting officer. Then she returned her attention to Nick. "Thank you," she said, pressing her lips to his for what she intended to be a quick kiss.

"You're welcome," he whispered as he ran his tongue over her bottom lip before tipping his head to delve deeper. As he kissed her, he arranged her so she straddled him and took her by surprise when he pulled back to whip the sweater up over her head.

Sam shivered as cool air hit her fevered skin. "Nick—I'm working—I can't right now." As she said the words, she reached for the hem of his shirt, but he stopped her. Moaning with frustration, she found his mouth for another frantic kiss and gasped when he released her bra. "Got to work…"

"Shh," he said, feasting on one breast and then the other.

Surrendering to the sensory assault, Sam gripped his shoulders and tried to convince herself that taking ten minutes for herself didn't make her a crappy cop.

"You have the most beautiful breasts," he whispered, trailing his tongue in circles around her nipple.

"They're too big."

"No," he said, laughing. "They're not. They're utter perfection. In fact, I could sit here all night and do nothing but what I'm doing right now until the sun comes up."

She tilted her pelvis tight against his throbbing erection. "Really? Nothing but this? All night?"

He groaned. "Maybe we could mix it up a bit." Helping her to her feet, he unbuttoned her jeans, hooked his fingers into her panties and divested her of both garments in one swift move before bringing her back to his lap.

"You're kind of overdressed," she said, tugging at his shirt.

"Patience, babe." Raining hot, open-mouthed kisses on her neck, he ran his hands up and down her back, sending shivers of desire dancing through her.

"I don't have any patience. Don't you know that by now?"

He propped her thighs on his legs and then moved his feet apart, opening her.

"What're you doing?" she asked, her words infected with a stammer.

"Touching you."

"I want to touch you, too."

"You'll get your turn." He cupped her breasts and ran his thumbs over nipples still sensitive from his earlier ministrations. "It was infuriating today to hear that bastard call you frigid." His hands coasted down over her ribs. One arm encircled her while his other hand slid through the dampness between her legs. "Feel that?" he whispered. "That's as far from frigid as you can get."

"I hardly ever came when I had sex with him," Sam managed to say. "It made him mad."

"We know you weren't the problem, right?" he asked as he drove two fingers into her.

Sam cried out.

"Did you mess up my desk on purpose?" he asked, his fingers coming to a halt deep inside her.

Laughing, she said, "Maybe!" She wiggled her hips, begging him to continue.

""Fess up or you won't get what you want."

"Yes! I did it!"

"That was easy," he chuckled. "Now you must be punished."

She moaned as he found the spot that throbbed for his touch.

He shifted the arm he had around her so his hand gripped her ass, holding her still for his gliding fingers. When he captured her nipple between his teeth, the combination lifted her into a powerful orgasm that stole the breath from her lungs and brought tears to her eyes.

"So hot," he whispered against her lips. "So, *so* hot."

His fingers continue to tease, and Sam was astounded to feel another climax building. Somehow she marshaled the energy to tear at his shirt, lifting it up and over his head. She ran her hand down his chest to his belly and below, dragging her finger over his steely length.

He inhaled sharply.

"Nick, *please*. I want you."

"You have me, Samantha. I'm all yours. Forever and always." He kissed her as if it was the first time all over again, exploring her mouth with deep, penetrating sweeps of his tongue.

When she couldn't stand the burning need another minute, she worked her way off his lap, pulled him up and stripped him in record time. Dropping to her knees, she took him into her mouth.

"Sam…" He buried his fingers in her hair. "Babe, wait. This was about you. Come up here."

"You said I'd get my turn," she pouted, dragging her tongue over him as she looked up to find his eyes bearing down on her.

"And you will." He helped her up, returned to the chair and brought her down to straddle him once again. "I love you."

She tilted her hips and took him in. Leaning forward she touched her lips to his. "I love you, too."

"I'm never going to get tired of hearing that."

"I'm never going to get tired of saying it."

"Promise?"

She nodded and rolled her hips to take him deeper.

Releasing a long deep breath, his eyes fluttered closed.

Sam kissed the bandage above his eye and rode him slowly, each movement taking them both closer…so close.

Suddenly, he wrapped his arms tight around her, stood up and carried her to the sofa without losing their connection.

Hooking his arms under her knees he held her open

for his fierce possession. Caught up in the thrill, Sam came with a sharp cry of release that dragged him right down with her.

"Damn," he whispered a minute of heavy breathing later. "Just when I think it can't get any more perfect..."

She brushed the damp hair off his forehead. "It does."

"We're going to kill ourselves if it gets any more perfect."

Sam laughed. "Hell of a way to go."

With his eyes fixed on hers, he kissed her softly.

"I have something I need to tell you," she said, her stomach twisting as she said the words.

"Now?"

Filled with a kind of fear she hadn't often experienced, she bit her bottom lip and nodded.

"SO ARE YOU going to clue me in on what I'm doing here?" Elin Svendsen said as she paced the fancy hotel room.

"I told you," Freddie said, keeping a tight rein on his libido as he watched her move back and forth. "It's for your safety."

"Are you *sure?*" Her teasing smile shot lust straight through him. He was glad he'd kept his trench coat on. "I'm starting to wonder if you made this whole thing up to get me alone in a hotel room." She sashayed up to him so that her breasts were right at his eye level.

Desperate, he said, "One of John O'Connor's ex-girlfriends was murdered."

Elin gasped. "For real?"

"Would I lie about murder?"

"I don't know. Would you?"

"I never lie about murder."

"I don't get it. He wasn't married or anything."

"Well, he sort of was."

Elin spun around. "What do you mean?"

Freddie told her about the woman and child who'd been banished to the Midwest twenty years ago.

"So you think it's her?"

"We suspect it could be, and we want to keep you safe until we find her."

Elin crossed her arms in a protective gesture that tugged at his heart. "I can't believe he had this whole other secret life."

"Apparently, no one knew. Not even his closest friend."

"I don't sleep with married guys. I know you probably think I'm easy, but I do have morals."

"I never suspected otherwise."

She tilted her head to study him. "You're pretty cute, you know that?"

Freddie cheeks heated with embarrassment. "Thanks. I think."

Smiling, she added, "We could make this little 'protection mission' of yours a whole lot more fun if you're game."

He swallowed hard. "What do you mean?"

She bent over, her top sliding forward to reveal a tantalizing view of her spectacular breasts. A hint of the Cupid tattoo was visible over the top of her low-cut bra. "Sex, Detective," she whispered. "Dirty, raunchy sex."

Feeling as if he was being tested, Freddie shifted to relieve the growing pressure in his lap. "I'm on duty."

"Who would know?"

"I would." *Sam would know. Somehow, she'd find out, and I'd be screwed in a whole other way.*

Shooting him an "are you for real?" look, Elin

shrugged and reached for her bag. "I'm going to get changed."

As soon as he heard the bathroom door close behind her, Freddie closed his eyes and counted to ten. God help him, but he wanted to grab her, toss her down on the bed and have his way with her. Reminding himself that he was *working*, he willed his throbbing erection into submission.

Elin emerged from the bathroom wearing a purple silk nightgown that just barely covered her shapely ass.

Freddie suppressed a groan as she passed by him, leaving a fragrant cloud in her wake.

"Are you *sure* you don't want to have some fun?" she asked as she got settled in the other bed.

"Positive," he said through gritted teeth.

She flipped off the light. "Your loss."

Freddie fell back on the second bed and released a tortured deep breath. He was definitely being tested.

NICK GRABBED A BLANKET from the back of the sofa and spread it over them, arranging them so they lay facing each other. He traced a finger over Sam's frown. "I don't know what's causing you such concern, but whatever it is, we'll get through it together, Sam."

She rested her hand on his chest.

Nick's heart galloped under her touch as he waited for her to gather her thoughts.

"When I was with Peter," she said tentatively, "we tried for a long time to have a baby. We were about to go for infertility treatment when I got pregnant."

Imagining what she was going to say, Nick ached for her.

"I was so excited, even though Peter and I were already having a lot of problems. I know it was foolish to think a baby could fix it, but I still had hope then."

His heart breaking, Nick wiped away a tear that spilled down her cheek.

"I miscarried at twelve weeks."

"Sam…I'm so sorry."

"It was a bad miscarriage. I lost a lot of blood, and it took me a really long time to bounce back. Peter was so devastated. He kind of retreated into himself."

"So you went through it alone."

She shrugged and sat up, moving out of his embrace. "I had my sisters, my family. Angela had Jack a short time later, and he saved me in so many ways. He's my baby as much as he's hers. She even says so."

"He's adorable."

"He's my little man." She wiped her face with an impatient swipe, as if the tears were pissing her off. "A couple of months later, the doctor told me we could try again. Things with Peter had seriously disintegrated, but we both still wanted a baby so we made an effort to fix what was wrong even though I already knew it couldn't really be fixed. For a while, though, things were better. A year after the miscarriage, I got pregnant again, but I didn't know. It was an ectopic pregnancy. Do you know what that is?"

Nick sat up, reached for her hand and tried not to be hurt when she brushed him off. "I've heard of it."

"It's when the embryo implants outside the uterus. In my case, it was in one of the fallopian tubes. I was home alone when the tube erupted. I had almost bled to death when Angela found me."

"Jesus, Sam."

"I was in the hospital for more than a week that time. It was the most painful thing I've ever been through—physically and emotionally. I lost the tube and one of my ovaries. Because of some other problems I'd had with endometriosis, my doctor told me it was unlikely that I'd ever conceive again."

All at once Nick understood what had her so worried. "It doesn't matter, Sam. Not to me. If that's what you're worried about, don't."

"But you want a family. You *deserve* a family after growing up without one."

"We'll have one. We can adopt. There're millions of kids out there in need of homes. It doesn't matter to me how we get them."

"But—"

He leaned over and kissed her. Hard. "No buts. You're the key to everything. I knew that years ago when I first met you, and I know it even more now after living without you for so long. You're what I need most. We'll figure out the rest." Caressing her cheek, he added, "You've already given me so much that I've never had before. I don't want you to spend another second worrying about the one thing you can't give me."

"I told you I'm on the pill, but I'm not. I don't need to be, but I couldn't very well blurt this whole thing out when we were about to make love the other day. I'm sorry I lied to you."

"That doesn't even count as a lie, babe. When the time is right, and we're ready to have a family, we'll work something out."

"You should think about it. You should take some time to make sure—"

He stopped her with a finger to her lips. "I don't need to think about it."

The tension seemed to leave her body in one long exhale, and when he reached for her, she came willingly back into his arms.

"Do you feel better?"

She nodded. "I felt like I was deceiving you by getting so involved with you and not telling you this."

"You weren't deceiving me. It's part of you, Sam. It's part of what's made you who you are, and I love everything about you."

She ran her finger over the stubble on his jaw. "I used to dream about you when I was married. I wondered where you were, what you were doing, if you were happy. We only had that one night together, but I thought about you all the time."

The reminder of what they'd been denied made him ache with regret. "I thought about you, too. I read the paper obsessively, looking for the slightest mention of you."

"I did, too! I knew you were working for O'Connor. I even watched hours of congressional coverage, hoping for a glimpse of you, but you kept a low profile. I hardly ever saw you."

"My profile is probably going to get even lower."

"What do you mean?"

"I checked my voicemail at the office today. Got a few job offers."

"Like what?"

"Legislative affairs for the junior senator from Hawaii, communications for the senior senator from Florida. Oh, and director of the Columbus office for the senior senator from Ohio." With a teasing smile, he added, "What do you think about living in Columbus?"

She curled up her nose. "Is there anything that wouldn't be a major step down?"

"Nope. But that's how it works in politics. Your fortunes as a staffer are tied up in who you work for. If they go up, you go up. If they flame out, so do you."

"Or if they die…"

"Exactly."

"So what're you going to do?"

"I've got some money put away, and there's that money coming from John, too, so I'm not going to make any hasty decisions. In fact, it might be time for a change."

"What kind of change?"

"I used to toy with the idea of going to law school. It's probably too late now, but I still think about it."

"If it's what you want, you should do it."

Nick chuckled as he tweaked her nose. "So you'd be willing to put up with a professional student for a couple of years?"

"Whatever makes you happy makes me happy."

He shifted so he was on top of her. "*You* make me happy."

Sam's arms curled around his neck to bring him in for a kiss full of love and promise. She wrapped her long legs around his hips and arched her back, seeking him.

As Nick slid into her, he was so overwhelmed by love for her it took his breath away. Trying to get a hold of his emotions, he stayed still for a long moment until she began to wiggle under him, asking for more. What had earlier been frenetic was now slow and dreamy. He leaned in to kiss her, managing to hang on to his control until she gripped his ass to keep him inside her when she climaxed.

"Sam," he gasped as he pushed into her one last time, unable to believe they had managed to top perfection.

THIRTY-FOUR

SAM WAS TRYING to shake off the sex-induced stupor and open her eyes to go back to work when her phone rang. Checking the caller ID, she saw it was Gonzo. "What've you got?"

"A bloodbath," he said. "They're both dead."

Giving herself a second to absorb the news, she said, "How?"

"Noel was shot twice in the head at close range. Just like the other one, she was tied to the bed and tortured."

"I'm on my way." Sam sat up and started pulling on clothes.

"What's wrong?" Nick mumbled, half asleep.

"Noel and Natalie Jordan were murdered in their house."

He gasped. "Oh my God."

"I've got to get over there."

Reaching for his jeans, he said, "I'll come with you."

"No! There's no need. Peter's locked up, and I have to work."

"I promise I'll stay out of the way."

"You *never* stay out of the way."

"I knew these people, Sam. Don't make me stay home."

He looked so uncharacteristically vulnerable that her heart went out to him. She understood all at once that more than anything he didn't want to be alone just then. "Okay, but you *will* stay out of the way."

"I promise."

ON THE WAY to Belle Haven, Sam arranged for surveillance on Elin Svendsen's apartment building in case Patricia showed up there looking to make Elin her next victim. To Nick, she said, "Can you call Christina? I need the full list of every woman John dated during the years she worked for him."

"All of them?"

"Every one. I want names, addresses and phone numbers. Patricia has been gathering the same info we have. She's had someone digging into his past. I want to know what else she found—or rather *who* else."

"Christina might not have all that."

Sam shot him a withering look. "She was in love with him. You think she doesn't have the full lowdown on all the women he dated? Give me a break. She's probably got every detail down to their bra size in a spreadsheet. Tell her to email the list to me."

While Nick made the call, Sam ordered first shift to be called in early. Rounding up all of John's Barbies was going to take some serious manpower. Her cell phone rang, and Sam took the call from Detective Jeannie McBride.

"We've checked every hotel in the city," Jeannie said. "No hits for a Patricia Donaldson. Do you want me to start checking the burbs?"

Sam thought about that for a moment. "Try Patricia O'Connor, and get some extra people on it. I need that info ASAP."

"You got it, Sergeant."

Sam ended the call, but clutched the phone as they sped toward the Jordans's house. "I can't believe I didn't get to her sooner."

"She was the love of his life. Why would you think it was her?"

"He was the love of *her* life. Not the other way around. If a guy loves a woman the way she told us he loved her, he's not banging everything he can get his hands on when he's not with her. I think maybe she was still caught up in their teenage Romeo and Juliet romance, but he'd moved on. I'd sure love to talk to their kid. Thomas."

"He must be somewhere local with the funeral the day after tomorrow."

"If he is, we'll find him—and his mother. I just hope we get to her before she gets to another of John's girlfriends."

By the time they arrived, the Jordans's Belle Haven neighborhood was overrun with emergency vehicles.

Gonzo met them, his usually calm demeanor rattled. "I got here as soon as I could after Cruz called to tell me you wanted her picked up. The door was open. I saw him lying in the foyer and immediately called it in. We're getting some shit from Alexandria, so you'll have to talk your way in."

Calling on every ounce of patience she could muster, Sam explained to the Alexandria Police that the Jordan murders were possibly tied to Senator O'Connor's killing. After some territorial squabbling and just as she was about to get ugly with them, they agreed to let her view the crime scene. They made Nick wait outside.

Noel had been taken quickly in the foyer. Sam deduced that he'd opened the door and was shot before he had time to even say hello to the caller.

"He's the number two guy at Justice," she said with a smug smile for the cocky Alexandria detective who'd tried the hardest to keep her out. "You might want to let the attorney general know that his deputy's been murdered."

Flustered, the young detective said, "Yes, of course."

Pleased to have defused some of his arrogance, she went upstairs to see what had been done to Natalie. She'd been bound in almost the exact same fashion as Tara. And like Tara, the blood between her open legs told the story of sadistic sexual torture. "Is that a *hairbrush?*" Sam asked, staring at the object that had been left in Natalie's vagina.

"I think so," the medical examiner said.

Sam grimaced. Judging from the ligature marks on Natalie's neck, she too had been strangled after suffering through a prolonged attack.

Patricia was exacting revenge, one woman at a time.

The Alexandria Medical Examiner estimated time of death at about three hours prior. Sam's gut clenched at the realization that Noel must've just gotten home from the polygraph when they were attacked. If she'd only pieced this together a little sooner, she might've been able to save them.

Since it wasn't her crime scene, she stepped outside after asking the detectives for a courtesy copy of their report.

Nick was once again leaning against the car, waiting for her.

"Same thing as Tara."

"Christ," he whispered. "I didn't like Natalie, but the thought of what she must've gone through..."

Sam ran her fingers through her long hair, fighting off exhaustion that clung to her like a heavy blanket. "I know."

"I've been thinking..."

She glanced up at him to find his face tight with tension and distress. "About?"

"Graham and Laine."

The statement hung in the air between them, the implications almost too big to process.

Sam tossed the keys to him. "You drive while I work."

As they flew across Northern Virginia, Nick's big frame vibrated with tension. "You don't really think..."

"That she'd go after the people she blames for ruining her life? Yeah, I really think."

"God, Sam. If she hurts them..." His voice broke.

She reached for his hand. "We may be way off." But just in case they weren't, she gave the Loudon County Police a heads up about potential trouble at the senior Senator O'Connor's home. She also forwarded the list of ex-girlfriends that Christina had grudgingly sent to HQ with orders to place officers at each woman's home. The officers were provided with photos of Patricia Donaldson and Thomas O'Connor—just in case she wasn't acting alone. Issuing a second all-points bulletin for both of them, Sam could only pray that the cops got to the other women before anyone else was harmed.

"Should've seen this," she muttered, hating that it had taken her so long to put it together. "So freaking obvious."

"Don't beat yourself up, babe."

"Hard not to when the bodies are piling up."

"I'll bet I know why he was killed on the eve of the vote," Nick said.

Sam glanced at him. "Why?"

"He decided the week before he was killed that he was definitely going to run for re-election. He probably told Patricia that. Maybe he'd promised her one term to satisfy his father and then it would be their time If I'm right about that, she wouldn't have wanted him to have the chance to bask in the glow of his big victory on the bill. Not when he was screwing her over—in more ways than one."

"That makes sense," Sam said, buzzing with adrenaline as all the pieces fell into place. Certain now that she was on her way to cracking the case, she called Captain Malone and Chief Farnsworth at home to update them on the latest developments.

"Get me an arrest, Sergeant," the chief said, groggy with sleep.

"I'm moving as fast as I can, sir."

After she ended the call, Nick reached for her hand. "Why don't you close your eyes for a few minutes?

She shook her head. "I'd rather wait until I have a couple of hours. How about you? Are you okay to be driving?"

"I'm fine. Don't worry about me."

"Too late." She rested her head on his shoulder and went through the case piece by piece from the beginning. All along she'd suspected it would be a woman, one he was close to, who had a key to his place, who he wouldn't have been surprised to find waiting for him in his apartment.

Her cell phone rang. "What've you got Jeannie?"

"Unfortunately, nothing. We can't find them anywhere in the city."

"Damn it. They must've checked in under other names."

"That's the hunch around here. We're expanding into Northern Virginia and Maryland. I'll keep you posted."

"Thanks."

A Loudon County Police cruiser was positioned at the foot of the O'Connors's driveway when Sam and Nick arrived. He rolled down the window.

"Everything looks fine," the young officer said. "The house is dark and buttoned down for the night. I walked all the way around but didn't see anything to worry about."

"Thanks," Nick said. "We're just going to take a quick look and then be on our way."

"No problem. Have a nice evening."

As Nick drove slowly up the long driveway, Sam studied him with new appreciation. He'd handled the young cop with aplomb—thanking him for checking but letting him know they were going to take their own look—without insulting the officer. "Smooth," she said.

"What?"

"You. Just now."

"You sound surprised that I can actually be diplomatic when the situation calls for it."

She snorted with laughter.

"What's so funny?"

"You are when you get all indignant."

"I'm not indignant."

"Whatever you say."

They pulled up to the dark house, and Nick cut the engine. "I want to take my own walk around."

Sam retrieved a flashlight from the glove box and reached for the door handle.

"Why don't you stay here?" he said. "I'll be right back."

"The way you stay put when I tell you to?" She flipped on the flashlight in time to catch the dirty look he sent her way. "Let's go."

They walked the perimeter of the house, finding nothing out of the ordinary. In the backyard, Sam scanned the property. "Seems like everything is fine."

"I want to see them to make sure."

"Nick, it's two-thirty in the morning, and their son's funeral is tomorrow."

He scowled at her. "Do you *honestly* think they're sleeping?"

Realizing he was determined, she followed him to the front door and cringed at the sound of the doorbell chiming through the silent house.

A minute or so later, Graham appeared at the door wearing a red plaid bathrobe. His face haggard with grief, Sam deduced that he hadn't slept in days.

"What's wrong?" he asked.

"Nothing," Nick said, his voice infected with a nervous stammer. "I'm sorry to disturb you, but there's been some trouble tonight. I wanted to check on you and Laine."

Graham stepped aside to invite them in. "What kind of trouble?"

Nick told him about Tara and the Jordans.

"Oh God," Graham whispered. "Not Natalie, too. And Noel..."

"We think it's Patricia," Sam said, gauging his reaction.

Graham's tired eyes shot up to meet hers. "No… She couldn't have. She loved John. She'd loved him all her life."

"And she'd waited for him—fruitlessly—for her entire adult life," Sam said.

"We think he told her he was running for re-election," Nick said.

"So she assumed he was choosing his career over her and Thomas," Graham said.

"That's the theory," Sam said. "And we think she recently learned there were other women in his life."

"Why are you worried about us?" Graham asked Nick. "We haven't seen her since Thomas was born."

"Because if she's settling old scores, she certainly has a bone to pick with you," Nick said.

Graham ran a trembling hand through his white hair. "Yes, I suppose she does."

"I'd like to arrange for security for you and your wife until we wrap this up," Sam said.

"If you think it's necessary."

Knowing what had been done to Tara, Natalie and Noel, Sam said, "I really do."

Nick hugged Graham. "Why don't you try to get some rest?"

"Every time I doze off, I wake up suddenly and have to remember that John is gone…I keep reliving it, over and over. It's easier just to stay awake."

Nick embraced the older man again, and when he finally released him, Sam saw tears in Nick's eyes. "I know what you mean."

"Yes, I suppose you do."

"I'll see you in the morning. Don't hesitate to call me if you need anything."

Graham patted Nick's face. "I love you like one of my own. I hope you know that."

His cheek pulsing with emotion, Nick nodded.

"There's something I need to talk to you about after the funeral," Graham said. "Save me a few minutes?"

"Of course."

"Drive carefully," Graham said as he showed them out.

SAM SLIPPED HER ARM through Nick's and led him from the house, taking the keys from his coat pocket on the way to the car. "Are you okay?" she finally asked once they were in the car.

After a long moment of silence, Nick looked over at her. "He's never said that to me before. I've always sort of known it, but he's never come right out and said the words."

"You're an easy guy to love—most of the time."

His face lifted into the grin she adored. "Gee, thanks."

"We've got to do something about your inability to follow orders, however."

"Best of luck with that." He linked his fingers with hers as she drove them down the long driveway. "Thanks."

"For what?"

"For understanding why I needed to see with my own eyes that they're okay."

"They're your people."

"They're all I've got."

She squeezed his hand. "Not anymore."

THIRTY-FIVE

ON THE WAY BACK to Nick's house, Sam arranged for security at the O'Connor home and participated in a conference call with other HQ detectives to map out a plan for coverage of the funeral in the morning. If Patricia or Thomas showed up at the cathedral, they were prepared to snag them going in. Sam planned to wear a wire so she could communicate from the inside if need be. Because she knew Nick needed her support, she hoped she could get through the service without her job interfering, but she knew he'd understand if she had to leave. He wanted John's killer caught as much as she did.

As she followed Nick into his house, she glanced at the front shrubs, recalling once again the sensation of being hurled through the air by the force of the bomb. She shuddered.

"What's wrong, babe?"

"Nothing," she said, trying to shake off feelings that were magnified by a serious lack of sleep.

"It's going to take a while before we can walk in here and not think of it."

"I'm fine," she assured him, amazed once again by how tuned into her he was. "I just need a little more computer time."

He hung their coats in the front hall closet and then stepped behind her to massage her shoulders. "What you need is sleep."

"But—"

"No buts." He steered her up the stairs to his bedroom.

Sam wished she had the energy to fight him as he undressed her and tucked her into bed.

"What about you?" she asked, smothering a yawn.

"I'm going to grab a shower. I'll be there in a minute."

"'K," she said, her eyes burning shut.

While she waited for him, Sam's mind wandered through everything that had happened during that long night, replaying each crime scene as she tried to hold off on sleep until Nick joined her. All at once, she snapped out of the languor to discover that nearly half an hour had passed since he'd left her to take a shower.

She got up and went into a bathroom awash in steam. Opening the shower door, she found him leaning against the wall, lost in thought. Quietly, she slipped in behind him and wrapped her arms around his waist.

He startled and then relaxed into her embrace. "You're supposed to be sleeping."

"Can't sleep without you. You've ruined me." She pressed a series of kisses to the warm skin on his back. "Come on."

He shut off the water.

Sam grabbed his towel and dried them both. Taking his hand, she led him to bed. Wrapped in his arms, she was finally able to sleep.

WALKING INTO THE National Cathedral for the first time in her life the next morning, Sam gazed up at the soaring spires like an awestruck tourist from Peoria.

She wondered if staring at the president of the United States and his lovely wife like a star-struck lunatic made her any less of a bad-assed cop. In all her years on the job and living in the city, she had caught occasional glimpses of various presidents, but never had she been close enough to reach out and touch one—not that she would because that would be weird of course. Not to mention the Secret Service might take issue with it.

But as President Nelson and his wife Gloria approached Nick to offer their condolences, Sam could only stand by his side and remind herself to breathe as he shook hands with them.

"We're so very sorry for your loss," Gloria said.

"Thank you, Mrs. Nelson. John would be overwhelmed by this turnout." He gestured to the rows of former presidents, congressional members past and present, Supreme Court justices, the chairman of the Joint Chiefs of Staff, the secretaries of state, defense, homeland security and labor, among others. "This is Detective Sergeant Sam Holland, Metro Police."

Sam was struck dumb until it dawned on her that she was supposed to extend her hand. To the president. Of the United States. And the first lady. *Jesus.* "An honor to meet you both," Sam said.

"We've seen you in the news," the president said.

Sam wanted to groan, but she forced a smile. "It's been a unique month."

Gloria chuckled. "I'd say so."

Since both men were speakers, they were shown to seats in the front, adjacent to the O'Connor family. While Nick went over to say hello to them Sam scanned the crowd but saw no sign of Patricia or Thomas. Seated behind the O'Connors were most of John's staff and close family friends whom Nick identified for her when he returned to sit next to her.

She glanced over to find him pale, his eyes fixed on the mahogany casket at the foot of the huge altar. He hadn't eaten that morning and had even refused coffee. Looking back at the throngs of dignitaries, she couldn't imagine how difficult it would be for him to stand before them to speak about his murdered best friend. Disregarding her PDA rule, she reached for his hand and cradled it between both of hers.

He sent her a small smile, but his eyes expressed his gratitude for her support.

The mass began a short time later, and Sam was surprised to discover Nick had obviously spent a lot of time in church. Since she'd been raised without formal religion, the discovery was somewhat startling.

John's sister Lizbeth and brother Terry read Bible passages, and his niece and nephew lit candles. When both of them ran a loving hand over their uncle's casket on their way back to their seats, Sam's eyes burned, and judging by the rustle of tissues all around her, she wasn't alone.

President Nelson spoke of his long friendship with the O'Connor family, of watching John grow up and his pride in seeing such a fine young man sworn in as a United States senator. As the president left the pulpit, he stopped to hug John's tearful parents.

An usher tapped Nick on the shoulder. With a squeeze for Sam's hand, he got up to follow the usher's directions to the pulpit.

Unable to tear her eyes off Nick as he made his way

to the microphone, Sam was swamped with love and sympathy and a jumble of other emotions. She sent him every ounce of strength she could muster.

"On behalf of the O'Connor family, I want to thank you for being here today and for your overwhelming outpouring of support during this last difficult week. Senator and Mrs. O'Connor also wish to express their love and gratitude to the people of the Commonwealth who came by the thousands to stand in the cold for hours to pay their respects to John. He took tremendous pride in the Old Dominion, and the five years he represented the citizens of Virginia in the Senate were the most rewarding, challenging and satisfying years of his life."

Nick spoke eloquently of his humble beginnings in a one-bedroom apartment in Lowell, Massachusetts, of meeting a senator's son at Harvard, of his first weekend in Washington with the O'Connors and how his exposure to the family changed his life.

Sam noticed the O'Connors wiping at tears. Behind them, Christina Billings, Nick's deputy and the woman who'd suffered through unrequited love for John, rested her head on the communication director's shoulder.

Nick's voice finally broke, and he looked down for a moment to collect himself. "I was honored," he continued in a softer tone, "to serve as John's chief of staff and even more so to call him my best friend. It'll be my honor, as well, to ensure that his legacy of inclusiveness and concern for others lives on long after today."

Like the president before him, Nick stopped to embrace Graham and Laine on his way back to his seat.

Sam slipped her arm around him and brought his head to rest on her shoulder. At that moment, she couldn't have cared less who might be watching or who might gossip about them later. Right now, all she cared about was Nick.

The mass ended with a soprano's soaring rendition of "Amazing Grace," and the family followed the pall-bearers down the aisle and out of the church.

Dignitaries milled about, speaking in hushed tones as the church emptied. Watching them, Sam realized this was as much an official Washington political event as it was a funeral.

With Nick's hand on her elbow to guide her, they worked their way through the crowd. He stopped all of a sudden, and Sam turned to see who had caught his eye.

"You came," Nick said, clearly startled to see the youthful man with brown hair and eyes and an olive complexion that reminded Sam of Nick's.

"Of course I did." After a long pause, he added, "You looked real good up there, Nicky. Real good."

An awkward moment passed before Nick seemed to recover his manners. "This is Sam Holland. Sam, my father, Leo Cappuano."

"Oh." Sam glanced up to take a read of Nick's impassive face before accepting Leo's outstretched hand. He seemed far too young to be Nick's father, but then she remembered he was only fifteen years older than his son. "Pleased to meet you."

"You, too," Leo said. "I've read about the two of you in the paper."

Nick winced. "I meant to call you, but it's been kind of crazy..."

"Don't worry about it."

"I appreciate you coming. I really do."

"I'm very sorry this happened to your friend, Nicky. He was a good guy."

"Yes, he was."

Neither of them seemed to know what to say next, and Sam ached for them.

"Well," Nick said, "the family's having a thing at the Willard. Can you join us?"

"I need to get back to work," Leo said. "I just took the morning off."

Nick shook his hand. "Give my best to Stacy and the kids."

"You got it." With a smile for Sam, Leo added, "Bring your pretty lady up to Baltimore for dinner one day soon."

"I will. I have Christmas presents for the boys."

"They'd love to see you. Any time. Take care, Nicky." With a smile, Leo left them.

"Dad?"

He turned back.

"Thanks again for being here."

Leo nodded and headed for the main door.

Nick exhaled a long deep breath. "That was a surprise."

"A good surprise?"

"Yeah, sure."

But she could tell it had rattled him. What would it be like to expect so little of your father that you'd be shocked to see him at your best friend's funeral? Sam couldn't imagine.

On the way out of church, numerous people stopped Nick to compliment him on his heartfelt eulogy. He accepted each remark with a gracious smile, but Sam could feel his tension in the tight grip he kept on her hand. When they finally made it outside, he took a deep breath.

Gonzo met them. "No sign of either of them."

Removing the ear piece she'd worn during the funeral, Sam took a measuring look around at the crowd. "I really thought they'd be here, if nothing more than to pour salt in the O'Connors's wounds. She told Cruz they were planning to attend."

"We'll keep looking," Gonzo assured her.

"Any word on autopsies on Tara or Natalie?"

"Nothing yet."

"Get with Lindsey and put a rush on Tara's. We'll have to bug Alexandria for Natalie's." Sam glanced up at Nick, whose attention was focused elsewhere. Lowering her voice, she said to Gonzo, "I need to hang with him for a while longer. Call me if anything breaks."

"You got it."

"Thanks." Taking Nick's arm, she directed him to the row of taxis lined up at the curb.

"It was a good idea you had to take the Metro in this morning," he said once they were in a cab.

"I knew security would make it tough to park anywhere near the cathedral." She snuggled into him and wrapped her arm around his waist. "Are you okay?"

"I've been better."

"You were really great up there, Nick. I was so proud of you, my heart felt like it might burst."

He hugged her tight against him and touched his lips to her forehead. "Thanks for coming. I know you had other things to do—"

She tilted her face to kiss him. "I was exactly where I needed to be. Where I *wanted* to be." Glancing up at him, she found him staring out the window. "Can I ask you something?" she said tentatively, not sure if this was the best time. But she needed to know. For some reason, she *had* to know more.

"Sure you can."

"What you said about growing up in Lowell with your grandmother..."

"What about it?"

"If you lived in a one-bedroom apartment, where did you sleep?"

"The sofa pulled out to a bed."

She bit her bottom lip in an attempt to deal with the sudden need to weep. Her every emotion seemed to be hovering just below the surface, and it wouldn't take much for the floodgates to swing open. "Where did you keep your stuff?"

"I didn't have a lot of stuff, but what I had I kept in the hall closet."

Her heart cracked right in half. "That's why you're so particular about the things you have now, isn't it? And I've made fun of you for that. I'm so sorry, Nick."

"Don't be sorry, babe. You're right to razz me. You lighten me up, and I need that."

"I had no idea..."

"How could you? But it doesn't bother me at all when you tease me about being anal. I swear it doesn't, so please don't stop." He tipped up her chin and flashed the cajoling smile she couldn't resist. "Please?"

She returned his smile with a pout. "If it doesn't bother you, that takes some of the fun out of it."

He laughed. "I love you, Samantha Holland, and all your crazy twisted logic."

Wanting to give him absolutely everything he'd ever

been denied, but satisfied for now to hear him laugh, Sam closed her eyes and pressed her lips to his neck. "I love you, too."

THIRTY-SIX

THE CAB CAME to a stop in front of the Willard Intercontinental Hotel, two blocks from the White House on Pennsylvania Avenue.

"The O'Connors reserved the ballroom, and the food here is amazing," Nick said, hoping to convince her to stay for a while.

"I really need to get to work."

"I know. I'm just being selfish wanting you with me."

Sam studied him. "Let me check in with HQ. Maybe I can stay for a few minutes."

Nick watched her while she talked on the phone and wished he could take her home to decorate the Christmas tree he planned to buy. He'd never bothered with a tree before, but this year he wanted the bother. This year, everything was different.

"I'll be there shortly," Sam said as she ended the call. "I'm only a couple of blocks away at the Willard."

"So you can come in?" Nick asked when she had returned her phone to her coat pocket.

She hesitated, but only for a second. "Sure. There's not much else I can do until we get a sighting of one of them."

Before they entered the hotel, Sam rested her hand on his arm to stop him. "You know it's going to be like this, right?"

"Like what?"

"I'll want to be with you, especially on a day like this, but I'll need to be somewhere else a lot of the time."

Nick smiled, touched by the hint of vulnerability he detected. "I know what I'm signing on for, babe."

"Do you? Do you really?"

Something in her tone and the expression on her face told him this too had been a problem in her marriage. He leaned in to kiss her. "I really do. I'm sorry you can't spend the day with me, but I understand you have a job to do, and in this case, I have a vested interest in you getting it done."

"Okay," she said with a sigh of relief.

"I'm never going to hassle you over your work, Sam," he said as he guided her inside with an arm around her shoulders.

"Never say never. It has a way of screwing up plans, vacations, meals, sleep…"

"I'll do my best to understand, but I'll always be sorry to see you go."

She looked up at him, a small smile illuminating her beautiful face. "I want to be with you today."

"I know, and that counts for a lot."

They checked their coats and wandered into the elegant ballroom where Graham and Laine greeted each guest as they entered the room.

Nick embraced them both.

"You did a beautiful job, Nick," Laine said, grasping his hands.

"Thank you." Nick had such admiration for the aura of dignity the older woman projected even in the darkest hours of her life.

"No, thank *you*, for everything this week. I don't know what we would've done without you."

"It was no problem."

Laine shook Sam's hand. "Thank you for coming today."

"The service was lovely," Sam said.

"Yes," Laine agreed. "I thought so, too."

"Any developments?" Graham asked.

"A few," Sam said. "I'm heading into work shortly, and I hope to know more by the end of the day. I'll keep you informed."

"We'd appreciate that," Graham said. "Nick, look me up in half an hour or so, would you?"

"Sure." With his arm around Sam, Nick steered them through the crowd toward one of the bars in the corner. "I know you have issues with them, so thank you for that...just now."

"This isn't the time or the place."

"Do you plan to do anything about them lying to you?"

"What would be the point? If they had told me the truth, it would've saved me some time. I don't have anything to gain by going after them." She glanced over at the O'Connors who were greeting the senior senator from Virginia and his wife. "In fact, I kind of pity them."

"Because of John?"

"That, too, but also for what they've missed out on with Thomas. And for what?"

"I wonder if they regret what they did," Nick said as he accepted coffee for himself and a soda for her.

"They will if we can prove Thomas's mother murdered John."

Nick shook his head. "What a tangled web."

"It amazes me that people think they're going to get

away with trying to hide a baby. A secret like that is a time bomb looking for a place to detonate."

"True. I see it all the time in politics. The stuff people try to keep hidden usually blows up in their faces during a campaign."

Sam took a measuring look around the room. "I wonder where the cops who are supposed to be protecting the O'Connors are. I don't see anyone."

"Could be undercover."

"If there was a cop in this room, I'd know it."

Lucien Haverfield, the O'Connor family's attorney, approached them. "There you are, Nick. I've been looking for you."

"Lucien." Nick shook hands with the distinguished older man and introduced him to Sam. "Nice to see you."

"Fine job you did today at the funeral."

"Thank you."

"The will is being read tomorrow at two at the O'Connor home. I need you to be there."

"Why's that?" Nick asked, surprised.

"You're a beneficiary."

"But he left me money," Nick stammered. "Insurance money, and a lot of it."

"Can you be there at two?" Lucien asked, clearly not willing to shed any light in advance of the reading.

"Yes, of course."

"Great." Lucien patted Nick's shoulder. "I'll see you then."

"Wonder what that's all about," Nick said to Sam.

"I guess you'll find out tomorrow."

"Yeah." He noticed Graham signaling to him and

led Sam over to a table where Graham sat with the Virginia Democrats.

"We'd like to have a word with you upstairs, if you can spare us a few minutes, Nick," said Judson Knott, chairman of the party.

"Sure," Nick said with a perplexed glance at Sam.

"I'll, um, just wait for you here," she said.

"You're welcome to join us," Graham said. "This involves you, too."

Sam looked at Nick, who shrugged. "Okay," she said.

They followed the other men to the elevator and then to the Abraham Lincoln Suite. Nick took a moment to check out the incredible blue and gold suite, thinking he'd like to bring Sam there sometime when they could be alone. He accepted a short glass of bourbon from Judson. Sam declined a drink. Richard Manning, the party's vice chairman, had also joined them. "What's this all about, gentlemen?"

They gestured for Nick and Sam to have a seat at the dining room table.

"We have a proposition for you, Nick," Judson said.

Nick glanced at Graham and then at Sam. "What's that?"

"We'd like you to finish out John's term," Graham said.

Nick almost choked on the bourbon. "What? *Me?*"

Under the table, Sam grasped his arm.

"Yes, you," Judson said.

"But you have any number of people better suited. What about Cooper?"

"His wife was recently diagnosed with stage three breast cancer. He'll be announcing his resignation from the legislature the day after tomorrow."

"I'm sorry to hear that," Nick said sincerely. "How about Main?"

"He's been carrying on with his son's first grade teacher for years, and his wife filed for divorce yesterday. It'll be hitting the papers any day now."

"The party's having some troubles, Nick," Manning drawled. "We need someone of your caliber to step in and get us through to next year's election. We're hoping Cooper's wife will have recovered enough by then to free him up to run."

Nick couldn't believe they were serious. He wasn't the guy. He was the guy *behind* the guy. He named ten other Virginia Democrats he considered better suited to the job and was treated to a variety of disqualifying details about their personal lives that he could've lived without knowing. She's expecting twins, he's gay and in the closet—wants to stay there, he's got financial problems, she's caregiver to a mother with Alzheimer's. It went on and on.

"Listen, you guys," Nick said when he had run out of names to float. "I appreciate you thinking of me..."

"You struck a chord this morning," Judson said. "With your talk of humble beginnings. The data is highly favorable—"

"You've *polled* on me?" Nick asked, incredulous. *"Already?"*

"Of course we have." Richard seemed insulted that Nick even had to ask. "Most of Virginia and the rest of official Washington watched the funeral. You made quite an impression." Richard directed a charming smile at Sam. "Between that and your very public relationship with the Sergeant—"

"Don't bring her into this," Nick snapped. "She's off limits."

Graham rested his forearms on the table and leaned in to address Nick. "You know how this works. Nothing's off limits, *especially* your personal life. But the party is prepared to throw its support behind you if you want it. By this time tomorrow you can be a United States senator. All you have to do is tell us you want it, and we'll make it happen."

"Your name recognition is off the charts right now," Richard added. "Factor in youthful vitality, obvious political savvy, a well-known connection to the O'Connors and you're a very attractive candidate, Nick. Governor Zorn thinks it's a brilliant idea."

A United States senator. It boggled his mind. "I don't know what to say…"

"Say yes," Judson urged.

"It's not that simple," Nick said, thinking of Sam and their fledgling relationship. Could it handle the pressure that would come with a job like this on top of a job like hers? "I need to think about it."

"For how long?" Judson asked. "The governor is anxious to act."

"I need a couple of days."

"Two," Judson said. "I can give you through Christmas, and then we'll need to know."

"Why don't you want it?" Nick asked, beginning to worry about Sam's total silence and the sudden pallor gracing her cheeks.

"Hell," Judson said, "I'm too damned old to keep that kind of schedule. Richard is, too. We want to spend our spare time golfing and hanging out with the grandbabies. We need someone like you to get us through this transition. We're asking for one year, Nick. Give us that, and for the rest of your life you'll be known as Senator Cappuano."

The title sounded so preposterous, it was all Nick could do not to laugh.

Judson and Richard got up to leave. Both shook hands with Graham.

"Sorry again for your loss, Senator," Judson said.

To Nick, he added, "Let me know what you decide by the twenty-sixth."

Nick nodded and shook hands with them. When he heard the door click shut behind them, he turned to Graham and Sam.

"What do you think, Nick?" Graham asked.

"I'd like to know what Sam thinks."

"I, ah, I have no idea what to say."

He could tell by the wild look in her blue eyes that she was having a silent freak out and decided to wait until they were alone to address it further with her.

"You seriously think I can do this?" he said to Graham.

"If I had any doubt, we wouldn't be here."

Nick studied the other man for a long moment. "This was all your doing, wasn't it?"

Graham shrugged. "I might've suggested that the best man for the job was the one who knew John the best."

"I didn't know John as well as I thought I did."

"You knew him as well as anyone."

Nick looked over at Sam, wishing he knew what she was thinking. No doubt the offer had shocked her just as much as it had shocked him. Standing, he offered his hand to Graham. "Thank you for the opportunity."

Graham held Nick's hand between both of his. "I have nothing but the utmost faith in you, Nick Cappuano from Lowell, Massachusetts. I was so proud of you up there today. You've grown into one hell of a man."

"Thank you. That means a lot coming from you."

A knock on the door ended the moment between the two men.

THIRTY-SEVEN

"I'LL GET IT," Nick said. He strolled to the door, opened it and gasped at the face that greeted him. John's face. Rendered speechless, Nick could only stare at the young man. He had a wild, unfocused look to him that put Nick on alert.

"I'm Thomas O'Connor. I understand that my, um, grandfather is here?"

Recovering, Nick said, "Yes. Please. Come in."

As he ushered the young man into the room, Nick experienced the same prickle of fear on the back of his neck that he'd felt once before—the day he walked into John's apartment and found him dead. Sam, he noticed, had stood up and was watching Thomas's every move as he approached Graham.

"Who are you?" Thomas asked Nick.

Surprised that Thomas didn't seem to recognize him or Sam, he said, "I'm Nick Cappuano, your father's chief of staff, and this is my girlfriend, Sam." Nick met Sam's steady gaze with one of his own, using his eyes to implore her to go along with him. Until they knew what Thomas wanted with Graham, he didn't need to know she was a cop.

"You've taken me by surprise," Graham finally said as he sized up the grandson he hadn't seen since the day he was born twenty years earlier.

"I imagine I have."

"I thought we might see you and your mother at your father's funeral," Graham said.

"She got tied up in Chicago and couldn't make it," Thomas said.

Sam and Nick exchanged glances, and he knew she was picking up the same uneasy vibe.

Thomas turned to them. "You two can take off. I came to see my grandfather."

"That's all right," Nick said, the tingle on his neck intensifying by the minute. "We've got nowhere to be."

Thomas pulled a gun from the inside pocket of his winter coat. Pointing it at Sam and Nick, he said, "Then take a seat and shut up." He gestured to the sofa.

"Thomas," Nick said, taking a step toward him, "you don't want to do this. What difference will it make now?"

The younger man stared at him, his eyes even more wild and unfocused than they were when he first arrived. "Are you serious? What *difference* will it make? My *grandfather* ruined my mother's life. He shipped her off like unwanted garbage to protect his political image."

Sam rested her hand on Nick's arm to pull him back. Nodding her head, she signaled for him to take a seat with her on the sofa.

Once they were seated, Thomas turned back to Graham. "All you cared about was yourself."

"That's not true. I cared about your father, and you, too. I sent money. For years. I made sure you had everything you needed."

"Everything except my father and my family! You took everything from us. We got him for one lousy weekend a month, and you know what he was doing the rest of the time? Fucking his way through Washington with one stupid bitch after another."

Watching Thomas gesture erratically with the gun, Nick's heart slowed to a crawl.

Sam poked his leg to get his attention.

He watched as she raised her pant leg and removed the small clutch piece she had strapped to her calf.

She pressed it into his hand and drew her primary weapon from the shoulder harness she had worn for the funeral, keeping the gun hidden in her suit coat in case Thomas turned to them. Mouthing the word "wait" she used her finger to indicate that he should go right while she went left.

Nick nodded to let her know he understood.

"You know what he told me a couple of weeks ago when I introduced him to my girlfriend? He advised me later that I shouldn't get 'tied down' to one woman. That a man needs to 'mix it up,' that 'variety is the spice of life.' It was a real touching father-son moment, and it was the first time it ever occurred to me that he'd been unfaithful to my mother. She'd waited her *whole life* for him. Ever since you banished her, she's done nothing but wait for him and settle for whatever scraps he tossed our way. And then he comes and tells us he's running for re-election! He actually expected us to be *happy* about his big news. He'd promised us one term. One term for you, his beloved father. Then it would be our turn. He lied about *everything*. Everything!"

"He loved you."

"No, he loved *you!* You were the only one he cared about."

"You killed him," Graham said in a whisper. "You killed my son."

"He had it coming! He was a fucking *whore!* I've got the investigator's report to prove it. You should see what he got done in just two weeks' time. It was truly revolting."

"That doesn't mean he deserved to die," Graham said. "Natalie didn't deserve what you did to her, either."

Thomas moved so quickly, Sam and Nick couldn't react in time to stop him from pistol-whipping his grandfather.

Graham went down hard, blood spurting from a wound on his forehead.

"Get up!" Thomas shrieked. "Get up and take what's coming to you like a man!"

"You talk about being a man!" Graham screamed back at him. "But what kind of man rapes and murders women?"

Sam held Nick back, giving him the one-minute sign.

"I made them pay for what they did to my mother. They got exactly what they deserved."

"You're a monster," Graham whispered, the blood loss weakening him.

Thomas aimed the gun at his grandfather's chest.

Sam gave Nick the thumb's up.

They rushed Thomas from behind, each of them pushing a gun into the young man's temples.

"Freeze," they said in unison.

Sam glowered at Nick. "I'll take it from here." She had Thomas disarmed, cuffed and immobilized less than a second later. With her free hand, she tugged her radio off her hip and called for back up.

"What the fuck?" Thomas screamed, fighting the restraints. "You're a fucking *cop?*"

"Surprise," Nick said, unable to resist a smile as

adrenaline zipped though his system. Watching her work never failed to fire him up. "Meet my 'girlfriend,' Detective Sergeant Sam Holland, Metro Police Department. You really ought to read a newspaper once in a while."

"Son of a fucking bitch."

"You said it, buddy." Sam tightened her hold on Thomas. "You're under the arrest for the murders of John O'Connor, Tara Davenport, Natalie Jordan and Noel Jordan. You have the right to remain silent."

Nick stayed with Graham while Sam dragged Thomas out of the suite to turn him over to Gonzo for transport to HQ. Nick pressed a handkerchief to the wound on Graham's head.

Tears spilled down the older man's cheeks. "This is all my fault. I caused this. I forced John to lead a double life."

"You did what you thought was right at the time. That's all any of us can ever do."

"Will you find Laine for me? I need to see her."

"As soon as the paramedics get here, I'll get her to the hospital."

"Call Lucien," Graham said. "Have him send someone over to represent Thomas."

Nick stared at the older man. "You can't be serious."

"He's my grandson. What I did to him and his mother drove him to this." Graham closed his eyes and took a deep, rattling breath. "Make the call."

Even though he didn't agree, Nick said, "I'll take care of it." He rested his hand on top of Graham's. "Try not to worry about anything."

"You're going to make an outstanding senator."

"I haven't said yes yet."

"You will." The older man held Nick's hand until the EMTs arrived and whisked him away.

The moment they left with Graham, Sam returned to the suite.

"Whew," Nick said. "That was something."

A cocky grin lit up her gorgeous face. "Just another day at the office."

"For you, maybe."

"You did good—for a rookie."

"Gee, thanks." He wiped the sweat from his forehead, his legs still rubbery. "You called Chicago to check on Patricia?"

"They're on their way to her house as we speak. Thomas had her credit cards in his wallet."

"I feel sorry for her," Nick said. "She's lost them both."

"The whole situation is too sad, but his lawyer will probably mount an insanity defense."

"He was going to kill us all, wasn't he? That's why he said all the stuff he did in front of us."

"I suspect that became his plan when we insisted on staying. I just can't believe I didn't figure this out sooner. I was so sure it was a love affair gone wrong."

"Well, it sort of was when you think about it."

"Yeah, I guess you're right."

"I'm just glad we were here when Thomas confronted Graham." He shuddered. "I don't even want to think about what could've happened."

"It's probably better if you don't think about it."

Nick slipped an arm around her shoulders. "We need to talk about what happened before Thomas showed up."

"Later." She hip checked him. "No PDA in front of the colleagues."

He slapped her on the ass. "Screw that."

Sam attempted a dirty look but failed to pull it off.

"We make a good team, you know that?" he said.

"As long as you remember who's in charge."

Nick took great pleasure in hooking an arm around her and escorting her down the hallway full of hooting cops. Not even the elbow she jammed in his ribs could detract from his euphoria at having her by his side and John's killer on his way to jail.

In the elevator, she looked up at him, her clear blue eyes full of love. "Thanks for having my back in there."

Hugging her closer to him, he kissed her cheek and then her lips. "Samantha, I'll *always* have your back."

EPILOGUE

NICK GOT HOME from the reading of John's will just after five on Christmas Eve and went straight to the kitchen to dig out the bottle of whiskey he'd kept on hand for John. He poured himself half a glass and downed it in one long swallow that burned all the way through him. Pouring a second shot, he took it with him to sit in the living room where a seven-foot Christmas tree waited to be decorated. Under the tree were six festively wrapped gifts for Sam.

He hadn't heard from her all day, and after her refusal to discuss the Virginia Democrats' offer when they finally got home late last night, he had good reason to wonder if she would keep her promise to spend this evening with him. She hadn't even called to tell him that Marquis Johnson had been remanded over to trial—without incident. Nick had to hear about it on the news.

Still hopeful that Sam would keep her promise to spend tonight with him, Nick went into the kitchen to make the dinner he'd shopped for earlier. By nine o'clock the pasta was rubbery, and he had given up on her. Could she really be *that* freaked out by his job offer? Didn't she know that if she wasn't in favor of it, he wouldn't do it? Disappointment mixed with disbelief. That she would let him down like this, that she would let *herself* down like this…

He stretched out on the sofa with another shot of

whiskey. The empty tree was a stark reminder of how his plans for this evening had failed to materialize. Without Sam, what did it matter? What did anything matter?

He must have dozed off because the ringing doorbell startled him awake an hour later. His heart surged with hope as he got up to answer it. He swung open the door, and there she was.

"Hey," he said.

"Hey."

"I thought you weren't coming."

"I almost didn't."

Nick stepped back to let her in and took her coat.

"What do I smell?" she asked, surprised. "Did you cook?"

He shrugged. "Nothing special."

"Did you leave any for me?"

"All of it."

"You didn't eat?"

"I was waiting for you."

Snuggling into his embrace, she said, "I'm sorry. I totally freaked, and I handled this all wrong."

Nick hugged her close, overcome with relief at having her back in his arms after a day filled with uncertainty. He brushed his lips over hers. "Tell me what you're thinking, Samantha. Tell me the truth."

She looked up at him with those blue eyes he loved so much. "I'd be a liability to you. I'm messy and loud and I swear and sometimes I even tell white lies—I don't mean to, but they sneak out before I can stop them. I'm dyslexic, infertile and my stomach runs my life. And then there're the lovely people I come in contact with on a daily basis: drug dealers, prostitutes, murderers, rapists. There's the whole fiasco with the Johnsons—and my ex-husband is headed for prison..."

Even though he was amused by her speech, Nick knew she was dead serious and fought back a smile. "That's not your fault. He tried to kill us both."

"Which will lead people to wonder what kind of woman marries a man like him. They'll question my judgment and yours for getting involved with me. They'll rehash Johnson and every other ugly case I've ever had—and there're a lot of them. It'll reflect poorly on you."

"I'm not running for office, Sam. It's being handed to me for one year, and then it's done."

Rolling her bottom lip between her teeth, she mulled it over. "We'd attract a lot of media attention after everything that happened this week."

"I can handle it if you can."

"I'd hate to be responsible for causing you trouble. I'd hate that."

"I can deal with that, too."

She rested her hands on his shoulders. "You want this, don't you?"

"My life was just fine before. If I say no, it'll be fine after."

"That doesn't answer my question."

"It's something I never dreamed of, something I never even considered before yesterday."

"My dad and Freddie think it's so cool," she said with a shy smile. "They say it would work out fine for us. My dad even thinks it could be a 'grand adventure.'"

Her skeptical scowl amused Nick. "They're very wise men. You should listen to them."

Looking up at him, she said, "Can we eat? I haven't eaten all day, and I'm starving."

He decided not to push his luck since she seemed to be coming around to a decision in her own peculiar way. "Sure."

"Oh!" she said on the way to the kitchen. "You got a tree!"

"I told you I was going to."

"When did you have time?"

"I did it this morning, along with a few other things."

"What other things?"

"A little Christmas shopping," he said with a mysterious smile as he poured her a glass of wine. "And some real estate shopping."

Her eyebrows knitted with confusion.

He served her the reheated shrimp fettuccine Alfredo and carried a tossed salad to the table. "You said you couldn't live way out here in Virginia, right?"

"Uh huh." She dove into the meal as if she was, in fact, starving. "You never told me you could cook like this! It's amazing!"

"You never asked, and I'm glad you like it." After lighting the candles on the table, he sat down across from her. "Anyway, since you can't live here, I bought a place in the city."

"What place did you buy?" she asked, astounded.

"The one that was for sale up the street from your dad's. I looked at it on Sunday when you were at work, I offered this morning and they accepted. I'm meeting with a Realtor after Christmas to list this place."

She sat back in her chair to stare at him. "Just like that?"

"I knew you'd want to be close to your dad and to work."

"Won't you need to maintain a residence in Virginia?"

Implied but not stated was if he became a senator. "John took care of that. He left me the cabin. That's why they wanted me to come today."

Her eyes went soft with emotion. "Nick…That's wonderful. You love it there."

"I was so surprised and delighted." He reached for her hand and brought it to his lips.

"How's Graham doing?"

"Better. They let him go home today when his blood pressure returned to normal."

"That's good."

"I feel sorry for them. They've got a long road ahead of them coming to terms with all of this. And the media is clamoring for info about John's illegitimate son."

"They should just come clean at this point."

"I think that's the plan. Laine wanted me to tell you how very sorry she is for lying to you about Thomas. She said she panicked when she saw you had his photo."

"It's in the past now. I'm over it."

When they finished eating, Nick picked up their wine glasses and led her to the sofa. "John had so many secrets. Hell, I had no idea until today when the lawyer was doling out his millions how insanely wealthy the sale of his business made him. There were a lot of secrets, but he loved his father. So much. Despite everything. He loved him."

"I can understand that. There's not much my father could do to change how I feel about him."

"You're lucky to have him."

"And I know it."

He studied the face that had become so essential to him. "What're we going to do, Sam?"

"Well, tonight we're going to decorate that tree." She glanced at the tree and then down at the gifts under it. "What's all that?"

"One for every year we missed."

Smiling, she shifted to straddle him. "That's so incredibly sweet."

He pulled her in close.

"Tomorrow," she said, touching her lips to his, "we're going to Tracy's for dinner. The next day, you're going to tell the Virginia Democrats that you're their new senator."

He cradled her face in his hands. "Am I?"

"It's just a year, right?"

"One year."

"It'll be a total mess. You know that, don't you?"

"I *love* a good mess," he said with a teasing grin. "In fact, I *live* for messes."

She smiled. "We're really going to do this."

"We really are."

"I love you, Senator Cappuano."

"I love you, Lieutenant Holland. Merry Christmas."

"Same to you." She leaned her forehead against his and looked him in the eye. "It's gonna be one hell of a New Year."

"I can't wait."

* * * * *

ACKNOWLEDGMENTS

When I first began work on the book that became *Fatal Affair*, I quickly realized that I couldn't begin to replicate the District of Columbia's complex Metropolitan Police Department. So the department portrayed in *Fatal Affair* is my version of the MPD and is in no way intended to mirror the real thing.

I want to thank my husband, Dan, who loves a good excuse to surf the web. He did tons of research for me, and I appreciate his help. My children, Emily and Jake, put up with me when I'm writing and have learned not to ask me any important questions when I'm lost in thought.

To my friends Christina Camara, Paula DelBonis-Platt and Lisa Ridder, thank you for reading, critiquing, editing and proofreading early versions of this book. To Julie Cupp, thank you for braving the cold to take me to Eastern Market, for answering my many questions about Washington and for your help, as always, in naming characters. Since *Fatal Affair* was first published in 2010, Julie has become my full-time assistant, and I'm deeply grateful for all the many ways she makes my life easier. She's the best!

Thank you to Newport, RI, Police Captain Russell Hayes for reading the book, providing critical input and taking me on a memorable ride-along. To my friend, Newport Police Sergeant Rita Barker, thank you for reading and introducing me to Russ. Thanks to Theresa Ragan for coming up with the perfect name for the book. Special thanks to my agent, Kevan Lyon, and my first Carina editor, Jessica Schulte. Both of you helped to make this a much better book than it would've been otherwise, and I'm grateful for your contributions. To Angela James and everyone on the Carina team, thank you for taking a chance on the Fatal Series way back when. I still can't believe everything that's happened since then.

Finally, my profound thanks to all the readers who have embraced Sam and Nick's story: I can never tell you what your loyalty and dedication to my books means to me.

To discuss the Fatal Series with other avid readers, join the Fatal Series Reader Group on Facebook at facebook.com/groups/FatalSeries/. To dish about the details in *Fatal Affair*, with spoilers allowed and encouraged, join the *Fatal Affair* Reader Group at facebook.com/groups/FatalAffair/. I love to hear from readers! You can contact me at marie@marieforce.com. Thanks for reading!

xoxo

Marie

Turn the page to read about Sam and Nick's "memorable" one-night stand in ONE NIGHT WITH YOU, a Fatal Series novella.

ONE NIGHT WITH YOU

ONE

SAM HOLLAND WALKED into the dank hole-in-the-wall that was O'Leary's Bar and gave her eyes a second to adjust to the gloom. After hours outside in the broiling sun, the cool, moldy atmosphere was just what she needed. Well, that and a cold one with her dear old dad.

Skip waved to her from the far end of the bar, and when she walked over to him, he jumped up to hug and kiss her. "Hey, baby girl. You're late."

"Awwww," Captain Malone said, "Daddy's wittle girl is here."

Since she'd known Malone for most of her life, she felt entirely comfortable giving her superior officer the middle finger, which made him howl with laughter.

"She's all yours, Skip." Malone threw a twenty on the bar. "God help you."

Skip tightened his arm around Sam's shoulders. "Wouldn't have it any other way."

"See you guys tomorrow," Malone said on his way out.

Sam took the stool Malone had abandoned and popped a handful of beer nuts into her mouth as she signaled the bartender for one of what her dad was having. "You really gotta do that?"

"Do what?" Skip was the picture of innocence when he knew damn well what she was talking about.

"The whole 'baby girl' schmoopy schmoop in front of other cops."

Skip's brows stretched to his hairline. "What in the name of fuck's sake is schmoopy schmoop?"

"The hugging, the kissing." Sam waved her hand to indicate the full scope of his greeting. She was already regretting this line of conversation, because she knew exactly what he would say.

"You're my daughter."

"I'm also one of your junior officers."

"You're my daughter first."

"Dad! Seriously. It's hard enough for me to deal with my dad being the deputy chief without you acting like my dad every chance you get."

"Honestly, Sam, I *am* your dad, and I'll damn well act like it until the day you bury me."

Not wanting to think about burying him—ever—she nodded her thanks to the bartender when he delivered her beer and a fresh one for Skip. "You're not making it easy for me."

"Isn't that what you wanted? If I recall correctly, your exact words were, 'Hands off. Let me do my own thing.'"

"Yes! Hands off. No schmoop!"

"Sorry, that ain't gonna happen." He took a deep drink from his mug. "So I see you're taking another half day."

As he laughed at his own joke, she rolled her eyes at the almost daily comment. "Another eleven-hour half day."

"Slacker. You know I expect better from you."

"Yeah, yeah."

"Is that any way to talk to a superior officer?"

"It's the only way to talk to my old man."

"Who you calling old?" He pushed the beer nuts closer to her. "Want to get some dinner tonight?"

"I'd love to, but Angela talked me into going to a stupid party that I have no desire to go to, and now I'm committed, although I still hope to get out of it."

"What's up with the party?" Skip asked.

"A man of interest, apparently."

"Is that right? Well, thank goodness. I thought she was going to mourn that jackass Johnny for the rest of her life."

"Don't go celebrating quite yet."

"I'll require a full report tomorrow. Meet for coffee?"

"After three years of meeting for coffee every day before work, you still have to ask?"

"Best part of my day, baby girl. Very best part."

"Mine, too." Sam smiled at his unabashed affection for her. She knew she'd made him so proud by joining the department, and continuing to make him proud was her only goal as a police officer—well, that and relieving Lieutenant Stahl of his corner office in the Homicide detectives' pit. That was her other primary goal. Someday…

"So Angela's actually showing interest in a guy who isn't Johnny the douche bag?" Skip asked.

"Yeah."

"You're going to that party."

"You can't actually make me go."

"Yes, I can." The look he gave her reminded her of the many times she'd tried to challenge his authority while growing up. Skip Holland got a lot done with that eyebrow.

"I *really* don't want to go." Newly promoted to detective with the Metropolitan Police Department in Washington, DC, Sam had sore feet and a sunburn after working a full day plus a three-hour construction detail following her regular shift. She wanted a cool bath, another cold beer and a soft bed—in that order.

Her sister had called her at work earlier to make her case.

"*Please*, Sam," Angela had said. "When was the last time I asked you for anything?"

"Um, yesterday when I dropped off and picked up your car from the garage—and paid for the repairs."

"I'll pay you back, and you know I appreciated your help."

"So, we're square. I don't have to go to this party tonight."

"You do have to. Spencer is going to be there, and he wants me to meet him. I can't go alone. That would be so awkward. All I need you to do is come with me so I don't have to walk in alone and stay long enough to make sure I find him."

"That's not all I'd have to do. There would be showering, hair drying, makeup application and torturous shoes that most likely won't go on over my swollen feet."

"*Sam...*"

"*Angela...*"

"I'm begging you. I've called everyone I know, and they're all busy. I *need* you."

Sam had been on the verge of begging herself when Lieutenant Stahl walked by her cubicle, glaring at her when he saw her sitting with her feet on the desk as she talked on the phone. Even though she was officially off duty, she dropped her feet to the floor, sat up straighter and raised her middle finger to his departing back.

"I really, really, *really* like him, Sam. Really. Remember when I dated him for a short time when Johnny and I were taking a break? I never forgot him, and I always regretted going back to Johnny after I met Spencer."

Since Angela hadn't sounded excited about any guy since the painful breakup with her high school boyfriend a year ago, Sam began to waver. "How long would I have to stay?"

"No more than an hour. I promise."

"All right," Sam said with a protracted groan.

"I owe you big."

"You already owe me big."

"I owe you bigger."

"Yeah, yeah. Just wait until I start cashing in all these chips."

"Anything you want," Angela said, her voice bright with euphoria Sam hadn't heard in a very long time. It was well worth the sacrifice of her tortured feet stuffed into heels if it would bring back Angela's smile. She hadn't been herself since Johnny decided he wasn't done playing the field and couldn't think about getting married until he'd sown his wild oats. Unfortunately, he'd chosen to use those exact words when he ended his long relationship with Angela.

At times over the last year, Sam and the rest of their family had wondered if Angela would ever get over the heartbreak Johnny had left behind when he moved on without her. So if an hour in heels made Angela feel better, Sam was more than willing to forgo her night in the tub.

"Pick me up?"

"I'll be there at eight." The line went dead. Angela knew better than to give Sam time to change her mind.

"Goddamn it," Sam muttered under her breath as she stood to gather her belongings. After eleven hours at work, there wasn't much gas left in her tank. But since there was nothing she wouldn't do for either of her sisters, Sam trudged out of HQ into humidity that made for another stifling summer day in the nation's capital.

And then she'd remembered her plans to meet her dad for a drink on the way home. This day kept getting better and better.

"Where'd you go?" Skip asked as he took a sip from his beer.

"Just thinking about Ang and this lame-ass party I agreed to go to with her. It'll be a bunch of players trying to score."

"Want to borrow my Taser?"

"Yes, in fact, I would."

Skip's deep laugh rumbled through his chest, drawing a smile from her, too. His laugh was infectious, and she loved making it happen. She downed the last of her beer. "I gotta go beautify. Can I get this round?"

"Absolutely not." He never let her pay. "Don't let any of those players get their hands on my baby girl."

"Don't worry. I'll kick their asses if they so much as try."

"That's my girl. Take care of Ang. She's not made of the same tough stuff you are. She's soft on the inside."

"I know," Sam said with a sigh. "I'll keep an eye on her. Don't worry."

"That's like telling me not to breathe." He pointed to his cheek.

Sam looked around to make sure none of the other cops sitting at the bar was looking before she planted a quick kiss on his cheek.

"Love you, baby girl."

"Love you, too, Skippy. See you in the morning."

"I'll be there."

After leaving the bar, she drove home to the less than fashionable townhouse she shared with three roommates in the Capitol Hill neighborhood where she'd grown up. Sam liked the convenience of living close to her dad and sisters but had chosen to live on her own rather than move in with Angela after graduate school. It'd been time for her to grow up and stand on her own two feet, and Angela would've wanted to take care of and keep tabs on her "baby" sister.

Sam had been ready to bust loose after slogging through years of school while battling dyslexia. The last thing she'd wanted was anyone keeping tabs on her. So she'd answered an ad for roommates and ended up living with two guys, Peter Gibson and Dave Maxwell as well as Dave's brother John, who crashed there more often than Dave did. Of course, her dad, the deputy police chief, had run background checks on all of them before he let her sign the lease.

She'd learned it was futile to remind him that she was an adult now and didn't need or require his approval.

Peter was watching SportsCenter when she came in, dropping her backpack inside the door and kicking off her shoes as she made for the fridge.

"Hard day at the office, dear?" he asked.

"Long day at the office, made longer by an endless detail in the broiling sun." Sam cracked open a bottle of water and chugged it down before reaching for another one. If she was going to be expected to drink any more alcohol tonight, she needed to rehydrate.

"Want to get a pizza?"

"I'd love to, but Angela talked me into going out, so I have to go get ready."

"Where're you going?"

"Some party she was invited to. Apparently, there's a guy involved."

"Ahh, I see. Where's the party?"

Sam shrugged. "No idea. I'm just along for the ride. Better hit the shower and get my act together. She'll be here soon." As Sam trudged upstairs, she thought about how interested Peter always was in what she was up to. She wasn't sure if he was interested in *her* or just naturally curious. He was cute in a boyish sort of way, with sandy hair and blue eyes that lit up when he laughed.

Since their other roommate, Dave, an associate gunning for partner at a local law firm, was hardly ever home, she'd shared many a pizza and night in front of the TV with Peter and had begun to think of him as a friend.

Sam spent more time than she should have standing under the cool water in the shower and had to rush through the hair drying and makeup portion of the program. She hated being rushed and didn't look as good as she could have, but so what? This was Angela's big show. Who cared how she looked?

Because she didn't care, she turned off the flat iron and decided her hair could be wild and curly tonight. Normally, she hated the wild curls, but she couldn't be bothered with the effort it would take to tame them. The summer sunshine had added blonde streaks to her toffee-colored hair, which was currently longer than it had been in years. Who had time for haircuts between work and the extra details she regularly signed on for to pay off her student loans?

It was all she could do to get five hours of decent sleep every night. Sam's philosophy was you're only young once, and paying off the staggering debt from college and graduate school was a top priority. Of course, it didn't hurt that all her volunteering for overtime made her look good to the brass. She'd made detective a year earlier than she'd expected and now had her eye on the rank of detective sergeant in a few years.

Naturally, she'd heard a few rumbles about favoritism after she earned the gold shield, but Sam tried to ignore that crap. So what if her dad was the deputy chief? She knew—and he knew—that she'd worked her ass off to earn that promotion. No one had given her anything she hadn't deserved. Even though she respected him more than anyone in the world, it wasn't always easy to be Skip Holland's daughter in that department. People held him in very high regard and had equally high expectations for his daughter. It was a lot to live up to, but Sam was equal to the challenge.

Wearing a short summer skirt, a lightweight top and sky-high heels that made her feet scream for mercy, Sam eyed her bed and wished with every fiber of her being that she were a less faithful sister. She wanted nothing more than to slide naked into that bed and blast the air-conditioning for the next eight hours. But it was not to be.

A horn blaring in the street let Sam know Angela had arrived. "Here goes nothing." She grabbed her purse and headed downstairs, her feet protesting every step of the way. "See you later," she called to Peter on the way out.

"Have fun. Don't do anything I wouldn't do."

"Very funny. I'll be back before that can happen."

"I'll keep your spot on the sofa warm."

"Excellent." Sam rushed out the front door into the oppressive humidity and felt her hair get bigger in just the few seconds it took to get into Angela's car.

This was going to be a long night.

TWO

"WHY'S THE CREEP watching you leave?" Angela asked, eyeing the house suspiciously.

"What?"

"Peter. He's in the window watching you. He gives me the willies."

"You're being ridiculous. He's my friend."

Angela pulled the car away from the curb and hit the gas. "Your friend who wants you bad, if you ask me."

"He does not. He's a buddy. That's all. He's got a girlfriend."

"Have you met her?"

"Not yet."

"You haven't seen the way he looks at you when you're not looking at him. It's creepy. Tracy thinks so, too."

"So you guys have been talking behind my back about me and my roommate?"

Angela made an erratic lane change that had the driver of the car behind them laying on the horn. "Well, yeah, of course we have."

"How about you get us there without getting us killed?" Sam asked, holding on to the handle above the passenger door.

"Don't be so melodramatic."

"You've got cop courage."

"What the hell does that mean?"

"You drive like a maniac because you can drop my name or dad's to get out of a ticket."

"Whatever. I'd drive like a maniac even if you guys weren't cops."

"Lovely. Where is this party anyway?"

"Somewhere in Georgetown. I have the address in my purse. Now, back to Peter the creep. I think you should move out of there, and so does Tracy."

"Please tell me you didn't share those thoughts with Dad."

"We haven't. Yet."

"Don't. I don't need him on my back. It was bad enough when he insisted on running background checks before I could move in there. I'm twenty-eight, for crying out loud, and a cop in my own right. Why do I need my daddy checking out my roommates?"

"Because you'll always be his baby girl no matter how old you are."

She thought of their conversation earlier in the bar and knew Angela spoke the truth. "Why doesn't he treat you and Tracy that way? It's bizarre."

"Come on, Sam. You know you've always been special to him."

"You guys are, too."

"We know that, but we always belonged to Mom. You were his."

Sam couldn't deny that either. She and her dad had shared a special bond all her life, and she'd gone out of her way to make him proud. She'd never forget the tears in his eyes the day she took the oath as a member of the Metropolitan Police Department. "Still, that doesn't give him the right to micromanage my life."

"Try telling him that."

"I have told him that. A thousand times. He just smiles and goes about minding my business for me, so please, for the love of God, do not mention to him that you and Tracy think Peter is creepy. A, it's not true. And B, I don't need the aggravation."

"We won't say anything to him, but you need to keep an eye on Peter. Something about that guy rubs me the wrong way."

"Good thing then that you don't have to live with him."

"I still don't get why you didn't want the extra bedroom at my place. It would've been just like old times."

"Right, with you minding my business in addition to Dad. That's just what I didn't need."

"That's so not true! I wouldn't have bothered you."

Sam let her withering look speak for itself. Angela and Tracy had been mothering Sam since the day she was born.

"I wouldn't have! You should move in with me. I don't like you living with that guy."

"That guy has been nothing but nice to me, and I'm not moving out of there. I signed a lease for a year, and I'm staying put."

"Suit yourself, but don't tell me I didn't try to warn you when it turns out he is, in fact, a creep."

"I won't." Sam watched her city go by in a blur as Angela darted in and out of unusually light DC traffic like a seasoned stock car driver. Having a cop riding shotgun definitely gave her permission to drive like a lunatic, knowing the ticket wouldn't stick if they were pulled over. "So when did you hear from Spencer?"

"It was the funniest thing! I was at work today, and he came in for a meeting with one of the partners. I'd forgotten how hot he is and how much fun we had during my break from Johnny the asshole. I definitely let a good one get away when I went back to Johnny, so when he asked if I wanted to get together, I said I'd love to. He's got this party tonight with his college friends, so he asked me to meet him there."

"And thus my plans for the evening were changed, too."

"Oh, stop your whining. You had nothing better to do."

"Right, just a bath and eight hours horizontal."

"*Boring.*"

"Sounds like heaven to me. I've been working like a demon lately. I'm freaking exhausted all the time."

"You don't have to pay off all your loans at once, you know."

"I want them off my mind."

"If you kill yourself doing it, what good will it do?"

"I'm not killing myself, but I was looking forward to a night at home."

"I already get that I owe you for the rest of my life for coming tonight, but how much do you want to bet that tomorrow you'll be thanking me because you had such an awesome time and met so many incredible people?"

"I'll take that bet. Twenty bucks?"

Angela held out her hand. "Make it fifty."

Sam shook her sister's hand. "You're on. Be prepared to pay up this time."

"Yeah, yeah. Why break with tradition?"

THE PARTY WAS as awful as Sam had expected it to be, full of simpering women and men on the make, getting loaded and looking to hook up with any random vagina.

It reminded her of the two fraternity parties she'd been talked into attending in college, both of them hideous experiences she tried not to think about—ever.

Now, as a badge-carrying police officer, it was nearly impossible to attend events like this and not view them through a law enforcement lens. It wasn't her place, she told herself, to bust the two guys smoking pot in the kitchen or to run a check on the white powdered substance she noticed on the nose of another loser.

If she wanted to be a total asshole, she could've called it in and had the place raided, which would get her out of here and home to bed. But she couldn't do that to Angela, who'd been so excited about connecting with Spencer again. Seeing Angela excited about anything had Sam refraining from making the call, but she couldn't bear to breathe the pot smoke coming from the kitchen.

She went through sliding doors to a huge deck that was full to overflowing with more bodies. *Is this thing strong enough to hold this many people?* Sam would bet money she was the only person on the deck wondering about its structural integrity. The rest of them were too busy drinking and boasting and bullshitting and generally trying to score.

How had she managed to skip this entire phase of her upbringing? She'd gone from high school to adulthood in the blink of an eye, when her mom left her dad for another guy the day after Sam, their youngest child, graduated from high school. Shit like that causes a person to grow up quickly. Plus, she'd never been one to suffer fools easily, and this party was chock full of fools.

A few of them were good-looking. She'd give them that. Many of them were also well dressed, having come directly from work. But the packaging didn't make them more appealing. It only made their behavior seem more vapid, since some of them clearly had careers and something to lose by acting like frat boys after hours.

She found a corner to occupy while she kept an eye on Angela, who was talking to a group of guys across the deck. She didn't think any of them was Spencer, but she wasn't sure since she couldn't see their faces. She'd met him once before and thought she'd recognize him if she saw him. Angela was smiling and laughing and engaging in the conversation, so Sam left her alone and let her do her thing.

Hopefully, Spencer would show up soon and Sam could have a word with him before leaving. At times like this, she enjoyed making sure a guy was aware of what she did for a living so he'd know better than to fuck with her sister.

She'd made the mistake of relaxing into her corner of the deck when one douche bag pushed another douche bag, sending beer flying out of a red plastic cup and all over her. *Motherfuckers.*

"Oh my God," one of them said. "I'm so sorry. Let me help."

"Hands off," Sam growled at him.

He backed up immediately, hands in the air. "My apologies. What can I do? Napkins? Paper towels? What's your pleasure?"

"A paper towel or three would be good," Sam said as she held her soaking wet skirt away from her body.

"Coming right up."

Since she fully expected never to see him again, she wrung the beer out of her skirt, grimacing at the nasty smell and the stickiness it left behind on her hands. Now she really wanted to get the hell out of here.

A starched white handkerchief entered her line of vision. She glanced up at its owner and every thought that wasn't about his supreme hotness left her brain in one big whoosh. He was tall—easily six-foot-four or five—with olive-toned skin, kind hazel eyes, thick dark brown hair that curled at the ends and a mouth that had her immediately thinking about how long it had been since she'd had sex.

"I saw you take a direct hit," he said in a deep voice that had her leaning in closer so she wouldn't miss a word. "Thought this might be useful."

And then she realized he was offering her his handkerchief and waiting for her to take it from him. "Oh, um, that's really nice of you, but I'd hate to ruin it. Looks like a nice one."

He shrugged. "I have others."

Rattled by his presence and the way he looked at her, she took the cloth from him and used it to mop up some of the liquid still dripping from her skirt. "NDC," she said of the navy blue initials embroidered on the white linen. He wore a navy pinstripe suit with a crisp white dress shirt and no tie.

"Nicholas Domenic Cappuano, at your service, but I go by Nick."

"So you're Irish, huh?"

Even his laughter was sexy. "Full-blooded."

"Me, too. Sam Holland."

"Nice to meet you, Sam Holland."

Was it possible to come from the way a hot guy said your name? Sam never would've thought so before now. "You, too. Thanks for the assist."

"My pleasure."

Did everything he said scream "sex," or did he only have that effect on her? The thought nearly made her laugh out loud. Who was she kidding? There wasn't a woman alive who wouldn't want to jump all over him. He probably had to beat them off him with a stick.

"That's probably as good as it's going to get," Sam said of her stained skirt. "One of my favorites, too."

"I can see why. So what brings you here tonight?"

Appreciating the smoothly delivered compliment, she said, "My sister." Sam nodded at Angela, who'd apparently connected with Spencer while Sam was being doused with beer. Angela beamed with happiness as she talked to a handsome guy who hung on her every word. "I'm her wing-woman tonight. What about you?"

"Some guys from the gym talked me into coming when all I wanted was a steak, a glass of red and bed—in that order."

She marveled at how similar to her dream evening his had been—only hers had been more of a pizza and beer variety than steak and red. "Sounds so much better than this meat market."

He chuckled at the term. "I take it you were a reluctant attendee, too?"

"You could say that. I worked eleven hours today, three of them in the scorching sun, and all I wanted was a cold shower and eight hours unconscious."

"What do you do?"

"I'm a cop with the Metro PD. Recently promoted to detective, in fact."

"Congratulations. That's fantastic. Aren't you young for that rank?"

"Not you, too," Sam said with a groan. "My dad is

a bigwig in the department, so all I hear about is nepotism and special favors. No one likes to think I earned it the old-fashioned way. I busted my ass—and continue to bust my ass every day."

"I have no doubt you earned it. Your dad must be proud."

"You could say that," Sam said with a small smile, indicating the understatement of the century.

"Who's the dude talking to your sister?"

"He's the reason we're here."

Nick took a closer look at Spencer, who was listening intently to Angela. "Doesn't seem like a total douche bag."

"Not total," Sam said with a smile, digging him more by the minute. The last thing she'd expected when she came to this party was to meet someone like him. "So many of these guys…They're all such…*players*. Do they think we can't see right through their shit?"

"Truth?"

"Of course."

"Most of them don't realize they're full of shit."

Sam laughed harder than she could recall having laughed in recent memory. The beer on her skirt was forgotten, along with the stink and the stickiness and anything that didn't involve him and all his gorgeousness and charm.

"You wanna get out of here?" he asked.

"More than I've wanted anything ever."

He nodded toward Angela. "Are you her ride?"

"She was mine."

"Even better." He pulled keys from his pants pocket and held them up for her to see. "Shall we?"

"You're not like a serial killer posing as a successful DC yuppie or something, are you?"

"What if I am?"

Very subtly, she looked around to make sure no one was paying any attention to them. Then she lifted her skirt ever so slightly so he could see the service weapon that was strapped to her thigh.

His eyes widened and then heated with interest.

"But wait, there's more." From her purse, she withdrew the shiny gold shield that represented her proudest accomplishment. "Any questions?"

"Just one."

She raised a brow.

"Do you believe in sex at first sight? Because that was like the hottest freaking thing I've ever seen in my life."

Flustered but pleased by his reaction to her little demonstration, she decided to play along. "Like *ever*?"

"*Ever.*" He leaned in closer and spoke directly into her ear. "Go tell your sister you're leaving."

With her entire body buzzing from the high of her encounter with Nick, Sam made her way across the crowded deck to where Angela giggled madly at something Spencer had said. Then she noticed Sam and grabbed hold of her arm, pulling her into their circle.

"You remember my little sister, Sam, right?" she asked Spencer.

He shook Sam's hand. "Of course. Good to see you again, Sam."

"You, too."

Angela wrinkled her nose. "Have you been bathing in beer?"

"Some asshole dumped a cupful on me." Sam leaned in closer to her sister. "Listen, Ang…I'm going to split. Looks like you've got things under control here."

"You can't leave by yourself! Wait for us."

"Angela, for Christ's sake. I'm a cop. I can get myself home, and besides…I met someone. I'm going to grab something to eat with him."

"Who did you meet?"

"A guy. No one you know."

"Where is he?" She craned her neck, looking all around the deck as if she'd be able to pick the guy Sam had met out of the crowd.

"Will you please stand down? I met a guy who was nice to me after some other jerk spilled beer on me. We're going to get food, and then I'm going straight home to bed because I've got another twelve-hour day ahead of me tomorrow. I did my part by coming with you, and now I'm out of here."

"I want to at least meet him."

"You're not meeting him, and I can take care of myself."

"Old habits, you know?"

"Always the big bossy sister." She kissed Angela's cheek. "Are you going to be okay to get home?"

"I'll take her," Spencer said.

Sam was standing close enough to her sister to feel the shiver that went through her. Yes, Angela was in good hands. "Talk to you tomorrow."

"Sam…You're sure about this guy you're leaving with?"

Sam thought about the monogrammed handkerchief he'd sacrificed for her, the smile, the charm, the "sex at first sight" comment and nodded. "Yeah, I'm sure." She hadn't reached the rank of detective without developing a fairly good sense of people. "Call me in the morning."

"Oh, you can bet I will, and Sam…Thanks for this." Angela hugged her and whispered in her ear, "I'm so happy to see him."

"Good." She said good-bye to Spencer and battled her way through the crowd again, throwing an elbow or two along the way, half-expecting super-fucking-hot Nick Cappuano to have been snapped up by some other woman while she'd been gone. But he was standing right where she'd left him in their little corner of the deck, with no other women in sight.

The profound sense of relief she felt at that should've been concerning to her, but it wasn't. She liked him and wanted to get to know him better. That was all this was and all it would ever be. She had more than she could handle on the job. There was no time left at the end of most days for the distraction of a boyfriend or even a fuck buddy, for that matter.

Sleep was her lover these days, and how sad was that?

Nick held out a hand to her. "Ready?"

"Ready." She took his hand because he was much bigger than she was and could blaze a trail through the crowd for them both. Well, she also took his hand because she was dying to touch him.

THREE

HE WAS AN effective trailblazer. People got out of his way. For once in her life, Sam was glad to be a follower. She was too exhausted after the day she'd put in to fight any more battles.

"I think I must be getting old or something," he said the minute they were free of the apartment and heading down two flights of stairs.

"Why's that?" Sam wondered if she ought to let go of his hand now that they were out of the scrum. For some reason, she held on, and he didn't let go.

"Parties like that one aren't as fun as they used to be. Present company excluded, of course."

"Of course," she said dryly.

"I just mean the crowds, the booze—"

"The fake hookup bullshit?"

"That, too. Once again, present company excluded."

"Ha! You're very smooth."

"I try. So was it a clean getaway? With your sister, I mean."

"Sort of. She gave me the third degree about where I was going and who I was going with. Typical big-sister crap. She can't help herself."

"It's nice that she cares."

"I wish she cared just a tiny bit less than she does. What about you? Any siblings?"

"Nope, just me."

"You're so lucky."

He replied with a small smile, but there was something else to it.

No, not going there. It's not like I'm ever going to see him again. She decided to keep the conversation focused on safer topics. "So what do you do?"

"I work for Congressman Delehanty of Kentucky."

"Oh, that's cool. I guess."

He let loose with a deep, rich laugh that made some of her most important parts stand up and take notice of what was going on.

Welcome to the party, girls.

"What you're saying is it sounds frightfully boring, right?"

"I never said that. I never even *thought* that." *No, I was too busy thinking about my nipples to be bored.* Sam wished she could find the off switch for the running commentary in her brain.

"Believe it or not, it's actually kind of fun. Most days. We solve a lot of problems for people who don't have anywhere else to turn. I like that part of it. But I'm sure it's nowhere near as exciting as being a cop."

"Is anything as exciting as being a cop?" she asked with a cheeky grin.

"You did mention something about three hours in the sun..."

She waved that off. "That doesn't count. It was a detail."

"What does that entail, exactly?"

"Extra duty directing traffic at a construction site. We do it for the money. In my case, to pay off beastly student loans that are going to hang over my head forever at this rate."

"Ah yes, the burden of the twentysomethings."

"You, too, huh?"

"Um, well, not really. I had a scholarship, but it didn't pay for everything, so there's some debt. Not a ton like some people have, though. I'm lucky that way."

"Yes, you are." She nudged him with her shoulder. "Egghead scholarship or jock scholarship?"

"Ohhh, what a *loaded* question!"

"So which is it?"

"The school I attended doesn't do athletic scholarships."

"Egghead! I knew it! You've got that whole buttoned-down smart thing going on over there. And what kind of college doesn't do athletic scholarships?"

"Um, how to say this..."

Sam stopped short and turned to him. "The kind with ivy on the walls. Am I right?"

"Perhaps."

She tipped her head to study him more closely. "Which one?"

"There's more than one?"

Tossing her head back to laugh, she said, "Oh my God. Say it isn't so."

"It is so. Is this a deal-breaker?"

"We had a deal?"

Nick put his arm around her. "We definitely had a deal. What do you feel like doing?"

Sam was afraid if she told him, he'd think her a total slut. "Truthfully? Or should I go for socially correct?"

"By all means, give me the truth."

She looked him dead in those incredible hazel eyes. "Your place or mine?"

His eyes widened for a fraction of an instant before he recovered. "Roommates?"

"Two. And a squatter brother. You?"

"None."

"You win."

A smile stretched across his gorgeous face. "I was a winner the second I saw that guy dump beer all over you."

"There needs to be food at some point."

"I can do that."

"And protection. I don't do anything unprotected."

"No, I don't imagine you do."

"Is that a problem?"

"I don't have a problem in the world, but I do need to make a stop on the way home."

"That's fine. So was it Harvard or Yale?"

Laughing, he said, "Harvard." He kept his arm around her on the way to the car he'd parked several blocks away.

"I can live with that."

THE CAR WAS a silver Acura with black leather seats. It was so clean, you could eat off the carpet, a thought that nearly gave Sam the giggles in light of what they were about to do.

"I don't do this." The words escaped from her lips before she took a second to think them all the way through.

"Do what?"

"Pick up guys at parties and go home with them."

"Oh. Well…Good. I don't either."

"You don't pick up guys at parties?"

His laugh was as sexy as the rest of him. "You know what I mean, smart aleck."

"So you're not out at yuppie parties every weekend? Different week, different girl?"

Rolling his eyes, he said, "Hardly. I've been off the meat-market circuit since I graduated from college eight years ago."

That made him about thirty, which was what she would've guessed. Two years older than she was. A full-grown adult, or so he seemed. Looks, she knew after years of dating, could be deceiving.

"You should have a little wife and two-point-five kids by now."

"Says who?"

"The yuppie timetable. It's well documented."

"You're funny, Sam Holland. Has anyone ever told you that?"

"Sure, I'm a good time had by all. What can I say?"

"I thought you just said you weren't a good time had by all?"

And he was smart and quick, too. When mixed with insane hotness, it was all a little too good to be true. "So what's wrong with you then? Thirty years old, still single, presumably no girlfriend if you're taking me home with you…"

"You're just full of charm, aren't you?" he asked, laughing again. "For your information, *Detective*, there's *nothing* wrong with me. And no girlfriend, or I wouldn't be taking you home with me."

"Guys like you who are still single always come with baggage."

"Is that so? And where have you conducted your research on this matter?"

"It's a project my girlfriends and I have been working on for years now. The evidence is irrefutable. Thirty and reasonably good-looking, decent job yet still unmarried and unattached...You're either still living with your mother or you've got a weird and disgusting habit like collecting all the belly button lint from your whole life into a baggie or something." Sam glanced over to find him staring at her, incredulous, as they waited for the light to turn green. "How close am I?"

"You're off your rocker. One, I most definitely do *not* live with my mother, and two, belly button lint is gross."

Sam crossed her arms. "It's something else then."

"Are you trying to talk me out of taking you home with me?" Despite the question, his pretty eyes were still full of amusement and what might've been desire.

"Not at all. I thought we were just making conversation."

"Is that what we're doing?"

"What would you call it?"

"An interrogation?"

"Nah, this isn't even close to that. You ought to see me when I really get going with a perp."

"I think I'd like to see that."

"Maybe I'll let you sometime."

"Maybe I'll take you up on that."

How was it possible they were already talking about more than a one-night stand? Sam was suddenly desperate to get things back on the sex-only track. "So where are we going anyway?"

"Looking for a store that has what we need."

"Oh."

A few minutes later, he pulled into the parking lot of a convenience store. "Need anything?"

"Nothing other than the obvious."

He flashed a grin at her. "Be right back."

While she waited for him, a flutter of nerves attacked her sensitive stomach. *What am I doing? This isn't me. I don't do this shit. Not anymore*...It occurred to her that she could get out of the car and be gone before he returned. There was still time to call it off, but then again, she could call it off at any point with him. She already knew he wasn't the kind of guy who wouldn't take no for an answer.

But there was something about him that compelled her to stay, to refrain from bolting even when the inclination to run had her reaching for the door handle. Then he came out of the store, seeming frustrated—and empty-handed.

"They didn't have them?" she asked when he was back in the car.

"They didn't have the right ones. I know somewhere else that has them."

There were right ones and wrong ones? Since when? "Um, okay."

After he struck out at two more stores, Sam began to wonder if this was a ploy of some sort. "Look, if you're really not into this—"

The sentence was forgotten when he reached across the center console and dragged her into his arms for the single most potent kiss she'd ever received in her life. There was no slow buildup, no teasing strokes or hints of passion to come. No, this was all fire and heat and crazy need wrapped up in a kiss she'd never forget.

"Any more questions about my level of interest?" he asked many minutes later when the beep of a nearby car horn thrust them out of the sensual haze they'd slipped into.

She was a cop, for Christ's sake, making out like a horny teenager in a convenience store parking lot. Rubbing her fingers over her tingling lips, she shook her head. "No, no more questions."

"Good. If the next place doesn't have what I want, I'll settle for something else."

"Okay." He'd kissed the sass right out of her. With every brain cell in her body now focused on the throb between her legs, Sam had nothing else to say.

At the next store, he apparently struck condom pay dirt, emerging with a bag in hand and a big smile on his face. He got in the car and tossed the bag to her. "That, my friend, is the Cadillac of condoms, the grand pooh-bah, the top banana."

Snorting, Sam said, "Top banana? Is that a metaphor?"

"You know what I mean."

To her, they looked like regular old condoms, except for the extra-large size noted on the box. Sam swallowed hard as the tingling between her legs intensified. "How far to your place?"

"Ten minutes. Fifteen if the traffic is bad. How do you feel about fast food?"

"In general or as a quick solution to our pressing need for fuel?"

"The latter."

"I'm all for it."

"Excellent." They hit a McDonald's drive-thru and chowed down on burgers and fries while he drove. "I haven't had fast food in ten years."

"Seriously?" she asked.

"Uh-huh. Desperate times..."

She loved, absolutely *loved*, that he was feeling desperate enough to get her home to his place that he broke a ten-year ban on fast food. Sam was surprised when they headed out of the city, crossing the 14th Street Bridge. "Whoa, where are you taking me?"

"To an outpost known as Northern Virginia," he said between mouthfuls of french fries.

"You don't live in the District?"

"You say that like something is wrong with me for not living in the city."

"We've already determined something has to be wrong with you. This could be the sign I was looking for."

"You're too much, Sam," he said, laughing again. "Do you go on many second dates?"

That made her laugh, too. "A few. Here and there."

"That's shocking to me. Truly."

God, I like this guy. He was the full package, *and* he seemed to get her sense of humor. That made him a rare man, indeed. The fact that he made her panties melt every time he looked at her or flashed that irresistible grin only made him that much more appealing. *Keep looking for the flaw. Thirty and unattached. There's got to be something...*

As they headed into the guts of Arlington, Sam glanced over her shoulder. "I feel like I should've left bread crumbs or something. I'll never find my way home."

"I'll take you home whenever you want to go."

Since she never left the house unarmed, Sam would be able to defend herself if need be. But that didn't mean she let down her guard very often, especially with men.

This one…Well, he could be different. He rang every one of her bells—smart, sexy, funny, handsome, successful, educated and confident. So far she hadn't found a single thing about him not to like, except for maybe the fact that he lived outside her precious city.

They finally arrived at a townhouse complex, and he pulled into a parking space. Assailed by a sudden bout of nerves, Sam hesitated before reaching for the door handle.

"You still want to hang out?" he asked, tuning into her hesitation.

"Is that what we're going to do?"

He reached over to stroke her hair. "We can do—or not do—whatever you want. I've had more fun on the ride here than I've had in years. The evening is already a huge success from my point of view."

"You're good," she said grudgingly. "I'll give you that."

Waggling his brows and smiling, he leaned in to kiss her cheek. "You ain't seen nothing yet."

The nerves were overruled by the insistent throb between her legs that had her full attention.

"You want to go home?" he asked. "I'll take you."

"No, I don't think I do."

"Excellent decision." His hand moved to her jaw, turning her toward him for another kiss. This one was softer and more patient than the one before, but it packed no less of a wallop.

Sam curled her hand around his nape, drawing him in closer as their tongues dueled fiercely. Then he bit down lightly on hers, and Sam ignited. She pulled his hair, trying to get closer, and let go only when he winced.

"Sorry."

"I'm not at all sorry. What do you say we take this conversation inside?"

"I say that's a great idea."

FOUR

SAM LIKED THAT he didn't come around the car to get her but rather met her at the front, extending his hand to her. With his hand wrapped around hers, he led her to a white-clapboard-fronted townhouse that had a black front door and shutters.

The second the door closed behind them, he dropped his work satchel as well as the bag from the pharmacy and reached for her.

Sam went to him willingly, wrapping her arms around his trim waist.

His mouth came down on hers as he lifted her into his arms in a move that seriously wowed her. She was no wilting flower, and that he lifted her so effortlessly was a huge turn-on. Then he topped himself by pressing her against the wall in the foyer and positively devouring her.

Sam had never been kissed quite like this, as if his very existence was tied to her. She looped her arms around his neck and held on for dear life as he took her on a wild ride. Held against Nick's wall by the powerful force of his body, Sam forgot all about how tired she'd been after the long day, how much she'd wanted to stay home tonight. Instead, she gave thanks to Angela for dragging her out and to the guy who'd spilled beer all over her. He deserved some credit, too.

Her shirt disappeared down her arms, her bra sprang

free and her skirt was suddenly bunched around her waist. He worked quickly and efficiently on her clothes and then went to work on the buttons of his shirt, all without missing a beat in the kiss.

"Is that your gun, or are you happy to see me?" he asked in the second before he bit down on her earlobe and nearly made her come.

Rattled and undone, Sam said, "Put me down. Just for a second."

"One second."

She used the time to remove the weapon from her thigh and placed it in her purse.

He tugged on her skirt, letting her know he wanted it gone. "Panties, too."

Sam noted a slight tremble in her hands as she complied with his gruffly issued directive. When she stood bare before him in the milky darkness, she reached for his belt buckle and went to work on freeing him. Before his pants dropped, he removed a condom from his pocket. "Someone planned ahead."

"I had time to kill in line."

"Such a good little Boy Scout."

"Not so little."

Normally a cocky comment like that would irritate her, but when his erection surged into her hand—long, full and thick—she couldn't take issue with the truth. She stroked him, and he got even harder. Her mouth watered at the thought of all that hardness pounding into her.

With a groan, he pulled her hand away, quickly rolled on the condom, cupped her buttocks and lifted her again. "Here or in bed?" he asked in that same gruff tone that told her he was right there on the edge with her.

Since finding a bed would've taken time she didn't want to waste, Sam said, "Here. Right here."

"Would've been my choice, too." He dragged his fingers between her legs to test her readiness. "Next time, I'm going to kiss you here first. I want to kiss you everywhere, but right now..."

"*Yes*, right now."

He surged into her, stealing the breath from her lungs and every thought from her mind that didn't involve the sublime sensation of being taken by him. His fingers dug into the dense flesh of her bottom and held on tight as he withdrew and entered her again, harder this time.

Sam grasped a handful of his silky dark hair, needing to hold on to something. In this position, he had all the control, and she yielded to him willingly because he knew exactly what he was doing. He had her on the brink of release faster than she'd ever gotten there before, and he didn't let up, pounding into her repeatedly.

She drew him into another tongue-tangling kiss and dropped her hand to where they were joined, giving herself the push she needed to reach the peak. The orgasm ripped through her, more powerful than anything she'd ever experienced with any other man.

Gasping, he tore his lips free of hers and went with her, surging into her and then sagging against her, still throbbing inside. For a long time, they were silent, both breathing hard in the aftermath.

He broke the silence with a single word: "Wow."

Sam laughed. "That about sums it up."

"I've never had sex against a wall before."

"Neither have I."

"I'll never look at this wall the same way again." He kissed her, softly and sweetly. "That was so hot."

"Mmm, very hot."

"Hottest sex I've ever had."

"Yeah?"

"Without a doubt." He nibbled her neck and had her thinking about round two when her normal inclination was to say thanks for the lay, see you later. But not this time. This time, once wasn't going to be enough. Hell, six times might not be enough with him.

"Me, too."

"Hold on." Keeping his tight grip on her ass, Nick lifted her off the wall and walked them into his dark house.

With her arms around his neck, she held on as he headed down a hallway and into a bedroom that was faintly lit from the streetlights. He laid her on the bed and kissed her. "Hang on a sec." Gripping the condom, he finally withdrew from her. "Be right back."

Sam wanted to turn the light on so she could see his room—and him when he returned—but she stayed put. The muscles in her thighs quivered, and her sex pulsed with aftershocks. All in all, he'd blown her away, and that wasn't easy to do. Her friends teased her about being "the guy" in every relationship. She always went home after sex and didn't see the need for cuddling or other foolishness. Sex was about the release and nothing else.

But he'd made her curious enough to find out if round two would hold up to round one. As he came back into the room, the bag from the store in hand, her entire body tingled with awareness. In the shadows, she could see his erection stretching nearly to his navel. Her mouth watered in anticipation and at knowing he was thinking about round two as well.

"Drink?" He held out a glass of ice water.

Sam sat up to take it from him. "Thanks." She took a couple of sips, the cool liquid coating her throat. "Did I scream? Before?"

"A little."

"That must be why my throat hurts."

"You won't hear me complaining."

"I'm not usually a screamer."

"You're not usually with me."

She handed him the glass, which he placed on the bedside table. "You're feeling rather pleased with yourself, aren't you?"

"Aren't you? Pleased with yourself?"

"I'm pleased with both of us. We do good work together."

Laughing, he came down on the bed next to her. He placed his hand on her belly. "Yes, we do, but I'd hardly call it work."

"Consider it a metaphor, then."

"Are you cold?"

"No, the AC feels good after sweltering all afternoon."

"You're sunburned," he said, tracing his fingertip over the V at her neckline where her uniform had left her exposed to the sun.

"Maybe a little."

"I bet you're hot in your uniform. I'd like to see that sometime."

"That might be possible."

"Come here. You're too far away over there."

"I'm like two inches from you."

"Too far."

Oh, she liked this guy. She liked him a whole lot. As a rule, she didn't really like anyone. She put up with people, especially guys who were usually all talk and no action. This one had the goods to go along with the words. And he was sweet and funny and sexy as hell. Offering to take her home any time she wanted had earned him major points, and that was before he fucked her lights out against a wall.

Sam rolled onto her side so she was pressed up against him. "Better?"

"Getting there." He put his arm around her and slid his leg between hers. His erection lay hot and heavy against her belly. "Now that's better."

With her face pressed to his chest, she nuzzled his chest hair and dabbed his nipple with her tongue, earning a sharp inhale from him.

"I want to do that to you."

"You'll get your turn." Taking charge, Sam kissed her way down the front of him, spending extra time on his well-defined abs. He had the lean, muscular body of a man who took good care of himself but didn't spend more time than necessary pumping iron for the sake of pumping iron.

She used her tongue to trace the outline of each hill and valley in that spectacular field of abdominal muscles and thrilled when they quivered in response. Naturally, she had to do it again since the first time had been so rewarding.

"Sam..."

He sounded tense, on edge...She liked him that way, so she kept up the torture for a while longer before moving south to the sexy V-cut muscles that framed his hips.

The entire time, she pretended like his huge erection wasn't getting bigger by the second.

Blow jobs had never been her favorite thing to do, but she had a feeling he could change her opinion on the subject. For one thing, she'd never wanted to do that more than she did right now. Deciding to have mercy on him, she wrapped her hand around the thick base and stroked him.

The tortured groan that came from him only made her more determined to go for it. What the hell? This was one night of debauchery, and she'd already crossed a number of lines she hadn't crossed in years. What was one more at this point? She took him into her mouth slowly, going for maximum effect as she sucked on the broad crown.

"*Fuck*," he whispered harshly. His fingers combed through her hair, fisting and pulling ever so slightly as she took more of him into her mouth.

Curiously, the harder she worked to pleasure him, the more turned on she seemed to get. Never before had this act killed two birds with one stone. The slick heat between her legs had her full attention even as she took him deeper into her throat, swallowing slowly and lashing him with her tongue.

"*Holy fucking shit.*"

She wondered if he even knew that he was now pulling her hair—hard. The tingling pain from her scalp seemed to be connected directly to her clit, which throbbed insistently.

Nick gave a swift tug that dislodged his cock from her mouth. And then she was on her back. That he handled her like she was light as air was a huge turn-on since she was hardly "light." She was a long, *long* way from fat, but she was certainly no stick figure.

Hovering above her, he propped himself on one elbow while he rolled on a new condom. All the while, he stared down at her with those gorgeous hazel eyes that seemed to see all the way through her. Under normal circumstances, the thought of being "seen" that way would've freaked her out and had her running away. But nothing about these circumstances was normal for her, so she stayed put, wanting to see what would happen next more than she wanted to flee.

And oh what happened next...

Whereas the first time, against the wall, had been hard and fast, this time he was all about slow and sultry, taking his time as he started at her lips, devouring her with his teeth and tongue and leaving her bereft when he broke the kiss. He seemed to be in no particular rush as he kissed her neck and throat and the upper slopes of her breasts.

Sam had never been more aware of her nipples or the way they tightened in anticipation. She fisted a handful of his hair and tried to direct him there, but he wouldn't be rushed. He was killing her.

"Nick..."

"What?"

"I..."

"Talk to me. Tell me what you want."

She cupped her breasts in both hands and offered them to him, knowing she wouldn't soon forget the way his eyes widened with surprise and then pleasure as he gave her what she wanted. And oh did he give it to her, licking and sucking and biting...The biting was new and was nearly enough on its own to make her come.

Her breasts had never been more sensitive. Waves of heat traveled from her chest to every corner of her body. Right when she thought she couldn't take the exquisite torture for another second, he moved down and set out to torture her belly with the same exceptional attention to detail he'd shown her breasts.

Just like blow jobs had never been her favorite thing—before tonight, anyway—receiving oral was another thing that hadn't done much for her in the past. Most of the time, it was all stabby and pokey and overly enthusiastic effort that led to absolutely nothing for her except a general feeling of disappointment and chafing in the worst possible place.

As Nick worked his way down, down, *down*, she had a feeling her opinion was about to change. The first sign that she might finally have found a man who knew his way around the female genitalia came when he propped her legs on his broad shoulders, opening her wide before him. She resisted the urge to cover herself with her hands, knowing he would only push them away. Rather, she clutched handfuls of the comforter and waited to see what he would do.

She was fairly trembling with anticipation by the time he finally looked his fill and lowered his head to get down to business.

Holy Christ...He skipped all the preliminaries and sucked her clit, triggering an orgasm that made her scream with surprise and nearly unbearable pleasure. She'd never come so easily in her entire life, and she could easily become addicted to the full-body orgasms he provided.

He brought her down slowly, gently, and then took her back up again by driving his fingers into her at the same time his tongue found her clit. In a matter of seconds, she was coming again, which had never, ever happened twice in such a short amount of time. Before she had even a second to recover from the powerful, full-body release, he entered her. In keeping with the slow theme, he tortured her by pressing into her fully and then retreating completely.

He did that over and over again until Sam was about to lose her mind. "Please..."

"What do you need?" he asked, propped above her, sexy as all hell. The guy was seriously ripped, and every one of those muscles was beautifully engaged in what he was doing to her.

"You know!"

"Tell me anyway."

Sam wasn't much for talking during sex. She preferred to let her body do the talking for her.

He continued to hover, the tip of his cock just inside her while he waited for her to tell him what she wanted.

She raised her hips, trying to force him to get the show on the road, but he wouldn't be forced into anything.

His low chuckle would've infuriated her if every one of her brain cells hadn't been currently focused on what was happening—or not happening—between her legs. "Use your words."

"Are you always like this?" she managed to ask.

"I'm never like this."

She wanted to ask him what he meant by that, but posing the question would've taken effort she couldn't seem to summon when she was being held hostage by his powerful body and the thick press of his cock.

"Words," he reminded her. "Give them to me, and then I'll give you what you want."

"Fuck me. Just do it, will you?"

"How hard was that?"

"Hard. Yes, hard would be good."

Laughing, he gave it to her hard and fast, so fast and so hard that the bed banged against the wall as his body slammed into hers. So good…So fucking *perfect*. She'd never had sex like this before, the kind that made her question every choice she'd ever made in the past when it came to men.

This one had been different from the word go, and he was proving how different he was with every thrust of his big cock. Then he reached down to where they were joined to coax her into joining him in another of those full-body orgasms he doled out so effortlessly.

Sam saw stars— honest-to-God *stars*—as she came with him deep inside her, clinging to her as he let go with a deep groan of pleasure that echoed all the way through her.

As he came down on top of her, still throbbing deep inside her, Sam wrapped her arms around him to keep him from getting away. That too was new. She was usually the one to turn away afterward, eager to reclaim her space and to separate herself from the man of the moment.

But this man, this one…She wanted to hold on to him and the way he made her feel for as long as this perfect night lasted.

He raised his head off her chest and looked down at her, seeming to take inventory of her features. "That was…" He shook his head. "Amazing."

Sam nodded in agreement. She was unaccustomed

to being so undone by sex. To her, it was a physical act, a way to blow off steam and de-stress. She'd had more than one guy act hurt when she got right up afterward to get dressed to go home. She didn't see the point of lingering when she'd gotten what she wanted.

With his eyes open and fixed on hers, Nick kissed her before he withdrew. "Don't go anywhere," he said as he left the bed.

This would be the perfect opportunity to get up, find her clothes and ask him to take her home. She had an early morning, and this had been fun, but it was time to get back to reality. Except…She couldn't seem to move her arms or legs, nor could she find the wherewithal to make her escape.

So she stayed in his big comfortable bed until he returned with another glass of ice water. Still beautifully naked, he sat on the side of the bed and held the glass for her.

Sam propped herself up on an elbow and let him feed her sips of cold water that felt heavenly on her parched throat.

"You want to go home?" he asked.

"Not particularly."

Was that relief she saw on his face? Whatever it was, it was gone as fast as it had arrived.

"Do you have to be somewhere in the morning?"

"Um, yeah. Work."

"It's Saturday."

"I'm a cop. No such thing as weekends in my world."

"That's awful."

"Believe me, I know."

Putting the glass on a coaster on the bedside table,

he reached for the alarm clock. "What time do you need to get up?"

"How long will it take to get back to the real world from here?"

Rolling his eyes at her slam on Northern Virginia, he said, "On a Saturday morning, about fifteen minutes."

"Set it for five thirty, then."

The same hazel eyes that had rolled with derision now nearly popped out of his skull. "As in five thirty *a.m.*?"

Sam laughed at his horrified reaction. "You heard me right."

"That's extremely uncivilized."

"You've made me all dirty. I have to go home and shower before I meet my dad, the deputy chief, for coffee."

She definitely didn't imagine the slide of his Adam's apple in his throat. "Your dad is the deputy chief…of police?"

"The one and only."

"Well…That's…Nice."

Sam laughed so hard she had tears in her eyes. "Said no guy who dated any of Skip Holland's daughters. Ever."

"So he's kind of a badass, huh?"

"The baddest of badasses. He carries a gun, a Taser *and* a billy club—and isn't afraid to use any of them."

"Good to know."

Sam smiled at him. He was truly adorable and the sexiest guy she'd ever slept with—hands down.

Nick set the alarm, put the clock back on the table and slid into bed next to her.

Before she had a chance to wonder if he was into

snuggling, he had wrapped his arms around her and made her comfortable with her head resting on his chest. His hand traveled up and down her back in soothing circles that had her relaxing into his embrace.

"I don't do this," she said, breaking the long silence.

"Do what?"

"Snuggle. Sleep over." She hadn't really intended to share that with him, but the words were out before she could take the time to decide if she should tell him that. The usual rules of gamesmanship were all out of whack with this guy, who seemed to be as nice as he was sexy.

He tightened his arms around her. "I'm glad you've decided to make an exception."

"I've made quite a few exceptions tonight."

"I know that crossing the 14th Street Bridge was a big deal for you..."

Sam laughed. "Yes, that was the biggest of the exceptions."

"Sorry to drag you out of your city. I hope I've made it worth the trip."

She slid her leg between both of his and flattened her hand on his abdomen. "It was definitely worth the trip, and I do like to get my passport stamped once in a while."

"I want to see you again."

FIVE

"You do?"

He nodded, looking adorably uncertain.

"You mean you want to see me naked again, right?" She could get onboard with that.

"No…I mean, yes, of course I do, but that's not all I want. For some strange reason, I like you." This was said with a twinkle of amusement in those sexy hazel eyes.

"Ha! What's wrong with you? No one likes me, and *I* like it that way."

"Your particular brand of prickliness is a turn-on to me. What can I say? I must be a masochist."

"You certainly are."

"So…You want to see me again, too?"

"Maybe."

"Ouch."

"Ohhh, sorry, did I injure your proud male ego by being noncommittal? I bet that doesn't happen very often."

"You wound me, Sam. You really do."

"Just trying to keep you humble." She hesitated, glancing at him to find he was watching her closely. "You're a nice guy. A really nice guy."

Wincing, he said, "Double ouch."

"No, really," she said, laughing. "I mean that sincerely. And let me tell you, with the element I deal with at work, *nice* is a very good thing."

"I suppose I should take the props where I can find them with you. Something tells me you're not very free with the compliments."

If he hadn't been holding her so close to him, Sam might've squirmed from the way he read her so accurately. "The thing is…I don't do the whole boyfriend-girlfriend thing. I don't have time for a relationship. I work all the time."

"All work and no play will make Sam a very dull girl."

"Indeed it does."

"For what it's worth, I'm busy as hell, too. In fact, I'm leaving the day after tomorrow—or I guess it's today now—for a four-week trip to Europe with the congressman."

"Four weeks in Europe," Sam said with a sigh. "Sounds like hell."

"It would be for someone who considers Northern Virginia a foreign country."

"Crossing the Potomac is, in fact, *overseas,* but since you have DC in your initials, I won't hold the Northern Virginia thing against you."

When he laughed, Sam discovered she'd only scratched the surface of his supreme sexiness. That deep laugh opened up a whole new frontier.

"That's very kind of you. Truth is, I was rather looking forward to the trip until this incredibly sexy woman had beer spilled all over her, and I had no choice but to come to her rescue. Now four weeks in Europe is looking rather…boring."

"You give good compliment."

"Why, thank you."

"You give good *everything*."

"Is that right?" He nuzzled her neck while cupping her breast, and just that quickly, Sam wanted him again. Despite the zing of desire that had her motor running as if it hadn't been recently—and repeatedly—satisfied, she had the presence of mind to realize tomorrow would be a flat-out disaster if she didn't get some sleep.

"I hate to say this—and I do truly *hate* to say it—but I have to sleep, or the District's criminal element will have their wicked way with me tomorrow."

His deep, dramatic sigh made her smile. "If you're going to be that way about it…"

"Sorry."

"Don't be. Tonight was fantastic. Best time I've had in…well, ever."

"Me, too."

He stroked a hand over her hair in a soothing, protective way that made her want to sigh with pleasure. "Go to sleep. I'll make sure you're up in plenty of time to get to work."

"You should sleep, too."

"Me and sleep have a complicated relationship."

"Really?" She had all kinds of questions she wanted to ask about that bit of insight he'd shared with her.

"Shhh. Go to sleep. I'll tell you all about it some other time."

Knowing there would be another time, maybe more than one, filled her with the kind of giddy anticipation she'd never experienced with any other man. She definitely wanted more of this man, and suddenly, the idea of not seeing him for the four weeks he would be away was profoundly depressing.

Her last thought before she dropped off the cliff into sleep was at least she'd have something to look forward to during the dog days of summer in the District.

SAM RESURFACED SOMETIME LATER—it could've been minutes or hours for all she knew—to the feel of lips on her back and hands cupping her ass. It all came back to her in a rush of awareness. She was in Nick's bed somewhere in Northern Virginia after the best sex of her life with, apparently, more to come.

She opened her eyes for the brief second it took to ensure she hadn't overslept. Seeing she was down to mere minutes before the alarm would go off, she closed her eyes again, losing herself to the sensual storm he was creating behind her.

God, he knew what he was doing. He played her like a maestro trained to please her and only her. And wasn't that a terrifying thought? This was supposed to be a one-night thing, and now she was beginning to wonder if he was the guy she'd been meant to find after years of dating all the wrong men.

If this one was wrong, she didn't want to be right.

He moved her effortlessly until she was positioned on her hands and knees, her legs spread and her ass propped in the air by the two pillows he pushed under her. He touched her everywhere, starting with her calves and working his way up to her thighs. When his tongue entered the party between her legs, Sam startled and gasped before she moaned.

She'd never been one to take a passive role during sex, but he hadn't given her much choice with this position.

He left her teetering on the edge of release when he

withdrew from her only long enough to roll on a condom. Then he was back, hands on her hips, holding her in place as he slammed into her in one deep thrust that made her scream from the orgasm that detonated from her core and ricocheted through every cell in her body.

"Holy shit, that was hot," he whispered as he bit down on the tendon that connected her neck to her shoulder. "You almost took me with you with that one."

That was when she realized he was still hard and thick inside her.

"Hang on tight, babe. This is going to be fast."

With his fingers grasping her hips, he pounded into her, making her feel every exquisite inch of him. "You got one more for me?"

"No way."

"Wanna bet?" He reached around her, his fingers finding her clit, and the combination was so powerful, so intensely erotic that she was coming again before she could begin to form a protest.

He was right there with her, surging into her in a moment of perfect harmony that would stay with her long after this exquisite night with him was only a memory.

The rattle of the alarm broke the silence, providing a harsh welcome back to reality.

Still buried deep inside her, Nick reached over to turn it off.

"You give good wake-up," Sam muttered from beneath him.

"So do you." He kissed between her shoulder blades and then withdrew, squeezing her bottom one last time as he went. "Time to get up."

Sam groaned loudly. Every inch of her body felt used and abused—in the best possible way, but still, she was sore as hell. She moved slowly and was sitting on the edge of the bed considering her next move when he came into the room holding the clothes she had abandoned just inside his front door. Had that really been last night? It seemed like a week ago.

She took the clothes from him, feeling shy and uncertain all of a sudden. "Thank you." Then she did a double take. "Is this skirt *clean*?"

"Maybe."

"You *washed* my skirt."

"Possibly."

"For real? When did you do that?"

"You were sleeping. I was awake. It was no big deal."

Except it was a big deal. It showed that in addition to being incredibly nice and sexy, he was thoughtful, too. What a powerful combination.

"I didn't want you to have to wear a stinky skirt home."

"It's really very, very nice of you to do that. Thank you."

He shrugged off her praise, seeming slightly—and adorably—embarrassed. "You know, if you took a shower here, that would give you a head start on your day."

She eyed him skeptically. "I don't dare get soapy *and* naked with you. I doubt I have time for your kind of shower."

"I'll be on my best behavior. I promise."

"You're just a regular Boy Scout, aren't you?" she asked for the second time.

"Since you're so interested, I should tell you I was actually an Eagle Scout."

"Of course you were."

Smiling, he held out his hand to her.

Sam eyed it for exactly one second before she took it and let him pull her up. With her legs protesting every step of the way, she let him tow her into the bathroom, where he started the shower and produced a couple of clean towels. At first glance, his place seemed immaculate, nothing at all like the bachelor pads she was used to from the guys she dated.

In the shower, he was true to his word and kept his hands to himself. "Shampoo? Conditioner?"

"I'm not going to wash my hair. I just did it last night."

"Damn, I was hoping I'd get to do that for you. Rain check?"

There he was again, alluding to future encounters. Sam shivered in anticipation of more of him. "Sure."

Once again, he took hold of her hips and kissed the back of her neck that had been left exposed when she put her hair up. "I do plan to collect."

"Good to know." She'd believe it when she saw it. After years and years of dating the wrong guys, only time would tell if he was the right one. But damn, he was certainly off to a good start.

Stepping out of the shower, he wrapped her in a thick towel that smelled like fabric softener and left her to get dressed in private.

Sam emerged from the bathroom to find him wearing a Harvard T-shirt and basketball shorts. He was every bit as sexy now as he'd been in a suit the night before.

"Ready?" he asked.

Sam nodded, suddenly feeling shy and awkward as the morning-after weirdness set in. Had she really picked up a guy at a party and had him every which way to Tuesday all night long? Yes, she had, and she'd enjoyed every mouthwatering second of it.

He held the car door for her and waited until she was settled to close the door and go around to the driver's side. With the sun about to rise, she could see more of his neighborhood this morning. It was one of those upwardly mobile communities that were all over the DC area, each one less distinctive than the other.

They were quiet on the ride across the bridge into the city, where the monuments were lit by the first glow of morning sunshine.

"So pretty this time of day," Sam said.

"I never get tired of this view."

"Neither do I."

He glanced over at her and smiled.

Following an impulse, she reached for his free hand and took hold of it. "I had a really great time."

"So did I. You're going to give me your number, right?"

"Are you asking or telling?"

"Asking, of course."

Sam laughed and released his hand to use the pad and pen she always carried with her to write down her home phone number. Since her cell phone was department-issued, she was always afraid of Stahl trying to nail her for using it for personal calls, so she never gave out that number, which she explained to him as she tore out the page, folded it and placed it in a cup holder. "There you go."

"I'll call you as soon as I get back to town."

"Okay." Again, she'd believe it when she saw it. But he'd given her ample reason to hope that he might be different from all the losers who'd come before him. It occurred to her that she also owed Angela fifty bucks, a thought that made her laugh.

"What's so funny?"

"I bet my sister I'd have a shitty time last night, so thanks to you, I owe her fifty bucks."

"Sorry about that."

"I'm not. It was well worth it."

He took her hand again and gave it a squeeze. "It certainly was."

They arrived at her place on Capitol Hill far too soon for her liking. As Nick put the car in park, Sam was hit with an unreasonable feeling of foreboding, as if something awful was about to happen and she was powerless to stop it. God, what the hell had brought that on? She shook off the odd feeling to give him her full attention.

"Thank you again for a wonderful time."

He leaned across the center console to kiss her. "The pleasure was all mine."

"Not entirely all yours."

His smile was the sexiest thing she'd ever encountered. "I'll call you when I get back."

"All right, then. Safe travels." She reached for her door handle, but he stopped her from escaping.

"Sam…I *will* call you. I promise." He kissed her one more time and then let her go, seeming as reluctant as she felt.

"Thanks for the ride…All of them."

He was still laughing when she got out of the car and waved before skipping up the stairs to her place.

She was surprised when the door swung open before she could use her key. "Oh, hey," she said to Peter. "What're you doing up so early?"

"Couldn't sleep. Where were you?"

"Out with friends, but you won't believe what happened. I met the most *amazing* guy."

"Oh yeah?"

"Uh-huh." Still locked inside the dream state she'd been in for hours now, Sam helped herself to the coffee Peter had made. "I think this one might be different. I really do."

"You'll have to tell me all about him."

"I'll tell you the PG parts after work," she said with a wink. "Right now, I gotta get going." She downed the coffee and rinsed the mug. On the way out of the kitchen, she caught him watching her with an odd expression on his face. "What's wrong?"

"Nothing. Nothing at all."

"Okay, then. Talk to you later." Sam ran upstairs to get changed before the coffee date with her dad. She wondered if he'd be able to tell that something momentous had happened to her since they'd seen each other the day before. Of course he'd be able to tell. He read her like the proverbial book.

For once, she didn't care if her dad knew something she'd prefer to keep private—for now, anyway. Nick had made her giddy with excitement, and she had no idea how she'd survive for four whole weeks until she could see him again.

* * * * *

ABOUT THE AUTHOR

Marie Force is the *New York Times* bestselling author of 50 contemporary romances, including the Gansett Island Series, which has sold more than 2.2 million books, and the Fatal Series from Harlequin's HQN Books, which has sold more than 1 million copies. In addition, she is the author of the Green Mountain Series as well as the new erotic romance Quantum Series, written under the slightly modified name of M.S. Force.

Her goals in life are simple—to finish raising two happy, healthy, productive young adults, to keep writing books for as long as she possibly can and to never be on a flight that makes the news.

Join Marie's mailing list on her website at marieforce.com for news about new books and upcoming appearances in your area. Follow her on Facebook at www.Facebook.com/MarieForceAuthor, on Twitter @marieforce and on Instagram at www.instagram.com/marieforceauthor/. Contact Marie at marie@marieforce.com.